THE BLACK WIND

MARSHA CANHAM

OLIVERHEBERBOOKS

This book is dedicated to my son Jeffrey.
He brought love and laughter into my life and blessed us all with two
beautiful grandchildren, Austin and Payton.
I miss him every day of my life.

PROLOGUE

The two ships were less than a mile apart. Hunter and the hunted were light frigates mounting three masts, both driven by tall pyramids of canvas stretched into hard curves to catch the wind. The *Hyperion* flew the Union Jack from the topmast, her officers visible on the fo'c's'le in all their gold-braided finery. While the navy's determination to cripple the rebels' war effort could boast modest success in stopping ships and supplies moving in and out of ports along the American eastern seaboard, it was the privateers who proved to be stubbornly effective in breaking through the lines.

The *Hyperion* had one such rogue within cannon range now.

In the two years since war had been declared, the *Cygnet* had run the blockade into Savannah three times. This last endeavor had caught the attention of the British frigate which had been carrying cargo bound for Florida. It had veered off course in order to give chase to the privateer, but the arrogance of the British was such that her captain seemed not to take into account the *Cygnet* carried thirty-two guns compared to the *Hyperion's* twenty. Or that the privateer's lines were sleek and trim, making her faster and quicker to respond to the helm.

He would soon discover that her gunners were well-trained and confident. So confident they barely flinched when a warning salvo from the *Hyperion* whistled by overhead.

Apart from that deadly shriek there was total silence on board the *Cygnet*. The gun crews crouched alongside their iron monsters, lit fuses glowing red in the hands of the lead gunners. Their attention was fixed on the quarterdeck, where the ship's captain stood watching the British ship through a leather-sleeved long-glass. Concentration was broken briefly to glance at the ineffectual waterspout that erupted off the stern, but the glass soon went up again, and on a quiet command, the sailing master was ordered to trim sail and come about.

When they completed the wide turn and were beam-on, the glass came down once more. "Have your crews blow up their matches, Billy. Ten guineas to the crew who takes out her main mast."

The gun captain grinned and vaulted over the rail to land on the main deck.

The British, meanwhile, heeled up into the wind, boldly presenting her broadside. Her thunderous volley was impressive, but most of the shots fell wide or short. A full two minutes passed before a second broadside was unleashed, spitting red flames and raising clouds of drifting smoke. This time one lucky ball punched through the *Cygnet's* upper topsail, another bounced off the hull tearing away a splintered chunk of wood.

Only then did a gloved hand go up in a spinning motion. On a shouted command, the crews on both decks gave a rousing cheer and let loose with all guns.

The tremendous force of the blasts rocked the *Cygnet*, but even before she settled back, the guns were reloaded, primed, and firing again. Not a single shot appeared to miss. The *Hyperion* staggered under the barrage of round and grapeshot. Smashed wood and bodies flew everywhere. Men screamed, cut in half where they stood. On the third broadside, delivered almost within the same minute, the *Hyperion's* main mast took several direct hits and cracked in half before slowly crashing over the side, taking cables and rat lines with it. With the weight of sails and rigging dragging in the water, the ship's ability to maneuver was severely hampered, leaving her exposed to more deadly volleys. The fo'c's'le exploded, sending the officers in their smart braided uniforms somersaulting into the air and landing in a tangle of splintered rails and boards.

By the time a fifth round was loaded and ready to fire, the British flag was being hastily hauled down into the wreckage of the main deck.

The order to cease fire was quickly relayed to the *Cygnet's* gun crews, giving the men the opportunity to rub the burning smoke out of their eyes and to assess any damage.

There was very little to report.

One man had dropped a twenty-four-pound ball on his foot. Another had burned his hand on a smoking fuse. The ship itself suffered hardly more than a few scratches.

"Well done, Billy, well done," the captain said, clapping a hand to the shoulder of the gun captain. By their side, the tall black ship's master roared the order to "Bring us around! Make ready to board."

With no one easing their vigilance, the *Cygnet* glided gracefully through the oyster-colored water until the men were able to throw a score of grappling hooks across the gap to lock the two ships together. Planks were thrown over the rails and the crew cheered again, waving their cutlasses as they poured across and swarmed the deck of the *Hyperion*. They spread out like an army of ants, dividing and streaming down the hatchways.

The planking was red, slippery with blood, littered with bodies and wreckage. The captain was dead, as were several of his officers.

Formal surrender was offered by the last remaining figure of authority, a junior midshipman too young to have fuzz showing on his chin, or to bear such a burden as he held his sword out in shaking hands.

"How old are you, boy?" asked the captain of the *Cygnet*.

"F-fourteen, sir." Watery brown eyes looked quickly up. "I mean...ma'am."

The captain smiled. She was wearing a wide brimmed hat cocked up on one side, pinned by an emerald broach holding twin ostrich feathers. She reached up and took off the hat, offering a formal bow to the young man as her long red hair tumbled forward. "You fought bravely today, young sir. You may keep your sword."

"B-be advised, I shall use it to slit your throat should the opportunity present itself."

Pale silvery-blue eyes regarded the lad for a long, solemn moment before she snugged the hat back on her head and nodded. "I would expect nothing less from a fine British officer. We will, however, attempt to avoid such an occasion if at all possible, for I am certain Duardo, here, would take offence and peel the skin from your body."

The lad looked owl-eyed at the ship's sailing master. His head was as bald as a melon, his skin smooth and shone like oiled ebony in the waning afternoon light. His chest was an armored wall of sculpted muscle clad only in a sleeveless leather vest with two wide cross-belts that held an assortment of knives and pistols. His face and arms were heavily tattooed with tribal symbols that bespoke his African heritage.

He stood a good three heads taller than the lad and carried easily three times the amount of bulk across his shoulders and chest. His dark eyes looked the boy up and down and he grinned, baring huge white teeth, some of which looked strong enough to crack bones. "Aye, Captain. I might even carve a little flesh for the stew pot."

The lad's bravado drained into his toes and his legs crumpled. When he regained consciousness, he had been flung, like a sack of flour, over the giant's shoulder and was being carried on board the *Cygnet*.

PART I

1

BARATARIA BAY

T he newcomer stood just inside the doorway of the clapboard tavern. Despite the gloomy, smoke-filled atmosphere, the lustrous green velvet of her frockcoat bespoke a richness that identified the captains and crews of the most successful privateering ships. There were ornate scrolls of gold embroidery on the elegantly-sculped deep cuffs and standing collar. The waistcoat beneath fit like a corset, made of fine green and gold striped satin with a row of gold buckles down the front. Smooth black nankeen breeches were molded to the tops of her thighs, met by high, supple leather boots laced to the knee.

She wore a fine brace of pistols tucked into her belt, and as she brushed the spickets of dew off the lapel of her frock coat, the light from a nearby candle flared briefly off the polished blade of her sword.

Pale silvery-blue eyes scanned the noisy crowd a moment before settling on a table in the most private corner. Two men sat there, deep in conversation. A third shadowy figure stood to one side, leaning indolently against the wall.

The pair who were seated matched the descriptions she had

been given. Joseph Sauvinet was a customs agent who worked exclusively to handle the sale of trade goods and prize cargo that passed through the warehouses here in Barataria before being moved up the Mississippi. He was a small man with piglet brown eyes and a penchant for exaggerated fashion. On this night he wore blue striped trousers and a gray broadcloth coat with a triple-layered cravat flowing down over a ruffled shirt front.

Seated across from Sauvinet was Jean Lafitte. The self-proclaimed pirate king was dark-haired with a swarthy complexion. He wore long muttonchops that led down to a neatly trimmed goatee. His clothes were the opposite of flamboyant; dirty gray shirt, brown coat, rough cotton trousers.

Lafitte had established this base in the Bay of Barataria and had under his command nearly a hundred well-seasoned captains helming as many ships. From the outset of the war with Britain, it was Jean Lafitte who provided ... with Sauvinet's help ... the continuous flow of black-market commodities up the Mississippi. His privateers prowled the Caribbean like hungry panthers, capturing merchant ships, bringing their cargoes to Barataria, and filling the enormous warehouses. Lafitte's fleet of flat-bottom barges ferried the goods through the swamps to New Orleans and from there to riverboats that traveled north into the heart of the country.

Since the embargo, his profits had tripled.

His most valuable commodity, however, was information. He had a network of spies that stretched to every corner of the Caribbean and as far north as Canada. His emissaries took many forms and came from all walks of life: clerks, fishermen, soldiers, whores and priests alike, keeping him well-apprised of the goings-on locally, as well as in the northern States.

Thus, it was not entirely unusual in Jean Lafitte's world to have a deliciously beautiful and mysterious young woman whisper a cryptic message or deliver a packet of letters in the dead of night.

It was, however, unusual to have such a beauty enter a tavern full of unwashed, drunken pirate crews. So unusual that both men scraped to their feet as she approached their table.

"M'sieur Lafitte, I presume?"

"You presume correctly, mam 'selle." Lafitte nodded cordially. "This gentleman is my associate, M'sieur Sauvinet, and the dour-faced fellow holding up the wall behind us is Captain Sebastien Fonteyne."

Whether the captain's expression was dour or the result of the contents in the large tankard he held, it was difficult to tell. At Lafitte's introduction, he offered up a low grunt and pushed away from the wall, then went to stand at the plank that served as a bar. The woman's eyes followed his broad back for a moment but showed no outward reaction to the name that, even when whispered, made grown men quake in their boots.

Lafitte spread his hands affably. "Alas, I must offer an apology on Captain Fonteyne's behalf; he has been at sea these past three months and forgets his manners in the presence of a lady."

"The apology is mine to make, M'sieur Lafitte, for intruding on your conversation."

"I assure you it is no intrusion." Lafitte's sharp ears noted her manner of speech as being refined, her clothing expensive, yet her focus, apparently, was not easily unsettled in a tavern full of coarse ruffians. "Will you sit, mam'selle? Perhaps take a glass of canary to ease the chill from the night air?"

"Thank you, Captain Lafitte. I will. But I prefer spirits over diluted wine, if you please."

Lafitte arched an eyebrow, but reached out and dragged an empty chair over to their table. When they were all seated, a glass of amber liquid was poured and slid across to the newcomer, which she drained in a single swallow. As she tipped her head, the dull orange light from the hurricane lamp banished the shadows cast by the brim of her hat and for the second time in as many breaths, Jean Lafitte's eyebrow twitched upward with curiosity.

Her face was oval-shaped with clear, smooth skin. Eyes were an unidentifiable color in the gloom, but they were large, complemented by a slender nose and a mouth that was perhaps a trifle too wide. Floating wisps of hair lay against her cheeks and throat, having escaped from the thick braid that hung down her back. The light from behind made the airy threads glow in a fiery golden-red aura.

"I confess you have intrigued me... Miss—?"

"Captain," she corrected him. "Captain Whitticomb."

Lafitte's eyes narrowed. "Whitticomb? I am not familiar with the name, should I know it?"

"If you traveled frequently to Tobago, you might," she agreed. "Or Barbados. Or Martinique. Or if you had very good taste in rum ... which I see that you do. Perhaps you might know me better by my maiden name: St. Clare."

Lafitte tore his gaze away from her face long enough to glance at the thick green bottle sitting on the table. He read the label and looked at her face again, this time with unconcealed surprise.

"You are related to Alexander St. Clare?"

"My father."

"Ahh." Lafitte leaned back and smiled as a memory clicked into place. "It has been quite a few years, but I do seem to recall; a skinny, freckle-faced child with mischievous eyes and a habit of putting snakes and lizards in my boots when I did not pay her enough attention. Little Rosie with the red ringlets."

Her own smile skewed slightly. "I prefer Rose now."

"Honoring your great-grandmother?"

"Honoring who and what I am," she answered.

"Might I be allowed to share in the recollections?" Sauvinet asked, clearly unaccustomed to being left out of a mystery.

Lafitte poured Rose and himself another dram of rum then tapped on the bottle. "Who produces the finest rum in all of the Caribbean?"

"Why, the Pirata Lobo Company, of course."

"And the family that has made Pirata Lobo rum for the past two hundred years?"

Sauvinet started to say the name, stopped, and looked at Rose. His chest swelled and his nose twitched like a startled hare. "My most profound apologies, Miss St. Clare. I have done business with your father on several occasions. He is well?"

"Very well, thank you. He is currently on his way home from London."

"And your brother, Ramsey?"

Her eyes betrayed the slightest glint of irritation. "Not in London and not here, as you can see. And as far as he knows, I am not here either."

"Not—? Oh. Oh, I see. Yes, of course. In his position, I can understand the need for caution. Forgive me." He picked up his ale and took a swallow.

Lafitte leaned forward with interest. "Might I inquire as to how you did *not* get here?"

Rose turned and gave the pirate king a measured look. "On my ship, which is anchored in a cove about a mile outside the bay, alongside the *Hyperion*, a British supply ship that we captured three days ago."

Lafitte stared for a moment then turned his head slightly as if the deafness in his ears, caused by many years in close proximity to cannon fire, had made him mistake her words. "You ... attacked an English ship?"

She took another small sip of rum and shrugged. "Her

captain attacked first, which was not much of an attack. He thought to give us chase when our paths crossed in the Straits."

"Indeed. And?

"And ... the crew needed a little persuasion before they let us board her."

"The *Hyperion*," Sauvinet muttered after searching his memory. "A light frigate, eighteen guns, if I recall."

"Twenty," she corrected him. "And as I said, I was not the aggressor. The British captain fired the first shots. The *Cygnet* was simply defending herself against possible capture or impressment of the crew."

Jean Lafitte took a moment to refill his glass of rum, obviously buying himself time to think. The legalities of capturing a ship flying the French or Spanish or even the Dutch flag did not particularly trouble him. But so far, protecting his claim of neutrality in the conflict between the Americans and the British, his privateers were warned to steer well clear of any vessels flying either the Stars and Stripes or the Union Jack. "And so you brought a captured English ship here...for what reason?"

Rose looked at him. "I was hoping we might be able to come to an arrangement."

Lafitte pursed his lips and expelled an exaggerated sigh. "What possible arrangement could you be proposing, my dear? The major ports of Charleston, Savannah, Norfolk, as well as those as far north as Chesapeake Bay and Delaware, are locked up tighter than a virgin's thighs. Britain is determined to cut the upstart colonies off from all trade. Thus. the reason why you find us sitting here pondering the poor state of our enterprises."

She scoffed. "I should think you are making even more enormous profits off the conflict. Merchants from both sides of the Atlantic are still able to trade their goods in the islands of the West Indies, where business can be conducted in neutral ports. Some of those ports you control, do you not? Those same ports allow your ships to bring embargoed cargoes here to Barataria and from here, the goods are transferred to New Orleans." She leaned in and smiled again. "Whoever controls what comes into the port of New Orleans, controls what goes up and down the middle of the Americas. And you, Sir, control New Orleans."

Lafitte's dark eyes narrowed. "You seem to know a great deal about my business. Ah, but then I must remind myself that you are the sister of the Crown-appointed governor of Tobago, Ramsey St. Clare, who has the ability to issue or rescind the letters of marque that allow trade in the islands." He waved his hand airily. "Even so, you give me far more credit than I am due. I have recently been branded a pirate and a scoundrel and my presence in New Orleans has been heartily discouraged."

"False modesty does not do you credit, Captain Lafitte."

"One could say the same about false bravado." He took a sip of rum and studied Rose's features in the soft lamplight. "In this case, there is nothing false in the sorry condition in which we find ourselves. My own dear brother, Pierre, has been arrested and currently resides in a fetid gaol cell under charges of piracy. I barely escaped in time to avoid being locked in the cell beside him! The governor, Claiborne, has placed a five-hundred-dollar reward on my head! Tempting enough for my own men to look at me with a nefarious eye."

Sauvinet was clicking through his memory and interrupted. "The *Cygnet*, you say? Surely not the same vessel rumored to have run through the blockade into Savannah."

Rose nodded. "We ran it three times."

"Indeed." Sauvinet's piglet eyes widened. "I was not aware. Nor was I apprised that her captain was a woman."

"My husband is the ship's captain of record. Unfortunately he passed away three years ago from island fever but I saw no reason to correct the registry."

"Does it not foster ... discontent ... amongst the members of your crew?"

"My crew has seen me standing alongside them in battle, burned and bleeding, feeding shot into the smoking mouth of a cannon. They have seen me in the rigging setting sails in gale force winds. And they have seen me carve a wandering eye out of its socket and stuff it down the offending bastard's throat. Thus, to answer your question: no, my presence on board my ship does not foster discontent. I pay them well and treat them with respect."

Lafitte drew a deep breath and blew a stream of rum-soaked breath across the table to interrupt the conversation. "I confess I am intrigued, but exactly what kind of *arrangement* have you come to propose, my dear? I already have a wife. And a mistress."

"And I have neither the time nor inclination for such fuckery. I wish to propose a business arrangement, Captain. My *Cygnet* is a strong, bold vessel; her crew is second to none. With the British prowling the open water like vultures, it seems the wiser choice to be part of a wolf pack rather than running alone and howling at the moon."

"I see. And what of your brother, the governor? Or your father? Do they support your wolfpack aspirations?"

There was the slightest hesitation before she answered. "My brother Ramsey and I share very different opinions of the war between England and America. He was an officer in the Royal Navy for nearly a decade and sailed under Admiral Nelson before being appointed governor, thus it should come as no surprise that his loyalties lie with the Crown. In truth, he might still be sailing under the Union Jack had he not lost half his leg at Trafalgar."

"I gather he would not be pleased to know you were here?"

"He is not often pleased with me, so this should hardly warrant another spin of the whirl-a-gig."

"And your father? In which direction do his loyalties lean?"

"They lean toward freedom of choice, Captain, whether it be a country or a person making that choice. He does have a shipping company to run, however, and because he shares his time equally between London and the islands, he leans toward caution."

Lafitte chased a drop of moisture down the side of his tankard with his thumb. "I should not like to get on the wrong side of Alexander St. Clare."

"Nor would I, Captain. But as I said, he supports freedom of choice. Both my brother's and mine."

"Even so, would he not be risking a great deal regarding the future of his company if his name is associated with acts of piracy?"

Rose smiled. "Our family name has been associated with piracy since the days my ancestors sailed with Francis Drake. Putting family histories aside, however, I have kept my husband's name for that very reason. Thus, I have come in good faith to offer up the *Hyperion* and the cargo she carries, as well as the skills of one of the finest ships and crews in the West Indies."

Lafitte's dark eyes held hers for a full thirty seconds before his gaze strayed lower, to the shape of her bosoms where they were defined by the exquisitely brocaded corset-waistcoat.

Then he leaned back and laughed.

He laughed so long and so loudly that patrons in the tavern went silent for the second time, as shadowy faces turned to stare.

"I applaud your boldness, my dear. But a female captain in my fleet? In the brotherhood? Have you come to Barataria to make me a laughingstock?"

Rose felt her neck prickling as a flush heated her cheeks. "I have come, Captain Lafitte, because if there is going to be a fight to defend New Orleans against the British, I want to be part of it."

"What leads you to believe there will be a fight for New Orleans?"

"Are you telling me you do not think there will be? That the British will not attack New Orleans in order to take command of the Mississippi?"

"The city council feels the city is safe."

"The city council is wrong."

When he said nothing, Rose reached to an inside pocket of her coat and produced a thin sheaf of folded papers.

"These documents were on board the *Hyperion*. They give details of a British expedition force comprised of ten ships carrying twenty thousand troops under the command of an Irish Admiral named Nicolls. They are reported to be en route from the Azores to Florida with orders to land at Pensacola and from there to make preparations for the invasion of New Orleans."

Lafitte shook his head and sighed. "Mam'selle, there have been rumors of such an invasion fleet for the past three months."

"Have these rumors carried with them the news that Washington City has been sacked?"

Lafitte's smile faded and his expression hardened. "Sacked? When? How?"

She slid the documents across the table. "The full details are written here, but I can tell you as much as I know. The British landed in Maryland and overwhelmed the American militia. They marched to Washington City and set fire to the government buildings, including the President's House, which was burned to the ground. Fearing what else might fall into enemy hands, the American forces destroyed the naval yard and ammunition stores and then retreated, leaving the rest of the city undefended."

Lafitte snatched the papers and tipped them toward the light to read. "*Fools!* I have been warning President Madison for months that the embargo is not just there to disrupt trade, the blockade is there to keep American naval ships hobbled in port. The Crown's goal is to avenge the loss they suffered in 1776 and take America back into the Empire."

"Louisiana is the soft underbelly of this country," Rose said. "If the British attack in force, and if they capture New Orleans, they will win the Mississippi. They will be able to move their armies straight up into the interior and crush the rebellion from both sides, from land and sea."

Lafitte slapped the papers down angrily. "I have sent letters to the president, to every general with the wits to see the danger of leaving the delta undefended. In return, I get platitudes. Worse, I get accused of piracy and profiteering and am harassed by warrants for my arrest!"

"Having said that, however," Lafitte flexed his hands to calm himself, "and as much as I appreciate your offer, Rose St. Clare, this is not the time to bring any disruptions into my fleet ... and not just because you are a female, though that would give more than a few of my men pause to contemplate my sanity. While your family, past and present, may have been broad-minded when it came to females standing before the mast, I'm afraid my brethren are a superstitious lot and regard a woman on board as bad luck. If that were not enough to have them pinning my ears to the mast, my captains are a distrustful lot of bastards. With your brother being who he is, they might well suspect you were hiding a British flag somewhere on your ship."

"I can assure you—"

"As I said," he held up a hand to cut her off. "If there is truth in this news you bring, then this is not the time to bring discord amongst my captains. I will happily accept your gift of the *Hype-*

rion, but it is with profound apologies mam'selle, I must refuse your generous offer of joining my league of privateers."

"I was not giving you the *Hyperion* as a gift. I captured her; she is mine. I was bringing her with me, should you accept my ship into your fleet."

"Which I have already explained is not possible at this time. It would be equally not possible for you to sail out of Barataria unscathed should I decide to take *both* of your ships. Thus, you would be wise to leave while I am still in a generous enough mood to respect your family name and permit you to sail back to Tobago with your *Cygnet*."

The chair fell back and crashed to the floor as Rose surged to her feet. Her eyes were blazing, her jaw rigid, and her hand instinctively curled around the grip of one of the pistols tucked into her belt. Before she had even thought the action through or considered the lunacy of drawing a gun on Jean Lafitte, she felt the barrel of a pistol press into the side of her neck.

"I would not advise it if I were you."

The voice was as cold and hard as the steel against her throat. For the span of two ... five ... ten heartbeats she did nothing, but then slowly, her fingers uncurled, and her hand fell away. An arm, clad in black, reached around and withdrew both pistols from her belt.

Lafitte, if anything, was merely amused. "If you have taken offense at my refusal, perhaps we should ask Captain Fonteyne, here, how he would respond to a request for you to join *his* fleet of ships." The cold black eyes looked up at Fonteyne. "Sebastien? What say you? Am I being unfair to deny this sweet little girl her request? Would you be willing to have her on board your ship?"

"That depends on how truly sweet she is," came the husky rejoinder in her ear.

"Alas, she claims to need no more warmth in her bed."

"A pity," Fonteyne murmured, stroking the barrel of the gun along the curve of her neck. "But to answer your question, the only way a woman joins *my* fleet is if she becomes captain of my ship... and that would only happen over my dead, worm-ridden body."

Lafitte smiled at Rose and spread his hands through a shrug. "There you have it, my dear. And now, Sebastien, perhaps you will oblige me by escorting the young lady to the door and see that she safely gets back to her ship?"

"I'm quite capable of managing on my own, Captain Lafitte," she said through her teeth. "But I thank you for your cavalier concern."

"Tut tut. It must be nearing midnight, well past the hour for a *decent* woman to be walking alone. Especially here on the riverfront. Barataria is full of unsavory types."

He turned and started talking Cajun French to Sauvinet, taking up the conversation they'd been having before Rose interrupted. She felt strong fingers grip her elbow as Fonteyne drew her away from the table. She shrugged her arm free after a few steps, her feathers bouncing and her boot heels clacking sharply on the clapboard floor as he led her through the warren of tables to the door.

Outside in the damp night air, she jerked on a pair of soft leather gloves. "Is that little blacksmith-turned-pirate always such an arrogant bastard?"

Fonteyne tucked his pistol into his belt and glanced sidelong at her. "I thought he was being rather polite. He isn't usually so forgiving when someone intrudes on his business conversations."

"Nor am I," she said and started walking.

2

———

Fonteyne was very tall and had very long legs that caught her up with ease. He was dressed all in black, even to the gloves he wore. Not much of his face had been visible in the shadows of the tavern, and out on the street his features remained mostly shielded from the light glowing through the open windows of the taverns and whorehouses they passed. Surrounded on three sides by swamp, there was always a thick, soupy fog hanging over the Bay after dusk, making the air redolent with the tang of rot and mud and the creatures that slithered through the marshes.

But Rose knew. She knew exactly what Sebastien Fonteyne looked like in daylight and in darkness.

"You could have helped me back there," she said, her words muffled by the thick, hazy air.

Sebastien Fonteyne chuckled softly. "Now why would I do that?"

"Oh, I don't know. Old times sake? Or a favor owed perhaps?"

"A favor? You will have to remind me of your largesse?"

"Five years ago, I could have cried rape and you would likely still be looking at the world through iron bars."

"As I recall, the only thing you were crying was my name."

Rose ground her teeth. "A momentary lapse in judgement."

"A four-hour long lapse?"

"Oh for pity's sake." She stopped and faced him. "I was young and stupid and you took advantage."

"You could have sent me away after the first kiss. Or the second. Or—"

"It was a foolish choice I have regretted every hour of every day since."

"You think of me that often, do you?"

Instead of rising to the bait, she tipped her head and sighed. "I don't think of you at all, Captain Fonteyne, except to regret that it was you I recklessly took between my thighs that night. Although, as I have since discovered on several occasions, your efforts hardly warranted any remorse I may have felt afterward and surely never gave reason why I would revere the memory."

She started walking again, cursing inwardly at her own foolishness.

Five years ago, Fonteyne had dropped anchor in Port-Louis. He had been stopped and boarded by a British warship in open water east of Tobago and while he was not carrying any contraband at the time—or perhaps because he was not—the British captain removed three of his crew, claiming they were deserters from the Royal Navy.

In a rage, Fonteyne had demanded an audience with Ramsey St. Clare, the ranking naval officer at the time, who had offered no recompense, stating the marines were well within their right to board vessels and search for fugitives.

In an attempt to assuage his anger, for Ramsey was all too aware of Fonteyne's reputation, he invited the privateer to a ball that was being held that same night. He hadn't really expected the privateer to attend, but minutes before the clock struck midnight, Fonteyne strode into the ballroom, dressed as richly as any gentleman present. With his long black hair unfettered by any powder or wig, with the twin gold loops in each ear, and the broad chest encased in the finest black silks and velvet, he had exuded such an air of danger and savagery that women had actually swooned.

For her part, Rose had been intrigued. Not so much by his appearance, although it was certainly worth one or two skipped heartbeats, but by the knowledge she was in the same room as one of the most feared and successful privateers in all of the Caribbean.

Against her brother's express orders, she wrested an introduction, and with the focus of a hawk, maneuvered her prey out into the gardens. He seemed amused enough to allow her to ramble on about ships and guns, even answered some of her questions on strategy and handling of a ship in battle. But when she mentioned it was her intention to outfit her own ship and crew, he laughed outright and drew her into his arms.

In hindsight, it was probably the most devastating kiss she'd ever had. There was no finesse, no subtlety, no attempt at gentle seduction. It was raw and primal, as savage as the pirate-beast himself, quickly evoking a response from every nerve, every sense, every tiny hair that prickled to attention on her body. The kiss exposed her passions to the core and before she knew it, they were in the garden house and they were both stripping to bare flesh.

He had snuck out the next morning and sailed away from Port-Louis without so much as a wave farewell. A rose on the pillow was all he left behind. She had not thought to ever have to face him again. Not until she had seen him standing in the tavern tonight.

She heard footsteps behind her. He caught up in three long strides and pulled her into the shadowed niche of a doorway.

"What the hell do you think—?"

"I think I need to give you a very sound piece of advice. Do as Lafitte says. Get back on board your ship and sail home to Tobago. The news about the sacking of Washington City did not go unheard tonight and by morning the rumors will be flying. Few here have any love or respect for the British, even fewer will have respect for the sister of a governor whose loyalty lies with the Crown."

"Let go of me, damn you."

Instead of letting go, he pushed her deeper into the corner of the doorway and pressed his big body against her. Her hands went to her waist searching for pistols that were not there, and she was pinned too tightly to draw the knife she kept tucked in the top of her boot.

"There is no challenge here, madam, as to whether you are competent to stand at the helm of a ship. There is only the question of whether you have the sense to see that sometimes a retreat is the more prudent option."

Despite Rose's anger at being manhandled *again* by this lout, half of her wits were distracted by scent of leather, sweat, and saltwater that came off his body. Unwanted memories flooded back, and as she dared to tilt her head up, she found him staring at her so intently, she could hear her heart thudding in her ears. For a long, breathless moment, she thought he was going to kiss her again, but she placed her hands firmly on his chest and pushed.

It was like pushing against a solid wall.

When he muttered something under his breath and started to press even closer, to crowd her more tightly into the corner, the sudden presence of cold gun barrel digging into the back of his neck stopped him.

Rose pushed again and this time was able to twist out of his grasp. "Did you think I was foolish enough to approach Lafitte's den of thieves alone?"

Fonteyne, who had backed away and raised his hands in response to a second forceful dig from the gun barrel, was grudgingly impressed. He had not seen or heard anyone following them from the tavern, yet he now sensed a presence as large as himself, if not larger, looming behind him.

"I have never thought of you as foolish," he admitted.

"Suggesting you think of me often?" she asked, throwing his words back at him.

"More often than I should," he murmured too softly for her to hear.

He turned his head slightly, attempting to see who was holding the gun against his neck, but the muzzle bit deeper into tender flesh, discouraging him. The brief movement caught enough light to reveal the high forehead, the Romanesque nose that had been broken more than once. His mouth was a cynical curve. Unshaved stubble darkened the line of his jaw and the front of his neck

Rose tugged on her waistcoat to straighten it. "I thank you for your escort, Captain Fonteyne. Heaven knows what might have befallen me had you not been by my side."

Her sarcasm caused his mouth to twitch again. "The night is far from over."

He lowered his hands slightly and made a sudden whirling motion, intending to lash out at whoever was standing behind him, but the tall black shadow anticipated the move and struck out with the butt of the gun, catching Fonteyne hard on the temple. It was a solid blow and the pirate captain was thrown off balance. He fell heavily to his knees, where he swayed a moment, undoubtedly watching stars burst behind his eyes before he crashed down onto his side, knocked out cold.

Rose blew out a breath. She quickly searched left and right along the boardwalk to see if they had been observed, then leaned over to reclaim the pistols Fonteyne had taken from her in the tavern.

She tucked the guns back into her belt and, on a further thought, relieved Fonteyne of his pistols, as well as the three daggers she found secreted in his clothing and boot top.

And just for the insult, she took his leather purse, fat with coins.

When she straightened, she shook her head.

"Well, Duardo, so much for thinking we might be welcomed here, that we would have something to gain by working *with* the infamous Jean Lafitte."

The *Cygnet's* sailing master smirked. "The meeting did not go well?"

"The meeting went as well as I should have expected. The Pirate King of Barataria Bay is an arrogant, self-serving prick who believes women are only good for filling his brothels."

Duardo growled ominously. "He said this to you? Shall I kill him?"

Rose had no doubt the former slave would do exactly that if she asked him to, but even though the thought was tempting, she shook the idea away with a curse.

"Lafitte is of no use to us dead. Kill him and we would become pariahs in every port friendly to him."

A groan and the scrape of a foot had the two of them looking down at the sprawled figure of Sebastien Fonteyne. Duardo leaned over and placed a hand on his neck, pinching a nerve in the captain's neck until he stopped groaning. He then dragged the heavy body into the shadowy niche where it would not be easily seen by anyone passing by. As a further deterrent, he bound Fonteyne's wrists and ankles with leather thongs and tied a gag around his mouth.

"We should probably get back to the ship," Rose said. "The captain will not be in good humor when he wakes up."

"I can see that he does not wake up at all," Duardo offered as he fingered the thin bamboo tube he wore around his neck. He carried two types of darts in his arsenal; one induced a full night's sleep; the other made the sleep permanent.

But Rose was not listening. She was looking out over the harbor, where dozens of ships lay at anchor. A forest of bare masts stood silent in the fog-blurred darkness, their muted deck lamps glowing like faint yellow blooms through the mist. One glowed brighter than the others, her rigging lines festooned with lanterns. The ship was easily recognizable by the black paint on her hull and the gold gilding around her gun ports.

The *Pride* was Lafitte's ship.

Rose's eyes narrowed. "How many men came ashore with us?"

"Two longboats, ten in each."

"That should be enough," she murmured.

"Enough for what?"

She smiled. "Enough to show the puny little man exactly what a mere woman is capable of doing."

Duardo frowned. "Am I going to like this?"

"Probably not. How quickly can you round up our men?"

"They could not be very drunk yet. But they will not be happy getting dragged away from the whores so soon."

Rose waved away the comment. "Find as many as you can and meet me at the longboats."

3

———

Twenty minutes later, all but one of the *Cygnet's* crewmen were standing at the longboats, quietly grumbling. With no time to waste on soothing their interrupted carnal needs, Rose quickly outlined her plan, then split them into two groups. She took to the bow of one of the longboats, Duardo the other. With the mist forming a milky layer over the surface of the water, they were almost invisible as they rowed silently out into the bay, maneuvering stealthily between and around other ships. When they drew close to the *Pride*, they lifted the oars out of the water and drifted, coming close enough to hear men on the aft deck talking and laughing.

Rose had heard much about the pirate king's ship but until now had not seen it up close. Once a proud vessel in the Spanish treasure fleet, it had the telltale high fore and aft castles rising from the deep well of the main deck. She was two-masted, built to carry the weight of thirty heavy guns. The original figurehead in the bow of the Catholic ship had been that of an angel with spread wings, but Lafitte had removed it and replaced it with a demonic figure surrounded by flames, whose face bore a striking similarity to his own.

Duardo made a soft hissing sound to gain her attention. Communicating by hand signals, he slipped quietly into the inky water and swam the short distance to the *Pride*. There he climbed the anchor cable and swung himself by handholds onto the narrow balcony that spanned the stern. The upper deck of the ship was brightly lit, but aside from a dull glow emanating from a gallery of slanted windows, the rest was in darkness.

Darkness and mist was something that favored their business tonight.

Even so, it was risky. And would be more so if Fonteyne regained his senses and escaped his bindings to raise an alarm.

Rose's plan was to get on board, cause some mischief, and steal some prized possessions ... logbooks if she could find them, or manifests. Something that would prove she was not to be so cavalierly dismissed.

Reckless? Possibly so, but she was also not one to ignore an opportunity when it was presented.

Duardo's gleaming head rose out of the dark water beside the longboat.

"I have opened a gun port amidships; easy access for the men. I have also dropped a rope from the stern gallery."

"Lafitte's crew?"

"Aside from four playing dice, there are two on watch in the bow, both asleep, stinking of rum, and sleeping more soundly now."

Bolstered by Duardo's wide grin, Rose nodded. "Go forward with your men; my crew and I will board by the stern."

His black head sank back under the water and he swam away.

Rose drew a few deep breaths to quell the excitement racing through her veins, then quietly ordered the men in the longboat to row toward the *Pride*.

She was first up the knotted rope Duardo had hung. The

gallery windows rose as high as her head, and emblazoned above was the name of the ship in gold, the lettering as tall as a man and slanted elegantly to the right. The balcony itself was more for decoration than any useful purpose. Narrow doors at both ends opened into the captain's quarters.

A single lamp glowed through the dimpled waterglass, revealing what appeared to be the captain's private sleeping quarters. The shadows were too thick to see much beyond the circle of light thrown off by the lamp but although the image was wavey and distorted, Rose thought she saw what might be an open logbook on the desk.

She went through the gallery door and stood for a moment to take in her surroundings. Rose's own cabin aboard the *Cygnet* was stark and practical, built with collapsible inner walls that could be taken down and stowed during battle. Her berth was suspended over a demi-cannon, as was her desk, both of which could be removed so the guns could be manned by the crew during an attack. The floorboards were bare, free of any wax or polish that might make them slippery.

By contrast, Lafitte's cabin could have been mistaken for an ornate room in a brothel. As Rose turned the wick up on the lamp, the shadows were pushed back to reveal crimson-cushioned chairs with thin gilded legs sitting on a thick Persian rug edged in gold tassels. An enormous canopied bed occupied fully a third of the cabin space, the four corners hung with gold striped draperies. The desk was huge and solid, the sides carved with Chinese symbols. There were paintings in gold frames hung on two of the brocaded walls. A sideboard filled with gold and silver artifacts was crowded into the remaining wall space.

The chair behind the desk was ridiculously throne-like with intricate depictions of two rearing dragons locked in battle, their scaled tails curling down to form the arms. The book she had seen through the windows was, indeed, Lafitte's logbook opened to the page marked with that day's date and a simple "meeting with S" penned below.

To one side of the desk was a tall bookcase, and on one of the shelves there was a row of leather-bound books sandwiched between two white marble bookends carved like the heads of ancient Roman Gods. She took one of the books down and thumbed it open, and when she tipped it toward the lamp for a closer look, she needed a moment to understand what she was seeing.

It was a ledger filled with names and numbers, dates and manifests. There were lists of Lafitte's contacts and the amounts of bribes he paid to city officials. Rose glanced up and counted a dozen more books on the shelf, all likely filled with Lafitte's chicken scratch handwriting.

Meanwhile, the rest of the crew from the longboat had climbed aboard and filed quietly into the cabin, each of them gawping at the expanse of crimson and gold. One man reached up slowly to snatch the cap he was wearing off his head.

"An' we take the piss fer 'avin' a woman fer a captain," he muttered.

Rose reluctantly set the ledgers aside. Pistol in hand, she led the men across the cabin to the door. The latch lifted easily and swung open on well-oiled hinges.

The adjoining day cabin was not only larger than the sleeping quarters, but it was decorated even more garishly, if that was possible. Gold candelabra sat on a long mahogany dining table polished to a mirror shine. Each of the dozen Louis XIV chairs had plush velvet cushions for seats. Cabinets on the wall held gold plates and crystal glasses. A rack stretched floor to ceiling contained various bottles of wine and spirits. A sideboard, she noted with a smirk, had two bottles of Pirata Lobo rum on ornate silver trays.

Reminding herself that an alarm could be raised at any

moment, Rose sent five of the men below to secure the armory and powder magazine; both of which were crucial to secure before any of Lafitte's crew became aware of their presence. The rest of the crew from the longboat, pistols drawn, followed Rose's hand signals and bled off to search the smaller cabins.

In the dead of night, it was safe to assume most of the pirate king's crew would be asleep in their hammocks on the lower deck and not wandering around the ship.

Rose returned to Lafitte's private quarters and sat in the dragon chair tapping her finger thoughtfully on the logbook. The same shelves that held the ledgers had wooden bins below them, each filled with rolled-up maps and charts. The desk itself had several pigeonholes filled with correspondence, most written in some bastardized version of Cajun and English. There were three drawers down one side, all of them locked, and she was about to attack the brass plates with the tip of a blade when Duardo came into the cabin.

He was shaking his head in disgust. "Ten men. The six on deck and four more below. Our men have locked them in a cargo bay."

"Alive, I hope?"

"Sleeping," he said, patting the bamboo tube.

Rose frowned. "Only ten men? You searched everywhere?"

"Everywhere anything bigger than a rat could hide, Captain."

"I'll be damned."

He nodded. "Arrogant even for a pirate king."

Nibbling at the edge of her lip, she returned to the day cabin and poured two glasses of rum then handed one to Duardo.

He accepted the glass but was wary of the bright gleam in her eyes. It was an all-too-familiar gleam that usually meant trouble.

"I do not like what you might be thinking even more than I did not like what you were thinking before."

"What do you think I might be thinking?"

"That merely taking a few ledgers and logbooks is not enough."

"There are twenty of us on board," she said, the eagerness hard to conceal. "Easily as many as we put on any prize ship to sail it."

Duardo refrained from comment. His big hand squeezed the delicate crystal glass and he downed the harsh spirits in a single swallow. "If we take the ship, even if we manage to get her out of the harbor without any alarm being raised ... what do we do with her then?"

"I haven't thought that far ahead yet. Let's just see if we can get her out of the bay first."

ROSE DISPATCHED half of the crew to man the heavy capstan and haul up the anchor. She doused the big deck lamps along with the lanterns strung along the rigging, plunging the ship into darkness. She didn't dare lower any sails. Instead, she put men back in the longboats and attached tow ropes to both in order to pass through the harbor as quietly as possible. The thick mist aided their task by turning into a sudden downpour that was common in the humid heat of the marshes. Sheets of rain cloaked their movements, dampening any sounds that were made as the *Pride* glided out of the bay.

Once they had cleared Barataria Bay and left the outer island of Grand Terre behind, they piled on sail to catch the wind as it came around the headland. An hour later, they were in the open water of the Gulf where they retrieved the *Cygnet* and the *Hyperion* from the cove where they had been safely snugged away. Most of the *Hyperion's* crew accepted Rose's offer to disembark along with the unconscious crew of the *Pride*. Fully a third, however, lured by the promise of shared profits, signed articles and joined the *Cygnet's* roster.

With the smear of dawn light barely edging above the horizon, Rose lowered Lafitte's flag from the mast of the *Pride* and raised her own: a snarling female wolf on a hunter green field.

4

———

Jean Lafitte scratched a muttonchop whisker, yawned, and kicked Sauvinet hard under the table to stop him snoring. Judging by the clang of pots and pans from the back of the tavern, it was coming into morning. The bottle of rum ... or was it the second or third?... was empty and Jean's head was starting to feel as if it was floating up near the ceiling.

It had been a profitable week by Sauvinet's calculations. Two prize ships had been taken off the coast of Bermuda by Captain Jefferson Jayson, one of Lafitte's privateers, their cargo bays filled with a rich trove of wool, and English linen. All three of Fonteyne's ships had been equally laden with valuable contraband.

Offloaded to the storage sheds, the cargo would be sorted and transferred onto the flat-bottomed barges that could maneuver through the reedy waters of the swamps and mangroves where the deeper keels of British patrol ships could not venture. In turn, the crews would take on bales of cotton and tobacco for the run downriver to be loaded onto other ships bound for England and the Continent.

A thousand dollars a week clear profit was not unheard of and in that respect, Lafitte hoped the war dragged on for another year or more. However, the news that Washington City had been overrun and the President's House burned to the ground was admittedly disturbing. If the girl was right about the imminent arrival of a British fleet in the Gulf, it was only a matter of time before the English bastards turned their efforts to gain control of access up the Mississippi.

Lafitte was not particularly patriotic, but if New Orleans fell into British hands, he could piss every sou of profit away on the dung heap.

Up to now, the British representatives in Louisiana assumed Lafitte's trade was mostly in cloth, sugar, rum, and assorted household goods; supplies in demand since the embargo had been put in place. And until recently, as long as they got their share of the profits, the revenuers left him alone. Unbeknownst to anyone outside of Barataria however, his barges had also been transporting gunpowder and guns, squirreling the caches away, anticipating a time when such stores might be needed.

The bay containing Barataria was fifteen miles long and twelve miles wide, protected by two barrier islands, Grande Isle and Grande Terre. The land flanking the bay was mostly swamp and marshland, riddled with a maze of inland waterways that made it prized territory for privateers and smugglers. Several times in the past the British had tried to flush Lafitte out, but with no success. The Pirate King's warning system rivaled that of Elizabeth's legendary coastal beacons that had alerted England to the approach of the Spanish armada over two hundred years ago. At the first sign of trouble, vast quantities of contraband could be made to disappear into the marshes leaving no trace behind.

Lafitte stretched to ease a kink in his neck and jumped

slightly as the door to the tavern flew open and slammed into the wall. Sebastien Fonteyne thundered into the room like a black wind, his hat crushed in one hand, his other holding a wad of cloth to the side of his head. An expression of pure murder darkened his already ominous features.

Lafitte could see the cloth was spotted with blood.

"What the devil happened to you?"

"That little bitch happened. She had someone waiting outside to jump me. I've a lump on my head the size of the fist I plan to greet her with the next time I see her."

"The hell you say." Lafitte grinned. "A righteous little firepot. Clever, too, if she managed to get the best of you. We must mark this day down in the logs."

"That might be difficult."

"Meaning?"

"Meaning ... the *Pride* is gone and I assume your logbooks have gone with her."

Lafitte blinked. "What?"

"Your ship. She's gone. She's not in the harbor. And unless you ordered your crew to move her ...?"

Lafitte stood up so quickly the table tipped and crashed onto its side, taking Sauvinet with it. He ignored the accountant's spluttering and strode to the door, knocking aside a man rolling a barrel of beer into the tavern. The rain had slowed to a drizzle but was cool enough to clear some of the rum-soaked cotton out of his head.

He ran a short way along the boardwalk until he could see the full expanse of the harbor and the black, empty mooring where the *Pride* had been at anchor all week.

His lips moved with a litany of curses in a mixture of French, English, and fiery hot Cajun.

When Fonteyne walked up beside him, Lafitte's rage had

turned his face purple. "Who? Who would dare do such a thing?"

"I am not a great believer in coincidences, are you?"

Lafitte whirled around. "The girl? *Are you suggesting the girl took my ship?*"

"She *was* a little angry when she left the tavern."

"Angry enough to sign her own death warrant?"

"Angry enough to make a point."

"*And to do this she stole my ship?*"

Fonteyne looked out over the harbor. "So it would seem."

Lafitte was almost apoplectic. "I want my ship back! I want my ship and I want the girl! I want to see her lashed to the rigging, stripped naked, and flayed to within an inch of her life!"

Fonteyne touched the throbbing lump on his head. "It will be a pleasure to wield the cat myself!"

"That you will, my bold captain, just as soon as you catch her."

"*Me?* My crew has just come in from three months at sea. Two of my ships are on their way to Galveston for repairs."

"Are you saying you need all three to find one little girl and get my *Pride* back?"

Fonteyne drew a deep breath. There was no sense arguing with Lafitte when he was hopping around like a bantam cock, and in truth, he did have his own score to settle with Rose St. Clare.

At the same time, it was difficult not to admire the sheer guts it had taken to board Lafitte's prized ship in the middle of a harbor full of cutthroat pirates, overpower the crew of the *Pride*, and sail it away without causing so much as a ripple.

He growled low in his throat. "Give me a day to roust my crew out of the brothels and we'll hunt her down."

"Bring her back, 'Bastien. Bring her back in irons. And,

presuming you don't have to sink her to do so, you can add her bold little ship with it's thirty-ott guns, to your fleet."

"And the *Hyperion*?"

"That too," Lafitte nodded.

5

In the harsh light of day, the enormity of what she had done gradually transformed Rose's sense of giddy triumph to a more realistic sense of potential doom.

She had not only stolen Jean Lafitte's ship—which was an insult to his reputation as well as his pride—but she had stolen the logbooks, manifests, and ledgers that mapped out his entire business empire.

In the wrong hands, the information contained in just one of those dozen ledgers could destroy him. Or see him thrown in jail with no hope of ever seeing daylight again.

Sitting in his cabin, sipping his fine French wine out of a solid gold goblet, Rose was scanning another book marked 'captains'. Inside were the names of all the captains under Lafitte's command, their ships, the prizes they captured, the cargos they had brought to Barataria to be traded, sold, and dispersed. The captains and crews were well compensated for their efforts and loyalty. In the twenty or so pages she thumbed through, there was only one instance where a captain was caught cheating and his ships had been confiscated. At the bottom of the page there was an inked sketch of a hangman's noose, indicating his fate.

Curiosity made her look for Sebastien Fonteyne's page ... or pages, as it turned out to be. She recognized the name of at least one of the Spanish ships he had captured, the *San Raimundo*, a heavy warship used to transport the bullion that was still being mined and minted in Nombre de Dios. It was rumored to have been sunk in a storm, but apparently the storm came either before or shortly after the Spanish vessel crossed paths with Fonteyne's small fleet of three ships, led by the thirty-eight-gun frigate, the *Black Wind*. The *San Raimundo* was only one of a score or more he had captured on raids in the Caribbean, proof of the firepower and superb tactics that made him one of the most successful privateers in Lafitte's company.

Of all the men Duardo could have clocked over the head, Fonteyne was probably the last one she would have chosen to knock out and hog-tie, but what was done was done.

There was no doubt both he and Lafitte would come after her with a vengeance.

Rose swallowed the last of the wine in a gulp and pushed out of the chair. She returned the ledger to its slot and then snatched her hat off the berth where she had tossed it.

She found Duardo on the quarterdeck conferring with the ship's helmsman, Jose Mercado, who had been brought over from the *Cygnet*. A big man with a chest like a barrel and hands strong enough to crush the shell of a coconut, he was a Spaniard who understood English perfectly but refused to speak it.

Before climbing up to join them, Rose took a moment, as she always did, to admire the tall pyramid of sails overhead. The wind was strong from the north, swelling every sheet of canvas into a straining white curve. Regardless of who owned the ship, the beauty of those sails against the brilliant blue sky, the freedom they represented, the adventure, and yes, even the danger never failed to make her heart beat a little faster.

They also helped cleanse the crimson garishness of Lafitte's cabins out of her brain.

A quarter mile in the *Pride's* wake, the *Cygnet* had trimmed her sails so as not to overtake the heavier ship. She rode as serene and graceful as the elegant bird whose name she bore. Sailing alongside, trying valiantly to keep apace, was the *Hyperion*.

"We might have to cut her loose," Rose said to Duardo as she joined him by the binnacle. "I hate to do it but she will slow us down."

"The elf claims to know a place where we can hide her."

"Hide her?"

"Aye. Hide 'er. Leastwise 'er cargo." The voice came from the level of Rose's waist and she looked down to find the *Cygnet's* navigator and pilot standing beside her. First impressions often mistook him for a child, but under the mop of wiry brown curls, Stubb McCray was well into his third decade, most of which had been spent at sea. Stunted from birth, he had not grown above three feet in height, a handicap which might have hampered a lesser man. But he turned his vertical disadvantage to a lethal advantage in a fight, for he was able to slash through the tendons and tissues of an opponent's knees and calves before they knew he was there.

Most of the crew moved with equal wariness around the diminutive navigator, for they were conscious of his ability to creep silently through tiny dark places, seeing and hearing everything that went on aboard the ship.

"The *Hyperion* be lumberin' like a bloated sow on account 'er belly's full o' copper sheathing an' iron ingots," Stubb continued. "There be a war goin' on in case ye hadn't noticed. That cargo be worth a bloody fortune to either side."

"I am well aware of her cargo," Rose said. "It's unfortunate

Lafitte was in such a hurry to dismiss me as a nuisance... or a plaything for someone's bed... that he lost his chance to reap a share of the profits."

Stubb grinned and cast a sly glance around the deck of the *Pride*. "I vow ye taught 'im a lesson he'll not soon forget."

"One that I doubt he will let go unanswered. More like as not, he will send half his fleet of pirates after us and I would rather not be caught dragging a leaking hulk behind us."

"We should sink both ships," Duardo said.

Stubb gasped. "The *Pride* be worth ten *Hyperions*!"

"Both are worth nothing if we are all hanging from the yardarms."

"An' for that ye'd sink fifty thousand pound sterling in copper an' jaysus knows how much coin in prize monies for Lafitte's floatin' brothel?"

Rose listened to them bicker back and forth for a moment, then turned and looked out over the main deck. The *Pride* was scrubbed and well-tended, her boards were solid, her bulwarks and carved rails showed no signs of battle scarring or repairs. The ship had not seen action for a very long time. The rigging lines were taut, with nary a worn or frayed cable and the sails bore no patches or signs of weather wear.

Once a fearsome fighting ship, she had been reduced to a gilded show piece.

"She might be worth more than just prize money to us," Rose said.

The two men ceased arguing and looked at her.

"Think you Lafitte would order his hunters to shoot at and possibly sink his prize possession?" she asked. "Or would he rather have her returned in the same condition she was when he went ashore?"

Duardo's brow remained creased with doubt; it was Stubb whose eyes danced with a dawning glint.

"Ye mean keep her as an 'ostage?"

"A bargaining chip. I would be willing to wager a year's profits that Lafitte would not want it known that she was stolen and blown to splinters by a female captain and her crew."

"But once he gets her back?" Duardo asked. "What then?"

Rose smiled. "Then he might get his ship back but we will hold onto his ledgers, logs, and manifests ... all of which will be removed to the *Cygnet* for safekeeping."

"Like as we should be removin' the *Hyperion's* cargo," Stubb insisted. "For safekeepin'."

Rose sighed. "Have you any idea how many tons of copper are in her holds? We don't have the time to waste offloading it."

"Bah! The waste would be in squanderin' such a fine cargo, hard won!" Not waiting to hear any further argument, the little man kicked Mercado in the shin to move him out of the way and climbed onto the crate he had placed at the base of the binnacle. He poured over the chart for a long moment before stabbing it with a fat finger. "There."

Rose leaned in. "There is nothing *there* but open water."

"Nay, nay. There be an atoll, dead bare, n'owt more'n a barnacle o' rock stickin' up from the ocean floor. Don't even 'ave a name. Never so much as a tree or bramble be growin' on it. Flat an' wide as Duardo's nose."

The black man scowled at him but Stubb only snickered. "Ships sail past wi'out takin' the trouble to mark it on any chart on account there be n'owt to see. No fresh water to be fotched, no soil to plant, nary enough scrub or brush to build a fire. No damned thing calls it home but snakes an' lizards an' them be none too pleased to welcome guests."

"Sounds appealing," she said wryly.

Stubb cackled. "For what we want, aye, that it is. The atoll be shaped like this." He formed a crab claw with his pudgy hand to illustrate. "Inside be a tidal pool 'bout three fathom deep. We could sink the copper in the pool an' none would be the wiser. None would even spare a thought to take a look."

"It would take hours to winch it out of the cargo bays and row it ashore."

"Three ships we 'ave, with three stout crews. Wave a few pieces o' silver at 'em an' they'll 'ave the lot out an' sunk afore ye can take a good shite."

Rose glanced at Duardo. "What do you think?"

The big man plucked Stubb off the crate like a bug and flicked him aside so he could study the chart. "Two days sail if the wind holds."

"One if we cut through the Twin Sisters," Stubb declared, scrambling to wedge himself back up between them.

Duardo flexed his jaw muscles and adjusted his estimates. "One day's sail, then, to the atoll, but two more to unload the copper."

Rose pondered the map and the danger involved in taking those extra days away from running before the wind. Then she looked at the faces of the two men whose experience and opinions she trusted most on the ship. She was also aware of the big ears listening to their conversation and knew that within minutes, the entire crew would be alerted to what they were discussing.

"It might be worth the risk."

"Worth it an' then some," Stubb insisted. "I can hear yer father now if he learns ye sunk her with a full load o' cargo."

By way of demonstrating, he shoved his hands into the armholes of his vest and stomped across the deck shaking his head in an admirable imitation of Alexander St. Clare. "Ye did what, girl? Ye did what? Copper? *Copper*? Ye know what that shite be worth?"

Duardo cuffed the little man on the shoulder then looked at Rose. "Decide soon, Captain, before the *Hyperion* makes the decision for you and sinks. The men patched her as best they could but the hull leaks like a sieve. Might not even make it as far as the atoll. But if it did, the cargo would be worth its weight in gold, and the thought of what their shares might be worth would inspire the crew to keep her afloat."

Rose glanced out over the main deck. There was no one working, no one talking. The men had fallen silent to hear the whispers being relayed back about the conversation on the quarterdeck. Their potential profits were being discussed and they were all ears.

"Alright. Set a course for the atoll," she decided. "I will give you *one* day to offload as much as you can. In the meantime, get some men over the sides with paint to cover all the damned gilding on the rails and gun ports. The sun or moonlight hits any of it and we'd shine like a beacon in a lighthouse." To Duardo she said, "Signal the *Cygnet* and bring Billy Burr on board here to run out the guns. We don't know when they were fired last and if we have to use them, I don't want any of them cracking or exploding. Check the powder stores and supply of shot as well. I don't expect this floating brothel is too well provisioned if she was only used to parade back and forth from Barataria to New Orleans."

While the mismatched pair set about issuing orders to the crew. Rose gripped the rail and looked out over the wide expanse of the sea. She turned her face to the last rays of warmth from the fiery orange ball of the sun where it was making its descent. Streamers of light were cutting through the distant scatter of clouds that rode low on the horizon, and where the rays touched the sea, they turned to surface into molten lava.

She did not expect to see anything, but she held a spyglass to her eye and searched slowly and carefully for any hint of sails riding low in the distance.

There was nothing to see.

Nothing but water and sky and golden shafts of waning sunlight.

Duardo stood at her shoulder. "You are convinced he has sent his hunters after us?"

"I am convinced there will shortly be a black wind blowing in our direction."

6

———————

Sebastien Fonteyne stood on the fo'c's'le of his ship, the *Black Wind*, and watched the last golden rays of sunlight fade below the horizon. Every scrap of canvas was set, every sail filled and curved like sheets of marble in the steady wind. With daylight fading, most of the men were winding down from their daily tasks, some sitting shirtless on crates and barrels to dry the sweat earned from a hard day's work. Some lit their pipes. Some stood holding their tin cups by the barrel of grog waiting their turn with the wooden dipper.

To a man, they warily eyed their captain, all too familiar with the ominous look on his face.

Unfettered, Fonteyne's long black hair blew forward over his cheeks as he scanned the unbroken line of the horizon. Eyes the color of dark amber scoured the demarcation where water met sky, occasionally peering through the brass long-glass, almost demanding to see another set of sails or, with the eastern horizon already darkening, an errant light winking in the distance. His mouth was set in a grim line; the muscles in his jaw were clenched so tight, the veins in his temple stood out like cords.

The girl had a two-day head start. It had taken him that long to provision his ship and find enough sober crewmen to work the ship. The *Black Wind* normally carried one hundred and seventy men; there were three quarters that number on board now, but Fonteyne had gone into battles with less. As long as there were enough to keep his battery of guns firing, Fonteyne was confident.

Two days was one hell of an advantage but not insurmountable. Over the past year or more, Lafitte's *Pride*, had rarely ventured beyond the stronghold of Barataria Bay. Her hull had not been scraped in months and was likely crusted a foot thick with barnacles that would shave several knots off her top speed. Captured from the Spanish, the ship had been built in Cadiz, made of solid oak timber, her decks reinforced to carry the weight of armaments. Lafitte had removed a goodly number of the heavy cast guns and modified her rigging to gain more maneuverability. Conversely, he had kept all of the ornamental carvings and extravagant gilding which marked most galleons in a treasure fleet. Her silhouette would be easily identifiable at any distance.

The lump on Fonteyne's head ached like the devil and each time he scratched without thinking, a bloody scrap of scab was torn away. He had worn a bandage the first day, but that had proved to be an even greater nuisance. After two decades and countless battles at sea he knew his flesh healed fast.

His temper, however, did not.

He had a two-day disadvantage and four points of the compass to consider as the hunt began.

North was discounted at once, for that way lay only mangrove swamp and sandy coastlines; nowhere to hide a ship as recognizable as the *Pride*. A westerly heading would take her toward Panama and into shipping lanes that were heavily patrolled by the Spaniards. Since breaking ties with Napoleon and the French allies, Spain had become increasingly territorial as they watched the conflict escalate between the Americans and the British. Spanish royalty had been engaged in battles with England since the days of Elizabeth's reign, and they had every reason now to be wary of the Americans, They undoubtedly suspected it was only a matter of time before the land-hungry colonists turned their greedy eyes to the vast, rich plains that stretched west of the Mississippi into Mexico and California.

To the south lay the wealth of the silver and emerald mines of Columbia, riches that proved tempting to French, Dutch, Portuguese, and English pirates. Fonteyne himself had embarked on several successful raids along the coast of Cartagena and Granada and had needed the guns of all three of his ships to blast his way back to home base.

He doubted Rose St. Clare would find sanctuary there.

Eliminating the North, South, and West points of the compass, left the long chain of islands in the East. Hundreds of them, big and small, some inhabited, some barren, some lush with vegetation, others dry as volcanic rock. The islands of the West Indies lay in a sweeping crescent that extended downward from Florida almost to South America.

Rose St. Clare's ancestors had once established a stronghold on one of those islands. If fables and old seamen's tales were to be believed, Pigeon Cay had provided the Dante pirate clan an impenetrable base for over sixty years. Spanish raiders had eventually found it and destroyed the harbor and the warehouses. They had looted everything of value and scorched the earth before taking the islanders captive. But a century later, it was still not marked on any chart or map. Many, following tall tales of vast hoards of treasure left behind, had tried to find the island over the years but none had achieved any success—none who had lived to report it, at any rate.

Stories of the infamous *pirata lobo* ... the Pirate Wolf ... had filled penny sheets with spine-tingling adventures and heart-pounding romances for decades, few of which Fonteyne gave any credence. Buried treasure on a hidden island and men who could make themselves invisible were just more legends alongside tales of Kidd's hidden cache of Spanish gold and Blackbeard's hoard of jewels secreted somewhere on the island of Jamaica.

The Dante-St. Clare Shipping Company had bases in Tobago, and London. The patriarch of the family, Alexander St. Clare, ran his fleet of merchant ships between the two ports and from there, to all points of the globe. The girl and her brothers had grown up at sea, so it would be reasonable to assume she would have an intimate knowledge of the Caribbean.

One thought lingered and nagged at the back of his mind: What if Pigeon Cay did exist, and what if Rose knew where it was? Lafitte could send every one of his hundred ships to scour the islands and never find it ... or her.

The first time Sebastien had met Rose St. Clare at the ball in Port-Louis, he had been genuinely intrigued. She was a seventeen-year-old beauty, slender and shapely, with curves in all the right places. She had stood out like a beacon in the crowd of powdered and pale women who spent all their daylight hours hiding away from the tropical sun. Rose's skin was tanned, her arms firm with muscles not gained by pushing embroidery threads through pillowslips. She hadn't stared, she hadn't fawned, her tongue hadn't tied in knots when she spoke to him.

And she hadn't known that Fonteyne had been in such a rage with her brother, that seducing her made the evening twice as pleasurable as he had anticipated it would be.

His duel that night had been with bodies, not swords, and he had come away the victor.

He certainly never expected to see her again, most definitely not striding into Lafitte's stronghold claiming to be the captain of her own ship. In all his years, Fonteyne had encountered only one other female captain, a woman as broad across the beam as a shithouse, with a face as repulsive as the odor of her black and rotting teeth.

Rose St. Clare, however, was as intriguing and possibly more beautiful than he remembered. Seeing her walk into the tavern had caused an unexpected reaction ... one that forced him to move away from the table and stay at a distance until his blood settled to a dull roar. The girl had nerves of steel sailing into Barataria Bay and a hundred times more so daring to sail away with Lafitte's ship ... a feat few men would have tried, let alone accomplished. It was difficult not to admire her resourcefulness as well as her audacity, and it was apparent she had the blood of her piratical ancestors flowing through her veins. It would be a damned shame to have to spill it all over her deck.

"You'll push your eye into the socket if you keep pressing that glass against it."

Fonteyne acknowledged the comment with a low, throaty growl.

"Ah. The usual succinct response when your mind is a thousand miles away."

Fonteyne lowered the long-glass and snapped the telescoping sections together. "Two days, Archie. Two damned days head start and only half a clue where to start looking."

"Half is better than none."

Ever the quick-witted optimist, Archibald Penman III was the ship's doctor and one of the few men Fonteyne called friend. Tall and lean, with wavy gold hair, the only time he was seen without a standing collar and cravat, an embroidered silk waistcoat and pristinely tailored jacket was when he was in the surgery, up to his elbows in blood. His boots shone and his snow-white breeches were fitted tight to his thighs and smooth.

The current rumor amongst them had it that Penman was a member of the English aristocracy who had run away to sea to avoid a charge of murder. But the rumors changed as often as he changed his cravats and he neither acknowledged nor refuted any of the whisperings.

Indeed, he rather enjoyed hearing the colorful tales he was supposedly involved in.

"I have been dispatched to fetch you. Cook has laid out a fine supper of roasted suckling pig and warns that if his talents are wasted and the feast not eaten while the crackling is still … ah, crackling … he will hang himself from the nearest yardarm."

Fonteyne frowned. "I doubt we have a yard stout enough to hold all three hundred pounds of him."

"Each pound well-earned to judge by the smells coming from the galley and the drool running down my chin."

"That isn't drool."

Penman wiped the slick of grease off his lip. "I was only testing the quality of the goods. And if you delay another five minutes, the crew will launch an assault on the galley and you'll be lucky to get a boiled turnip for your supper."

Fonteyne laughed. "Fine. I will come and eat the pig."

He handed the glass to the helmsman, then followed Penman down the stairs and through the hatchway to the corridor leading to the cabins in the stern.

His quarters were utilitarian, a small space made smaller when crowded with his desk, his berth, his sea chests, and a long dining table. His plates were wood or pewter, his candles sat in dull brass sticks. There was no linen cloth on the table and the six chairs around it were mismatched and well worn. The wall behind his desk was festooned with the flags and pennons from the ships he had captured; a rack held an assortment of swords surrendered by their captains.

He unbuckled his sword belt and hung it over the post of a

straight-backed pilgrim's chair before he sat. He set his pistols on the table with a thud and poured two glasses of wine, one of which he slid across to Penman.

The doctor swirled the wine gently around the bowl of his glass and glanced at Fonteyne. "I quite understand the concept of hunting on land, and the ability to track prints and spoor by following broken branches, trampled grass, and whatnot. But how do you hunt on the sea when there are a thousand places to hide in a thousand different directions and no tracks left on the water to follow?"

"A combination of best guess and sheer luck."

"And what would be your best guess?"

"The St. Clare home base is on Tobago. It could be that she will head in that general direction."

"Would she not anticipate you thinking that exact thing?"

"Perhaps. Being the brazen little minx that she is, I wager it would be hard for her to resist showing off her prize to her brother. Ramsey St. Clare would pop all of his buttons if he had Lafitte's ship in his possession. The British would elevate him to Viceroy and make him a peer." He frowned into his wine and added, "Which might be exactly why she would avoid it. With her wanting to join Lafitte, I gather she and Ramsey are not on the same side of the conflict."

"Are you aware your eye twitches every time you say his name?"

Fonteyne shrugged. "Ramsey St. Clare and I have a history. A party of armed British officers boarded my ship while it was docked and removed three of my men, claiming they were British deserters. St. Clare refused to help get them back, so I followed the vaunted Royal Naval vessel out of port, blasted their incompetent gunners to silence, and not only took my men back, but kept the ship."

Penman looked around the cabin. "This ship?"

Fonteyne's grin was wide and white. "She's built of stout English oak, solid as iron from stem to stern. It was not her fault she was crewed by striplings barely a month out of their cadet jumpers. I have given her a few modifications, but all to good effect."

Penman laughed. "Surely you must see the irony in pursuing Rose St. Clare for doing much the same thing."

Fonteyne took a sip of wine. "You admire the chit, do you?"

"Anyone who can send that wretched little blacksmith into apoplectic fits must surely warrant a few huzzahs. Unless, of course, your vexation comes more from the lump she left on your head rather than any umbrage she caused Lafitte?"

Sebastien's reply was delayed as the door opened to a parade of three cabin boys carrying trays of food. First to reach the table was a large portion of a suckling pig, roasted and glistening, accompanied by bowls of turnips, cabbage and biscuits.

Regarding the fragrant bounty, Penman instantly forgot what they had been discussing, but Fonteyne did not. He sipped his wine and watched the doctor carve the meat and fill their plates, but his thoughts were back up on deck overlooking a sea as deep and unfathomable as Rose St. Clare's eyes. He'd not heard the chit had married and the name Whitticomb roused no memory of a captain by that name. Dead these past three years? Probably from sheer frustration trying to rein in a firebrand like Rosamund St. Clare.

I have accepted the challenge, girl. Wherever you have gone, I will find you. And when I do ...

FAR TO THE south and east, Rose felt the whisper of a shiver run up her spine. She glanced over her shoulder, half-expecting to see a tall black-haired devil standing behind her, but there was only sky and ocean, the latter dotted with marching whitecaps. She chided her own foolishness and tucked her neck into the standing collar of her jacket to ward off any further chills.

As a precaution, however, she doubled the lookouts in the tops before going below to her cabin.

7

The atoll was every inch as barren and desolate as Stubb had described. Much like an iceberg, the bulk of the island lay underwater, sloping so far out that a ship could not come within three hundred yards without scraping the keel. Half a mile long, the highest point rose a mere forty feet above the surface of the ocean, removing any possibility of a vessel using it as a shield to hide behind.

On the leeward side, there was a break in the solid sheets of rock, a crevice barely wide enough for a longboat to row safely through. Once past the outer pincers of the 'claws', the rock widened in the middle to formed a rim around an egg-shaped tidal pool, the centre of which was inky dark. The pool was open to the sea, the water undrinkable, useless to passing ships. As Stubb had said, there were no trees crowning the atoll, nothing taller than patches of scrub brush growing out of crevices.

Even with crews from the three ships working steadily to offload the *Hyperion*, the heavy bundles of copper sheathing were taking far too long to haul up from the cargo bays, winch across to the longboats, and ferry to the atoll. Rose grew increasingly anxious when cables snapped or a boat capsized from attempting to load too much weight. She spent every hour on the crest of the knoll, her long-glass searching the western horizon, the direction from which any hunters would likely appear.

To the east, lying out of sight below the horizon was the southern tip of Hispaniola. Rose was fairly confident they could not be detected as they worked feverishly to transfer the copper, but the Spanish island was still too close for comfort. While her fleet of three ships might present an imposing sight at a distance, the salvageable guns on board the *Hyperion* had been transferred to the *Cygnet*, rendering the English vessel with no means to fight or defend itself. The guns on board the *Pride* were still in the process of being reamed out and cleaned, leaving only the *Cygnet* fully capable of any kind of defense. The fact those defenses had been increased from thirty-two guns to forty was little comfort.

Rose was not eager to cross wakes with any patrolling galleons. It was enough to wonder how long it would take Lafitte's trackers to catch their scent.

Each time she speculated on who might be following in their wake, an image of Sebastien Fonteyne's face came to mind and her pulse quickened. In some small, incautious part of her mind she hoped it would, indeed, be him, for if she wanted to show she was capable of sailing with the best, she had to prove she could outfox the best.

If it *was* Sebastien Fonteyne chasing her down, he was undoubtedly furious over what had happened at Barataria.

In truth, she had not yet allowed herself to acknowledge the shock of standing chest to breast with him after so many years. Crowded into that doorway, his big body pressed against her, she had felt her heart racing like a wild thing. If she closed her eyes she could see his face, smell the leather and bay rum on his skin, feel the warmth of his breath on her cheek.

Five years ago, with their bodies stuck together with the

sweat from their exertions, he had thought it a joke that she wanted to captain her own ship.

"You can't be serious."

"I am completely serious. I have been sailing with my father since I was six years old. I have stood at the helm, I have fired and swabbed the guns; I have learned to navigate by the sun as well as the stars, and I can wield a sword as well as any man."

"Aye, but have you killed another man?"

"Yes. I have."

Her head was in the crook of his shoulder, his hand was toying with strands of her hair. Hearing her answer, his fingers stopped moving, trying to decide if she was serious or being a minx. "I suppose you can also shoot the eye out of a rat at one hundred paces?"

"With a musket at fifty, aye."

He laughed and rolled her onto her side, then onto her back, keeping his body firmly wedged between her thighs. "Then, despite all your questions earlier tonight, I warrant you have nothing left to learn from me."

"Well, there was one thing. But I am now quite thoroughly enlightened."

He had been just about to kiss her again, but stopped and raised his head. His hair had fallen over his forehead, his flesh still full and thudding softly inside her.

He leaned further back and when he read the meaning behind her sly smile, his gaze followed the valley between her breasts down to below her belly where their bodies were joined.

"You were a virgin?"

She had debated lying, but knew he would see through it. "I thought a man could tell."

"Not always," he said quietly. "Not when they are too …"

"Intent on satisfying their own pleasure?" she finished for him.

He pushed himself all the way up and she frowned as the warm slide of his flesh abandoned hers. He stretched out beside her and stared up at the ceiling.

"Virgins are a complication I usually try to avoid."

"I certainly have no wish to be a complication. I merely thought, if I am to live and work on board a ship with a hundred men for months on end, it was important to recognize a man's motives, to not fall into a swoon like an addled schoolgirl every time I was looked at a certain way or forced into a compromising position by word or gesture."

He turned his head to frown at her. "I am glad I could be of service."

"And now you are angry. Or insulted?" She sat up and gathered the folds of the bedsheet around her. "Because I used you exactly the way you wanted to use me to get back at my brother for not helping you get your men back?"

He had stared at her, she had stared at him, and he hadn't denied the charge.

Rose blinked and snapped her spyglass closed along with the memory.

"This is taking far too long. I never should have let you talk me into this.

Standing beside her, Stubb mouthed her words silently in unison as she said them for the hundredth time. Aloud he asked, "When do ye ever do aught on my advice alone? It were the crew what voted an' the crew what convinced ye to stay an' let them work the extra day."

"You standing over them brandishing your pistols had no influence over them, I'm sure."

"I were cleanin' them."

Rose reached down and pinched his ear hard enough for him to squeak out a curse.

"Oh please, let me help," came a voice from behind.

Rose turned as Billy Burr joined them at the top of the knoll and flicked Stubb's other ear. He clapped his hands over both ears and cursed again.

The *Cygnet's* gun captain was as tall as Rose and shared the distinction of being the second woman on board the ship to hold a position of command normally dominated by men. Her hair was dark and cropped short, her arms and legs were corded with muscle, her hands rough, thick with calluses. Her skin was bronzed from years spent under the tropical sun; large green eyes looked at the world as if everything was a challenge to be conquered. She might have been a beauty, had the right side of her face and neck not been scarred by powder burns.

Billy never spoke of her past. The lilt in her voice hinted at a mixture of British, Spanish, Dutch, and French—all languages she could speak fluently. She claimed to have spent four years disguised as a man on board a Dutch East India ship, but when she heard there was a female captain taking on crew, she shed the bands around her breasts and lined up to join Rose's company. Her skill and knowledge in handling weapons of every kind had quickly dispelled any rebellion amongst the men.

Billy made another pinching motion toward Stubb and chuckled as the little man flinched and scrambled out of arm's reach. Tormenting him was one of her small pleasures.

"Have you had a chance to take a good look at the guns on board the *Pride*?" Rose asked, in no mood to watch the two spar.

"If any of them have been use any time during the last year, I'll fuck a shark. I found bird nests in three of them and rust inside most. I have my crews cleaning and reaming them out but I won't know how sound they are until I can fire them."

"Powder and shot?"

"More than I expected, less than I hoped. Enough to see us through one good fight but two would be a stretch. Most of the cloth charges were rotted, so I've put the sail makers to work making new cartridges from silk, which should cut down on the debris they leave in the barrel. Other than that, hell, for all I know the muzzles will explode with the first broadside. The twenty-fours are so corroded I would like to just tip them over the side. I'd feel better if we could test them."

Stubb sighed noisily, knowing that when Billy started talking about guns and cannon, the discussions were never very short. He shaded his eyes with a pudgy hand.

"Storm be comin'. Big bitch too, by the way my ballocks be achin'."

As one, Rose and Billy looked up at the sky. It was a clear, searing blue, and while the seas were rough, the wind was hot and steady.

"It be comin'," Stubb insisted. "Tonight, I warrant, if not afore. My sacs be as hard as goose eggs, an' when they be like that, ye can be sure a big blow is comin'. We should put toe to heel an' not linger longer than need be."

Rose glared an icy reminder that he was the one who persuaded the crew to stay the extra day to save more of the copper.

"How long can we keep the *Hyperion* afloat?" she asked. "I would rather not sink her this close to the atoll."

"She be a mort lighter with twenty ton o' copper gone, but she won't last long. We took most o' the men off the pumps on account it were just wastin' energy."

Rose nodded and glanced at Billy. "Looks like you'll be getting that chance to test Lafitte's guns."

"Or blow up yerself an' the brothel tryin'," Stubb snorted.

Billy's smile was lopsided because of the scars. "One of these days, gnome, I will pin your pointy little ears to the mast and use *you* for target practice."

Unfazed, he chuckled and walked away, whistling through his teeth to signal the men that the work was done and they should gather up the ropes and winches and return to the boats.

WHEN THE LAST of the copper was unloaded into the tidal pool and they were certain no trace of their presence had been left behind, the empty longboats and their exhausted crews returned to the ships. Two of the boats were rowed to the *Cygnet*, one to the *Pride* and one to the *Hyperion*. With the waves getting rougher and the wind picking up, all three ships were tugging restlessly on their anchor cables as if anxious to leave as well.

As his boat approached the hull of the *Hyperion*, Duardo twirled his finger in the air, alerting the men to put their backs into the anchor windlass and raise the heavy iron hook. It was decided he would take the helm of the balky English ship until they found a good place to sink her. The *Cygnet's* helmsman, Jose Mercado, was put in temporary command of the *Pride*.

Having already transferred the charts, ledgers and papers from the *Pride* to the *Cygnet*, and having endured quite enough of the crimson nightmare that was Lafitte's cabin, Rose returned to the welcome familiarity of her own ship.

When she walked through the gangway, Stubb was already on board and greeted her with a partially devoured chicken leg clutched in his fist.

"Hard work 'at was," he said around a mouthful of meat. "An' a mort o' greedy hands in the stew pot afore I got there. Be n'owt much left aside from biscuits an' broth, but ol' Barney saved a piece o' capon an' put it in yer cabin."

Rose's stomach rumbled to remind her she had not eaten

since ... since she could not remember when. But the sky was still a brilliant, pristine blue, with a clear horizon stretching out for miles. Hoping to ease the persistent scratch across the nape of her neck, she climbed up the rigging to the topmost yards and perched there with the spyglass aimed to the western horizon. Her sight-line was elevated just enough for her to see over the crest of the atoll and allow a slow sweep from one side of the vast expanse of the ocean to the other.

She frowned a little, thinking of the notation scripted along the border of old sea charts.

Beyond this place, there be dragons.

Dragons? Or black-haired devils?

She sighed and tucked the long glass into her belt. Her eyes were dry and burning, scorched by the sun. She had not slept more than a mouse in a cat's cage over the past forty-eight hours, so it was her berth, more than the thought of food, that had her start to shinny back down to the main deck.

"Sails Captain! Sails off the larboard beam!"

Rose stopped, climbed to the topmost yard again, and raised her glass. She blinked hard and rubbed a fist across her eyes but could see nothing through the glare of the lowering sun.

"Where, dammit?" She caught a breath, then: "Never mind, I see it."

What she saw was smallest wink of white peeking sporadically between the distant waves. It was little more than a tiny pinprick easily lost in a sea of glittering pinpricks as the sun bounced off the distant whitecaps, but it was there and it was a ship. It was impossible to see any pennants or flags that would identify her, but the brush of ghostly fingers down Rose's spine told her exactly who it was.

She cupped her hands around her mouth and called down to Stubb's upturned face. "Signal the other ships. Let go the sheets and braces. Make all sail."

"Be there one ship? Two?"

"I can only see the one, but there may be more below the horizon coming up behind her. One or twenty-one, we've no time to waste!"

"Aye, aye." Stubb tossed the gnawed chicken bone over the side and relayed orders even as he scrambled nimbly up the ratlines. He joined Rose at the very top of the mainmast, one hundred and sixty feet above the deck, and helped her untie and unfurl the topgallant sail. It opened with a shudder and a loud snap as it caught the wind and belled outward in a hard curve.

Job done, Rose swivelled around on the yard, and her temper bristled slightly knowing the *Cygnet's* sails would be winking back across the leagues. She could almost hear the shouts of a sharp-eyed lookout on board the distant ship.

There was the possibility it was a galleon making its way to Havana. It was also possible it was a British patrol skulking around the islands, searching for potential smugglers. There were always merchants and couriers travelling to and from the other side of the Ocean-Sea, for not all nationalities were involved with the conflict between Britain and America and trade carried on as usual, though most kept a wide berth.

But Rose knew it was none of those. It was Lafitte's hunter and whoever her captain was, he was undoubtedly roaring orders to his crew to pile on sail.

8

———

In the sudden chaos that erupted on board the *Black Wind*, orders were shouted back and forth between the riggers as they scrambled onto the yards by twos and threes. The upper deck was cleared of anything that did not belong ... crates, barrels, tasks the crew might have been working on before the cry of "sails ho!" was relayed across the decks. Any sails not already unfurled were released, lines were caught and pulled tight by men waiting below who attached them to the mooring pins that ran along both sides of the ship.

Sebastien Fonteyne watched with a critical eye, roaring commands when he saw a slack cable. If not for the roughness of the waves lifting the *Black Wind* twenty feet higher than normal and an experienced lookout who spotted the distant sails between troughs, he would likely have carried on due south to outrun the storm clouds rapidly approaching from the northwest.

On orders from the helm, the massive canvas sheets were maneuvered to bring the *Black Wind* into a sweeping turn. Sebastien felt the surge beneath his feet as his ship leaped into the chase and he felt the rush in his blood knowing his instincts had not failed him and his quarry was in sight.

Full credit was given where it was due: she had eluded him for almost five days and he could only suppose that one or more of her ships was responsible for slowing her down. He doubted it was the *Cygnet*. From the information Sauvinet had provided, he knew she was a three-masted light frigate with a top speed rumored to be sixteen knots. She carried a compliment of thirty-two cannon, most of them twenty-four pounder long guns capable of deadly accuracy at long ranges as well as close combat.

According to the customs agent, the first two years after she was launched, the *Cygnet* had carried half her current armaments and, under the auspices of the deceased Terrance Whitticomb, had been harmlessly conducting trade between the islands. Three years ago, her purpose had changed, her battery of guns had increased, and the *Cygnet* had been credited with taking half a dozen ships in prize. How or when the unfortunate Whitticomb had died was not noted in any records, but in hindsight, it could be left to assume it was when Rose had taken the helm.

The more he learned about the *Cygnet* and her captain, the more intrigued he became. While it was true that Rose St. Clare had done what few of Lafitte's own company of brigands had managed to do by running the blockade lines three times, it only served to increase suspicion as to whose flag she was sailing under. The pirate king was convinced, that she *must* be working with the British. She *must* have been sent to Barataria by her brother in order to spy! How else to explain why a mere scrap of a girl could sail around the Caribbean unscathed unless she was in the employ of the Crown!

So she had come to offer her services against a British invasion fleet? It was more likely she had come to infiltrate and report the extent of the defenses around Barataria Bay!

To Fonteyne's way of thinking, however, three years was a long time to pretend you were something you were not. If she had been sent to Barataria as a spy, and if captain and crew were, indeed, loyal to the Crown, there was no company on this earth, not even his own, that would have kept such a ruse secret for so long regardless how breathtaking their captain looked in her figure-hugging corset and skin-tight breeches.

Breasts were no match for the promise of gold. Any secret mission would have been sold out long ago by a judas on the crew seeking his thirty pieces of silver. It was rumored to have been just such a betrayal that had cost the Dante ancestors the destruction of Pigeon Cay a hundred years ago.

Perhaps Lafitte should have taken the girl more seriously. Considering Fonteyne's own personal history with Rose St. Clare, it was doubly unfortunate that Sebastien was the one to have to drag her back to Barataria on her knees.

He had to catch her first, however, and with ominously dark thunderclouds swiftly blowing up behind them—weather she might not be able to see from her vantage point yet—it was imperative to close the gap between hunter and prey as swiftly as possible.

When it was full dark, he had the crew bring up the black canvas sheets which would allow them to sail almost invisibly through the night. Orders were given that no lights, not even the smallest red glow from a pipe would be allowed above or below deck.

In the end, Fonteyne had no reason to worry about lit pipes or errant lights. The storm came on them strong and savage, tossing the ship from wave to wave like it was a child's toy. Rain fell in torrents, pounding the decks, waterfalling down hatchways, swirling along corridors and soaking everything in its path. Wind-driven needles of salt spray battered the crew as they wrestled to haul in sail and secure the heavy sheets before they were torn from the yards. Timbers groaned and ropes snapped, whiplashing across the deck to become fouled in tangles of twisted rigging. Jagged streaks of lightning smashed overhead, striking all three masts multiple times.

Twice, the *Black Wind* heeled over so sharply a man could have reached an arm over the rail and touched the angry black sea wall. Foam-crested waves crashed over the deck, the weight forcing the keel into troughs so deep the following sea rose as high as the topmost mast.

Standing on the quarterdeck, a sodden black demon in his own right, Sebastien Fonteyne tied himself to the wheel and stood firm through everything the sea threw at him. At times he could be heard above the wrath of the storm, cursing, laughing, and cursing more.

9

The storm raged for two nights and two days. When dawn arrived on the third morning, it was difficult to believe they had just been through a maelstrom. The air was perfectly still, the surface of the sea was smooth as glass. A thick fog bank had enveloped the *Black Wind*, blanketing the ship in gray clouds. The air was gray, the sea was gray, the eerie veils of mist that shifted with any movement on deck were gray. Water dripped constantly from the rigging and sails, which hung sodden and limp from the yards.

There were broken spars overhead and the top fifteen feet of the mainmast had been split down the middle by a lightning strike. The gate at the gangway was missing, blown off its hinges, and two of the big guns that had been unseated lay at odd angles to the gunports. Anything not securely fastened before the storm struck was gone, swept overboard by the fury of the sea. The rudder was slow in answering the helm, which meant it likely bore damage below the water.

Fonteyne had run dry of curses. Neither he nor his navigator, Nathanial Reed, had any idea where they were or how far off course the storm had thrown them. For all they knew, when the ghostly miasma lifted, they could be sitting a mile off the shore-line of Havana, surrounded by a fleet of Spanish galleons. Making matters worse, they had no idea in which direction Hispaniola even lay, for the glass casing around the binnacle had been smashed and the compass needle was gone. The fog and clouds overhead blocked any possibility of taking a reading from the sun ... assuming they could even find the horizon.

Archibald Penman joined Fonteyne and Reed at the rail and stared at ... nothing.

"Do either of you have a best guess where the devil we might be?" he asked.

Reed shrugged and spat over the rail. "Until I can see the sun or stars, I can only go by what my gut tells me."

"And what does it tell you?"

He lifted a finger. "Bow's pointing that way."

Penman pursed his lips and nodded. "Helpful."

Reed was a tall, lean man with snow white hair braided to his waist. He had been at sea for thirty years and had lost half a leg in battle. He wore a wooden peg fitted with leather straps that buckled onto his belt, a handicap that did not hamper him in the least. There wasn't much he hadn't seen, and rarely anything that spooked him but judging by the way his eyes flicked constantly left and right, he was spooked now.

"Capt'n—?"

Fonteyne nodded. He felt it too, a sensation like the sticky filaments of a spider's web dragging down his spine.

"Double the lookouts," he ordered quietly. "Put men with the keenest eyes and ears into the tops where they might be able to see or hear something above this mess."

Reed touched a forefinger to his brow and went to relay the orders. A dozen men scrambled immediately up the ratlines and vanished within a few rungs of the shrouds, swallowed into the dense fog.

Sebastien felt an irrational urge to step back from the rails as the fingers of mist circled his ankles like shackles. He was not an overly superstitious man, not on most days at any rate, but there were tales of ships getting lost in thick fog banks like this. One such story recounted how an entire fleet of treasure galleons had vanished off the coast of Bermuda without a trace of wreckage ever being found.

He frowned and blew out a breath. "What of the crew? Any serious injuries?"

"Two goats missing, likely washed overboard. One lad with a broken arm," Penman said. "Otherwise mostly bruises and scrapes. It could have been much worse, I suppose."

Sebastien took the remark as a subtle criticism for taking the risk of leaving the main sails up for so long. He glanced to the side, but the surgeon's face was as placid as ever. Penman's cravat was crisply tied, and while he was not wearing a formal jacket, his waistcoat was buttoned over a shirt so white, the fashionably full sleeves glowed against the eerie gloom of the fog.

Immune to the steely glare, Penman adjusted the ruffle on his cuff. "By way of consolation, one must suppose our quarry has found herself in similar straights. Lafitte's ship, like the man himself, wallows like an overstuffed pig and would not have borne up well under such high winds and seas."

Sebastien said nothing. His last glimpse of Rose St. Clare's three ships had put her on a course heading south and east but he had no way of knowing if she had outrun the storm or, like them, been blown in circles.

"Should we, perhaps, light the big deck lamps and try to burn off some of this vile mist? We can—"

Fonteyne held up his hand to silence Penman. "Listen."

Penman fell obligingly silent. The fog was muffling what few whispers of conversation that were passing between the crew. Beyond that, he could hear the faint gurgle of ripples lapping gently against the hull. Overhead, the massive canvas sheets were still shaking off spickets of water that fell in a patter to the deck.

"What am I supposed to be—?"

"Listen! Close your damned eyes and *listen!*"

Penman turned his good ear to the fog ... which was not much better than trying to hear out of his bad ear. But even though he closed his eyes to help focus on sounds, he detected nothing aside from the faint clinking metal from a loose cleat rattling somewhere overhead.

"Sebastien, I'm not—"

"Watch out!"

Penman's eyes popped open in time to see a mermaid, her long hair streaming back like flames, emerge from the fog and hurl herself straight toward them. She was bare-breasted, her body gleaming from the moisture of the heavy fog. The scales on her lower body were iridescent silver, blue, and pink.

Sebastien shoved him out of the way a moment before the top of Penman's head would have been taken off by the carved wooden figurehead. Half a breath later, both men were thrown across the deck as the reinforced prow of another ship slammed into the side of the *Black Wind*, crushing through the rails.

A loud roaring sound followed. Whether from Fonteyne's throat or the timbers of his ship as she canted suddenly to the side, it was difficult to tell, for the roar was accompanied by the shouts of men above deck who lost their footing on the slippery yards, and from men below who were tipped out hammocks and tossed onto the boards. One long scream marked the descent of one of the lookouts, who, because of the tilt of the ship, splashed into the sea.

Fonteyne and Penman lay sprawled on the deck. They watched, stunned, as a score of grappling hooks came spinning out of the fog to bite into anything solid. Even before the two ships were solidly locked together, there were ghostly shadows swinging across on ropes that came out of the fog and seemed to be attached to nothing. Fonteyne reached instinctively for a sword that was not at his hip, for though he had brought it up on deck with him, it lay across the top of the capstan where he had set it down while relieving himself over the side earlier. There had been no warning of an impending attack, nothing to indicate another ship was lurking out in the fog.

More shadowy figures swarmed across on planks like a pack of wolves, cutlasses and pistols to hand. Dozens of them, scores of them, armed to the teeth came aboard screaming like banshees. They spilled across the decks and ran down the hatches, shocking the already fuddled crew into submission before anyone knew what was happening.

Two minutes.

That was all the time it took for the *Black Wind* to be overrun, for her crew to be put on their knees, for the few stalwart defenders to be disarmed, their efforts knocked into submission.

Fonteyne staggered to his feet, blinded in one eye by blood pouring out of a deep gash on his forehead. Instinctively, he snapped a dislocated thumb into its socket, then looked for Penman, who had been flung hard against the base of the mainmast. He, too, was stumbling to his feet, dazed, disoriented by the fog, by the pain of a bruised hip, and by the sudden influx of armed attackers.

One of those attackers leaped onto the deck, landing with a mighty thud. He towered nearly seven feet in height, his bald head gleaming like ebony. His chest was a fearsome wall of bulging muscle, bare but for a slender bamboo tube suspended between the two leather crossbelts that held a brace of long-snouted pistols. Eyes like two black pits scanned what little area of the deck was visible before settling on Sebastien Fonteyne.

Stark white teeth flashed in a grin. "And so, we meet again, Captain."

Fonteyne angrily dashed the blood out of his eyes. He was fairly certain he had never seen the black giant before, but he most assuredly knew that voice. He had heard it moments before he'd been knocked out cold on the waterfront at Barataria Bay.

The giant raised his clenched fist in a signal and seconds later, three hissing globes of light emerged from the fog. A trio of enormous ship's lamps burned cavernous gaps into the mist as they were carried on board and set in a hot yellow triangle around Fonteyne and Penman. They were followed by another figure who swung easily down off the bowsprit—now lodged firmly into the crush of broken rails and warped planking— and landed with a cat's grace on the *Black Wind's* deck. Light from the lamps reflected off the sword held in one hand and the pistol brandished in the other.

There was no mistaking where Fonteyne had seen the velvet frockcoat, the corset waistcoat, the long, lithe legs clad in thigh-high leather boots. Her features were shadowed by the wide brim of her hat but, after a long moment filled only with the hiss of fog melting on the sides of the lanterns, a throaty chuckle brought Rose St. Clare's face tipping up into the light.

"My compliments, Captain Fonteyne. You found us."

Fonteyne glared and said nothing.

Rose studied his face a moment before turning to Duardo and issuing a series of orders in a bastardized island dialect too rapid for Fonteyne to keep apace. The giant nodded and vanished into the thicker fog beyond the ring of golden lanternlight.

Sebastien dashed a hand across the blood that continued to stream over his eye. He clenched his teeth so hard it was a wonder they did not snap off at the gums. The attack had been swift and brilliant. Not a single shot had been fired, not a throat had been cut.

"How the devil did you locate us in this soup, let alone build enough speed to ram us?"

"Oh, come now, it was barely more than a nudge. In truth, I was aiming to come alongside, but we take what we can get. And I cannot reveal all of my secrets, Captain Fonteyne. Suffice it to say I have lived all of my life in these waters and have some knowledge of wind and currents. Some say both are as unpredictable as a woman's temper, so it would stand to reason I would understand them."

As if it had been an accomplice all along, the breeze strengthened, thinning the fog, sweeping hazy drifts of it across the deck. A scant few moments later it had dispersed enough to reveal the ghostly shape of the *Cygnet* and the spider's web of cables and ropes lashing the two ships together. There were men lining her rails, armed and wary; more with muskets and trumpet-shaped blunderbusses up in the yards. Gun crews stood at the ready behind the cannon, thin spirals of smoke rising from glowing linstocks.

As the initial shock wore off, Fonteyne's head started to throb like the devil. The blood was rushing through his ears, pounding in his temples. She was saying something else but her words were muddled into shapeless sounds by his anger.

"Do you have a doctor on board?" she asked again, pronouncing each word slowly as if she was speaking to an addled child.

Penman stepped forward. He ran a hand through his hair then gave the hem of his waistcoat a tug to straighten it. "That would be me, madam. Dr. Archibald Winston Claridge-Penman III, should it please you to know."

Rose blinked. "I am duly thrilled. You, however, don't look in much better shape than your captain."

"I assure you, madam, I ..." he stopped, took a small breath to steady himself, then squared his shoulders and tugged on his waistcoat again. "I am perfectly fine. I saw the mermaid and thought ... well, it doesn't really matter what I thought. With your permission, I should like see to the wounded."

"See to your captain before he bleeds all over my deck."

Fonteyne's head jerked up. "*Your* deck?"

"In case you hadn't noticed, my men have taken control of all the decks as well as the armory and helm, Captain. So yes, I am assuming command of this ship and claiming her as my prize. I would advise you to discourage your crew from causing any trouble or trying anything foolish. Duardo, with whom you are already acquainted, has no patience for insurrection. I have seen him snap a man's spine in two for merely thinking to offer a challenge."

Without warning, she cocked her pistol and pointed it at the white-haired Nathanial Reed, who had been trying hard not to be noticed. "You there. What are you holding behind your back?"

Reed brought his hands forward and took a reluctant step apart from the rest of the crew gathered behind him.

"Just a chart. I was in the middle of trying to figure out where we were when—"

She glanced briefly down at the wooden peg leg. "You're the navigator?"

"Reed ma'am. Nate Reed. Navigator, aye."

She uncocked the serpentine lock on the pistol. "At the risk of losing your tongue, I prefer to be addressed as Captain. Can I rely upon you to pass my orders to your fellow crewmen?"

Reed looked at Fonteyne, whose expression would have cracked a slab of granite.

When Sebastien showed no inclination to sanction the order, Rose moved closer to him, her pale, steely eyes so piercing, he felt the effect down in his belly. With the next breath he realized the sensation was caused by the tip of the razor-sharp dagger that was pressing up into the tender junction between his thighs.

"I suggest you tell your man ... all of your men ... to co-operate. I don't *need* your crew to sail this ship, Captain. Nor do I have any qualms about setting them adrift then slapping you in irons and hanging you over the deck in a cage which is, I suspect, what my fate would have been if the tables had been turned."

Fonteyne stared. His own fate was not a concern, but without knowing where they were, setting his crew adrift was not something he could risk. Not yet, anyway.

Without looking at Reed, he spoke through the grate of his teeth, "Do it. Do as she says."

Rose slid the dagger back into the sheath at her waist and smiled. "I knew, under all that glowering bluster, you were a reasonable man. Now ... shall we continue our discussion in your ... er, *my*... cabin, so the doctor can go about his business with needle and thread? I should hate to have you swoon in front of your men from loss of blood."

10

———

Rose was only slightly surprised at the spartan nature of Fonteyne's cabin. She tossed her hat onto his desk and immediately took a seat in the captain's big chair, forcing Fonteyne to sit at the dining table.

The two stared at each other in silence, their private thoughts crackling in their heads until Penman, accompanied by Duardo, appeared in the cabin several minutes later.

Without taking his eyes off Rose, Fonteyne asked, "How fares the rest of the crew?"

Penman nodded to acknowledge Rose before he answered. "Nothing that cannot be fixed with a needle and thread. The lad who fell into the sea has been retrieved, unharmed. They are mostly suffering from shock and ... well, to be frank ... embarrassment."

Rose, noting the look on Fonteyne's face, reached around to a sideboard and fetched a bottle of rum and some short glasses. Her intent was halted briefly by the display of captured pennons nailed to the wall.

Doubtless he had expected to hang hers among them.

She poured out four measures of rum, two of which Duardo placed on the table in front of Fonteyne and Penman.

Both men took the offering and drained their cups in a single swallow, the heat and burn of the potent liquor barely causing a squint.

Penman leaned in to inspect Fonteyne's wound and made a clicking sound with his tongue. With thumb and forefinger, he pulled a fat sliver of wood out of the torn flesh, which exposed the white of the bone and started a fresh streak of blood flowing over the captain's left eye.

"What do you intend to do with my ship and crew?" Fonteyne asked, his gaze still locked on Rose.

"That depends entirely on you," she said.

"How so?"

"First things first. Let the doctor make you a pretty new scar, then we can talk without fear of a needle stabbing you in the eye."

Penman cast a crooked smile over his shoulder. "I assure you, my hand is quite steady."

"It isn't your hand I'm worried about."

Fonteyne maintained the glare that had sent many a grown man cringing into a corner but seemed to have no effect on Rose St. Clare.

"Get on with it, man," he growled at Penman.

The doctor had already threaded a needle. He swabbed at the blood and pinched the raw edges of the gash together then proceeded to close the wound with a row of tiny stitches. Rose watched for the first few weaves, then thumbed casually through the logbook Fonteyne had left on his desk.

When Penman was finished, he snipped the thread close to the last knot, then looked to Rose.

"Might I trouble your man for another tot of rum?"

"Duardo is not anyone's man," she said coldly. "So if you wish another *tot* of rum, you can ask him yourself."

Penman looked at the giant black man. "My humble apologies, sir. Ill breeding on my part."

Duardo sneered and carried the crock of rum across the cabin, stopping so close that Penman had to tip his head back in order to see his face. When the doctor's cup was refilled, Duardo lifted the jug and poured several enormous mouthfuls of the liquor directly down his own throat before returning to stand by Rose's side.

Penman took a small swallow, but soaked the rest onto a square of linen, which he then pressed over the wound on Fonteyne's brow before binding it with a long strip of bandaging. When he started to wipe at the rest of the blood on Fonteyne's cheek and neck, his hand was pushed impatiently aside.

"I will ask again: What do you intend to do with my ship and crew?"

Rose offered up a faint smile. "How unfortunate we could not have worked together as allies in Lafitte's company. I suspect he will need all the help he can gather around him to block the British from taking New Orleans."

"What makes you think Lafitte would risk so much as a longboat defending a city that has turned its back on him. He was in a New Orleans jail cell for the past month, charged with piracy and profiteering. A warrant has been posted to put him there again alongside his brother, Pierre."

Rose frowned, then slid her glass over for Duardo to refill it. "What about you? Where do your loyalties lay?"

He waved his hand in a dismissive gesture. "I hold favor with neither the American naivete nor the British arrogance."

She leaned back and planted her boots squarely on the

corner of his desk, her ankles crossed. "Speaking of arrogance, it was rather pompous of you to come after us on your own."

"How can you be sure that I have?"

She smiled and tapped the open logbook on his desk. "Your entries are quite detailed. Mentioning the presence of a second or third ship in your company would surely be considered worthy of note. More worthy than—" she paused and leaned forward to read— "two barrels of fresh water lost in the storm."

Fonteyne shrugged. "Fresh water is important."

"As would be concern for another ship ...or ships ...if they were caught in heavy weather with you." When he said nothing, she smiled again. "Ramsey does the same thing. A habit he acquired while serving in the Royal Navy. Quite annoyingly, he keeps a record of everything said or done in the course of a day, counts every shilling spent, every bottle of wine consumed. But then ...if I recall correctly ... that was how the two of you met, was it not? You also served under Nelson?"

The tarnished gold eyes simply stared.

"I expect that was why you were so vexed when Ram refused to help you get your men back."

"In the end, I took them back without his help."

"You do realize that you had put him in an untenable position. He'd only been governor for a few months."

"Whereas I had been his friend for ten years. But he made his choice and I made mine, and here we are."

"Yes. Here we are. And to answer your question, if your crew submits to my command, if they make no attempt to overpower my men or take back the ship—an action that, I promise you, would fail—then we should have no reason to lock the lot of you in irons."

Fonteyne tipped his head as if calculating the weight of the threat against the vow he had made to Lafitte, that a woman would only become captain of his ship over his dead and rotting body.

Avoiding her gaze for the first time, he leaned forward and snatched up a pouch of tobacco that was lying on his desk. "For the time being, you have my bond that neither I nor my crew will offer up any resistance."

"For the time being?"

He took paper out of the pouch and rolled a line of shredded tobacco. "Aye, for the time being, for I confess you have aroused my curiosity."

"Curiosity can be a dangerous thing."

He licked the paper to seal it and twisted both ends tight. "No more dangerous than a woman's mind, I warrant."

"I think I shall take that as a compliment."

"Take it however you like." There were sulphur matches in a small Chinese urn on his desk, but reaching for it would have meant walking around behind her. Instead, he set the pouch and the rolled cigar to one side then stood and tugged the hem of his shirt out of his breeches. "You have no objections if I find a clean shirt?"

The blood from his wound had soaked the one he was wearing almost to the waist. She started to wave a hand in assent, then changed her mind.

"Duardo."

The big man walked over to where two large sea chests were pushed against the berth. In the first, he found two knives and a small throwing axe. In the second, he found a brace of pistols.

Fonteyne gave another little shrug. "I forgot they were in there."

Under Duardo's watchful eyes, he finished stripping the stained shirt over his head and tossed it into the corner. With his chest bared, every muscle and sinew seemed carved from solid oak. His skin was tanned dark from the sun, his shoulders and arms flexed with strength. The well-defined bands across his belly led the eye downward to where other shapes were equally well defined through skin-tight breeches.

There were also myriad scars criss-crossing his body, some of which Rose distinctly remembered tracing with her finger-tips. She forced herself to look away, refusing to let herself remember.

She leaned forward and reached for her hat. "Will I be able to trust your helmsman to follow my orders?"

"That would depend on what those orders might be."

"For now, simply to keep apace with the *Cygnet* and the *Pride*. My crew is perfectly capable of sailing her, but I should hate for an unfamiliar hand to set the sails wrong and snap another mast by mistake. Or run her aground. Or—"

Fonteyne cut in. "Nate can be trusted."

"Excellent."

She looked at Duardo and nodded at the rack of swords behind Fonteyne's desk. Duardo gathered them under his arm then carried them out of the cabin.

Rose offered up a crooked smile as she put a hand to the door latch. "I am prepared to take you at your word, Captain Fonteyne, that there will be no trouble on board. But make no mistake, sir, this ship is under my command now."

Fonteyne gave an exaggerated bow as she exited the cabin, but once the door was closed, his face hardened and he muttered under his breath, "For the time being, little Rose. For the time being."

ROSE'S BRAVADO lasted until she reached the upper deck. There, she grabbed the rail, drew a deep breath, and blew it out in a huff to ease some of the tension in her body.

Some, not all.

As shocked as Fonteyne had been that his ship had been taken so completely by surprise, Rose had been equally shocked that her audacious plan had worked. Billy Burr and Duardo had each thought her mad, even Stubb had protested mightily when he heard her intentions, but she had regarded the attack as possibly the only opportunity they would have to gain the upper hand.

The three ships had managed to outrun the worst of the wind and violent seas and found refuge in the sheltered bay of a small island. It was sheer bad luck that Fonteyne had been blown in the same direction. When the lookouts who had been posted high on the rocky peak reported seeing another ship less than a mile offshore, Rose's stomach had plunged down into her toes. The *Black Wind* was superior in firepower, manpower, and would likely have sent the *Cygnet* to the bottom of the sea had they met on open water. Further, if the fog cleared and the wind returned in his favor, Fonteyne would have seen them emerging from behind the island and he could easily have opened fire and reversed their fates.

But the storm, the windless calm, the murk of the shifting fog bank, combined with her own sheer audacity had been bolstered by Stubb's knowledge—given grudgingly— of the currents where they broke around the crescent-shaped island.

Rose had seen a bold opportunity and she had taken it. Now she not only had the finest, deadliest ship in the Caribbean under her command, she also had its most fearsome captain as her captive on board.

The memory she had carried in her mind for so many years was of a darkly sensuous lover full of passion, lust, and reckless bravado. The moment she had seen him stride into the ballroom at the governor's mansion, she had known exactly where and how she wanted the night to end. She may have been a virgin, but she was no ignorant miss who had no knowledge of what a man and woman did in bed. Nor did she want her first experience to be with any of the pale and powdered prospects her mother continually paraded before her.

Once again, she had seen the opportunity to take what she wanted and she had damn well taken it. To that end, the night of her dénouement had been a success. Butthe long nights that followed came with a thousand regrets.

During the intervening years, she had deliberately sought to burn Sebastien Fonteyne out of her mind, but when the candlelight was dim and her body was straining against a lover in search of relief, it was always Fonteyne's face she saw before her, Fonteyne's hands she ached to have stroking down her flesh, Fonteyne's big body she imagined lashed tightly to hers.

Utter foolishness.

She could see that now.

He was just an ordinary man made of flesh and blood. He could be cut and he could bleed like any other mortal being. The anger and resentment she saw in his eyes was barely a tenth of what she felt for the years she had wasted thinking him an untouchable warrior-hunter.

She had not only touched him, she had taken his ship, his prized possession without having to fire a shot.

She just wasn't entirely certain what to do with it now. They were at enough risk sailing through the islands with the *Pride* in tow. That risk was doubled having two impressive prizes, both easily recognizable, in her little fleet.

She felt a presence beside her and looked down. Stubb had dragged a cask over to the rail and was climbing up to see why she was peering so intently over the side. The fog had almost all blown away leaving a slightly blurred sea and varying shades of-blue sky above. The island that had given them temporary refuge was visible off the port side. The *Cygnet* had cut loose the grappling lines and was a half-pistol-shot distance off the *Black Wind's* beam, her gun ports still open, her crew alert for any signs of treachery. Twenty of the *Cygnet's* men remained on board the *Black Wind*, having changed positions with twenty of Fonteyne's crew who were now on board the *Cygnet*.

"I put a brace o' men in the tops with glasses in case there be other vultures nearby."

"There are no other vultures. He came alone."

"Alone?" His brows shot upward. "Now there be a puff-chested cock in full blood."

"Probably a good thing," she murmured. "Because that was luck. Pure, sheer, bloody luck. My hands are still shaking."

"Aye, since we be confessin' then, my breeks 'ave a few fresh stains as well. One o' these days, mind, ye'll come up with some bare-assed scheme that'll end with the lot o' us sinkin' down into Neptune's graveyard. For now though, after that wee trick, the crew be so chuffed wi' themselves, they'd take on a squadron o' Spaniards single-handed if ye ask't them to."

"You have had your fair share of bare-assed ideas," she said. "For most of them, I just hold my breath and pray."

Stubb chuckled. "Faugh! Only means we deserve each other's company."

Rose smiled, for she could see the little man swelling his chest with pride. Many had scoffed at the notion of her having any success standing at the helm of a ship crewed by misfits and scoundrels, but she had happily taken up the challenge to prove the naysayers wrong. Leading the pack of cynics was her own brother, Ramsey, who, she suspected, was more driven by jealousy than disdain. It would have given her a great deal of satisfaction to sail into Tobago with Lafitte's *Pride* and Fonteyne's *Black Wind* sailing under her pennon. It would almost be worth the risk just to see the look on her dear brother's face.

Unfortunately, once the shock passed, Ram would likely confiscate all three ships and toss the crews in the brig.

Four ships, however, were decidedly one too many. Her men were spread thin and even with half the *Hyperion's* crew added to their roster, they were heavily outnumbered should Fonteyne decide to take his ship back.

"It will be a shame to have to sink the *Hyperion*," she said.

"Worthless crate o' timber be leakin' like a sieve," Stubb declared. "N'owt worth a snork o' spit-foam in a bucket o' seawater."

Rose agreed. "We will waste no more effort trying to keep her afloat."

"I'll make sure the lads strip every cable an' cleat what might be useful."

Rose nodded absently then frowned. "Where the devil is Billy? I haven't seen her since we came on board."

Stubb chuckled. "She very near creamed herself when she seen the *Black Wind's* guns. I expect she's got herself rubbed all over one o' them big culverins by now."

Rose laughed. "Go and fetch her for me. She wanted to test the guns on the *Pride*, this is her chance to do so. She can use them on the *Hyperion*. The sooner we dispose of the wreck, the sooner we can leave this place. Despite what might be in Fonteyne's log books, I find it hard to believe Lafitte would only send one ship into the hunt. There could be more, perhaps without Fonteyne even being aware of it. What did you find in the way of damages?

"I sent a man down to look at the rudder. There be a tangle o' lines twisted 'round it from the storm, but it be clear an' fine now." He paused and looked up at the *Black Wind's* cracked mainmast. "We can brace that with tar an' cables fer the time bein' an' hope we don't run into any more foul weather, but we'll 'ave to pull up somewheres to fix it proper."

Rose clapped the little man on the shoulder. "I trust you can find us another hidey-hole somewhere? In the meantime get the carpenters working on any damage we did to the deck and rails."

"Aye, Capt'n. What about the rest of our guests? There be a mort o' them crowded into the bilges."

"Put them to work on the repairs. The captain has given me his bond they will make no trouble."

Stubb's eyebrows shot upward. "An' ye believe him?"

"Not for one half of one half second. Put men in the yards with muskets and give them orders to shoot anyone who lifts a finger the wrong way."

11

Billy Burr delayed the need to test Lafitte's guns in favor of using the big black beasts she found on board the *Black Wind*. Rose obliged her request by having Nate Reed tack the *Black Wind* into position at the mouth of the bay. From there, Billy and her gun crews enthusiastically poured five full broadsides into the listing *Hyperion*, smashing timbers and rails, cutting through masts and yards. The last round she sent thundering across the gap was for pure pleasure rather than necessity, for there was little left on the surface aside from floating debris.

At the end of the bombardment, the smallest thread of black smoke marked the spot where the English vessel had been, but that too was extinguished when the last scrap of timber sank beneath the bubbling water.

Rose had watched from the quarterdeck with Stubb, who had to stand on a coil of rope to gain enough height to see over the rail. Like most of the crew on deck, they had both stuffed twists of cloth into their ears, making it look like they were leaking clots of milk.

Without the plugs, the concussion from the heavy guns

would have rendered them partly deaf for several days. As it was, their voices sounded as if they were speaking from the far end of a long, watery tunnel, which in this case was not unwelcomed. Stubb had not stopped talking, squawking, criticizing, and generally pointing out how he would have made a better job of the sinking.

"Even so, a fair effort," he said to Rose, shouting so she could hear him through the tunnel.

She nodded and refrained from shouting anything back that might encourage him to start another analysis.

With the sun nearing its zenith, the heat was beating down in full force. She had tossed her hat and frockcoat aside and stood now in breeches and waistcoat with the sleeves of her white linen shirt rolled up above her elbows. Her hair shone red with sun-kissed gold threads wound through. The long plait had lost most of its woven definition and the loosened curls flew haphazardly around her face and neck.

She plucked the cotton plugs out of her ears when she saw Billy Burr below her on the main deck. "Well done, Billy."

Billy grinned and looked up. "The culverins are magnificent, cast in Spain by God himself. The barrels were so clean they whistled."

"Shall I assume the armory is better provisioned than the *Pride*?"

"There is enough shot and powder on board to fight the whole of King George's navy."

"Best put on sail," Stubb said. "The thunder of them shots will carry two miles or more an' we be a mort closer to Hispaniola than my liver likes."

Rose agreed. "Mercado can handle the *Cygnet*; I want you to stay on board here with me. Signal the *Pride*. Have Duardo prepare to get under way."

"Oh, aye, I found a good place to make repairs a day south o' here. Good harbor, friendly natives."

"Find another," she said after a moment. "We're going due east."

Stubb knocked a pudgy fist on his ear in case he hadn't heard correctly. "East?"

"East, yes. To Crooked Island and from there, up the Tongue toward the Straits."

Stubb's eyes widened. "The Florida Straits? Ye sure ye want to risk it? British revenuers be thick as thieves along the Tongue waitin' to pounce on ships comin' out o' New Providence."

"Exactly so. Hopefully they will be too busy chasing smugglers to see us slipping past."

Stubb's look was sceptical. He scratched his head hard enough to dislodge his cap, but although he opened his mouth to voice another objection, he bit back whatever he was going to say and jumped down off the coil of rope. "Aye, Capt'n. East it be. I'll 'ave to fetch my charts to plot a new course. Back in a blink."

"Take your time," she murmured as the tiny navigator descended the ladderway. her attention was diverted to where Billy now stood, bow in hand, a wooden quiver of arrows at her side.

Scores of gulls had been disturbed by the thundering broadsides and flew in screeching circles overhead. Billy nocked an arrow into the bow, drew the string back to her cheek and shot a fat one in the chest. Even before it had fallen to the deck, she fit another arrow and shot a second bird, then a third.

Rose came down from the quarterdeck and joined Billy on the maindeck. "Are food supplies so short we need to roast the flying rats for our supper?"

Billy loosed another arrow, shot another gull. "The hollow shafts of their tail feathers hold the perfect amount of powder to prime the touchholes of the cannon. Quicker to fit a quill in the hole than guess how much powder is needed or spill it all over the barrel in the heat and confusion of battle."

Rose knew the burns on Billy's face had been a result of excess black powder igniting in just such a way.

"Tell me what you know about making a bomb. The explosive kind."

"Is there any other kind?" When she realized Rose's question was serious, Billy lowered the bow. "Well ... the simplest way is to pack a metal tube or canister with gunpowder, then run a black-match fuse a safe distance away. The bigger the canister, the bigger the boom."

"And if that metal tube was packed around barrels of whale oil and other combustibles, then placed in a longboat?"

Billy's curiosity prompted her to lower the bow. "You would get a boom that would send hellfire exploding in all directions."

"Enough hellfire to seriously damage a ship?"

"You're describing a fireship. Aye, fireships destroyed more warships in the Spanish Armada than any rounds from British guns."

Rose pursed her lips thoughtfully and Billy followed her gaze to where the crew on the *Pride* was unfurling the big mainsail. "May I ask what ship you are wanting to blow up?"

"I haven't quite decided yet."

"I was hoping you might say the *Pride*. It would make me very happy to blow up that floating brothel."

"I'm not sure I want to vex Lafitte any more than I have already."

Billy snorted. "I admire your knack for understatement. As if stealing his ship out from under his nose or humiliating his favorite captain won't have vexed him enough."

"I stole his ship to prove a point, that we can be more advantageous as a friend than an enemy."

"And this?" She waved an arrow to indicate the sails overhead.

"Wasn't planned," Rose admitted, "But it certainly speaks to our worth."

"You would still petition to be part of Lafitte's fleet?"

"No. But I might accept an *invitation* to join his company of privateers."

"And just how do you plan to get him to do that?"

Behind them, Sebastien Fonteyne stood with his arms crossed over his chest and a scowl on his face. "I would be curious to know the answer to that as well."

ROSE AND BILLY spun around at the sound of his voice. Rose with a hand flying to her pistol, Billy with an arrow nocked and ready to fling at the intruder. Sebastien did not flinch, did not blink an eye at either threat.

After a full thirty seconds, Rose huffed out a breath. "Do you always creep up on people and listen to their private conversations?"

"Not always. Sometimes I like to end their conversations by clapping their heads together and splitting their skulls."

Billy increased the tension on the bowstring, but the cool gaze showed not a twinge of fear. Nor did they betray any reaction to the ugly burn scars that distorted the left side of her face. The terrible wounds had the opposite effect, in fact. His mouth softened slightly at the corners. "You must be Billy Burr. Did you enjoy firing my guns?"

"Not nearly as much as I would enjoy firing this arrow."

He glanced over at the bay, where only the smallest of ripples remained to show where the *Hyperion* had once been. "It took you five broadsides to sink her?"

"I wasn't counting."

"I was. I would have expected a new crew firing unfamiliar guns to take twice that many."

Billy eased the bowstring slightly, wary of the compliment. "My gunners can stand with the best."

"As, apparently, can your captain." Saying this, his gaze turned to Rose, but if he expected her to react favorably to the flattery, he was sorely mistaken.

"I did not give you leave to come up on deck," she said.

"There was no lock on the door. Moreover, I'm an inquisitive bastard. When my ship's guns are firing, I like to know why."

He had discarded the bandage Penman had wrapped around his head and rinsed the blood out of his hair. The shaggy black waves were tied smoothly into a damp queue at his nape, revealing features that were clearly defined: the broad forehead, the rugged shape of his jaw furred under several days worth of bearding. Dark lashes called attention to the shockingly direct boldness of his eyes though the flesh beneath was beginning to turn purple from bruising. Penman's neat line of stitching cut through the tail of the eyebrow giving it a slightly downward slant.

Rose was aware that her crew had slowly stopped what they were doing to turn and watch the exchange between the infamous Sebastien Fonteyne and their captain, who, without the bulk of her frockcoat padding her shoulders, looked half his size as she stood glaring up at him, her hands planted firmly on her hips.

Billy broke the tension by shooting another gull that flew overhead, bringing a flapping corpse down into the crew's midst. "Back to work, you laggards! You there, fetch the dead birds and have a care with the tail feathers, I need them whole. And bring me the spent arrows as haven't enough to waste."

"Ho, there, madam, might I put in a request for the bodies of the gulls when your men have relieved them of the feathers?"

Archibald Penman stepped hastily out from the shadows of the hatchway where he had been hanging back out of sight. He had followed Fonteyne out of the cabin but was evidently less keen to venture onto the open deck.

"The livers," he explained in response to Billy's stare. "After they have been dried, the powdered livers can be of some medicinal use."

Billy turned the damaged side of her face slightly away. "Aye, you can have what you want when I'm done. But if you call me madam again, it'll be your liver that'll be carved out and ground into powder."

Penman raised his hands. "Yes. Yes, my apologies, ma—er..."

"Billy. Just Billy." She turned and fired off two more arrows as she walked away.

"Billy is quite good with that bow," Rose said. "Not so good at holding her temper. Nor, for that matter, is the rest of my crew."

"Indeed," Penman said, casting a glance at the hard faces. "Point taken."

"You have yet to answer my question," Fonteyne said.

"And what question might that be?"

"Two, actually. The first is how you plan to get Lafitte to invite you to join his company of pirates and thieves; the second is how you intend to convince him to defend the good citizens of New Orleans who have so obviously *not* gone out of their way to accept his offer of protection."

She found herself focussing on the shape of his lips while he spoke and quickly looked away.

Some of the crew, she noted, had sidled discreetly closer to catch snatches of their conversation. Those snatches, she knew, would travel from one end of the ship to the other, top to bilges, before the last words had left her lips.

"Perhaps it is a conversation better had back in the cabin," she said.

Fonteyne had seen the glance she had cast around the deck and nodded in understanding. He crooked a finger at the helmsman, Nate Reed, who was standing nearby, shadowed by two of Rose's crewmen.

"The helm is yours again and you are to follow Captain St. Clare's orders."

"We will be getting under way shortly," Rose said. "Stubb is currently looking for a safe place to put in for repairs. The carpenters have done what they can for now," She paused and pointed up at the mainmast where the crack had been bound in thick cables. "We should not linger here in case someone heard the guns or saw the smoke."

Nate blinked. He looked from Fonteyne to Rose—who had already started to walk away—then back to Fonteyne. "Captain?"

"I have given my bond that we will all behave like gentlemen," he said, loudly enough for the crew to overhear. But quietly, he added, "And until I find out what the minx is up to, you will follow along with the charade."

Nate tugged at a snow white forelock and his Irish came out in a crooked smile. "Aye Captain. Until you tell us otherwise."

12

———————

When Fonteyne returned to his cabin, he found Rose seated at his desk with her boots propped up on the corner of the desk.

He stared at the flecks of dirt beneath the leather heels for a moment, then chuckled softly and went to the sideboard, where he poured two full measures of rum. He handed one of the cups to her, then dragged the chair from the dining table and turned it to face the interloper.

"Now then—"

"Would you mind opening some of the gallery windows? The air is dreadfully damp and musty in here."

Fonteyne considered telling her to open the damned windows herself, but in the end, he obliged.

When the slanted windows across the stern were swung open, they could hear the rush of water creaming in their wake as the *Black Wind* began to ride the wind. Gulls were circling and screaming, following the ship, persistent in their hopes of catching any discarded scraps.

Fonteyne settled into the chair and took a deep swallow of

rum. The gash on his brow had begun to throb, but he allowed no outward sign of discomfort.

"I confess I did not hear the entirety of your conversation with your gun captain, but I did hear mention of fireships. You were not, I trust, so vexed with Lafitte as to plot sending a fleet of them into Barataria Bay?"

Rose leaned back and smiled. "An interesting idea, but hardly practical. The Bay is what, five? Ten miles long?"

"Thereabout."

"I had a smaller target in mind."

"I am all ears."

Not quite, she noticed. With his hair pulled back she could see that he was missing the upper curl of his right ear, likely shorn off by the blade of a sword.

"I plan to sail up the Florida Straits and look for the fleet the British are sending to invade Louisiana."

He took a slow sip of rum before setting his cup carefully on the table beside him. "And if you find them, what then?"

"Ideally, I would like to blast them out of the water."

"There could be a hundred ships in the fleet. We have three."

Rose noted the use of the word 'we' but chose not to draw his attention to it. "The missive advised there were ten vessels on their way. And, as I said, attacking was what I would *like* to do. If that's not possible then perhaps there is something that can be done to slow them down or lower the odds slightly."

"Is that why you were asking about fireships?"

She flung his own words back at him. "I am an inquisitive bastard. I like to consider all my options before deciding on my course. I suspect the British are already aware that their eighty-gun ships-of-the-line would be of little use; their deep draughts would prevent them from crossing the Mississippi delta or sailing up the river. My guess is the majority will be sloops and light frigates carrying troops who would have to establish a base first at Pensacola. Despite it being Spanish territory, the British already have a foothold there which would give them the option of attacking New Orleans by land. That's assuming, of course, they plan to attack the city first."

"Where else would they be planning to attack? There is nothing of value along the coast of the Gulf, nothing but marshes and swampland on either side of the Mississippi."

"Not quite nothing," she said, tipping her head.

The throbbing in his temple was obviously slowing his thinking process and it was a full minute before he understood the anticipant look in her eyes.

"Barataria," he said.

"Huzzah," she said softly. "As long as Lafitte and his fleet of privateers has a commanding presence in the Gulf, the British will be wary of him allying himself with the Americans."

"Thus far Jean has shown no preference in favoring either side. In fact, he would be quite content to sit back and watch them destroy each other."

"Because regardless who wins or loses, there will be profits to be made in the aftermath?"

"Exactly so."

Rose tapped her fingers lightly on the desk.

"Had he given me a few more moments of his precious time, I might have been able to tell him that amongst the papers we found on board the *Hyperion* was a letter showing they were aware of the dispatches Lafitte has sent to General Jackson, warning him of the disaster that would befall the southern states should New Orleans be captured. Apparently, he has repeatedly urged the general to send troops to reinforce the city and I do not imagine the British were well pleased to discover the content of those letters."

Thoughtful eyes searched hers as he contemplated her words. "That would explain the warrants for his arrest. What isn't as easily explained is why you appear to be so cavalier about jeopardising the interests of your family. Your father's business operates in the Indies by way of letters of marque issued by the Crown. They could easily be revoked should he, or any of his family, be seen to openly support the Americans. Or to throw their lot in with Lafitte, for that matter. Your brother has already proven that his loyalties lie firmly with the Crown.

She pursed her lips and tapped a finger idlly on the desk. "Both he and Father are forced to walk a very fine line."

"Whereas, by sailing to Barataria and offering your services to Lafitte, you appear to have leaped right over it."

"My actions do not reflect on my family."

"Your name does."

"As your M'sieur Sauvinet noted, my name does not appear on any charter, nor deed of ownership, nor any letters of marque. All of those bear my husband's name."

"That was going to be my third question," he said quietly.

After considering her next words for a moment, she stood and walked over to the bank of gallery windows to stare out at the following sea. "Terrance Whitticomb and I were married for all of three months. He was from good, solid English stock, and exactly the type of man my mother wanted ... nay, *expected* me to marry. She believed he would settle me into the life of a happy little wife serving tea on the veranda and forgetting all about my passion for the sea. It would also avoid bringing any further embarrassment to the family, because you see ...apparently someone had seen a man coming out of the garden house the morning after the governor's ball, followed closely by myself looking visibly ... dishevelled. Since I refused to give a name, Mother sent for Terrence and put us in front of a minister a week later. I protested mightily, of course, but I was only seventeen and not quite as brazen as I may have made myself out to be." She glanced over her shoulder and offered up a half-smile.

"You would have to meet my mother to understand why one does not argue with her. At any rate," she turned back to the window, "We were immediately sent away, out of sight, out of mind, to celebrate our nuptials in Jamaica.

"Unfortunately, Terrance caught the yellow fever. I returned to Tobago, to the loving and sympathetic bosom of my family, only to be told I was to be sent to London, out of sight, out of mind again. I slipped away that very night, took command of the *Cygnet*— which had been part of the dowry—bribe—wedding gift or whatever you want to call it— and sailed out of port. I've not been back to Port St. Louis since."

She felt Fonteyne's presence behind her, felt the air seem to shift and shimmer like heat waves around her. Every nerve ending in her body prickled to attention, the ripples spreading with every warm breath that bathed the back of her neck.

"I am sorry. I had no idea."

"How could you know? You skulked away like a thief and I watched you and your ship sail out of port without so much as a by your leave."

"Which was exactly how I saw the British frigate leaving with my men on board. I had no choice but to leave on the instant if I hoped to catch him."

He was too close. His body was too warm, too solid, and when he placed his hands on her shoulders, there was only a thin layer of linen shirt to keep the memories from flooding back. The heat from those memories shivered downward, flowing through her body like ribbons and tangling together in the pit of her belly.

She twisted abruptly out of his grip and walked back to the desk to retrieve her cup of rum. "It is over and done, Captain Fonteyne. I am content with how my life has turned out."

His hands remained in mid-air, cradling a phantom pair of shoulders. Then his fingers curled and he lowered his arms and turned. "Happily for you, the inconvenience of a husband did not last very long."

"I did not wish any harm toward Terrence. He was actually quite sweet. And even-natured. He did not storm about like a black cloud."

Fonteyne smiled slowly. "I have no doubt you would have been content to spend the next forty years appreciating that sweetness while you served tea and exchanged gossip with a flock of plantation wives."

"I would have thrown myself off a roof first." She took another swallow of the strong spirits and slammed her empty glass down on the desk. "You really are quite arrogant, you know. Not to mention condescending."

"Some women find those qualities exciting. As you apparently did, at one time else why would you have dragged me into that garden house?"

"As I said, I was seventeen and foolish. And you were not dragged, sirrah. You walked rather eagerly to your doom on three legs."

His smile turned into a soft laugh. "Doom? Aye, that it was, for I will admit to more than a few sleepless nights when I wrestled with the notion of returning to Port St. Louis."

"God spare me, surely that is not an admission of being in possession of a conscience?"

"Not in the least, madam. I would have liked to return to give you a few well-needed lessons on toying with someone who should not be toyed with."

"Ah well, lost opportunities." With her knees threatening to falter, she looked down and shuffled a few papers on the desk. "Now, if you will excuse me, I have some reading to do. You should find yourself another cabin and rest your head; that lump on your brow must be aching rather fiercely by now."

"Something is starting to ache, but it is not my brow." He was looking at her in a way that made her bones feel as though they were melting down into her toes.

Her breath caught in her throat as she watched him walk slowly toward her, stopping so close she was forced to arch back against the desk to avoid contact. He reached past her shoulder and snatched up the bottle of rum.

"I will be in the navigator's cabin if you need ... or want me."

ONCE OUTSIDE IN the gloom of the companionway, Fonteyne leaned against the bulkhead for a moment and commended himself on his restraint. It was true, his head was pounding. His thumb was aching from being dislocated and summarily wrenched back into place earlier. It wasn't often a woman stood toe to toe with him and matched his verbal barbs thrust for thrust. In fact, it never happened. Nor did it ever happen that a woman made him feel pangs of guilt for his custom of making love to them and walking out the door without a backward glance.

He shook his head, but that only made it pound harder.

He pushed away from the post and walked toward the ladderway at the end of the short corridor. His intention was to go up on deck where the fresh air would clear his head and blow away the images of Rose St. Clare stretched out naked on the bed, the moonlight streaming through the open window making her eyes shine and the dampness on her body gleam.

The ship took a gentle roll to port and Fonteyne's distraction made him lose his balance. His shoulder struck the wood and he lurched forward, stretching out a hand to grope for something to brace himself with. His head struck the slanted wooden overhang of the ladderway instead and the compounded explosion of pain made him pitch forward and land face down on the planks.

WHEN THE CABIN door shut behind him, Rose released her breath on a curse. Thankfully he had left before seeing the rush of heated blood that flooded her cheeks, but Rose could feel it. Unaccustomed to blushing for any reason, she snarled and threw herself into the captain's chair hard enough to make it tip precariously back on two legs.

She was still fuming at his insolence several minutes later when she heard a tapping on the door and barked, "What is it?"

Stubb poked his head around the door. "No need to shout like a fishmonger. If ye be in a foul mood, tell me now an' I'll go t'row myself over the side to spare ye the trouble."

"I am not in a foul mood. And the day you actually do throw yourself overboard instead of merely threatening to do so, will be the day I run the length of the ship naked."

The little man chuckled. "Some might be willing to pay good coin for me to take the swim in order to see that."

"And how would you spend it from inside a shark's belly?"

"Fair point." He came all the way into the cabin and hopped up into a chair. "Wind be comin' up sharp, so we should be clear o' the Spanish shippin' lines by nightfall. Still a mite close fer comfort since we be not egg-zactly gambolling about in three small carracks. Mayhap if we only had Lafitte's brothel fer company we could slink past any curious eyes, but ho! Look where we be." He waved a hand. "Only on board one o' the most well know'd privateer ships in the Caribbee. Every brigand with a full ballsack would be after chasing us."

"If we get pushed into a fight, will the mast hold?"

"We wrapped a hundred feet o' tarred cable around an'

drove in some bolts. She'll hold. The way his sails be set, we could cope with jest the two masts if it came to that. But it won't." He leaned forward and grinned. "Coz damned if she don't 'ave two extra masts tucked down in the hold! Take us a day to winch the old one out an' fit the new one in."

"Have you found us a safe harbor?"

"Aye. Serpent's Tail. Dead east."

Rose nodded. "Signal the other two ships."

"Done it already."

Her mouth flattened. "Which rail would you like to be tossed over?"

Stubb cackled and hopped down off the chair. He glanced around the cabin seeming to notice for the first time they were alone. "Ho! Did ye finally toss *him* overboard?"

"I was tempted, believe me. But no. I merely told him to find another cabin and leave me to my reading."

"Ye let the bastard wander off on his own? On a ship he knows better than the back o' his hand?"

Rose swore and pushed to her feet. She was a few steps behind Stubb as he dashed out into the corridor, but they did not have to go far before they found Sebastien Fonteyne. He was lying in a crumpled heap at the bottom of the ladderway, his face awash in fresh blood, the bottle of rum smashed on the deck beside him.

13

Sebastien opened his eyes a slit. Something was squeezing his brains in a vice and when he groped his brow with a hand, he felt a thick layer of linen strips wrapped around his head.

"Pull those bandages off again and I vow I shall bind your hands down by your sides."

Sebastien opened his eyes wider and saw Penman's face looming inches above him.

"What happened?"

"What happened is, your head isn't as hard as you thought it was, and the blow you took on deck was exasperated by a second blow when you bounced off a beam and knocked yourself out cold. You tore your wound open again, ruining all of my excellent stitchwork. You were damned lucky you didn't break your damned neck."

"Your bedside manner is appalling."

"I try hard. How many fingers?"

He held up a hand, extending his forefinger and moved it slowly side to side.

"Two. And they are both blurry."

Penman frowned. "It should clear. I had to restitch the wound and your lump has a new lump. I can give you some laudanum if you need it to help you sleep."

"I don't want to sleep. I want to know what's happening. How long have I been lying here?"

"A few hours. I woke you several times to make sure you weren't bleeding inside your skull, but I gather you don't remember?"

Fonteyne frowned. "I remember losing my balance when the ship heeled, but nothing else."

Penman arched his eyebrows. "You lost your balance?"

"I was distracted." Fonteyne glanced around. The lamps were lit, the wicks turned low, but he could see that he was in his own berth, in his own cabin. Rose St. Clare was there, standing back in the shadows, but when she saw he was awake, she stepped forward into the light. Her hair was loose about her shoulders, but her face was distorted by the stark whiteness of the shirt she was wearing. It was obviously several sizes too big which spread the glare even more as she moved closer to the lamplight.

"You are wearing my shirt," he muttered.

"I haven't had time to fetch any of my own clothes from the *Cygnet*," Rose said. "And mine was stained helping to scrape you off the deck and lug you back up here."

Penman leaned over him again. "Drink this, it will help."

Sebastien recognized the strong, sweet smell of the liquid in the cup and pushed Penman's hand away. "I don't want any laudanum. It tastes like burned shoe leather."

"Suit yourself. Suffer away."

"Can he stand?" Rose asked. "If so, I'd like to move him to another cabin."

Sebastien grasped Penman's hand and brought the cup back. "Maybe a few sips. The floor and ceiling seem to be spinning together."

The doctor slid his free hand behind Fonteyne's neck to support him then held the cup to his lips. The tincture was as bitter and distasteful as Sebastien remembered. He made a face but emptied the cup, then pressed his head back down onto the pillow. He closed his eyes and kept them closed.

"Can he be moved?" Rose asked again. "I'd like to have some privacy."

"If possible, I would like to leave him be for the moment. Just until I'm certain his brains are not going to leak out of his ears. The laudanum should take effect shortly and he will sleep soundly for a few hours."

Penman set a small bottle of the brown liquid on the stool beside the berth. "I gave him a rather strong dose, but I will leave you with this, Captain, should he need it. No spirits, regardless how loudly he bellows. And if he becomes an annoyance, feel free to knock him on the head again but please do it on the other side."

"I'm right here," Fonteyne said, glaring through slitted eyes.

"Then do us all a favor and try not to act the fool again. If you strike your head a third time, I cannot promise your skull will not crack wide open."

Fonteyne managed a half-hearted wave of his hand. The laudanum was starting to take effect, spreading through his body in a warm, numbing wave. The stabbing throbs in his head faded. His eyelids grew so heavy he gave up trying to lift them. It went against every grain of his being to lie there like a puddle of pudding, but his thoughts became cloudy, his mind began to drift away with the gentle motion of the ship, and despite his best efforts to fight against it ...

WHEN HE WAS certain Fonteyne was asleep, Penman gathered up his wooden doctoring box and left the cabin. Rose stood by the berth for a moment and watched the steady rise and fall of Fonteyne's chest. With his head swathed in bandages and the stern lines around his mouth and eyes gone slack, he hardly looked like the dangerous, blackhearted pirate who prowled the Caribbean causing fear and palpitations in the breasts of his prey.

She leaned over and drew the blanket up to his chin. Somewhere in the back of her mind was the urge to climb into the berth and lay down beside him, to tuck herself against his big body and draw from his strength. To breathe in his scent. To let herself remember how it had felt with him moving inside her.

A more rational voice between her ears told her to cast aside any foolish thought of doing so. She stepped back, not entirely happy to see her hand was shaking slightly as she turned down the wick on the lamp beside him. She was bone tired herself and if she did not get some sleep soon, she would be useless.

All three ships were staying close as they headed into nightfall. The order had gone out for absolute darkness, no deck lamps, no lights above the orlop deck. The gallery windows had been hung with heavy black sheets of canvas and she checked them again to make sure there were no gaps or cracks.

It was a moonless, cloudless, clear night, and the ships were moving like dark wraiths through a sea of starlight, impossible to see where the horizon ended and the sky began. If the wind held and if Stubb's calculations were correct—and she had no reason to believe he would be wrong—they would see landfall by morning.

She yawned and arched her back to stretch out the knuckles

of her spine. There were blankets folded at the foot of the berth and she took one up and spread it on the boards. She had slept in worse places and she was too tired to sling a hammock. She kicked off her boots, laid down on the blanket and was asleep as soon as her head touched her folded elbow.

14

The island Stubb had set course for was a winding stretch of low peaks and shallow, curved bays five miles long and three miles wide. Most of it was covered with impenetrable green jungle that was home to thousands of colorful birds, snakes, and reptiles. There were signs that natives in the past had attempted to establish a village in one or more of the shallow bays, the gods only knew how long ago, for the skeletal structures of their huts were rotted and choked in a tangle of vines. Most of the inlets were without beaches of any kind; they were comprised of sheer rocky cliffs that stood gray and solid against the battering surf. The few bays that appeared to offer anchorage were littered with boulders and jagged outcroppings that would shred a ship's hull to splinters if it ventured too close.

Leeward, they found one deep-water cove ringed by a thick curtain of palms and scrub.

"Frenchies should 'ave sent Napoleon 'ere instead o' Elba," Stubb said. "Would 'ave gone screamin' mad afore he could have escaped. "There be mozzies big as buzzards in them trees. Sting a man until he swells up an' bursts, then carries him off to suck the rest of 'is blood dry later."

"An exaggeration, I'm sure," Rose said.

Stubb glared up at her. "Why do ye suppose all them huts we saw be empty an' rotted? Only ones who ever tried to live 'ere were head-shrinkers an' cannibals, an' then only on account o' they was meaner than the mozzies."

Rose focussed her glass on the top of the rise, scanning for any hint of life. "So you brought us to this charming place because ...?"

"Because it be marked with a big red X on most charts an' because neither the Spanish ner the Frenchies fancy 'avin' their heads shrunk or their livers roasted over a fire pit."

"And you thought we would?"

"Ye wanted a safe place to make repairs? None better outside o' Pigeon Cay."

Rose glanced around quickly to see if any of the crew was within earshot. The location, the very existence of Pigeon Cay was one of the best kept secrets in the Dante-St. Clare family. Rose herself had never seen it, never been there, though she had heard the many thrilling stories about the fabled lair of her ancestors, the base from which the Pirate Wolf and his pack sailed forth and wreaked havoc on the Spanish Main.

Stubb caught her furtive glance. "Bah. We might be talkin' about pigeon pie for all any o' these clod-eared numpkins know."

"Even so ..."

"Even so ye could shout it from the topmast an' none would pay heed."

She sighed. "Next you'll be telling me you've been there."

When Stubb only replied with a chuckle, she looked down at the little man. She knew his daily goal was to tease the nipples off her, and yet ...

He sensed her glance and chuckled again as she lightly boxed his ear.

"Reprobate."

"Better'n bein' a gullible firkin." He threw his head back and howled like a wolf before he jumped off the coil of rope and trotted happily away.

Ramsey had called the *Cygnet* a ship of mismatched fools, with a dwarf at the helm, a giant as quartermaster, and a female gun captain, but Rose could think of no better crew to have on board with her.

A splash of color on the lower deck drew Rose's attention. Archibald Penman was watching the three ships maneuver their way into the half-moon bay. His crisp navy blue shortcoat was without a wrinkle, the deep vee formed by the lapels allowed a view of the blue and yellow flowered silk waistcoat beneath. His neckcloth was rigid to his chin, the bow tied in precise, neat folds. Blond hair was smoothed back into queue and bound with a thin black ribbon.

Rose descended from the quarterdeck and joined him by the rail.

He turned and greeted her with a polite smile. "Good day to you, Captain."

She nodded. "Doctor."

"I took the liberty of looking in on the cap ... on Sebastien and he seems to have spent a quiet night. Did you manage to get any sleep?"

"I did, thank you. In spite of his snoring."

Penman smiled. "He can be somewhat of a ... er ..."

"Pain in the arse?"

"I was going to say bull in a glass shop, but yes. He tends to make his presence known even when asleep." Her gaze was so direct, he cleared his throat and looked over at the island.

"I vow I never tire of seeing the many colors of the ocean; the varying shades of blue from dark and impenetrable indigo, to pale and so clear as to count the grains of sand on the bottom."

They both peered over the side at a shout from the helm and a rattling of thick chains as the anchor was dropped.

"Will we be going ashore here?"

"Stubb says there is fresh water inland, so while the mast is being replaced, a party will top up the water barrels and forage for fresh fruit."

"Might I accompany them ashore?"

"Might I ask why?"

"I have discovered in our travels around the Caribbean that each island tends to offer something in the way of medicinal plants or bugs."

"You want to collect bugs?"

"Crickets, katydids, blister beetles, even cockroaches can be useful. Maggots, of course, for cleaning putrid flesh. And where there is fresh water, there is bound to be leeches."

"I see. Yes, you may go ashore so long as you do not wander away from the landing party. We will be leaving as soon as the repairs are made."

He laughed. "I can assure you, Captain, I am not one for wandering off into the jungle on my own."

"If I may be so bold, Doctor, you strike me as someone who should not even have sought a life at sea."

"In truth, when the cannons are blasting or when storms are tossing us about like corks, I have thought that myself. At the same time, I have learned more about doctoring in the seven years I have been on board the *Black Wind*, than I expect I would have learned in twice as many years in a high-born hospital in London treating ague and palpitations."

"Seven years? Then you know the captain well."

"As well as any man can know him, I suppose I do."

It was Rose's turn to laugh. "Don't look so ill at ease, Doctor, I am not going to ask you to tell me any of his secrets. In fact, I only have one question for you."

"Which I shall answer if I can."

"Setting aside the fact that he is a blackguard and a scoundrel, as well as a bull in a glass shop, can I trust him to keep his word when he gives it?"

His smile turned a little crooked. "That does seem like a great deal to set aside when weighing the worth of a man, but yes. In all the years of our acquaintance, I have never known Sebastien Fonteyne to break his word or renege on a vow or a promise once it has been given. Of course, you would now have to gauge the trustworthiness of *my* word as I give it, but as different as he and I might be in some regards, we put the same value on our honor. A man's—or woman's word once broken means nothing."

He paused and looked down at his hands for a moment. "Having said that, however, he's a proud bastard, and owing to the fact he is in the unique position of never having suffered defeat on board his own ship, I cannot vouchsafe that it would not be in his nature to make as much of a nuisance of himself as he possibly can."

"I cannot fault him for that, Doctor. I would do the same if I found myself in a similar position."

Billy Burr came up beside them cleaning black grease off her hands with a rag.

She was wearing loose canvas trousers and a ragged, filthy shirt. There was dirt in her hair and the acrid odor of tar clinging to her skin and clothing.

Penman caught himself staring, then stepped quickly to one side and offered up a polite bow. "Miss Burr."

"My name is Billy. Not Madam, not Miss. Just Billy."

"Billy. Yes, yes forgive me. A lapse in memory."

"A lapse in manners as well since you keep staring." She

turned her face and presented him a clear view of the melted skin that formed her scars. "Is this what you want to see?"

Penman's throat and cheeks turned a mottled red. "I assure you, I ... I was not staring for that reason."

"Then why?"

He cast an appeal at Rose, but was not going to get any help from that quarter. "If ... if I did have a lapse in manners, which of course, I did ... it was simply because I don't believe I have ever seen such an amazingly pure shade of green as your eyes. They truly are quite remarkable and bring to mind the darkest of emeralds found in Cartagena."

Billy stared.

Rose stared.

Through the awkward silence that followed, Penman groped for something else to say, but in the end, his cheeks flamed as red-raw, and he offered up a quick bow. "Captain. Billy. I am certain you both have important matters to discuss, I shall leave you to it."

"Thank you for the conversation, Doctor. I will send one of the men to fetch you when the crew is ready to go ashore."

"And I shall gather up my cricket boxes." He bowed one last time before he turned and walked hastily away.

Billy's gaze followed him across the deck until he vanished into the void of the hatchway.

Rose's mouth twitched slightly. "I think you have an admirer."

"And I think he's quite mad," Billy said. But she snuck another glance at the hatchway and Rose could swear she saw the veriest hint of pink warming the gun captain's cheeks.

~

TWO HOURS LATER, with the sounds of shouting, heaving, hammering, and sawing echoing around the bay, a small flotilla of longboats put to shore from all three ships. They carried empty barrels and large wicker baskets. Heeding Stubb's warnings, the crews rubbed a thick layer of mud on any exposed skin to ward off the swarms of stinging bugs that would greet them at the jungle's edge. Only one man scoffed at the notion as they cut their way into the vines and tangled brush; he was carried out shortly thereafter, his eyes swollen shut, his skin covered in red blisters.

Forewarned, Penman had changed out of his fine clothing and put on second, possibly third best before joining the shore crew. He covered everything, even the tawny locks of his hair with mud, earning a few hearty claps on the shoulder from the *Cygnet's* crewmen.

Duardo led the trek into the jungle, wielding a machete like a scythe to cut a path through the thick jumble of vines. They found the fresh water pool where Stubb said it was and filled the barrels while other men scoured the surrounding area, filling baskets with ripe mangoes, bananas, pineapples, and limes.

Back at the beach, the bounty was loaded into the longboats and rowed out to the ships, with most of the men swimming behind in order to rinse the mud and sweat off their bodies. Nets were used to winch the heavy barrels on board, and as soon as the longboats were secured on deck, and the carpenters on board the *Black Wind* had pounded the last bolt in place, the sails were raised on the new mast and they were on their way.

The wind was strong and remained in their favor through the rest of the afternoon and by the time the sky was showing hues of pink and purple, they were nearing the miles-wide channel known as Pirate Alley. A myriad of small islands and atolls lay on both sides. Many a merchant ship had been captured or lost here, as hunters could lurk out of sight and attack without warning.

The night promised to be moonless again and the wind sharp, giving Rose hope they could be well up the Alley before the sun rose the next morning. Once again, she ordered all lights out and the sails reduced to minimize the silhouette of the three ships. Like three ghostly galleons they cut through the dark water, their course charted by the great swath of the Milky Way above them.

15

———

Weary from having spent a full day on deck, Rose entered the cabin and came to an abrupt halt. Sebastien Fonteyne was sitting behind his desk studying one of the charts she had been marking calculations on before she went up on deck.

"Shall I assume you are feeling better?"

He looked up. The bandaging was off and his hair was loose. The bruising had spread across his brow and under his eyes, turning the skin a mottled black and blue almost to his chin.

"Much better, thank you."

"Good. Then there should be no reason why you cannot remove yourself to another cabin."

"I am rather fond of this one."

"So am I. It's much bigger than the one on the *Cygnet*. Unfortunately, I have not yet been able to enjoy the luxury of the extra space because I was advised against moving you in your ... enfeebled state."

"You were not in a much better state, madam. I woke a time or two and saw you curled up on the floor like a kitten."

"Cavalier of you to offer up the berth."

"I confess I did give a thought to sharing. But with the laudanum clouding my thoughts I could not guarantee my behavior having a soft body in bed with me. I have, however, restored myself with rum. Would you care to join me for a dram?"

Rose was not in the mood to play at a game of words and wits. She tossed her hat on the long dining table and unfastened the lacing down the front of her waistcoat as she crossed the cabin to the washstand. She poured water out of a jug into the thick porcelain basin and rinsed her face and hands, then ran a square of dampened linen across the back of her neck.

"Long day?"

"Long and hot and ... long," she said.

"And my ship? I understand you were able to seat a new mainmast?"

"Two days ago, your own carpenters insisted on making the repair. If you trust them to have done so correctly, then the mast is anchored soundly."

She heard what might have been a growl, but when she looked back, he had changed positions and was now seated at the table helping himself to a biscuit from the tray one of the lads had brought in from the galley. Rose's stomach rumbled and as she walked past, she grabbed the last two biscuits as well as a fat wedge of yellow cheese.

He had filled a second glass with rum and set it on the desk.

Rose chose not to acknowledge the courtesy as such. She took a seat in the big chair and savoured a long slow swallow of rum. It took a second and third swallow for the effect to reach her belly and when it did so, when her fingers and toes felt the restorative tingle, she leaned back, took a bite of biscuit, and studied Sebastien Fonteyne as she chewed.

"Better?" he asked.

"It will be."

He glanced down at the rolls of paper on the desk. "Those are damned fine sea charts, by the way. The details are rather ... astonishing."

"I had them brought over from the *Cygnet*. My family takes great pride in having damned fine charts."

"Lafitte has a framed copy of one drawn by *Le Cygnet Noir*, an ancestor of yours, if I'm not mistaken."

"Isabeau Dante. My great-great-great-possibly more greats-grandmother. It might interest you to know that her daughter, Juliet, also captained her own ship, the *Iron Rose*."

"So the sea truly is in your blood," he said quietly.

"Saltwater runs through my blood, bone, muscle, and sinew, sir. Did you think I was playing at this on a whim?"

"I confess it may have been my initial thought," he admitted. "Lafitte's as well. But no one who could run the blockade three times without taking any damage could hardly be accused of playing at it."

There was an odd note in his voice, and Rose smiled. "But they *could* be suspected of having too easy a time of it by working with or for the British."

He swirled the rum around his glass, watching the lamplight dance in the tawny liquid. "The notion did occur."

"Well, at least you're honest. Although Lafitte seemed more inclined to believe I should be working in his brothel."

A smile slowly overcame Fonteyne's stern expression. "I doubt I will ever forget the look on his face when he realized you had stolen the *Pride* out from under his nose. He actually turned purple and hopped up and down."

"I expect it was much like the expression on your face when you realized we had taken the *Black Wind* without firing a single shot."

His eyes narrowed and his smile turned a little brittle. "I was extremely angry."

"Was? Meaning you are not angry anymore?"

"Oh, I am still angry. Very much so. And while it is not in my nature to compliment someone for humiliating me and my crew—"

"That was not my intent."

"Yes, it was. It was revenge for having to suffer the humiliation of marrying some spindle-legged lout as a consequence for the night we spent together in Port Louis."

She opened her mouth to object but closed it again without a sound.

"Before you interrupted," he continued, "I was about to say I knew of no other *man* who would have had the courage or, indeed, the ballocks to execute such a perfect attack. Not one damned shot, indeed. I'll not live that one down so long as I draw breath."

She studied his face, looking for the trap. "Since it is not in your nature to give out compliments, I assume there is another reason for such largesse."

"Can it not simply be a tribute from one captain to another?"

"No."

He tipped his head back and laughed. "Your bluntness is refreshing. In truth, however, I have no hidden motive unless, of course, you count my own brashness in admitting my desire to take you back to bed ... where together we might find more reasons to lavish each other with compliments.

"Might I ask how were you going to persuade me to lose all grasp on my sensibilities?"

"The same way I did five years ago: by kissing you until you had no further need of sensibility."

She released a small puff of breath. "I see. Is this your idea of a seduction? Has it worked on many in the past?"

"Come now, Rose." He smiled in a way that would have loosened an old maid's drawers. "Our way of life is too short to waste on picking flowers and enduring endless days of coy flirtation. We live day to day, sometimes hour to hour, never knowing what the next will bring. At some point, every damn thing we have done was exactly what we wanted to do at that moment."

She mirrored his crooked smile. "Captain Fonteyne, at this moment, as impossible as it may seem that I could refuse such an ardent invitation so full of charm and profound insight, I do wish to go to bed. But I wish to do so *alone*. I would be grateful, therefore, if you could remove yourself to another cabin and find yourself another pillow on which to lay your head."

His eyes glittered above his smile, and she had the unnerving feeling he could see clear through her bravado to the wildly beating heart of that same seventeen-year-old who had melted in his arms and discovered pure passion.

In the end, however, he pushed to his feet and tugged politely on a wavy black forelock. "Another time, perhaps."

"Hope springs eternal," she quoted. "Goodnight, Captain. Do try not to fall down any stairs tonight."

FONTEYNE COMMANDEERED the quartermaster's cabin, a mere five paces away, and shut the door behind him. The girl had nerve, that was for sure. He hadn't expected her to tumble into bed with him at the crook of his finger ... although it happened more times than he cared to recount with most of the women he encountered. Old, young, fat, thin, married or not, they lifted their skirts and opened their thighs and welcomed him into their arms with grasping hands and eager sighs.

At the same time, he hadn't expected her to brush him away like an annoying fly.

Most of the cabins in the stern had the berths suspended over cannon. In battle, the berth could be raised and hooked to the wall and the gun pushed through the port. He tugged on the rope now to open the gun port a few inches, letting the cool night air rush into the cramped space. He lit the stub of a candle and set it on an iron sconce bolted to the wall. The light it gave off was weak and flickering.

"Try not to fall down," he muttered, swearing as he stubbed his toe against a wooden post supporting the berth. He sat on the edge and raked his fingers through his hair.

Rose's face came to him in the shadows ... those big, lovely eyes looking up at him, her hair spread across the bedding like red flames. The sound of the water creaming off the hull seemed to echo the whispered confession that she had been a virgin ....

He shook his head and growled inwardly. No regrets? Who was he kidding? He had regretted leaving her naked and sprawled out on the bed of discarded clothing, the faint dawn light washing over her body. He had gone to the window to clear his head and contemplate what he might say, what he *could* say when she awakened. But he had seen the *H.M.S. Savoy* gliding out of the harbor with his seized men on board, and in that precise moment it had been the right thing to do to leave Rose St. Clare and go after his men.

In the days, weeks, months that followed, he had convinced himself there had been no other choice to make. If he had stayed ... what then? Even if he had gone back ... what would he have done? Marry her? Not likely. He valued his freedom far too much to anchor himself to a wife.

But he did have a conscience, despite what she thought. Hearing that she had been forced into a marriage with Terrence Whitticomb had left him with a sour taste in his mouth. As sour as his mood had been since she had walked into the tavern

Later, he would blame his inattention on his urge to break something, for he swung his fist and struck the side of the berth hard enough to bring forth a curse. It was then, as the candle gave a violent shiver and nearly blew out, that he realized he was not alone. He had not heard the door open, nor was he aware of anyone entering the cabin until he heard the soft click of the latch.

He turned ... and felt the breath he had drawn get sucked straight out again.

Rose was standing with her back against the closed door.

"I knew I would not be able to sleep unless ... unless we talked about what you said."

"Which part of what I said?"

"The part about never knowing what the next day might bring. About having no time for picking flowers and petty flirtations. Regrets and recriminations, too, I should imagine."

"You have regrets?"

"Surely we all have regrets," she admitted. "Some minor and easily forgotten or of such little consequence as to not linger long in the mind."

"And others?"

"Not so minor. Not easily forgotten. Mistakes, even."

He stood up but she held out her hand to stop him from moving toward her.

"I am entirely to blame for what happened five years ago."

"As I recall, there were two of us in that garden."

"Well yes, but ..."

"But what?"

She looked up at him. "But I was the one who lured you there."

"As you pointed out, I did not offer up much resistance," he murmured.

She bowed her head again and blew out a half-angry breath. "Please don't make fun of me, or I'm likely to stab you."

He held up his hands in submission, but took a step closer.

"Aside from being stabbed, the very last thing I wish to do is make fun of you."

Her hair was unbraided and he was close enough now to reach out and gently push the dark waves back over her shoulders. He let his fingers run through the silky tangles to spread them, then tucked his thumb and forefinger under her chin and force her to look up at him.

"I feel as though I am about to make another mistake," she whispered.

"Then you probably should not do it."

"It won't change anything. I am still the captain and I am still in command of all three ships."

He moved his hand from beneath her chin and started to loosen the laces at the top of her shirt. "I have no quarrel with your ability to command. You have proven yourself to be more than capable."

"You gave your word not to make trouble."

"I did. And I will keep it. This ... particular kind of trouble ... has nothing to do with that promise."

He eased the loosened edges of her shirt aside and brushed the backs of his fingers down the exposed flesh. He sent one hand skimming beneath the cambric to cradle the lush swell of her breast, brushing his thumb across the crown as he felt the nipple tighten into a hard little bud. At the sound of her soft gasp, he bent his head to the curve of her neck, his lips finding the pulse beating wildly below her ear.

With his hand teasing her breast and his lips tracing a bold path to her mouth, the unexpected flush of desire that had prompted her to follow him to his cabin flared into a need so intense, she feared her knees might buckle. Her body came alive, flooding her with sensations she had tried to forget. When his mouth found hers, she welcomed it without hesitation, parting her lips, sharing her breath with his. Tongues slid together, exploring, remembering. The air around them grew still, and time was suspended as the world narrowed to two pairs of lips, two breaths, two beating hearts.

He broke away briefly and cradled her face between his hands. "You will likely regret this in the morning," he warned softly.

"I suspect we both might, but right now, at this moment, this is exactly where I want to be."

Fonteyne drew a deep breath and scooped her into his arms. He carried her the few short steps to the berth and when he set her down his mouth was fastened to hers again. Her arms were around his shoulders, and their tongues were lashed together. He stripped off her shirt and unfastened her breeches, peeling them down at the same time she was tearing at his shirt, exposing the bare breadth of his chest.

Naked, he joined her on the narrow berth and rolled onto his back, taking her with him letting her hair flow forward, wrapping them in a silken cocoon. He rolled again so that she was beneath him, their shared need so great there was no time for finesse. He was hard and she was sleek and wet. As he pushed inside her, she arched her body up, taking all of him without hesitation, pulling him deep. Her legs wrapped around him and held tight as her body moved into each thrust. She gasped with the stretching fullness of him, trembled with the waves of pleasure that built and grew and tightened until the sensations surged and crested.

Sebastien felt her spasms clench around him and he slid his hands down to her hips, lifting her, holding her as he continued to thrust. Her hands twisted up into his hair, then clawed at his shoulders and she climaxed, shuddering through a seemingly endless orgasm. When he could hold back no longer, he arched his back to gather himself for one last push, then surrendered to his own white-hot ecstasy.

THE SHIP EXECUTED a shallow turn and the motion woke Fonteyne. Cool air was sweeping through the open gun port along with a watery pale light. He lifted his head slightly to gaze down the length of his naked body. He was alone, surprised that he hadn't felt Rose slip off the berth and leave, although not surprised that she hadn't wanted to waken him. Waking him would mean she had to talk to him. Or look him in the eye.

He laid back and stretched the kinks out of his arms, then smiled as he scratched his hands up and down his chest. Until sheer exhaustion had claimed them both, they had taken full advantage of every hour they had been together. The berth was so narrow she had spent most of the night sprawled like a limp ragdoll on top of him ... until she wasn't and she was beneath him, straining and clutching at his body.

He was surprised she had been able to stand, much less walk away, stealthily or otherwise.

It was the first sign of weakness she had shown and, still smiling, he rolled onto his side and fell instantly back to sleep.

16

———

Back in her own cabin, Rose was startled awake by the sound of pounding of footsteps on the boards overhead followed by an almost simultaneous knock on the door.

"Sails off the larboard beam." Stubb poked his head inside. "Too far to see 'er flags."

Rose sat up, drawing the blanket up to her chin. "Has she noticed us?"

"We be runnin' due east, so a lubber-head would 'ave to be blind not to 'ave seen our silhouette against the dawn."

Rose cursed and swung her legs over the side of the berth. She had fallen into bed wearing only the oversized cambric shirt she had donned before creeping out of Fonteyne's cabin. She snatched up her breeches and pulled on her boots, stamping her feet in firmly.

"Where are the *Pride* and *Cygnet*?"

"The brothel had trouble with her rudder. Mercado put a tow line on 'er an' we cut our speed so they could pull ahead rather than be drug behind."

"When did this happen? Why wasn't I told about the rudder?"

"'Appened durin' the ghost watch." He avoided meeting her eyes. "Billy an' me thought it best to leave ye be."

Her cheeks turned ruddy but her voice was all business. "Is the *Pride* still under tow?"

"Duardo signaled the repairs be almost done."

Rose tightened the laces on the shirt then shoved her arms through the sleeve-holes of her waistcoat as she hurried to the desk. "Where the devil are we, anyway?"

"Passed Pirate Wells an hour ago an' now we be just shy o' the Nobbins."

Rose took a moment to glance at the open chart she had been about to study before ... well, before. The Nobbins were the first of two islands that formed the chain of over three hundred atolls and cays stretching up for almost as many miles. Stubb had dubbed them Big and Little Nobbin, with the bigger of the two identifiable by three distinct pitons.

"How far?"

"T'ree, maybe four hours."

As she passed Stubb on her way out of the cabin, he was still avoiding her eyes and she cursed inwardly. If he and Billy knew where she had spent the night, then it was likely most of the ship's crew knew as well. She had assumed it would be awkward seeing Fonteyne up on deck for the first time, but she hadn't anticipated a hundred men staring at her and snickering.

Out in the companionway, Rose shoved an arm into the sleeve of her coat and nearly fisted Sebastien Fonteyne in the face as he emerged from the quartermaster's cabin.

They both drew up short and stared for a full ten seconds.

"I heard the bell," he said. "Is there anything I can do?"

"You can stay out of my way." She pushed past and dashed up the ladderway to the main deck. The wind was brisk, the eastern sky was watery gray with the light starting to spread out across the sky as the dawn rose to chase away the night.

Billy Burr was waiting on the quarterdeck and handed her a long-glass. The first thing Rose did was check the position of the *Pride* and the *Cygnet*, estimating they were little more than a pistol shot ahead. Two sets of cables were stretched between them, but the lines were slack, indicating the *Pride* had begun answering to her own rudder again.

She swung the glass around and looked out over the stern. The distant ship was emerging from the west, presenting a full set of sails, a tower of white against the retreating night sky.

"Flags?"

"Too far to tell until the sun climbs higher," Billy said. "Carrack maybe or a schooner."

"Or one o' them revenuers who like to lurk like vultures up an' down the Alley." Stubb spat over the rail. "I warned ye we be takin' a chance comin' this way, an' ye know how much I hate bein' right all the time."

"So you keep telling us," Rose said and rolled her eyes slightly. "But one ship against three? For all we know, it could be another ship doing what we're doing: running up the Alley toward New Providence."

Rose felt a chill slither down her spine as she heard Fonteyne's voice over her shoulder. "May I take a look?"

Without turning or looking at him, Rose handed him the long-glass. He stepped to the rail beside her and made two, three slow passes along the western horizon before focussing on the distant speck of white. He lowered the glass and frowned in thought for a moment, then peered through the glass again.

"Not Spanish," he said. "Not French or Dutch."

Billy scowled. "A ship you might recognize, perhaps?"

Fonteyne lowered the glass and glared at Billy. "Are you asking me if I somehow managed to signal our course to another ship despite being nearly comatose on laudanum for the past day two days?"

Rose raised a hand before Billy could offer up a retort. "If she's not Spanish or French or Dutch, that leaves—"

"They," Fonteyne said quietly. "There are at least two and they don't seem to be too shy about it. They are showing lights on deck."

Rose snatched the glass back and raised it to her eye. He was right. The shifting light and mirror-like haze shimmering above the surface of the water had hidden the second ship, which was just now taking shape. Both vessels had lights winking from their decks.

"The American navy is spread too thin," Fonteyne said, his brow furrowed in thought. "At last count, they had seventeen frigates and corvettes, eight schooners, and three brigs. Most, if not all, locked in ports behind the blockade lines. The British navy, on the other hand, has a hundred ships patrolling that line and access to eight hundred more fresh from the war with France with admirals itching to bring the fight across the Atlantic. As you have previously pointed out, the Americans don't have a single tall ship free to protect access to New Orleans —a major oversight which, it may please you to know, I now happen to agree was a blatantly stupid miscalculation.

"The British know the quickest way to bring an end to the rebellion is to stop the supply of guns and powder going up the Mississippi, which is why agents of the Crown have put bounties on the heads of every privateer suspected of selling their cargoes to the Americans. Break the supply chain, end the war."

Stubb had his glass stuck through the spindles of the taffrail and made a clucking sound with his tongue. "God's left eyeball, 'ee's right. They be wearin' British colors, flyin' ol' St. George an comin' on fast. Most like to be revenuers tryin' to catch us up an' search us for cargo." He lowered the glass and looked up at Rose. "We could outrun 'em, so could the *Cygnet*. But the brothel couldn't outrun a dead snail."

Rose turned her glass to the islands they were approaching. The Nobbins were curved to suggest they once formed the top rim of a volcano. Separating the two eroded crescents, each four or five miles long, was a channel with shallow, rocky bottoms on both sides and a narrow path of deep blue water in the middle. The *Cygnet* and *Pride* had already fallen into a direct line with the *Black Wind* intending to take advantage of the stiff breezes and currents to sweep them safely between the reefs.

She swung around to check the position of the revenuers again. "We don't have to outrun them," she said. "But we can make it look like that's what we are trying to do. It's entirely possible they haven't seen the other two ships yet, hampered as we were by distance and morning haze. We can let them chase us for a while, until Duardo and Mercado are safely on the other side of the channel. Mister Reed!"

The *Black Wind's* helmsman stepped up sharply.

"I judge our speed to be seven? eight knots?"

Reed looked at Rose then at Fonteyne, uncertain who to address. "Thereabout, aye."

"Slow her down to five. Loosen the tops and the royals so they fall slack. Make it look as if we are in some difficulty."

Reed glanced at Fonteyne and caught the slight nod before he tugged on a forelock. "Aye Captain."

"Stubb! I need you to signal the *Cygnet*. The revenuers may think they have a grand prize within their grasp, but we're going to arrange a little surprise for them."

Stubb rubbed his hands together with glee and ran forward to signal the other two ships from the bow.

Rose turned and ran squarely into Fonteyne's chest. He put his hands to her shoulders to steady her and left them there a moment longer than necessary. Her hair was flying loose in the breezes, the silky red curls teasing the backs of his hands. Her cheeks were flushed, her eyes bright with excitement and Fonteyne found himself catching at his breath.

"I am sure you are aware that a ship does not sail well under two captains," he said after a moment. "You may be excellent at the helm of your own vessel, Rose, but you know nothing of how the *Wind* responds under battle conditions. I don't doubt for an instant you could cope, but wouldn't you rather be in command from the deck of your own ship?"

"Mercado is more than capable of commanding the *Cygnet*."

"If you are worried about me breaking away after we've dealt with the revenuers, or that I might turn my guns on your ship, I'll remind you that I did give you my bond."

"I am not worried about that in the least, Captain Fonteyne. Nor am I worried that there will be much of a fight."

"How can you be so sure? You said yourself, the *Black Wind* is a tempting prize."

She responded with a mercurial smile. "I am certain enough to make you a small wager, Captain. If they attack us with any measure of success, I will return command of your ship to you upon the instant."

She brushed past to hasten forward to the bow and he watched her over his shoulder for a long, dragging moment before turning and following. She had the glass to her eye and spoke without looking at him.

"A night in your bed has not addled my wits, Captain," she murmured. "It is as fair a wager as you are likely to get."

"And if they don't attack?"

She lowered the glass. "I went to Barataria Bay hoping to prove my worth to Lafitte. It has been my hope, since coming upon you in the fog, that if I proved myself, then perhaps you, as his most trusted and successful captain, would persuade him to set aside his disdain for women and accept me for my skill, not my breasts."

"If there is no attack," she said, gazing up at him, "I will still return command of your ship to you, but I will want your word, your *bond*, that you will agree to stand me in good favor with Lafitte. Back me in my request to join his company of brethren as captain of my own ship."

His eyes narrowed a fraction. There was no doubt a trap was being set, but he was not sure if it was for the revenuers ... or him. Either way, she was giving him back his ship, and they were still a long sail away from Barataria Bay.

"You have my word," he said. "But I will do you one better, Captain St. Clare. If Lafitte won't take you into his company, I will take you on as a member of mine."

THE CREW of the *Black Wind* was fast and efficient when whistled into action. The decks were cleared of any obstructions. Shot was brought up from the armory and stacked on brass monkeys. Buckets were placed alongside each gun holding cartridges of gunpowder measured for the weight of shot for each cannon. Another canister held Billy's newly crafted feather straws filled with powder for the touchholes.

Casks of sand and ash stood at hand to scatter and soak up any spilled blood that might make the planks slippery. Linstocks fitted with as yet unlit slow fuses were passed out to the gun crews, some whom were already stripped to the waist with bandanas tied around their heads to soak up the sweat. The ports remained closed, but the wooden wedges were knocked out from behind the wheels of the gun carriages and the heavy tackle lines were unclipped.

Coils of rope were placed beneath each of the three masts in the event a cable needed replacing; spare yards and sails were at the ready along with hatchets and saws for cutting away any damage that could hamper the ship's maneuverability in battle.

Apart from the men who were up in the rigging to work the sails, the rest of the crew crouched at their positions. A good many of Fonteyne's crew were still stinging from the way Rose's men had taken their ship and so were bristling for a real fight ... one they could handily turn on their captors if Fonteyne gave them the signal. To a man, they watched him closely, for mutiny was easily accomplished in the heat of battle, but so far he stood calmly on the quarterdeck, occasionally looking up at the sails and ordering a slight adjustment.

Rose was equally wary. Trust, in her experience, was something hard won and easily broken. Fonteyne was a pirate and a brigand with treachery tainting the blood that flowed through his veins. Wager or no wager, there was no guarantee he would keep his word and as a precaution she armed only her own crewmen with cutlasses and muskets. This did not half please him and he paced the deck like a panther, his black hair tangling and whipping in the wind. Watching him, Rose knew that soon he was going to be even angrier with her. He was going to feel tricked and duped but there was little she could do now to avoid it.

On board the *Cygnet* and *Pride*, similar preparations were being made for battle. Having exchanged a flurry of signals with Stubb, both ships had hauled in sail as soon as they had cleared the reefs and had taken up positions out of sight on either side of the channel, their ports open, the gun crews crouched and ready.

AN HOUR later and still two miles away, a smartly uniformed

lieutenant in the Royal Navy, lowered his long-glass and nodded. "There can be no doubt, sir. It is the *Black Wind*."

"What the devil is that pirate doing here? The last reports had Fonteyne a thousand miles away, hunting off the coast of Cartagena."

Lieutenant Ormond Bentley was in his eighteenth year, barely showing any chin hairs. Due to his family's wealth and influence with the admiralty, he had managed to avoid the bloody conflict in Europe and had been assigned to one of His Majesty's revenue ships, the *Renard*, patrolling the West Indies. The name Sebastien Fonteyne was shockingly familiar, as was the notorious privateer's deadly reputation. Tiny beads of sweat dampened the meticulously curled blond hairs at his temples as the high collar around his neck seemed to grow a little tighter.

"What shall we do, Sir?"

"Do? What shall we do?" Beside him, Captain Douglas Ashworth Templeton-Bing, picked a shred of breakfast ham out of his teeth. He was not five years older than his lieutenant, tall and stiff-necked with an air of pretention that had the crew wondering if he had been born with an iron rod up his backside.

Having been interrupted during his morning meal, his mood was one of acute petulance.

"What we shall do is catch the bastard and put him in irons. Fonteyne is a pirate and a petty thief. He is not half so fearsome as the penny sheets make him out to be. And his ship is as vulnerable to a few well-placed broadsides as any other."

"Yes, sir. Of course, sir. It's just …"

"Just what, Lieutenant? We have the weather gauge. The wind is at our backs and we have speed under our keel. Look how his tops and gallants are hanging. His mainmast shows a fresh repair and unless I am mistaken, that is raw timber on the rails. He has been in a fight recently and come away wanting."

It was not the answer he would have liked to hear, but the young lieutenant felt he ought to agree. "Aye, sir."

"Signal the *Daffodil* to close up and follow our lead. When we are within range, we shall fire a shot across her bow and by God, if that is, indeed, the *Black Wind*, we will dine well tonight Mr. Bently. On his own gold plate with jewelled forks!"

"But Sir ... he is headed into the channel and we have no way of knowing what lies on the other side. The lookout—"

"Yes, yes, the lookout thought he saw another ship ahead of the privateer, but ten other keen pairs of eyes saw nothing of the like. A ghost image caused by the heat rising off the water."

Once again, the lieutenant knew better than to argue, but his face was easy to read and the captain clapped him on the shoulder.

"Come now. Buck up, Lieutenant! We have forty guns between our two vessels and crews eager to use them. Mark my words, we will have the villain's flags before midday or my worth is not equal to the brass buttons on my coat!"

17

───────

The *Black Wind* sailed effortlessly through the channel. On the far side of the passage, she heeled to starboard to glide into the bay formed by the hooked crescent of land. On the western side of the volcanic bay, the *Cygnet* had taken up a firing position with her starboard guns aimed at the mouth of the channel. Beside her, the *Pride* was still dealing with a recalcitrant rudder, but Rose knew the ship would soon be in a firing position if Duardo had to push the hull around himself.

Once the *Black Wind* was in position on the eastern side of the channel, the three ships would be set to catch the revenuers in a deadly crossfire.

It was a straightforward mousetrap a blind man could have set up, so Fonteyne gave Rose no special credit for devising it. What did surprise him, however, was the presence of a fourth ship anchored in the bay, now a half pistol shot off the *Black Wind's* starboard beam.

Her sails were reefed, her gunports closed. The upper yards and rails were lined with men, some of whom had removed their caps and were waving and cheering as they watched the three new arrivals maneuver into position.

Fonteyne's frown was furrowed deep enough to stretch and endanger the line of stitching on his brow. "What the devil—?"

Stubb, who had been anticipating a good fight, took his cap off and threw it on the deck, glaring at Rose in disgust. "Did ye bloody well know he were bloody well here?"

Rose responded with an innocent shrug. "Not for certain. Not until I saw the signal light flashing from the top of the piton."

"An' ye didn't think to say aught?"

"Billy thought the crews could benefit from a drill."

"Billy!" Stubb sputtered and swore. "Ye told her, but the thought never touched yer brainbox to tell *me*?"

"It isn't often we get to surprise you," Rose said, smiling.

"I suppose lumber-nose knew as well?"

"Duardo? Of course he knew."

Stubb stomped on his cap in disgust and stalked off muttering to himself.

That left Fonteyne staring obliquely at Rose. "I don't suppose you might deign to tell me what everyone else seems to know?"

"That is my father's ship. The *Nighthawk*. We had agreed to rendezvous here before I left for Barataria Bay."

"Before? Meaning you were not anticipating a successful meeting with Lafitte?"

She sighed and shrugged. "Meaning my father humored me, but I lost a wager of two hundred pieces of silver."

"He suspected you would fail."

"On both counts, aye."

"Both counts?"

"The first, of course, was for Lafitte to let me join his wolf pack."

"And the second?"

"That I might be able to persuade him to become a silent

partner of sorts. Father cannot be seen to openly provide any aide to the Americans, but he does what he can from afar and if Lafitte had agreed to the partnership, Father could have done a good deal more. As it turns out, however, I doubt he'll be dancing a jig when he sees the two British revenue ships chasing us. So, if you will excuse me—?"

She called for a longboat and while it was being lowered over the side, she went below to fetch the packet of documents and dispatches she had taken from the *Hyperion*. She buckled her sword around her waist and shoved her arms into her short coat, then snatched up her hat and headed to the door.

When she emerged from the cabin, Fonteyne was waiting in the corridor, leaning a shoulder against the bulkhead. He looked every inch the pirate, for he had donned his black leather vest and jacket, as well as his own battered wide-brimmed hat. Tucked into his belt was a brace of long-snouted pistols ... pistols Rose was certain she had not agreed to let him carry.

Her hand went instinctively to one of her own guns. "What do you think you are doing?"

"I was thinking it was time to take my ship back."

"You were, were you?"

"Naturally, it would be far more civil and far less annoying if you simply gave it back."

"And why would I do that?"

"Three reasons I can think of offhand. One, because you need me as an ally, not an enemy. And two, you are going to want my help to convince Jean Lafitte that it would be in his best interests to help defend New Orleans. I have read most of the documents and dispatches you took off the *Hyperion*—or did you honestly think I was so clumsy that I would need to lie in bed for two days to recover my senses?"

"Instead, you went through my papers," she said calmly.

"As you did mine."

"You said there were three reasons why I shouldn't shoot you where you stand."

He pursed his lips and nodded. "The third is because I have an unexpected and totally illogical urge to shake the hand of the man who fathered such a complete lunatic. A brazen, clever, cunning, magnificent lunatic who seems to have more trouble trusting me than I do trusting her. Having said that, I would much prefer to be introduced as the captain of my own vessel, willingly offering my assistance in dealing with the British revenuers."

Rose hadn't moved, had not said a word to interrupt him. Her face was without expression, mainly because she did not know if she should be angry or relieved. Naturally, she would prefer to have his men, his ship, his guns by her side willingly. It was her father's reaction that worried her.

Alexander St. Clare was not someone likely to forgive the man who took his daughter's virginity five years ago then callously sailed off into the sunrise, leaving her to face the consequences alone.

She slid her hand away from her pistol. "I should speak to him first. Explain all that has happened. For you to present yourself to him before I do so may not be the best idea."

He reached up and brushed his forefinger along the curve of her cheek. "We have already had several ideas that, in hindsight, may not have been so brilliant. Where is the harm in one more?"

It was a fair point, one that was driven home by the tingling in her cheek ... and elsewhere ... at the touch of his hand. Before a blush could fully bloom across her face, she brushed past him and walked down the corridor. At the bottom of the ladderway she paused and cast a cool glance over her shoulder.

"Are you coming, *Captain* Fonteyne? I expect my father is as curious to meet you as you are to meet him."

ALEXANDER ST. Clare was in his fifth decade. A tall and imposing figure, his hair was iron-gray, his beard neatly trimmed. His broad shoulders were more accustomed now to tailored coats and ruffled cuffs than loose cambric shirts and leather crossbelts; nonetheless, he cut a formidable figure. Pale blue eyes dominated a handsome face that was still able to turn heads and cause women to whisper softly to themselves. And while those eyes held a thousand secrets of their own, the patriarch of the Dante-St. Clare Shipping dynasty had the uncanny ability to see through the trappings of a lie as if it stood naked before him. When that happened, when the blue turned to silvered ice, his gaze was as deadly as the blade of a knife.

But it was love and pride that shone from them now as he watched his daughter climb through the gangway of the *Nighthawk*. He had caught hell from his wife more times than he could count for giving Rose the freedom to sail her own ship, but he could no more have kept her pinned to the land as he could teach a butterfly to curtsy to the King.

Before they exchanged a word, Rose held out a small leather pouch jingling with coin. "I believe the wager was two hundred pieces of silver?"

"Ah. I did warn you Lafitte was a stubborn little prick, not easily persuaded to change his ways."

"He said that having a female captain join his ranks would frighten away the men who might not be able to match the successes of a better ship, a better crew, a better fighting force. His arrogance cut our conversation short."

Alexander laughed. "I'm sure it did."

"I repaid his misplaced sense of superiority by stealing his prized possession."

The blue eyes glanced over at the *Pride*. "So I see." A few seconds later his gaze turned frosty as Sebastien Fonteyne stepped through the gangway onto the deck. "I also see that his ship was not the only one of Lafitte's trinkets you brought back with you."

"A long story best told over a bottle of rum, Father. But it will have to wait, for we have two revenuers chasing up our wake."

Alexander nodded. "I am aware. They are still an hour or thereabouts away, so you can talk fast and we can spare five of those sixty minutes for you to tell me why you are keeping company with Lafitte's right-hand man."

Fonteyne stepped forward and introduced himself with a slight tipping of his head. "Captain Sebastien Fonteyne, at your ser--"

The pale blue wolf's eyes silenced him with a glare. "I was speaking to my daughter. You will have your turn, if and when I deem it necessary."

The tension between the two men was palpable and Rose cut through it by speaking quickly, recounting most of what had happened over the past fortnight, beginning with the capture of the *Hyperion*. She skimmed through the meeting with Lafitte and the subsequent taking of the *Pride*. "He insulted me and his ship was just there, so I thought ..." She then replayed the dash for open water, the stashing of the copper and getting swept up in the storm, ending with the unexpected luck in finding themselves in a position to sneak up on the *Black Wind* undetected.

"Unfortunately, we had to sink the *Hyperion*," she concluded. "But she was carrying papers that led us to believe a British fleet will be arriving soon to prepare for an attack on New Orleans."

St. Clare looked at Fonteyne. "If his ship was forfeit to you, why is he standing on my ship wearing pistols and grinning like a well-fed lion?"

"Because we need his help with Lafitte. And because he has offered it."

"He offered his help willingly?" Alexander's mouth curved up slightly at the corner. "Is that how his face got so bruised? Should I be checking your knuckles?"

"The bruising was caused by his own clumsiness, although I will admit there were moments when my fists were tempted."

Fonteyne arched an eyebrow but refrained from making any mention of temptations.

Rose spoke quickly again. "But he did agree to help convince Lafitte to throw his support to the Americans."

Fonteyne raised a finger to object. "That ... was not exactly what I agreed to. What I said was that you might *need* my help to convince him to defend New Orleans against both warring sides."

"Both?" Alexander frowned. "Are you suggesting the Americans would attack their own city? For what purpose?"

"Your daughter said it most succinctly: capture the city, you control access to the entire Mississippi."

"The Americans have already laid claim to New Orleans," Alexander said.

"Their grip is tentative and relies on a militia made up of shopkeepers and farmers. A far more experienced army defended Washington City but apparently could not hold it. The Americans have not known what to do with Louisiana since they purchased the territory from the French in '03? My guess would be at the first threat of a British attack, they would blow up the levee and flood the city, then run north. If they do that, if the British get a foothold on the Mississippi and land an army flushed with victory over defeating Napoleon Bonaparte ...?"

He left the sentence unfinished but Alexander St. Clare could guess the conclusion. He sighed and shook his head. "If they fail to hold the Mississippi, then they will lose the damned war."

"They will lose more than just the war," Fonteyne said quietly.

The discussion ended there as Alexander caught a flash of light from the top of the piton. "Best get back to your ship, Daughter." And to Fonteyne he added, "I assume your gunners can still hit a moving target?"

Sebastien caught the sarcasm in the older man's voice but smiled easily. "They can hit a stationary one as well."

"Excellent." Alexander turned and glanced up at his helmsman. "Mr. Fitch, you'll alert us if any fog starts to roll in that may hide more ships?"

Digby Fitch, who had overheard the entire dazzling tale of the *Black Wind's* capture ... as did half the ship's crew ... touched his forelock and grinned. "Aye, Captain. I'll be sure to put keenest eyes topside."

18

The sun was hot and brilliant overhead, bleaching the sails of the two British revenue ships a stark white as they neared the far side of the channel. Confident in their pursuit of their prized quarry, certain to have them trapped in the bay, the gun ports were open, the crews standing at the ready. Squadrons of red-coated sharpshooters were braced in the yards and lining the rails of the upper deck, their muskets primed.

It could only be imagined what the captains of both vessels thought when they sailed into the wide bay and saw not one but four battle-ready ships waiting to greet them. One of the forward gunners was so shocked, he touched his lit fuse to a five-pounder bow chaser mounted on the rail and a shot exploded from the muzzle in a minor spit of flame and smoke. The ball plopped harmlessly into the sea beside the *Black Wind*, sending a thin spout of blue water in the air fifty feet from her hull.

Watching from the quarterdeck of the *Cygnet*, Stubb chuckled. "Fairy farts they be sendin' over. I'm dreadful affeered for my life," he said in a shaky falsetto. "Best we haul down our flags an' surrender."

Beside him, Billy Burr smirked then looked to Rose, who nodded.

"Show them how it's done, lads!" Billy shouted. "Aim high and fire away!"

As one, five of the gun crews on the main deck touched the glowing tips of their linstocks to the touchholes and unleashed a thunderous volley at the *Renard*. They were loaded with chain shot—two heavy balls linked by chain—that spun like dervishes and screamed across the narrow distance to slice through the upper yards, shredding sails, and cutting cables, sending a score of sharpshooters scrambling to secure their footing as the broken yards fell into the sea.

Behind the *Renard*, the *Daffodil* came up too fast to avoid a similar round of scattered shot from the *Black Wind*. The fiery results were much the same: broken yards, scrambling men, sporadic and ineffectual musket fire from the soldiers lining the rails.

The uniformed officers standing on both quarterdecks stared in open-mouthed shock.

Rose St. Clare reinforced that shock by ordering a second round of shot that sliced through the remaining yards and rigging aboard the *Renard*.

Faced with the combined batteries of the four vessels, and with wreckage falling on their heads there was little debate. The revenuers took in sail and lowered their pennons then ran up a brace of white flags. Having signaled their capitulation, they followed the orders shouted through a speaking trumpet to bring their damaged ships to a limping halt and drop anchors in the deepest curve of the bay.

With the British officers confined and the crews disarmed and under heavy guard, Rose, Fonteyne, and Alexander St. Clare met again in the great cabin of the *Nighthawk*.

Rose and her father were intent on reading through the logbooks and documents Stubb had found on board the Crown ships. Fonteyne seemed more intent on enjoying a cup of rum and watching the patterns of sunlight dancing on the cabin ceiling.

The watery reflections held Fonteyne's attention until he could no longer resist the temptation to study the two people seated opposite him. The resemblance was unmistakable between father and daughter. They had the same high cheekbones, the same generous shape to the mouth. They shared the same silvery-blue eyes, though in Rose the shade seemed more exotic set against the red-gold color of her hair.

There was a fierce beauty to this woman derived from strength and confidence rather than feminine delicacy. Not that delicate would be a word that came instantly to mind upon first meeting her. Her jaw was a little too square, her gaze too direct. No downcast, fluttering eyelashes for this one. Her hands were too calloused for doing needlepoint, her thighs strong enough to hold his own captive until she took what she wanted from him. His first glimpse of Rose at the governor's ball in Port Louis those many years ago had won his interest and despite the five year separation, that interest had not waned.

Aye, he had remembered every detail from that night. It was imprinted on his memory alongside the most recent shock of seeing her stride into Lafitte's tavern on Barataria, any hint of delicacy belied by leather and steel, and the well-used pistols she wore on her hips.

Alexander leaned back in his chair and tapped his forefinger on the documents. "The troops who captured and destroyed Washington City were probably as inexperienced as the troops who failed to defend it. The fleet this Admiral Nicholls is bringing, however, will be filled with soldiers seasoned on the bloody battlefields of France. I'm afraid I don't know anything about the admiral himself, though the name seems oddly familiar."

Fonteyne shifted slightly, pulling his thoughts away from two naked, entwined bodies. "I had the misfortune to run into him back in '05, at Trafalgar. The ship I was on took heavy damage and limped into port with a useless rudder and few working sails. We managed to heel over so we only scraped along the length of his hull instead of hitting bow-on, but he took great offence that his paintwork was spoiled. He used it to his advantage, however, writing in a later report that the damage was done by a French vessel in the heat of battle."

"Are you implying he took no actual damage in the battle?"

"I'm *implying* nothing. I'm stating flatly that he never brought his ship within range of any French guns."

Alexander pursed his lips and nodded as if that was the only reference, he needed to form an opinion of the admiral's character. "This report mentions that the fleet was due to leave the Azores almost a month ago. Unless the ships are being rowed across, he should have made landfall by now. Most likely in Nassau to re-supply before carrying on into the Gulf."

"It was my thought to sail up Pirate's Alley and see if we could find them," Rose said.

Alexander pondered that thought for a moment then slid several folded papers across the table. "Both of you might want to take a look at this first."

The top sheet was a remarkably detailed map of Barataria Bay and the two islands, Grande Terre and Grande Isle, along with a myriad small inlets and bays depicted along the flanking coastlines.

Accompanying the map was a note, which said in part:

I recommend the approach likely to reap the most success is from the west, where an assault would be least expected. I would further advise a blockade of the eastern access and all other avenues of seaborne escape whereupon the pirates will have no choice but to surrender or scatter into the mangrove swamps. Once you have Lafitte and his two most capable lieutenants, Renato Beluche and Sebastien Fonteyne in chains, or better yet, swinging at the end of a rope, the pirates will be headless and gutless.

There was no signature on the note but Rose knew her brother's handwriting like she knew her own, the precision of each letter having been *whapped* sharply onto their knuckles by their shared governess.

From the grim set to her father's mouth, she knew he had recognized it as well.

Wordlessly, she slid the note across the table to Fonteyne. While the privateer studied the map and the note, Rose risked a glance at her father, but a slight shake of his head bade her hold her tongue.

When Fonteyne was finished reading, he pushed the papers away in disgust. "So much for the British wanting to negotiate with Lafitte in good faith. I did try to warn him, but he's a stubborn Creole bastard, often too full of himself to see what he doesn't want to see."

"I am led to understand he commands a federation of upwards of a hundred vessels?" asked Alexander.

"None of which are actually under his command, as such," Fonteyne said. "Jean is merely the middleman who distributes and sells the cargo our ships bring in. For easing us of that tiresome burden, he does command a certain amount of respect and loyalty."

"As well as a handsome share of the profits, I warrant?"

"No more so than usury fees and taxes collected despite so called free trade."

Alexander noted the distain in his voice. "Exactly how much convincing would it take to turn Lafitte's thoughts from profit to patriot?"

"I would be talking out of my arse to suggest he would be easily swayed. On the other hand, he is not well pleased with the way the city council and Governor Claiborne have been treating him. They have issued a warrant for his arrest on charges of piracy, thrown his brother in jail again, and confiscated the goods on a score of his barges."

"Have the Americans made *any* effort to reinforce defenses around the city?"

Fonteyne huffed at that. "They have two schooners patrolling all of the gulf coastline from Pensacola to Galveston. They have a few gun boats for show on the river, but nothing bigger than a twelve-pounder on board and no stores of powder or shot to fire them.

"Having said that," he added, "Lafitte has warehouses filled with enough guns, powder, and shot to start a small war of his own. To that end, he will defend Barataria with every last ball and ounce of powder in his possession. New Orleans, on the other hand, with its current council of pompous fools, I would not lay too high a wager on his wanting to extend a hand or a barrel of powder to help them."

"Do all of his captains feel the same way?" Rose asked. "Do you?"

"We are a fickle lot," Fonteyne admitted with a shrug. "The reason most of us stay with Lafitte is because he has half the judges and revenue agents in Louisiana on his payroll and he can move cargo inland on barges for a guaranteed profit. Threaten the flow of those profits and some of the captains will go elsewhere quicker than you can blink."

"You are saying their loyalty is provisional."

"I'm saying that for some, aye, the weight of their loyalty is equal to the weight of the gold in their pockets. Without it, his company of brethren would be considerably less in number."

"Lafitte knows this?"

"Of course he knows it. Mind you, he would cut out his own tongue before admitting it, but he is fully aware his hold over them is based on him retaining access to the Mississippi and continuing the flow of profits. One of the reasons why he is so outraged at the good citizens of Louisiana, and Claiborne in particular, for ordering the arrest of his brother Pierre ... is because it is an uncomfortable indication that he and all of his business enterprises might be just as vulnerable and—" he tapped the note—" we might all find ourselves facing the gallows."

"In that case, regardless which side he supports," Alexander said, "I suspect neither the British nor the Americans will be comfortable letting him remain in Barataria Bay."

Fonteyne agreed. "They would be fools to do so."

Alexander pursed his lips thoughtfully. "I understand Lafitte has written to President Madison inquiring about the possibility of amnesty for himself and his men should he throw his support in with the Americans."

"Several times. And he has been flatly refused each time."

"Madison is as obstinate as Lafitte and sounds just as arrogant. However, I have it on good authority that the President is contemplating sending General Jackson and his army south to Pensacola."

Fonteyne shook his head. "Florida is not the key. The British will happily let the Spanish and the native Indians keep Jackson's army occupied there while they go after the Mississippi, and, not to repeat the obvious, if they gain a foothold on the delta, it will not matter who has control of Florida."

It was Rose's turn to stare at him with an arched eyebrow.

"Why did you not say any of this to Lafitte when we were in Barataria Bay?"

"Because the idea of supporting either side has to come from Lafitte himself. You could have talked until your face turned as red as your hair and it would have had no effect. He will do nothing without the guarantee of some conditions."

St. Clare and Rose both waited.

Sebastien counted them off on his fingers. "Release of his brother from prison. Amnesty for himself and his men—in writing, from the President. And the guaranteed sanctity of Barataria Bay with the freedom to conduct his future business enterprises without interference."

Alexander pondered the conditions for a moment and opened his mouth to reply but the ringing of the ship's bell caused him to glance upward as if he could see through the boards. "We can continue this discussion later. For the moment, there are two Crown ships with their disgruntled captains and crews to deal with. Unfortunately, I cannot be seen to play any part in what you do with them. Much of our company holdings are on British-held territories and unlike you, Captain Fonteyne, whose letters of marque are issued in Columbia, mine come from the king and can be rescinded on a whim. That, plus the fact one of my sons is governor of Tobago, puts me in an awkward position should I be seen to be cooperating with you in any way."

He paused and smiled hesitantly at Rose. "As much as it will gall you, I would also suggest you remain out of sight and let Captain Fonteyne take credit for capturing the *Nighthawk* as well as the Crown ships. I took the liberty of sending that wretched little elf a message to take your pennon off the masthead and shield the identity of the *Cygnet* as best he could, though it may already be too late.

"As for the *Pride*," Alexander said quietly. "I doubt there is one sailor in twenty who is unfamiliar with her silhouette or provenance. If the British suspect she aided in capturing the two crown ships, or, indeed, was even present here today, it would not win Lafitte any favors. I would suggest, therefore, that the longer the captains and crews of the revenuers are deprived of their freedom, the better."

Fonteyne grinned. "I could deprive them of more than their freedom."

"I'm certain you could," Alexander said, "But I think it would suffice to maroon the officers on the islands and take their ships away with you."

Fonteyne glanced down at the note Ramsey St. Clare had penned. "If I leave on the morning tide, and with the wind in my favor, I can reach Barataria in enough time to warn them of any impending attack."

"I am coming with you," Rose said.

"I thought you wanted to have a look at the British fleet?"

"If I look and if I find them, I can hardly do anything on my own to stop them. I would rather go where I can be of some use."

Fonteyne waited for Alexander to protest but when no objection was forthcoming, he blew out a long, slow breath. "I can't stop you, of course, but I would rather you didn't. It will be difficult enough to convince Lafitte to play a hand he may be unwilling to play without trying to persuade him not to flay the skin from your back for stealing his ship."

"I am not afraid of a pompous little turd like Jean Lafitte," she said.

"Perhaps you should be. His word is law in Barataria."

"And I have *your* word you will convince him of my worth."

"I can but try."

Rose snorted rather inelegantly. "*Try* is a feeble word favored by feeble men."

Fonteyne's long fingers curled tight where they rested on the tabletop. A moment later he stood and plucked his hat off the table. "I had best play my part and make the necessary arrangements to put the crews ashore. Rose, a moment if you will?"

She glanced at her father, who nodded and waved her away.

Once she had joined him in the corridor and the partly closed door threw them into shadow, his arm snaked out and curled around her waist, forcing her to crush up against him. With no warning of his intentions, he bent and kissed her so fully and forcefully on the mouth, it drew the breath from her lungs and set her head to spinning.

When he released her, Rose gasped to regain her senses. "What the devil was that for?"

"I thought you needed a little reminder ... in case you were under the impression that a night in your bed would turn me into an obliging milquetoast."

"I was under no such impression," she said on a breath.

"Good. Because whether you come with me to Barataria or not will be my decision and my decision alone."

She blinked but then stared directly into his eyes for a long, heart-stilling moment. Instead of protesting, as he fully expected, or producing a threat to his manhood with another razor-sharp blade, she did neither.

She smiled.

It was no ordinary smile. It was one honed over the years she had spent dealing with narrow-minded, ale-swilling men who thought she should tremble and quake before their superior strength and brawn.

It was a smile that began to curdle the blood in his veins.

"Why of course, Captain Fonteyne," she said softly, sweetly. "It shall be as you command."

He eased his arms away and stepped warily back. "Rose... ?"

"Now if you will excuse me, *Captain* ... I must return to my dear father and inquire if he would like rose or hibiscus flavored tea served with his supper tonight."

She turned and walked back into the cabin, closing the door behind her with such a forceful slam it nearly broke the hinges.

Sebastien stared at the vibrating planks for a moment then cursed under his breath and crammed his hat on his head before heading for the upper deck.

FONTEYNE WENT through the motions of accepting the surrender of the two revenue ships after which he somewhat trepidatiously accepted an invitation from Alexander St. Clare to return to the *Nighthawk* to share the evening meal. He was relieved somewhat to hear that Nathan Reed and Archie Penman had also been invited, as had Duardo and Mercado from the *Cygnet* and *Pride* respectively. Digby Fitch, Billy Burr, and Stubb made up the rest of the group seated around the long dining table. The ship's cook brought out platters heaped with ham and mutton, fresh biscuits, cheese, and fruit, each course washed down with some very fine claret.

Keeping a wary eye on Rose's placid expression, Fonteyne relayed the information that he had advised the British captains that they, along with their crews, would be set ashore on the smaller of the two islands: Little Nobbin. There, they would be able to forage for enough fruit and fish to sustain them until they could hail a passing ship to pick them up. All three of the 'captured ships', which would now include the *Nighthawk*, would be taken in prize by the crew of the *Black Wind*.

The *Daffodil* with both masts broken and her sails shredded by chain shot, was by far the more damaged and her fate drew the most debate around the dining table.

"Bloody 'ell, just sink 'er," Stubb said around a greasy

mouthful of mutton. "It be 'ard enough 'avin' the brothel lumberin' our wake, never give a mind to draggin' two o' the king's finest behind us. Mores to the fact, we don't 'ave enough crew to manage 'em all. We be spread thin as hairs on a monkey's arse now."

Nathan Reed agreed. "Not enough crew by half if we run into trouble. Too many guns, not enough gunners."

"Even if I took two off each of your gun crews and ours," Billy agreed grudgingly, "There wouldn't be enough to work the batteries effectively on all six ships. Though it rots my tongue to say so, I agree with Stubb. While it makes for a pretty little fleet, we can't crew all six effectively."

"What's more, our men may'n't be too 'appy at the thought o' givin' away the two cutters," Stubb grumbled. "If we sail up the Tongue, we pass near enough to Kell's Bay to take 'em in, sell 'em an' put a little silver in their pockets."

Surprisingly, Alexander was in agreement. "Some of my crew can be 'forced' to remain on board to sail your prizes out of the bay, and when far enough away, can find a concealed bay to tuck the *Nighthawk* into along Pirate's Alley. I would also suggest that for appearance's sake, you set myself and the remainder of my men on shore with the others. Shared misery might loosen tongues of our British friends." St. Clare nodded toward his helmsman. "Mr. Fitch can remain on board the *Nighthawk* to bring her back when enough time has passed to rescue us."

Digby Fitch touched a forelock in acknowledgement, though he did not look well pleased.

"You have an objection, Fitch?" Alexander asked.

"Oh, nay, nay, Captain. I were just hoping ... I mean, it's been a long and boring voyage from London and I would've liked the chance to see some real action."

Alexander looked to Rose; she, in turn, glanced at Duardo, who was in charge of the crews. His black face split with a dazzling white grin. "Digby Fitch is welcome on board the *Cygnet*, if he wishes to learn how to sail a real fighting ship."

Digby mirrored the grin, for he and Duardo often engaged in a friendly rivalry. "Or give ye some points on how to improve your lot."

"Then it is settled. Mr. Russell, the quartermaster's mate, can take charge of the *Nighthawk*." Alexander said. "I will adapt a suitably enraged attitude at the theft of my ship whilst we commiserate with the captains of the cutters and watch our vessels being sailed away. Might I request we transfer a barrel or two of this fine red wine my younger son gifted us? It might help pass the time until we are 'rescued'."

Mention of her other brother earned Rose's attention for the first time. "Did you hear from Simon when you were in London?"

"By way of a twenty page letter," Alexander said, smiling. "He is still in France, though I suspect the monastic life is not all that he anticipated it would be. The wine you have before you now is, as you might agree, beyond anything I have tasted elsewhere. If I can persuade him to shed his cassock and throw in with us, it would be a fine addition to the Pirata Lobo name."

Prompted by his words, everyone at the table took up their wine glasses and enjoyed a hearty swallow. Only Archibald Penman refrained, though he did take up the glass and hold it to the candlelight to gauge the depth of dark claret red. And only Rose noticed that he set the glass down again without trying a sip.

19

___

The meeting broke shortly thereafter, with everyone returning to their respective vessels. Rose lingered behind to spend a little more time with her father for it had been almost a year since she had seen him last and the past few hours were hardly enough to make up for the lack.

They stood together at the rail watching the crowded longboats pull away. The night air was refreshingly cool after the tropical heat of the day. Lights twinkled on board all six ships and were reflected on the smooth surface of the water along with the myriad stars overhead. At Stubb's insistence, the sound of hammers and saws rang through the stillness and would likely echo through the night as repairs were made to the *Daffodil*. Word spread quickly about the intent to take the two British revenuers to Kell's Bay and the prize value for the ships quashed any complaints from the carpenters and sail makers, who would likely work through to the morning to improve the value of both cutters.

It was a good plan that had been fomented and Rose was heartily in favor of rewarding her crew, but she was frowning as she watched Fonteyne's gig being rowed into the darker shadows of the *Black Wind's* hull.

"If you have doubts about him, best voice them now," Alexander said quietly, aware of how far even the scantest whisper carried across the water.

"I suppose his arrogance has been duly earned through the years, and it isn't that I don't trust him, I just ..."

"Don't trust him. If those same past actions are anything to judge, I cannot fault you for your misgivings. I can, however, be suitably shocked that you have formed any manner of an alliance with him, however tenuous."

"We need his help, Father. Simply that. He is the only one who bend Lafitte's ear. And likely the only one who can get me back into Barataria Bay with the skin on my back intact."

"When you stole the blacksmith's ship out of his own port, what were you thinking would happen when he saw you again? That he would shower you with huzzahs?"

"I suppose I hoped the boldness of the act would prove I deserved more than a mocking dismissal."

"So you enraged the little pirate king and then compounded the matter by taking Fonteyne's ship as well ... a feat of undeniable recklessness that entire fleets of Spaniards have been unable to do, I might add. I should think you'd be more wary of Fonteyne's desire to avenge the humiliation than Lafitte's."

"Fonteyne was angry," she admitted. "Furious, even, yet he seems to have come around."

"At what cost?"

Rose looked up at him and saw the hard gleam in his eyes.

He had already guessed the cost. She didn't know how he knew, but he knew.

"Nothing I wasn't willing to pay," she said.

Alexander's hands gripped the rail tightly for a long moment before gradually relaxing again. "I am not going to insult you by offering any fatherly advice apart from saying you are a woman grown now, not a flighty seventeen-year-old with stars in her eyes."

"I never had stars, Father. You blame him for what happened that night, but I share the blame equally. He was intriguing and dangerous and made me feel more alive, more of a woman in that one night than I ever felt with Terrence Whitticomb. Being bedded by Terrance was like ... being bedded by an excited puppy."

Alexander cleared his throat. "While I do enjoy the frankness of our discussions, dear girl, there are times I would prefer some limits as to what you share. I'm sure I did not need to know your bedroom habits."

"Yes, you did. Because at the time, I hoped you would be on my side and not agree with Mother by forcing me to marry someone I did not want to marry. Especially since you and she were not married when Ramsey was born."

Alexander's chin jutted defensively. "A situation your mother was undoubtedly striving to help you avoid. And whether you care to believe it or not, I did you a favor."

"A favor! By marrying me off to a plantation owner's son who got seasick standing on a dock?"

"Whitticomb was not your mother's first choice of grooms. She thought you needed the firmer hand of someone like Sir Charles Stapleton."

Rose's jaw sagged as she stared up at her father. "Stapleton! He was past forty and had not bathed in as many decades! He had three teeth in his mouth! And his clothes were always stained with the meals he had eaten."

Alexander arched an eyebrow. "Then you acknowledge the favor I did you by putting young Whitticomb forward?"

Rose rolled her eyes and resumed gazing out over the starlit bay. "I acknowledge nothing aside from the fact that he was clean and had all of his teeth." She thought about it for a moment and added, "Aye, he was sweet and I was sorry he died of the fever, but even then, returning home as a forlorn, distraught widow—" she paused and glared as her father coughed— "I found no sympathy in anyone's heart. Not Mother's, not yours, certainly not Ramsey's. I was of half a mind to sail to France and seek refuge with Simon."

"I doubt the monks would have allowed a red-haired hellion in a seminary."

"I would have stormed the abbey and kidnapped him. It is difficult enough enduring the thought of my brother becoming a friar, let alone thinking of him living in a cold stone cell for the rest of his life."

"You made your choice which path in life to take; Simon made his."

"All through his boyhood years Simon fantasized about becoming a Templar Knight. We used to joust at palm trees, hacking melons and breadfruit as if they were the heads of Saracens. Discovering priests no longer carried swords probably came as an appalling shock once he was robed and tonsured. What is more, *I'm* shocked at Mother agreeing to let him go. He was ever her pet."

"Fiona loves all three of her children equally," Alexander said with a wry grin. "As do I. It's just that some of you enjoy putting that love to the test more often than others."

"And Ramsey? How far does he test you with his blatant pandering to the Crown? You know full well he wrote that note instructing the British how and where to attack Barataria."

"Your brother walks a very fine line ..."

"Yes, yes. An excuse I have given myself to explain some of his actions. But is holding the seal of the governor more important to him than loyalty to his family?"

Alexander's shoulders slumped slightly, for he had no real

answer. "I suppose we will discover the answer to that in the coming months."

"And in the meantime?"

"In the meantime, I want you to take every good care. I assume you are going to set out for Barataria regardless of Fonteyne's displeasure? The now crooked door to my cabin would suggest there was some difference of opinion?"

Rose clenched her jaw. "I don't need his permission to sail where the wind takes me. And if it takes me to Barataria in his wake, so be it. I have some leverage of my own if I need to deal with Lafitte."

"Even so, if you suspect the smallest reason not to trust Fonteyne, break away."

She turned her gaze to the silhouette of the *Black Wind*. "If I have the smallest reason to suspect him of treachery, Father, I will slit his damned throat."

Alexander let the comment hang in the air for a moment, then leaned on the rail again. "When you were in Charleston, were you able to speak to our friend again?"

"Briefly. He wasn't looking well. He was tired and drawn, with a cough that seemed to rattle every one of his ribs." She paused and frowned. "He is not pleased with the President's decisions on where to send his armies. Losing Washington City was a great blow."

"A city and the houses in it can be rebuilt. What cannot be replaced are the generals and the brave men who must win them back. Or hold them. Has he persuaded Madison to send him south?"

"Not in the strength he asked for. Which is why, curse their arrogant stubbornness, they will need Lafitte's help more than ever."

"Is the General in agreement?"

"He has ... reservations."

"In which case, my dear, you have your work cut out for you. You must convince Lafitte to throw in with Jackson and convince Jackson to accept his help. Which reminds me, I brought a little present for you, courtesy of the iron foundry in Liverpool. I'll have my men transfer it to your ship in the morning."

Rose laughed. "You needn't worry. Billy has had it moved across already."

"Rather presumptive of her."

"It was either that or she was remaining here on board with it."

"In that case, I applaud her initiative. Come. We have time for one more sup of wine before the play-acting begins."

ROSE WAS ALONE as she rowed the jolly boat across the dark waters, the oars dipping and swishing cleanly with each stroke. The day and evening had visibly drained her father and she left him to enjoy a last night of sleep in the warmth and comfort of his cabin. She had hugged him fiercely and knelt for his blessing, then climbed down to the gig and set off for the *Cygnet*.

How easily the words had spilled off her father's tongue: convince Lafitte to help Jackson, convince Jackson to take that help. Easy to say, so horrendously more difficult to carry out.

Major General Andrew Jackson had been a family friend for decades.

A young, adventurous Alexander St. Clare had been caught running supplies through the blockade lines in the Revolutionary War and served time in a prisoner of war camp in Camden, South Carolina. There he met the young Jackson, also a prisoner, and Jackson's brother, Robert. Both brothers contracted smallpox, and it was only through Alexander's ability to bribe guards, they were able to get extra rations and medicine.

Through a much bigger bribe, they were released and sent home, but Robert did not survive the pox. Andrew never forgot Alexander's help and they became fast friends. It was through Alexander, and more recently through Rose, that messages and information was able to be passed through yet another coastal blockade.

Anger at her brother gave her a fresh splash of resentment, for if not for his position as governor, she and her father would not have to resort to meeting on distant islands away from prying eyes and ears. Alexander wholly supported the Americans, but he had to appear to be loyal to the British. Perhaps her mother would not have to make such uncomfortable choices either, for despite her father's assurances, the relationship between mother and daughter had never really been close.

Fiona St. Clare had never understood Rose's penchant for sailing, or for thriving in the harsh conditions of life at sea. In truth, she'd almost fainted the first time she had seen her daughter wearing trousers and climbing the shrouds to perch on one of the upper yards. Rose loved her mother dearly, but Fiona tolerated the sea as long as she only had to see it sparkling in the distance, through a palm-shaded window.

In the years since taking command of the *Cygnet*, Rose had been forced to prove her mettle time and time again against men who thought she belonged anywhere but at the helm of a ship. Big, brawny, ugly men she'd had to fight to win the barest hint of respect. Men like Jean Lafitte and Sebastien Fonteyne, who thought the sea was a man's world and women had no place in it. And certainly not in possession of the necessary balls to defy them.

Faugh!

Halfway to the *Cygnet*, Rose dragged the oars in the water and changed direction. It was playing with fire, she knew, to go back on board the *Black Wind* but she did not want to leave

Fonteyne with the impression that just because he had bedded her, she had suddenly lost her mind and turned into a helpless, dependent female.

Nor could she take the chance that Fonteyne would slip out of the bay in the darkest hour of the night.

The jolly boat bumped into the hull and she quickly shipped the oars and tied it off to a mooring pin. The gangway on the top deck was open and there were no visible signs that the crew was making stealthy plans to get under way. There were the usual night sounds of creaking ropes and clinking chains. Snoring from the men who chose to sleep on deck rose and fell in familiar waves. Most of the lamps had been doused apart from the big fore and aft deck lanterns.

She noted the sentry on watch was one of her own crewmen not yet transferred back to the *Cygnet*. He touched a forelock and she nodded, then turned slightly when she heard voices coming from the bow. One of them was a woman's voice. Billy Burr? What on earth was she doing on board the *Black Wind*?

Curiosity got the better of her discretion and Rose moved toward the voices, careful to stay in the shadows. The smoothly aristocratic accent of the other hushed voice identified Archibald Penman and she recalled there had been more than a few glances and whispers passed between the two over the past several days.

She could certainly not fault Billy for the attraction. Penman was a handsome man and, as a doctor, was not in the least horrified by the scars that marred the side of Billy's face. He had likely seen ten times worse through the years. Even so, she had never seen Billy Burr give any man more than a passing smirk.

Not wanting to be caught listening in the dark, she retraced her steps as quietly as she could then hastened down the hatchway and along the companionway to Fonteyne's cabin.

Conscious of ears everywhere, she tapped quietly on the

door. When there was no answer, she tapped again, a little louder, but when there was still no response, she turned the latch and peeked inside.

A single lamp was burning on the desk, the wick turned low and the light weak. The berth was in shadow but she could see it was empty. He must have been somewhere else on the ship, and while she debated, for a fleeting moment waiting for him to return, she talked herself out of it. He would assume she was only there for one reason and that one reason could seriously undermine any argument she could put forth to accompany him to Barataria.

She turned and was about to leave when a slight movement in the shadows beside the gallery windows drew her gaze. He had been standing there staring out the window, at a view that would most assuredly have let him observe her approaching the hull of his ship.

"You wanted to see me about something?"

"No. No, not really." she frowned and bit the tip of her tongue. "No. I guess I just didn't like the way we left things between us. I'm sorry if I disturbed you."

"You don't disturb me. Not all of the time, at any rate." He moved closer to the desk where the dim light revealed that he was shirtless. He wore breeches but his feet were bare. "I am enjoying some of your brother's fine wine. I can see why your father would choose barrels of this over barrels of water to accompany him on shore. It puts Spain's claret to shame. Would you care to join me in a glass?"

"I should really get back to my ship. I should collect Billy as well. She's up top talking to Dr. Penman."

He looked briefly startled. "She is?"

"You don't approve?"

"Quite the contrary. Archie, despite his manners and grace, is not one to casually seek out female company." He poured half a glass of wine and stopped. "Not for lack of effort from the softer sex, I assure you. The women in Barataria fall over themselves just to win a smile from him."

Rose nodded slightly. "And for all her bluster, Billy is painfully shy and equally reticent when it comes to men."

"Then I would think they are well suited to spend some time together outside the realm of smoking broadsides and bloody surgeries."

He finished the pour and held the glass out to Rose. She had to walk forward to take it and when her fingers brushed his, she felt an instant shimmer of heat ripple up her arm and down her spine.

She suffered the sensation for a long moment before pulling her hand away.

"I haven't come to argue with you."

"That is refreshing."

"Only to say that I will be taking the *Cygnet* and the *Pride* back to Barataria. Whether you care to join our company or not is up to you."

"Lafitte will hardly give you a warm welcome on your own."

"Whereas I doubt he will even raise his voice in anger."

The wine glass paused halfway to his lips. "And how do you arrive at that rather naive conclusion?"

"Because as long as I have his manifests, ledgers, and logbooks in my possession, I don't imagine he will do anything to anger *me*. For a man claiming righteous indignation over accusations of piracy, he keeps surprisingly detailed records of all his business transactions. Entry upon entry of who sank what ship and captured what cargo. Also included are lists of judges and upright citizens of New Orleans who scream thief and pirate in public, but in private take full advantage of his black-market activities. If those lists happen to fall into the wrong hands, well ..." she shrugged and took a sip of wine.

Fonteyne watched her lick a bead of red wine off her lip. "I wondered when you would pull that card out of your sleeve."

"Your pages alone are quite impressive, Captain. The *San Raimundo*? A Spanish treasure ship supposedly lost in a storm? Dare I ask how much bullion was in her holds? No, wait ... the amount is there in the ledger, although I would wager what he told you was not the amount he sold it for."

He took a long moment to digest her words. "I would like to see those ledgers."

"I'm surprised you didn't find them when you searched my cabin on those days you were pretending to be knocked unconscious."

"I guess I didn't search in the right places."

She pursed her lips. "Even with the wind at our backs, it will take close to a fortnight to reach Barataria. That would leave a lot of time for reading."

He drew a deep breath. A vein popped into prominence on his forehead, just above the healed line of the cut over his eye. "If I agree—"

"If you agree to keep your word and present me to Lafitte as an ally, then you can do whatever you like with the ledgers. Give them back, burn them, throw them overboard, I could care less."

He gave his head a little shake. "You don't like taking no for an answer, do you?"

"It's a funny little word and triggers a funny little reaction down the back of my spine."

"Yes, I have noticed."

She shrugged. "You'll have to forgive me if I do have a mind of my own."

He drained the last mouthful of wine and leaned into the stronger light to refill it.

The glow from the lamp burnished his upper torso in gold. Every muscle, every curve, every prominent vein snaking down his arms spoke of power and authority that was firm and uncompromising, of violence held in tight rein. Despite the streak of rebellion that still coursed through her veins, Rose felt slightly unnerved. He was a dangerous man to toy with, and she felt suddenly very exposed and vulnerable.

Unwelcomed knots constricted her chest, making it suddenly difficult to breathe. She would be lying if she tried to tell herself she was unaffected by his sheer animal magnetism, by the scent of sea water on his flesh, by the nearness of the berth and the thought of what his hands, his mouth, his body could do to hers.

It was a weakness she could ill afford, and one that she had to command and control lest it control her.

There was only one sure way to do so.

She set her empty glass aside and removed her green velvet short-coat. Next, she loosened the lacing on her corset vest until it was easy to wriggle it down past her hips and kick to the floor. With her gaze locked unwaveringly on his, she grasped the hem of her shirt and lifted it up and over her head, baring herself to the waist. The action sent her hair scattering wildly around her shoulders and where the light caught the reddish strands, it seemed to surround her head in a halo of fire.

The air between them become as charged as the moments before a lightning strike and it was Fonteyne's turn to feel his mouth go dry and his body respond to her boldness. There was a fierce splendor in the deliberate way her eyes issued the challenge. She was exquisite and she was unique. She was a contrast in terms, impossible to measure against any other woman he had known. He had seen her lift a twenty-four-pound ball of iron and feed it down the throat of a cannon without flinching at the weight, and he had seen her breathless and shivering, whimpering like a newborn kitten as he ran his tongue between her thighs.

His body remembered the sleek, pearly welcome as he thrust himself deep inside her. His flesh remembered the strength of her orgasms, and the explosive heat of his own.

He threw his glass aside, barely aware of it shattering against the boards. A single step and she was in his arms. Their mouths slanted together in a kiss as powerful as the hungers fuelling it. Without breaking the bond, he slid his hands to her hips, lifting her, setting her on the edge of his desk where he reached down to remove her boots then peel away her breeches. He brushed her hair aside to reveal her breasts, naked and puckered with desire. He leaned down to take a nipple into his mouth, his hands guiding her down so that her torso lay on top of the charts.

His lips moved to her throat, then travelled the sleek path into the valley between her breasts, teasing both before travelling lower to the taut flatness of her belly, circling there a moment before descending through the soft thatch of red curls where a single stroke of his tongue found another valley to explore.

Rose squirmed under the deliberate assault as his tongue parted, swirled, and probed. Her hands searched for something to grab, to keep her from floating away, but found only papers and a heavy brass sextant. His tongue grew bolder and her hands flew down to grasp fistfuls of his hair; and when he slid his arms under her thighs and lifted her legs over his shoulders, her whole body clenched and shuddered as the waves of pleasure rushed through her. Her hips arched shamelessly to meet each thrust of his tongue; her fingers clawed and twisted, and when the urgency became almost too much to bear, she tried to speak, but only managed a harsh, guttural sound deep in her throat.

Sebastien lifted his head from between her thighs, his senses drowning in the taste of her. He saw in her eyes what she wanted, needed, and, after one last long slow lick, he released himself from his breeches, pulled her hips forward to the edge of the desk, and breeched her body hard and fast. So fast and so deep was the joining that he had to steel himself not to climax the instant he felt the greedy, grasping little muscles spasm around his flesh.

Beneath him, Rose was lost in a welter of pleasure so intense she could not think or breath. Her hands stayed tangled in his hair, her cries found echoes in his sharp, panted breaths.

Sebastien held back as long as he could. He felt his body tighten with a primal urgency. He drew on the last fevered shreds of strength for one final, magnificent thrust and surrendered himself to a deep, shocking release unlike anything he had experienced before.

IN THE THROBBING silence that followed, they could feel each other's heartbeats, feel the sticky dampness where their bodies pressed together. His weight should have been a burden, but Rose relished it. Her body was limp, without a shiver of substance; her legs hung limp over the edge of the desk, her arms were spread flat on the desk.

She was aware of the fact he was still very much inside her, but she made no move to dislodge him. A soft sigh escaped her lips, a deeply satisfied, saturated sound that sent a flood of warm contentment swirling through her body.

Drawing on some deep unknown reserve of strength, Rose managed to raise a hand and rest it on his upper arm. Having accomplished that much, her fingers curled and her hand slid gently back down onto the desk, the effort accompanied by a similar attempt to moisten her lips.

Sebastien lifted his head off her shoulder. When he

remained unmoving, she opened her eyes and saw that he was half-frowning, half-smiling as he looked at his own shoulder. Rose followed his gaze to the wide black smear on his arm. They both glanced aside to see where she had inadvertently knocked the inkwell over onto his sea chart. A wide swath of wet black ink was splattered from one side of the Gulf to the other.

"You realize we may now end up in Cartagena rather than Barataria."

Rose looked at her hand, covered in black ink. The reality of seeing herself splayed out like a strumpet on his desk might have made her laugh if not for the single word that brought her gaze up to his.

"We?"

He huffed out a breath. "I suspect I shall heartily come to regret it, but yes. We."

She frowned. "Not... not because of this, I hope."

He leaned up on his elbows and studied each facet of her face as if he might find the honest answer there.

"No. Not because of this."

"Good. I'm glad to hear it. Because *this* should not have happened."

"But it did."

"Yes." She pushed up against him and dislodge him from between her thighs. "But it will not happen again."

Amused, he watched her stand on unsteady legs, then bend with determination to start gathering up her discarded clothes. "You are right, it probably shouldn't have happened, but unless I misread all those begging little whispers in my ear, we both thoroughly enjoyed it."

She straightened and stared at him with as much dignity as she could muster. "I did no such thing."

"You did not whisper in my ear, or you did not enjoy?"

"I—" Her fists clenched around her clothes. "I have to get back to my ship."

She actually took a step toward the door before remembering she was stark naked. Cursing softly, she dropped her boots and pulled her shirt over her head. There was still ink on her hand and it smeared the cambric and left a black streak in her hair.

Sebastien tucked himself back into his breeches and watched Rose fumbling to pull on her trousers and boots. He wanted very much to grab her by the shoulders and stop her, hold her close, assure her that coming to him, wanting something from him and taking it with the confidence of a Valkyrie did not lessen his opinion of her.

Quite the contrary.

Before this day he had never put more energy into love-making than was required to ease his physical tensions and satisfy his appetites. Before this night he had never understood why the climax of the act was called the little death.

Now he knew.

"The *Cygnet* and *Pride* will be ready to sail on the morning tide," she said.

Before he could answer, or even nod, she was out the door and vanished down the dark corridor.

20

———

Long before the morning haze had burned away, the *Cygnet's* crew was a hive of activity. Men scrambled up the shrouds and onto the yards to await the orders to lower away the sails. The anchor crew winched the great iron hook off the sandy bottom and the bow of the ship was turning gracefully into the current. A healthy breeze funneled through the channel between the two islands, and as the six ships started to maneuver into position, each of their massive steering and main sails cracked forward as they filled with the wind.

Gliding regally forward under full sail, the *Black Wind* led the stately procession out of the bay followed by the *Pride*, the *Nighthawk*, *Daffodil*, and *Renard*. Rose's ship drew up the rear and was the last to pass out into open water. The stranded crews lined the shore and ran to the headland to follow their progress as the ships cleared the point. Standing on the quarterdeck, Rose caught glints of light from the tops of the pitons where British sentries with mirrors were flashing messages down to those in the bay, marking which direction the small flotilla took.

Other messages were flashing from the treeline as well, bidding good luck and godspeed.

All of the best and worst memories washed over Rose as she watched the Twin Nobbins grow smaller in the distance. She would have liked more time with her father, for she loved him dearly. She would have liked to have had him standing by her side like he had in the early days, when he was teaching her how to read the wind and the sea, how to navigate by the sun and by the stars, how to load and fire a cannon. Granted, the last lesson had met with some resistance, but she had planted powder-blackened hands on her hips and demanded he name another single captain who could not load and fire one of his own big guns.

She sighed at the memory and looked down at her hands. Try as she might, she had not been able to entirely remove the stain of black ink, which made the tiny hairs on her arms prickle to attention with the memory of how it had got there.

Shaking her head, she walked the length of the ship to the bow. The men paused in their work to tug respectfully on a forelock as she passed. She took pride in knowing the names of every member of her crew and knew they were loyal to the last man.

She remained on deck, her eagle eyes trained on the other ships to mark their speeds and handling. She only went below when the islands were reduced to specks on the horizon.

Sailing the British prizes to Kell's Bay would cost them at least half a day's sail off their set course, but Sebastien agreed the time would be well spent. The bay was accommodating to privateers who found it necessary to dispose of captured ships whose flags would brand them as pirates and jeopardize their letters of marque. It was also a stewing pot of merchants, privateers, and sailors fresh from crossing the Atlantic who gossiped like washerwomen around a town well. If there were rumors of an English fleet passing through the islands, the whispers would be heard there.

"Aye, we passed a fleet o' ships five days gone. Big bastards they was too, rollin' through the waves like fat sows."

Fonteyne leaned forward to refill the sailor's cup with rum. They were seated in a gloomy tavern that stank of fish, vomit, and sweat. The dozen or so rickety tables were crowded with raucous drunkards, many with a buxom whore on their laps. Fonteyne and Rose had come ashore at Kell's Bay, where Sebastien soon proved his worth by addressing the tavern keeper by name and tossing a handful of silver coins on the table to buy drinks for all the of the patrons ... most of whom knew his ship and him by name or reputation.

They took seats at an empty table and ordered tankards of ale. The casks of flowing spirits soon brought a crowd of sailors around them, happy to share news and information. Crews from both sides of the war between America and Britain were present, keeping their distance for the most part and respecting the neutrality of Kell's Bay. There were always some, however, who were deep enough in their cups to be bristling for a fight at the slightest insult, which made sitting between the two factions feel like being in the middle of a ring of lit powder kegs.

"We kept well clear," the sailor continued. "Captain were leery o' getting' too close."

"Cause he's a yellow-bellied cock," another chimed in, laughing at his own wit.

A fist slammed on the table, but the old tar quickly added, "Cause some o' them ships looked big enough they could carry the town o' London on board. One o' the bastards had t'ree decks above the waterline an' more guns than I ever seen afore on one ship."

Fonteyne exchanged a knowing glance with Rose. Three decks would mean a ship of the line. An admiral's ship.

"Did you count how many ships there were?" he asked the sailor.

"Near a hunnerd," said one voice.

"Don't be daft. Mayhap fifty."

A third sailor cackled and held up a hand that was missing three fingers. "More'n I could count. But they was in as long line as I couldn't see the end o' them."

"Weren't no merchant ships. Too many guns," said the first sailor. "Saw too damned many redcoats up on deck."

And that launched a volley of insults, which started fists flying.

Chairs scraped and shouts brought about flung tankards and spilled ale. Soon there were fights breaking out everywhere and Fonteyne grabbed Rose's arm to guide her through the surging mass toward the open door. Reed, Stubb, and Duardo, had been at different tables in the tavern being generous with their coin and feigning drunkenness to loosen more tongues. Reed and Duardo emerged seconds after Rose and Fonteyne; Stubb was last to leave the fray, having to weave his way around and through a sea of tangled legs. He had lost his cap and would have charged back into the fray if Duardo had not snatched at a fistful of his vest and hoisted him into the air to hold him back.

"Let me go, ye lubber-nosed black demon!" Stubb's arms and legs flailed for a moment but Duardo easily held him at arm's length. "Let me go, I say! That were my favorite cap. An' we've not had a good fist fight in months!"

He swung his fists in the empty air a few more times. At a glance and a shrug from Rose, Duardo set him down. He straightened his vest with a loud *har-umphf* and started to stalk back into the tavern but when a large wooden bench came hurling out the door, he hastily changed his mind and followed Rose and the others down to the beach where a crew from the *Black Wind* was waiting with a longboat.

"So the fleet is real," Rose said when they were on board. "Five days out, give or take."

"According to information which may be five days or more old already. Comprised of either a hundred or fifty ships, which probably means ten to twenty."

"Either way, they've likely stopped at New Providence," Nate Reed chimed in. "Closest port for resupplying food and water after a crossing."

Sebastien agreed. Once a thriving pirate stronghold, the island of Nassau had been taken over by the British a century earlier and was now a major port of call for ships coming in from the Atlantic. Commerce and trade had brought in wealthy landowners and merchants whose lavish homes now dotted the verdant slopes and hills. Fancy carriages filled streets that were lined with shops catering to elegant ladies with silk parasols. Sharing the wide span of the harbour, the Royal Navy had established a base that was easily big enough to accommodate a fleet of ships.

"Nicholls isn't a man who likes to rush into anything," Sebastien said. "He will be quite happy receiving a hero's welcome and linger long enough to fill his ample gut with good food and wine before he has to venture into a war. It's almost tempting to sail to New Providence and have a closer look."

"Almost?" Rose asked.

He looked at her and saw the sparkle of excitement that had flared in her eyes. "No! No, I can guess what you're thinking and no. There is not one chance in hell we are going anywhere near New Providence. We found out what we needed to know."

"That there was a sighting of possibly a British fleet of possibly five or fifty or a hundred ships? It doesn't tell us where they are heading or how many men and guns are aboard. We have time to take a closer look and get better information. As long as the fleet sits at anchor in New Providence, it means they are days behind us and both Barataria and New Orleans are safe from a surprise attack. And the more information we can provide Lafitte as well as General Jackson, the better prepared they can be."

Fonteyne crossed his arms over his chest. "And just how do you propose we sail into the harbor without causing a stir?"

"We still have my father's ship," she said. "Sailing her into the port of Nassau would hardly raise any suspicion. The St. Clare Shipping Company has warehouses in town and a house up on the hills where I spent a goodly piece of my childhood. A day or two at most and we could be in, find out what we need to know, and be gone again."

"Would no one question the absence of your father at the helm?"

"By the time anyone thought to question it, we would be long gone."

"The risk—"

"Would be well worth finding out everything we could about the fleet. Or do you not think the size and strength of the fleet would be the first questions Lafitte or Jackson would ask?"

Behind them, Duardo made a rumbling sound in his throat, but Stubb was all for it. He punched Digby Fitch in the arm then rubbed his hands together gleefully. "Ye wanted some adventure, Cock. Stick wi' us an' ye'll be havin' it by the barrelful."

Sebastien held up a cautionary hand. "I haven't agreed to anything yet. We could find ourselves trapped and thrown in irons should our presence draw suspicion."

"Then we must have a care not to draw any suspicion," Rose said. "We'll sail into port in broad daylight and leave the same way. Easy."

"If it's so easy, why are the hackles rising across the nape of my neck?"

"Because the thought of sailing into a British port under the noses of the British navy tempts you as much as it does me, and because it is too tempting *not* to do it."

Nathan Reed shook his head and muttered, "And because the pair of you are both stark starving mad."

21

———

Two days later, when the *Nighthawk* sailed into the wide harbor of Nassau, she was flying the Union Jack on her masthead and below it, in bright scarlet and green, the enormous flag bearing the crest of the Dante-St. Clare Shipping Company. Her gun ports were closed. Her crew was dressed in white shirts and red striped trousers with red kerchiefs around their necks. The decks were scrubbed clean and her yards were trimmed with fresh sails.

Standing on the fo'c'sle, Sebastien Fonteyne wore a black felted frockcoat over a crisp white shirt with a fount of lace spilling beneath his clean-shaven chin. His boots were polished to a mirror shine, his hands were gloved, and the unruly waves of black hair had been trimmed and tamed into a neatly gathered tail at the nape of his neck. The fancy clothes, borrowed from one of Alexander St. Clare's sea chests, were constricting across the chest and shoulders and the lace at the throat was an outright annoyance, but he tolerated the discomfort for the sake of looking like a perfectly aristocratic gentleman.

Beside him, almost as uncomfortable, Rose wore a softly flowing empire gown of watered silk, the blue complimenting the silver-blue of her eyes. The slightest movement, the smallest breeze molded the silk to the shape of her body which had caused Fonteyne's tongue to freeze to the roof of his mouth when he first saw her walking toward him. She had managed, with the magic of creams and powders, to lighten the tone of her skin from that of a bronzed sea urchin to that of a slightly sun-kissed traveller. Delicate lace gloves held an equally delicate lace parasol over a ruffled bonnet that hid all but the smallest scattering of fine red tendrils that framed her face. Her lips were rouged and her lashes darkened; an emerald the size of a robin's egg drew attention to the soft, deep cleft between her breasts, which were plumped and pushed up enough to threaten the confines of the silk.

"I thought the idea was to avoid drawing attention," Fonteyne murmured as he smiled and returned the waves from some sailors on a ship they were gliding past.

"The wrong kind of attention," she corrected him with a smile. "Our family has owned land in New Providence for over a hundred years. I have visited here several times."

"With your husband, I presume?"

"Heavens, no. Terrence rarely ventured off his family's sugar plantation. I warrant he never even set foot on New Providence, since sailing from port to port was not something he enjoyed. If ever he did find himself on board even just to supervise the loading of cargo, he tended to spend most of the time emptying the contents of his belly over the rails."

"The *Cygnet* was an odd choice for a wedding gift, if that was the case."

"The ship was always mine. Making it a wedding gift was the only way Father could release it from his fleet. Plus, I believe he held out hope I could turn Terrance into a sailor. I failed in that, quite miserably, but he had no objections to letting me enjoy my 'hobby'."

"In other words ..."

"In other words, I very much doubt anyone in the town of Nassau would even know what Terrance looked like. Indeed, it is equally unlikely that anyone knows of his unfortunate demise. He had no immediate family and both Mother and Ramsey were too mortified to admit to anyone that I had taken over the captaincy of the ship. Especially Ramsey."

She wriggled and adjusted the fit of the empire gown. Subsequent sea chests had revealed a wealth of silk and satin gowns Alexander was carrying home from London for his wife. While similar in height to her mother, Rose's body was more muscular and she felt like a monkey wearing party clothes.

"Stop fidgeting," Fonteyne said out of the corner of his mouth. "This was your grand idea."

She gave the dress a final tug then slipped her hand through the crook of his arm and pinched him hard through the layers of linen.

WHEN THEY DISEMBARKED, a carriage was waiting for them on the wharf, the polished mahogany doors stamped in gold with the imprint of the Dante-St. Clare Shipping Company. Speaking over the clatter of hooves and wheels, Rose pointed out buildings and warehouses along the waterfront that bore the Pirata Lobo signage above their doors.

The carriage moved slowly, weaving through the bustling traffic until it was free of the main thoroughfare and where the crush of buildings gradually turned into well-spaced homes and elegant manors. They slowed a mile past the city limits and pulled into a wide half-circle of white crushed stone, halting before a stately two story home with whitewashed columns supporting verandas that wrapped around both levels. Massive clusters of bougainvillea climbed up the columns and across the railings in varying shades of purple, red, and orange. Neatly groomed plantings of fragrant oleander grew between rows of tall palm trees that surrounded the house and provided shade from the searing heat of the tropical sun.

Before the large-spoked wheels came to a full stop, there were servants spilling out of the front doors. A houseman and three neatly dressed maids stood ready to welcome them. Speculative frowns watched Fonteyne step down into the sunlight, but their expressions soon broke into huge smiles when they saw him reach back to hand Rose down.

The major-domo hastened forward, his teeth gleaming white in a wide grin. He was tall and thin, his skin as black as Duardo's, wrinkled into folds and creases that bespoke his seven decades of living on the island.

"Why, Miss Rose!" He laughed and clapped his hands. "A real special pleasure to see you again!"

Tossing decorum to the wind, Rose ran up to the old houseman and threw her arms around him, hugging him so tightly his eyes bulged and he feigned a strangled sound in his throat. When she released him, they both laughed. She took his ancient hands into hers and felt a genuine surge of happiness. "How have you been, dearest Josiah?"

"Still wakin' up on the right side o' the grass, Miss Rose. And ain't you lookin' fit n' fine! Lord save me, Mr. Alexander was just here three weeks gone, an' never breathed a word you was comin'."

"I suppose he wanted it to be a surprise."

"That it is fo' sure." Josiah looked at Fonteyne and nodded courteously. "Welcome to Rose Hall, Mistah Terrance, Suh. A pure pleasure to finally make your acquaintance, though I'm of half a mind to take this young lady to task fo' waitin' so long to bring you 'round, and fo' surprisin' us like this."

Rose's jaw dropped open. "Oh! Oh, no, Josiah—"

Fonteyne cut her off. "The pleasure is all mine, Josiah. My dear *wife* is full of surprises these days it seems."

Rose gave him a look that would have drilled through stone but he only smiled and took her hand under his arm. "Shall we go inside, *dear*? I could use a tall cool glass of lemon water if some can be found."

Josiah shooed the three maids inside with orders to prepare food and drinks. He ordered one of the lads to fetch the cases from the carriage and carry them inside. Rose declined the lemon water and ran up the broad staircase to the second floor then along a corridor to the rear of the house. She half expected to find the furnishings in her old bedroom covered in dust sheets but everything was polished and clean, the bed linens looked as fresh as if they were newly laid.

Moreover, there were vases full of fresh flowers everywhere.

The explanation came clear when Josiah and Fonteyne came through the doorway behind her.

"You here fo' the Admiral's Ball tomorrow night?" Josiah asked. "Whole town's been buzzin' an' fussin', all excited to have a real navy hero in port. Some say Admiral Nicholls stood as close as you an' me to Bony-part when he surrendered. Wouldn't that've been somethin' to see?"

"Something, indeed," Rose said, exchanging a glance with Fonteyne. "How long has the admiral been in port?"

Josiah screwed up his face for a moment of calculation. "Seven days now. No, eight, that or thereabout. Got here nigh on a week after Mr. Alexander left and we've had two Sunday services since then. Touched in to take on fresh water an' supplies before he goes to join the war in America, so they say. Heard tell it was a bad crossing, sailed through some fierce storms. Lost one o' his ships but claims he still has more'n enough to sail on up the Mississippi an' level New Orleans to the ground."

"I didn't see any warships in the harbor," Fonteyne said casually.

"Likely anchored in the naval bay, further along," Josiah said. "Ten of them, so I hear, survived the storms."

Rose crossed over to the window and gazed out at the manicured lawns and gardens below. "I suppose they will have to ship out soon if they hope to join the war efforts."

"Yas'm. Day after the ball, I heard tell. Can't come soon enough, you ask me, an' thank the Lord fo' that. Proper folk can't hardly walk down the street without gettin' pushed aside by redcoats. Most o' them are drunk on whores an' rum. Respectable menfolk be keepin' their women to home, to save them bein' insulted or put upon. I keep our girls here behind locked doors fo' that same reason. Not safe fo' them to go wanderin' out by themselves."

"A wise decision," Rose agreed.

"Yas'm. Whole town has gone hero crazy. Mr. Ramsey even sent a wagon to fetch some o' Mr. Simon's good wine from the cold cellar."

Rose was in the process of untying the ribbon from her bonnet. Instead, she jerked the ends so tight she nearly sliced off her ears. "Mr. Ramsey ... my brother is *here*? In Nassau?"

"Yas'm. Got here two days ago. Only stayed here but the one night though afore he got invited over to the governor's mansion along with the Admiral an' officers an' other 'potent people."

She eased her grip on the ribbons but her face stayed flushed.

"I can send one o' the stable boys to go fetch him," Josiah offered.

"*No*. No, that won't be necessary." She turned and smiled. "I'm sure he and Governor Cameron are far too busy sharing stories and learning all the news from France to be disturbed. We can find him later. If there is time. Unfortunately, we won't be able to stay more than a night or two ourselves. We have business to tend to on the other side of the island."

Josiah's face folded into his wrinkles. In the next blink, however, he was smiling again. "In that case, I'll have Cook prepare your favorite meal. Least we can do. Is it still po'k an' pineapple or have you gone all fancy on us?"

"I will never be too fancy to stuff my belly with Cook's pork crackling."

Josiah grinned, offered a polite nod to Fonteyne, then exited the room, closing the door behind him.

Hearing his footsteps fade away down the hall, Rose expelled a huge breath and threw the bonnet onto the bed in disgust. "Dammit! Ramsey is here. Someone is bound to tell him the *Nighthawk* was seen coming into port."

"There are easily a hundred ships in port. I doubt the *Nighthawk* will draw any special attention. And if it does, what will he do?"

Rose paced back to the window. The sash was up and the breeze was rustling the folds of her skirt. The sun was bright and hot, rendering the silk almost invisible.

"If he finds out that I am here ...?" Her hands clenched into fists by her side and she shook her head, running through any number of possibilities. "He would not be happy to see me. Not unless he came with a warrant in hand for my arrest."

"Or mine," he said quietly.

She turned away from the window. "Good God, yes. He would be the one person on the island who would know for certain that Terrence Whitticomb is dead. And he knows you by sight."

"That he most decidedly does. So does Nicholls."

"Arresting me would only satisfy his arrogance. But arresting you would—?"

"Would not only give him immense pleasure but it would put a very large feather in his cap."

"Then we need to leave. We've found out what we wanted to know. The fleet is real, it's here, and it sails the day after tomorrow."

"We need to relax," Fonteyne said. He tucked a finger under his collar to loosen it and batted aside a drift of lace. "It's mid-afternoon now. The gentlemen at the governor's mansion will be well into their cups by now. I would hazard to say it would rouse more suspicion if we leave before we've brushed the dust off our boots."

She shook her head again. "How can you be so calm about this?"

"One of us has to be."

Her eyes narrowed. "You can be quite insufferable, you know. You were the one who did not want to come ... and now you do not want to leave."

"Not just yet, at any rate. As for being insufferable, you, Mrs. Terrence Whitticomb are testing my powers of restraint to the limit."

"Meaning what?"

"Meaning ... when you stand in front of the window like you are now, your gown is as transparent as a pane of glass and I'm about two steps away from picking you up, throwing you on the bed, and ravishing you until you haven't the breath or wit left to think, speak, or—heaven grant me—argue."

She blinked. "Is that all you can think about?"

"Not all, but an increasingly intriguing part."

She watched him take an ominous step forward. "You wouldn't dare."

He grinned slowly. "I'm surprised you still question what I

would and wouldn't dare. You're damned lucky I didn't ravage you in the carriage. Sitting there beside you, with your bosoms about to pop out of that bodice, was the most uncomfortable position I have ever been in. I half expected the seam of these trousers to slice off one of my ballocks."

"I thought you looked like you were eating a sour apple because you knew how ridiculous you looked with a bow in your hair and a stove-top hat."

He pondered her words for a moment then reached up and unfastened the ribbon that bound his hair. He shook the thick black locks free then took another step closer, forcing Rose to step back against the window.

"Josiah could return at any moment and wonder what we are doing."

"Does he have a wife?"

"Yes."

He smiled and reached out, hooking his fingers over the edge of her bodice and pulling her forward. "Then he'll know exactly what we are doing."

THE FIRST CRUNCH of crisp pork skin brought a soft whimper to Rose's throat. She chewed slowly, savoring every delicious crackle and burst of flavoursome grease. The cook had roasted a whole suckling pig and surrounded it with heaps of vegetables, cheeses, and fruits. Pineapple had been grilled over an open fire with honey and tamarind and was sweet enough to make her teeth ache with happiness. There were meat pies and flummery, and wonder of wonder, scraped ices flavored with lemons and limes.

Josiah kept their glasses filled with wine and fussed around them like a hen with chicks. Each time she glanced up, with her mouth stuffed full, she found Sebastien watching her, smiling. He had seen her eat before and was well aware that she did not nibble at tiny ladylike tidbits. He had even heard her belch with the enthusiasm of a dockworker.

A lady's maid had swept her hair up and pinned it into a mass of shining curls. She had changed into another of her mother's dresses, one with a whisper-thin shawl of lace around her shoulders to hide the pink, chafed skin between her throat and breasts. Each time Fonteyne glanced at her and each time his gaze fell to her bodice, she knew he was thinking about the past hours spent in the bedroom and she could feel her cheeks warming and her belly shimmering.

For two people who had declared they should not let themselves become distracted by such things again, they had certainly thrown all good intentions out the window.

She had also forgotten ... or deliberately pushed out of her mind ... the pleasures of sitting at a table that was not bolted to the floorboards, or the simple ease of drinking wine out of delicate crystal glasses that one did not have to catch if the ship rolled into a wave. At sea, she did not miss all the frippery and formality. Not really. She had made her choice and was happy with it, but even as she reached for her glass of wine, her gaze was drawn to the thin white scar that ran from her thumb to her wrist, a reminder of an encounter with a Spaniard who objected to her crew boarding his ship. There were other scars in other places, each marking a day, an adventure she would not have missed for all the wine and cracklings in the world.

Her thoughts were pulled back to the present when she heard a commotion out in the hallway. She drew her hand back and reached instinctively for the pistol that was not currently strapped to her hip.

When the double doors were flung open, Sebastien pushed to his feet and sent the chair rocking back on two legs.

Both gaped at the open doorway where Ramsey St. Clare stood, his arms wide apart, one hand clutching the edge of a door, the other holding his walking stick.

"I'll be double damned," he said quietly, his very cold gray eyes staring first at Rose, then at Fonteyne. "I did not believe my ears when I was told that my sister and her *husband* were on the island. I felt sure the fellow had been chewing too many banana leaves. Yet here you are and here I am bearing witness to a second unholy resurrection."

Rose folded her hands tightly in her lap. "Hello Ram. How lovely to see you after ... how long has it been? A year? Two?"

He held up the hand that was wrapped in a tight fist around his walking stick. "No. No, you do not get to make polite, civil conversation."

Sebastien reached back to straighten his chair but the cane came swiftly around to point in his direction. "Stay exactly where you are, Fonteyne." He said this without taking his eyes off Rose. "My mind needs to adjust to the sight of one phantom before trying to absorb a second."

Josiah melted into view behind him. "Shall I set another place at the table, Mr. Ramsey?"

"No, you should not." Ramsey turned and rather rudely shut the door, cutting off whatever Josiah was about to say next.

"The veins on your forehead are throbbing," Rose said. "Perhaps you should sit and have some wine before your eyes start to bleed."

A sound very much like a snarl came from Ramsey St. Clare's throat. He was tall and lean, handsome in a sharp-edged way, with a shock of dark auburn hair molded into a fashionable pompadour. His eyes were less blue and more gray than Rose and his nose was slightly tilted off centre. A scar tracked across his forehead from hairline to eyebrow, then continued down his cheek to his collarbone, a token from the same battle that had taken half his left leg.

Without saying anything, he went to the sideboard and poured himself a glass of wine, draining it in a few swallows before filling it again.

This time when he turned around, he had eyes only for Sebastien Fonteyne. "Your ballocks must be the size of cannon balls. I am surprised the weight of all that arrogance has not carried you to the bottom of the sea before now."

Sebastien smiled and offered up a polite bow. "A pleasure to see you in good health as well, Ram."

The color remained high in Ramsey's cheeks, but it was obviously taking a tremendous effort to temper the fury down to a mere rage.

"May I ask why? Why the devil are both of you here? And what unconscionable game are you playing to pretend you are husband and wife?"

"What makes you think we are pretending?" Sebastien asked.

Rose could not help the startled look she sent his way, one that Ramsey happily missed as he exclaimed, "The hell you say!"

Sebastien only shrugged and smiled.

Ramsey looked to Rose, who could think of nothing to say other than, "We saw Father. We met him at the Nobbins."

"And he approved of this ... this *farce*, did he?"

"He was happy to see me and not entirely hostile to Captain Fonteyne's presence."

Ramsey snatched the decanter of wine off the sideboard and carried it to the table. When he was angry, upset, or frustrated, he was less able to control the limp as he walked. At the moment, he was stumping his way to the dining table as if walking on an uneven log.

"You've not answered my first question. What the devil are you doing here? Are you aware there is a price on Fonteyne's head? A reward of ten thousand pounds has been posted by the Dutch East India Company. Apparently, they have taken offense at the number of their merchant ships he has relieved of their cargo. As for yourself—" He paused and looked at Rose. The face that was burnished by the candlelight was a face he had seen only in his memories these past few years. She had been the first person he'd seen when he had been carried off the ship on a stretcher, his body burning with fever. Craving her smile, her laugh, her brazen, ribald humor had been what kept him alive in the long voyage home after Trafalgar. She had looked after him, changed his stinking bandages, and nursed him back to health day by day, and even found a carpenter who could fit him with a new leg.

The anger bled out of him as if through an open cut. "Rose—"

She smiled softly. "I have missed you too, Brother."

He closed his eyes and bowed his head slightly, shaking it. "What the bloody hell am I to do with you now?" He looked up from under his brows. "Is it true you've been running the blockade lines to deliver supplies to the Americans?"

When she hesitated, he held up a hand. "No, please do not placate me with a lie." He raked a hand through his hair and sighed. "Fonteyne is not the only one carrying charges of piracy and treason. The *Cygnet* has recently been cited in several news sheets but, in a small mercy, at least the results of your antics these past months have been credited to your husband's name. I don't suppose Father mentioned the Whitticomb estates have been placed under threat of seizure?"

She bit her lower lip. "No. No, he didn't."

The heated color began to rise in Ramsey's cheeks again. "Not two miles from here there is a fleet of ten British warships.

Fifteen thousand troops are on board. Experienced troops fresh from victory in Europe and eager to claim a second victory against the rebelling Americans. Even now, the city is preparing to host a ball to give them a royal send off. The governor's mansion is filled with a hundred officers from the Royal Navy, not to mention judges, magistrates, and council members. A whisper in the wrong ear and this house would be surrounded by soldiers and there wouldn't be a damned thing I could do about it." He paused for a moment when another thought struck. "You came in on the *Nighthawk*?"

Rose nodded. "Yes."

"God spare me, is Father with you? Is he on board?"

"Um ... no. We left him and most of his crew behind on the Nobbins."

Ramsey's eyes narrowed to slits. "You—? Why—? No. *No, no, no, no!* I don't think I want to know why. Or how. Or if he agreed to this mad scheme. You need to leave here. Now. Tonight. Before too many people start asking questions."

Sebastien looked at her. "We should take your brother's advice and get back to the ship."

"Good God, man, I do not need you to take up my side in the matter," Ramsey said. "I am one thin thread away from skewering you where you stand."

"With what, pray? Your finger?"

Quicker than the eye could follow, Ramsey pulled the ornate silver wolf's head off the end of his walking stick. Twenty inches of gleaming steel was attached to the knob, a rapier-thin sword honed to a wicked sharpness. The tip flashed up beneath Fonteyne's chin, the point forcing him to tilt his head back.

The two stood frozen, eyes locked, bodies rigid.

Rose blew out a cautious breath. "Ram ... please."

"We were friends once," Ramsey said, his anger throbbing through a vein in his temple. "Great friends."

"Yes, we were. You saved my life a time or two, just as I saved yours. For that, I would save it again now by telling you to take that blade away from my throat."

Another long, chest-squeezing moment passed before the tip of the blade wavered ... then was lowered.

"You need to leave here," Ramsey said again. "You are putting this entire household in jeopardy. Gather your things, leave nothing behind that would indicate you were here. I'll have a word with Josiah then have one of the stableboys saddle two horses. A carriage might draw too much attention."

The tightness in Rose's chest eased a little. "Ram, I'm sorry to have put you in this position."

Ramsey slid the sword back into his walking stick, slapping it in the last inch to lock the blade in place. "You're my bloody sister, Rosie. Mother would have me hobbling on two wooden legs if I had you arrested. Him, on the other hand," he glared at Fonteyne, "Be advised, our slate is now cleared of favours owed. The next time I see you it will be with pistol in one hand and iron manacles in the other."

22

———

Heeding Ramsey's advice, Rose and Fonteyne quickly changed into shipboard clothing, happily casting aside the fancy garments for trousers. Josiah was sorely disappointed to see them leave so soon, but when he saw Fonteyne in leather breeches, leather waistcoat, and tall black boots, his protests died in his throat.

They mounted the waiting horses and took a circuitous route back to the harbour to avoid any unwanted attention on the bustling main streets. They appropriated a jolly boat tied to the wharf and rowed out to the *Nighthawk*, where quiet orders were issued to haul in the anchor and take her out of port. As a precaution, the gun crews were called up on deck, but there was enough movement of boats and ships in the bay that they glided along the shoreline without any trouble.

It was only when they drew near the naval yard that several longboats filled with redcoats approached and warned them to keep their distance. With the *Nighthawk* obligingly adjusting her course, Rose and Fonteyne stood in the stern and used long-glasses to confirm the number of ships and estimate the number of guns and firepower in the British fleet.

"Difficult to see the ships closer to shore," Fonteyne observed. "But most of the big bastards are anchored in black water, suggesting there is more below the waterline than above."

"If so, with a deep draught, they won't be able to cross the delta and sail up the Mississippi."

"Or sail close into to Barataria Bay. At low tide, the *Black Wind* scrapes her keel on some of the shoals." He lowered his glass. "Even so, it is a formidable display of power and purpose. If your brother was right, fifteen thousand soldiers is nothing to dismiss out of hand. It would help to know ..." His voice trailed off but Rose's ears had already perked to attention.

"Help to know where they are bound?"

"The base at Pensacola is the most logical landing place. The handful of Spaniards manning the fort would run at the first sight of a British flag, and fifteen thousand soldiers landing a stone's throw from Louisiana would pose a serious threat."

"I would think the American forces would want to know that."

His eyes narrowed and he turned to look at her. "I'm sure they would."

"We could follow them. With the ball planned for tomorrow night, we are at the very least two days ahead of the fleet departing New Providence. By the time we join up with our other two ships and send the *Nighthawk* on its way, we could easily shadow the fleet as it passes the tip of Florida."

"You don't think they would notice three ships following them?"

"Not three; perhaps just one. One light, fast ship that can stay far enough back in their wake as to not be seen."

"The *Cygnet*, of course."

"Of course. At the risk of repeating myself for the hundredth time, the *Cygnet* is not readily identifiable, not like the *Black Wind* or, heaven help us, the *Pride*. And we do sail under a Dutch flag. Even if they see us they will presume we are a merchant ship following close for protection against privateers and pirates."

"Your brother seemed well apprised of your blockade-running feats and suggested your ship may not be as unknown as you believe."

She thought about that for a moment before her frown cleared. "Assuming the British fleet set sail from Portsmouth, it would have left England two months ago. Before that, it would have taken a month or more for any news of the *Cygnet's* identity to travel from the blockade line back to London and the naval office. Assuming Admiral Nicholls had set sail directly from Gibraltar following Napoleon's surrender, he would still be two months behind any bully notes about the *Cygnet*."

Fonteyne considered pulling his hair out by the roots, but instead, reached to an inside pocket on his waistcoat and withdrew one of his hand-rolled cigars. He struck a sulphur match on the rail and studied Rose's expression over the small flare of flame and the resultant cloud of smoke.

"Would it do any good to point out the dozen or so flaws in your proposition?" He held up his hand to stop her from answering and gave a deep chuckle. "No, I don't suppose it would. But you will allow that some additional discussion on the matter might be warranted."

She tried not to smile. "I am always open for discussion. If the outcome is reasonable and I agree with it."

He was halfway through inhaling a lungful of cigar smoke when she said that and the resultant fit of coughing nearly had him falling over the rail.

～

A DAY later they were reunited with the other three ships. After crews had been restored to their respective vessels, it was decided that the *Nighthawk* should return to the Nobbins and "rescue" Alexander St. Clare. Before the last farewell *huzzahs* echoed across the water, Rose and Fonteyne had called their officers and gun captains to a meeting in the great cabin of the *Black Wind*. There, they divided the shares from the successful disposing of the two revenue ships in Kell's Bay, which would be distributed to the crews. Fonteyne also shared the information they had learned about the soldiers and firepower on board the British fleet.

"We have no way of knowing for certain where they are bound once they leave New Providence," he said. "Best guess is Pensacola, but Rose has suggested we follow them to make sure before we cross the Gulf."

"In truth, I would like to find a way to blow them out of the water," she muttered. "But I had a thought that we could lay off somewhere and keep watch, then follow them up the coast."

"Ten warships versus three?" Penman shook his head. "Please tell me neither one of you is that mad."

"At least one of us isn't," Fonteyne said, glancing sidelong at Rose.

"I have wrought what magic I can with the guns and rigging on board the *Pride*," Billy said, "and her maneuverability is much improved, but I would not trust her in a pitched battle, so we would only be able to count on two fighting ships."

"Ho!" Stubb chimed in. "That be far better odds. Two ships against ten."

Rose acknowledged Stubb's sarcasm with a frown. "One thought would be to send the *Pride* on ahead. I agree she would be fairly useless in a pitched battle, but she could carry a warning to Barataria, and in turn New Orleans. In truth, we have no way of knowing what has happened in the weeks we've been gone. General Jackson may have already arrived with his army in New Orleans."

"He might also have been informed of the British fleet," Fonteyne said, "and concluded, as we have, that the logical place for them to land would be Pensacola."

"In which case he might march his army to Pensacola, leaving New Orleans undefended," Rose said quietly. "Unless, of course, Lafitte can be persuaded to throw his support to the Americans. Since I expect he would be none too happy to see me sailing into his bay again, you, Captain Fonteyne, would be best suited to sail on to Barataria while my crew and I stay back and follow the fleet."

When that gave rise to a new wave of debates and arguments, Fonteyne stood and walked over to the gallery windows. He ignored the voices behind him and stared out at the afternoon sunlight rippling over the surface of the water. He had spent most of his life at sea, signing on as a powder boy when he was eight years old. Twenty-four years later he was still awed by the power of the sea, by winds that could make the difference in a victory or a defeat in battle, by the loyalty of men who put their lives in his hands and never questioned his decisions.

He changed his focus to the reflections in the glass noting Archie Penman's blonde hair shining under the lamplight. A doctor, an aristocrat, he could have spent his days tending wealthy women who were prone to fainting at the sight of any one of the little bugs or beetles he kept in jars in his cabin. Beside him, Billy Burr, a woman with more knowledge of guns and cannon than any man on board the *Wind*, which was the highest praise he could think to give.

At the other end of the table sat the imposing blackness of Duardo next to Nathan Reed, Stubb, and Digby Fitch, as unlikely a foursome of men as ever broke bread at his table. And next to them, Rose St. Clare, sprung from a dynasty that stretched back several generations, all of whom were born with wild adventures and seawater in their veins.

He turned and walked back to the long table and waited for the voices to fall silent.

"To be honest, I fail to see what more can be gained by following the fleet, so here is what I propose. Regardless where the fleet lands and where the army disembarks, it would seem to be more important to get well ahead of them to warn both Lafitte and Jackson and give them time to organize their defenses. I would suggest, then, that all three ships set a course for New Orleans, at whatever speed is deemed necessary. At the appropriate time, the *Wind* and the *Pride*, will break off and make sail for Barataria."

For once, there was silence around the table with everyone watching the two captains. Fonteyne's jaw was squared, obviously anticipating another verbal battle. Rose, for her part, took a deliberately slow sip of wine and set her glass carefully back down on the table.

It was Penman who cleared his throat and spoke first. "It sounds like a reasonable plan to me, er, not that my opinion counts farther than I can throw it."

When no one contradicted him, he sank lower in his chair and kept his tongue firmly between his teeth.

Fonteyne looked directly at Rose, who now seemed intent on swirling the dregs of wine around the bottom of her glass.

"We know the fleet will eventually land somewhere along the coast," he said, "be it Pensacola or the Mississippi delta or somewhere in between. Was that not your entire argument for sailing into Nassau? To learn the size of the fleet and the destination, both of which we now know."

"The destination we only think we know." She set her glass down and drew a deep breath. "But yes, I suppose that was the reason for stopping there."

"Unless you have a further objection?"

"None worth arguing over. I might only suggest that we part company as soon as it is no longer practical to hold back on our speed in order to stay together. And since the *Pride* is Lafitte's ship and you were sent to fetch it back, we shall, in good faith, place her safekeeping in your hands ... unless *you* have a further objection?"

Trapped by his own words, Fonteyne's eyelid twitched.

Nathan Reed cleared his throat discreetly. "I might be inclined to give the *Pride* half a day's head start. She still balks in heavy weather, should we encounter any storms or squalls."

Stubb snorted and chuckled. "She'd be needin' half a week to make up for her lumbering, more's the like."

Fonteyne frowned, and looked at Reed. "Whatever you think you need, since you will have her helm. You need to get as much speed out of her as you can."

Reed nodded. "Aye Captain. She's had some improvements so she might just surprise you."

Stubb started to make another comment, but the sound changed to a startled squawk as Duardo pinched a handful of sensitive nerves in the little man's neck and sent him sliding down in his seat.

Rose pushed to her feet. "It would seem as though we have a plan of sorts, and if there is nothing further to discuss, I suggest my crew and I return to our ship and make ready to sail at first light."

Without waiting for anyone to comment, she picked her hat up, placed it on her head, and walked brusquely out of the cabin. Billy was a pace behind, having passed a small smile to Penman before leaving. Duardo, Stubb, and Digby Fitch followed hastily in their wake.

When they were gone, Penman looked at Fonteyne. "Well, that went better than expected."

"Quite a bit better," Sebastien said, frowning. "So why do I feel like I've just had a canvas sack pulled over my head?"

LESS THAN AN HOUR LATER, with Nathan Reed not wanting to let any dust settle under his feet, the *Pride* weighed anchor and shook out her sails. While she was still lacking the speed or grace of either the *Black Wind* or the *Cygnet*, she was a slightly more graceful sow than when she had been stolen out of Barataria Bay. As they had done for the departing *Nighthawk*, the crews from the other two ships lined the rails and sent them off with a rousing cheer.

"If she encounters any trouble," Billy said, "I'm sure Reed is more than capable of handling it. I hand-picked a few of our own gunners to go on board and help where they can."

Rose nodded; her attention held by the diamond-like sparkle the sun cast on the surface of the western sea as it was sinking toward the horizon. "Good. That is good."

"With the modifications we made, the *Pride* has gained almost four knots on her speed. Her rudder has been rebuilt as well so there should be no floundering if she encounters heavy seas."

Rose nodded again, her gaze shifting to the silhouette of the *Black Wind*, "Good. That is good."

Billy luffed an eyebrow. "Cook is serving raw horsemeat for supper tonight."

It took a full minute for her words to draw Rose's attention away from the *Black Wind*. "He's doing what?"

Billy cracked a smile. "He's making mutton stew, actually."

"Ah. Sorry, my mind was ..."

"Focussed on someone standing on a deck about a thousand yards off the bow?"

Rose shook her head. "What is it about men? Arrogant blowhard captains in particular. Is it really so hard for them to believe a woman can function perfectly well without them telling us how we should think, what we should do, and how we should do it?"

"It must be because they fear their manhood is threatened. That's when they feel the need to beat their chests and order us delicate little creatures about."

"I believe the term is condescending."

"And the appropriate reaction to that is a desire to throttle."

"A very strong desire," Rose agreed.

"I thought you held your temper in check rather admirably back there."

"There is a time to argue and a time to just let them think they have won the day."

They fell silent for another moment and watched the *Pride* turn into the bronzed path of sunlight rippling under her keel.

"There are, of course, exceptions," Rose said. "Dr. Penman, for one. He seems like a good man and I suspect he makes you smile more often than he makes you want to pound him into the boards. The first time I heard you two laughing together on board the *Wind*, I wasn't even certain it *was* you; the sound was so foreign."

Billy objected. "I laugh all the time!"

"Not like that, you don't. When you laugh, every man on this ship feels their ass cheeks squeeze tight with dread."

"Only if they have a reason to dread it." Billy grinned. "But you are right. Dr. Penman is a very easy man to talk to. He doesn't seem to be bothered by—" she waved a hand absently across her damaged cheek— "by things that make other men cringe and turn away."

"For a gentleman keeping company with a band of pirates, he doesn't seem to be bothered by a lot of things."

"He has not talked much about his past, but I gather he was a tavern drunk when he met Captain Fonteyne and couldn't hold his hands steady enough to thread a needle. If you've noticed, he rarely drinks anything stronger than ale and that very sparingly. A sip or two to make it seem like he is drinking but most of it gets left behind or spilled onto the boards."

Rose leaned back, keeping her hands on the rail to stretch some of the kinks and tension out of her back. "I can only hope Fonteyne is a man of his word. Whatever happens in the coming days and weeks, I hope he sees how important it is to persuade Lafitte to join the Americans."

"Stubb doesn't trust Fonteyne as far as he can blow a plug of snot. He says his ballocks itch every time they are in the same room, and as you well know," Billy paused to raise her voice so that the curly-haired shadow lurking behind a bulkhead would hear her clearly, "his ballocks are the envy of every soothsayer and gypsy fortune-teller along the Spanish Main. Personally, I think it is merely lice, since his body has not seen soap or hot water for several months."

"Soap? Water?" Stubb's unmistakable snort of indignation brought him out of the shadows. "Both be the devil's own work an' are to be avoided beyond absolute necessity."

Billy flared her nostrils slightly. "I detect a great deal of necessity at the moment. I smelled you skulking in the shadows long before I saw you."

"Only because your nose holes be bigger than cannon muzzles! An' I do not skulk, I merely walk wi'out soundin' like a clod. As fer the Devil's Captain ayont, I say again, he is n'owt to be trusted." He looked directly at Rose and added, "No matter if his cock be as pretty as ever there were one."

Rose cast an icy glare at the little man. "Do you not have a beakhead to stick your nose into or a crack in the boards to pinch your ear against?"

Stubb planted his hands on his hips. "If it be not fer this nose an' these ears, ye'd not be knowin' the half o' what goes on aboard this ship ... or any other. Thus, ye should heed my words: He's already cast a spell over yer sensibilities, aye, as is plain to see by the addled look in yer eyes. Ye could not look more besotted if ye were standin' here naked an' leakin' wet down yer thighs."

Billy's hand fell to the hilt of her sword, but Rose belayed the movement. "What I do and with whom I do it is none of your damned concern, Mister Barnaby Stubb, and you would do well to keep that in mind."

Stubb swelled his chest and straightened to his full three feet of height. "Ye've just finished lettin' the blackhearted oaf give ye orders for what to do an' where to go, so aye, it be a concern to me. It be a concern for the rest o' the crew as well if we've been gelded."

Billy's eyes sparked. "Be careful what you're saying, rodent."

"I'll say the same thing to you if ye try to deny the blush in yer cheek an' the flutter o' them eyelashes every time ye see the addle-eyed physic. Do it! Say it be not so!"

With a deep, promissory snarl, Billy drew her sword slowly out of her belt. "You will be hard pressed to say anything at all when I carve out your tongue and hang it from the mainmast!"

Stubb clutched his crotch and made a lewd gesture. Before Billy could bring her sword slashing down, he dashed away and disappeared down the hatchway. Billy would have charged fast on his heels if Rose did not hold her back a second time.

"He isn't entirely wrong," she said. "And he's only saying what the rest of the crew is probably thinking; that we've given Fonteyne command of more than just his ship. He does, after all, have a well-deserved reputation as a pirate, a villain, and a thief. Rogues like Sebastien Fonteyne do not change into heroes and men of good character overnight."

Billy recognized the look in Rose's eyes. "You don't fully trust him either?"

"Not by the longest shot from the longest cannon we have on board. Once Duardo has set the watches, come join me in my cabin for whatever hellish-hot victuals our Jamaican cook has come up with for tonight. And yes, if you can let him keep his tongue a while longer, bring Stubb as well. We need to study a couple of charts."

PART II

23

Five hundred miles to the northwest, Jean Lafitte was cursing in a steady stream.

His temper had been on a short fuse in the weeks following the theft of his *Pride* and Sebastien Fonteyne's subsequent departure. His brother Pierre was still in jail. One of his ships had gone down in a blazing battle with a Spaniard off the coast of Panama. Add to that, three of his barges laden with black-market goods had been confiscated by the American authorities in New Orleans by order of the wart in his ass, Governor Claiborne.

His mood had only blackened when the knock came on his door, and a young pointy-nosed officer in British blues marched in at the head of a small delegation of four equally stiff-necked compatriots, all of whom stamped to a halt and saluted smartly.

The officer, stepped forward, snapped his hat off his head and tucked it under his arm, then handed Lafitte a leather portfolio. "Captain W. H. Percy sends his regards, M'sieur Lafitte."

"Who the bloody blazes is W. H. Percy? And who the bloody hell are you?"

"Lieutenant Andrew Ewert, at your service, sir. Captain Percy is the senior naval commander in the Gulf of Mexico. He sends his regards from our base in Pensacola and requests that you read the enclosed documents. He would be further pleased if you honor him with a reply as soon as possible."

Lafitte lifted the flap of leather on the billfold and peered at the thick sheaf of papers inside. "He expects me to read all of this?"

The pretentious look on the young man's face was mirrored in the smirks that passed between his adjutants, who supposed that Lafitte could not read at all. "I am authorized to relay the contents, if that is preferred."

Jean sat back down and propped his boots on the corner of his desk. "By all means, relay them."

The young man stared at the muddy boots for a moment, then restored his lickspittle smile. "Captain Percy wishes to advise you that, due to continued and unrelenting acts of piracy against merchant shipping vessels, he stands in receipt of an order to attack and destroy Barataria Bay. His fleet is prepared to act on his command."

"How thoughtful of him to warn me."

"However," the officer continued as if he did not want to lose his place in what he had memorized. "Should you and your Baratarians agree to join forces with the British, as our allies in the dispute with the American rebels, there will be no attack. Moreover, should you pledge loyalty to the king, he is authorized to offer each and every man amongst your company, from captain to powder monkey, amnesty for any involvement in past crimes. Further, at the resolution of hostilities with the rebels, you and your men will also be offered lands within His Majesty's colonies in America and forthwith be recognized as British subjects."

"Forthwith?" Lafitte spread his hands wide. "The king's generosity appears to know no bounds."

"As part of your cooperation of course, the navy would require the use of all the boats and ships under your command as well as the enlistment of all gunners and fighters to aid in the capture of New Orleans and the further invasion of Louisiana."

Lafitte said nothing. He looked at each of the stone-faced adjutants in turn, staring until their cocksure arrogance flickered and they lowered their eyes.

"As an added incentive," Ewert continued, "Captain Percy has the authority to offer a payment of thirty thousand pounds sterling to be apportioned ... at your discretion, of course ... for convincing your fellow captains to join our efforts."

Lafitte's eyebrow twitched. Thirty thousand British pounds was a great deal of money.

"Lastly, and as a gesture of good will, M'sieur, your brother Pierre Lafitte will be released from jail."

Lafitte's eyes widened out of their creases. "*Vraiment*? Such largesse. But surely your Captain Percy understands that I cannot speak for every man in Barataria Bay. The offers must be put before them and all must be allowed to voice their opinions and concerns. This will, of course, require time."

"Time, M'sieur Lafitte? How much time?"

Behind his small, dark eyes, Lafitte was trying to estimate how long it would take to empty his warehouses and safeguard their valuable contents.

Outwardly, he casually waved a hand. "My men are scattered here and there through the bayou and it will take, at the very least, a fortnight to gather them together."

"Two weeks," the officer said, frowning.

"A fortnight, *oui*. Even then, some may not be that easy to persuade. We shall of course require the thirty thousand pounds be delivered in coin rather than paper notes. But I shall surely read through all of these documents and present W.H. Percy's offers with as much enthusiasm as may be warranted."

When his flat smile gave no indication there would be any further discussion, Lieutenant Ewert offered a curt bow. "I will, of course, convey your requirements to Captain Percy."

"Along with my regards," Jean added, "and my thanks for his generous offers of amnesty and land grants which will also be in writing with all appropriate seals of authority from Governor Claiborne."

"In writing? Why yes. Yes, of course. In writing and filed with the local magistrate's court."

"In the meantime, I shall eagerly await my brother's safe return to Barataria. The scourge of being branded a pirate by these ungrateful Americans leaves a lasting bad taste in the mouth."

"We can fully sympathize," Ewert said with an obsequious nod.

"And now gentlemen, it would seem I have some important matters to discuss with my captains. You can find your way out?"

All five men snapped smartly to attention. "We shall convey your amiable reception of the Crown's offers to Captain Percy and hopefully win the disposition of your men to join us in our endeavor to reinstate British rule in the colonies."

"You will have my answer in two weeks time," Lafitte said.

THOSE TWO WEEKS had come and gone. During that same time, he had received a final rejection from the American council in New Orleans. They did not want or need his help. In fact, he was bluntly warned, if he showed his face anywhere near New Orleans, he would be arrested.

Following one last direct appeal to General Jackson, including an offer to support the American efforts with manpower and munitions, the surly response had gone one step further, branding him and his men 'a hellish band of pirates' who would all be hung from the gallows if caught.

Angered by both sides, he had made his own preparations. The captains of his merchant ships had been ordered to load as much cargo as they could from the bulging warehouses. He had watched as thousands ... tens of thousands of dollars worth of goods were removed. He loaded every barge, carrack, and long-boat with casks of powder and barrels of shot until the water splashed over the tops of the bulwarks. These he sent into the swamp and marshlands, ordering the men to hide the valuable caches of weapons and supplies where bigger ships could not follow.

After two weeks of sleepless days and nights, his men were exhausted and filthy. There were still ships in the harbor, desperately trying to take on cargo and make good their escape, but as the sun rose that fateful morning, they found both entrances to the Bay blocked by gun boats.

24

Being a lighter ship, the *Cygnet's* speed could easily outpace the *Black Wind*, though Rose was reluctant to insult Lafitte's premier captain by doing so. Instead, three days out from the Bahamas, Rose hung back more than usual and when questioned through the speaking trumpet, expressed concern that her ship was dragging. The helm seemed sluggish and slow to respond, possibly due to some undetected damage or fouling below the waterline.

When Fonteyne backed his sails and brought the *Black Wind* alongside, she further advised him that they were half a day's sail from Cayo Hueso and could stop there to make whatever repairs were needed. The cay was one of many small islands in the chain curving down from tip of Florida.

"I confess I am not familiar with the island," Sebastien said, looking over her shoulder at the chart laid out on the binnacle.

"Nay reason to be familiar with it," Stubb said, brushing a pudgy hand across the chart. "Sand an' palm trees, mostly. Natives from other cays used it as a graveyard for a few hunnerd year. Wind an' storms uncover hills o' bones, but mostly the cannibals 'ave moved to another cay."

Archie Penman blinked. "Did you say ... cannibals?"

"Aye. Bloody plague o' them used to be in these islands. Liked to boil sailors in a big pot then gnaw the meat off to the bone."

Duardo cuffed him on the shoulder and Rose shook her head with a beleaguered sigh.

"The repairs shouldn't delay us more than a day," Rose added, quickly rolling up the chart. "But since you want to get ahead of the fleet and reach Barataria with time to spare, there is no need to wait for us."

Fonteyne felt a scratch across the back of his neck. He had seen a small X on the chart before she swept it up and changed the subject. Stubb was beside her, hands behind his back, rocking on his heels. Duardo stood like a big black giant behind them, his face as blank as slate.

"Are there any signs of leakage below?" he asked. "I can send over a couple of my carpenters if you need them."

Rose looked up and smiled. "We're quite capable of handling any repairs that might be necessary."

"If you're certain—"

"I'm perfectly certain, Captain. But thank you."

She settled her hat on her head making the tall ostrich feathers dance. "How far do you suppose the *Pride* has gone in the past four days?"

"She's had a fair wind behind her," Fonteyne said. "Fair enough that we've not caught up with her yet, which is a pleasant surprise. Another two or three days I warrant, and she should be dropping anchor in Barataria Bay."

"Wouldn't your little pirate king be more convinced of any impending danger if he heard it from you?"

"Why, Captain St. Clare, if I was a suspicious man I might think you were trying to get rid of me."

"Not at all. I just see no reason for you to linger while we fix our rudder … and every reason for you to sail on ahead and warn Lafitte of a possible attack on Barataria."

"Lafitte is a stubborn bastard, but he isn't stupid. At this point he trusts neither the British nor the Americans, so it's more than likely he has already started emptying his warehouses of his most valuable and useful cargo. I know for a fact he's been squirreling away caches of guns and black powder all through the bayou for weeks."

"So for all of his supposed animosity toward the Americans, he might well have decided already to throw his lot in with them?"

"I did not say that. Nor would I say that, since his mind changes from one day to the next depending on which way the wind blows. Much like that of a woman."

"On the other hand, being always predictable can be tedious, can it not?"

"So can being predictably *un*-predictable."

"I'm not sure I follow."

He arched an eyebrow slightly. "For instance, if I was a suspicious man, I might think you were planning to do something foolish after I sail away."

"Something foolish? What could I possibly do on my own?"

"Oh, I don't know. Lurk behind your cannibal-infested cay until the British fleet sails past then cull one of the ships out of the pack perhaps? There is always one that lags temptingly behind."

"I give you my word I have no intentions of risking my ship by attacking the British fleet on my own. That would be—"

"Something foolish, indeed," he finished for her. "So what, exactly, were you planning to do? And don't insult my intelligence by carrying on with the porky about a damaged rudder."

Behind her, Stubb and Duardo moved discreetly toward the ladderway, and once there, scrambled down onto the maindeck.

Archie Penman watched them leave, then coughed a muffled excuse into his hand and followed them down.

Fonteyne, meanwhile, crossed his arms over his chest and glared at Rose.

"Well?"

"Well nothing. This is my ship. I can bloody well take her where I want to take her and do what I want to do with her. You said yourself that Nicholls is *probably* bound for Pensacola, but what if he has a different plan in mind. Lake Borgne is a hundred and fifty miles closer to New Orleans and deep enough to accommodate at least part of his fleet. What if he sails there instead, while General Jackson is valiantly marching his army overland to Pensacola? Fifteen thousand redcoats could overrun the city before Jackson was even aware they had landed."

"I grant you, your argument may be sound, but—"

"Thank you. Sometimes women do have the capacity to think without men around to help them."

He paused and glared. "What were you going to do if he does bypass Pensacola?"

Rose's gaze flicked for a moment past Fonteyn's shoulder, so he knew before he heard her voice that Billy Burr had come up onto the deck behind him.

"What is the one thing sailors fear above being shot or hacked to death with a cutlass?"

"Runnin' out o' rum." Stubb's voice came through the rails, proof he had not gone far enough to avoid being left out of the conversation entirely.

Billy ignored him and supplied the answer herself. "Fire."

Fonteyne's frown deepened. Fire was a genuine fear on board any ship. Hulls were wooden, sails were canvas, cables were hemp and soaked in pitch, all of which could burn out of control within minutes.

In the next instant, his brow cleared as he recalled the

conversation he had interrupted between Billy and Rose when he was still considered a captive on board the *Cygnet*.

"Fireships? You want to send fireships against them?"

"If they worked against the Spanish Armada, they could work against the British fleet."

Fonteyne took a step back, startled, but not entirely shocked for some unknown reason.

"*That's* your crack-brained idea? Just how were you going to get close enough to launch them? Dutch flag or not, they would see the *Cygnet* coming from ten miles away and every gun on board would be primed to blast you out of the water."

"We don't plan to let them see us coming."

Billy moved up beside Rose. "We'll use longboats. We load them with casks of powder and pack oiled rags around them. Add a mast and a sail for steerage and disguise them as small flotilla of fishing boats. Natives sail around and between the islands every day. They would hardly raise suspicion. Once the boats are close enough to the frigates, we light the fuses then jump overboard and swim away."

Fonteyne studied both determined faces then paced to one side of the quarterdeck, stared out over the turquoise water for a moment, then paced back.

"Do you have any idea how bloody dangerous that would be?"

"Bloody clever, too," Stubb voiced. "If'n it works."

"Oh, shut up," Fonteyne growled, glaring back at the disembodied voice. When he swung back to Rose and Billy, they were both watching him with unperturbed calm.

"It would work," Billy insisted. "If I pack some rockets and incendiaries in with the casks of powder, the boats will explode with enough force to send fireworks up onto the decks and yards. A crock or two of pitch will help stick the flaming cinders to the canvas sheets."

"Would I be wrong in suspecting you did not just come up with this crack-brained scheme today?"

"No," Rose said. "You would not be wrong. We've been debating it for days."

"So there is nothing wrong with your ship; there is no damage to your rudder causing her to lose steerage?"

Rose shrugged. "I was genuinely trying to avoid another argument."

He glared and planted his hands on his hips. "And you don't think you'll have one now?"

"No. I don't. Because the last time I checked, I was still the captain of this ship, still able to make my own decisions, and still able to come and go where I please without seeking anyone's permission or approval before doing so. What is more, I am sure you would rather leave my ship the same way you came on board instead of having Duardo toss you over the rail and make you swim back to the *Black Wind*."

The steely gaze flicked from one determined face to the other. It was a fierce, threatening stare that normally sent grown men crumbling to their knees. Yet neither woman crumbled. They both weathered the glare without evasion or fear, even mirrored it with a spine-chilling directness of their own.

Not for the first time, Fonteyne was torn between anger and admiration. He couldn't condone their hare-brained plan by any measure, and he was fairly certain it would fail miserably, but he had to admit it was gutsy and bold. As bold and gutsy as creeping through the fog and capturing the *Black Wind* without firing a single damned shot.

That still rankled.

"Very well," he said after a moment. He donned his hat and smiled thinly at Rose. "I will leave you to it then. Good luck. Good hunting."

Billy and Rose exchanged a wary glance. "That's it? That's all you're going to say?"

He took a step then looked back at Rose. "You said you wanted to avoid an argument and you seem to have your mind made up."

"I do, yes."

"Then once again, I wish you good luck and good hunting."

He descended the ladderway and walked along the deck to the gangway, collecting Penman along the way. Rose and Billy moved to the rail of the quarterdeck and watched until both men vanished over the side of the hull. They heard two solid thuds as the men jumped aboard their gig and moments later saw them being rowed across the clear azure water to the *Black Wind*.

Fonteyne did not look back when he was in the gig, nor did he look over once he was on board his ship. Instead, the faint echo of roared orders came across the water and within minutes, the sails were dropped and the tall ship was leaning into the wind heading west.

25

———

Cayo Hueso may not have been currently occupied by cannibals. But when the *Cygnet* reached it forty-eight hours later, it did have other unexpected occupants. In a bay on the leeward side of the island, there were men in the water bathing and fishing; men on the beach sitting around campfires cooking, laughing. And anchored in the deepest part of the bay was the *Black Wind*, the tops of her three masts festooned with palm fronds.

"What the bloody hell?" Rose muttered.

Stubb scratched his chin and chuckled at the palm branches. "Clever bastard. That be why we didn't see 'is masts stickin' above the trees. Rest o' the island be too damned flat to hide the big bitch proper-like."

Sparing any praise, Rose called for a boat to be lowered at once and for Duardo to row her ashore. There she was directed to a tent set back against the fringe of palm trees where Sebastien Fonteyne sat comfortably in the shade, in a makeshift canvas chair and smoking one of his rolled cigars.

Rose tramped alone through the soft sand, her anger up for a confrontation.

"What ... are you doing here?"

He shrugged. "I gave it some thought and decided it wouldn't be fair to let you have all the fun."

"I thought you said it was a crack-brained idea."

"I still think it is. But I also think it's crack-brained enough that it just might work. Lafitte needs time. Jackson most of all needs time and if we can buy them a little extra ...?"

"Plus, you can take all the credit if it does work."

"Hell no. The credit is yours. I'm merely here to watch your back."

"The day I believe that ..."

"... will be the day you finally, fully trust me. A day I look forward to with equal anticipation and trepidation." He flashed one of his most charming and disarming grins. "Now then, would you like a drink or something to eat? You're looking a little strained. I have rum, wine, lemon water if you prefer and the men just brought out a platter of freshly grilled fish."

Without answering, she turned on her heel and retraced her steps across the sand to the water's edge where Duardo was waiting with the jolly boat. The sun was high in the sky and blazing hot. The water was clear and sparkling. She stripped off her coat and waistcoat and tossed them in the boat along with her hat. She kicked off her boots and stockings and, wearing just a cambric shirt and breeches, waded into the surf and swam back to her ship.

OVER THE NEXT two days it became a game of preparation, then waiting.

Under Billy's supervision, the crew made good use of their time transforming several longboats into single masted fishing boats. The bottoms and gunwales were lined with casks of black powder. Fuses were tested as to how much time would be needed for a man to light them and swim clear.

When that was done, with no sign of the fleet on the horizon, the *Cygnet* was scrubbed and cleaned top to bottom. Rose would have liked to beach her and scrape her hull clean of barnacles, but that could take weeks, not hours or days. Instead, she challenged the crew to races to find the best swimmers and from that sadly small number, volunteers were chosen to man the fireships.

Men with the keenest eyesight built crow's nests atop the tallest palm trees located on the highest rise of land, but after four days of sighting nothing but empty sea, clouds, and gulls, the tension on board grew palpable.

Each night Rose met with Stubb, Duardo, Billy, and Digby Fitch in her cabin and each night they went over their plans to debate what could go right or very wrong.

During all this time, Fonteyne either remained on his ship or sat in the shade on the beach. Communication between ships was nearly non-existent.

Stubb shook his head. "Ye never should 'ave give the bastard 'is ship back."

"You seem to think I had a choice," Rose said.

"Ye would 'ave if ye'd've kept 'im bound in irons instead o' wrappin' yer legs around 'im an' thinkin' that would change 'is nature. Ye bloody well know he 'as no loyalties, cept to the color 'o gold. Mark my words, he be not 'ere to help, but to hinder. First chance he gets, he'll double-cross ye. He be like a bloody big cat just bidin' 'is time afore he pounces."

Duardo shot the little man a warning glance and growled low in his throat, but Rose lifted the tips of her fingers off the table to restrain him. "I am not his keeper, nor is he mine. As for trusting him, if you think so little of me to believe I would allow a man's body to command the way I think or act, then you obviously do not know me at all and have wasted the last five years on board my ship."

With four pairs of ice-cold eyes glaring at him, Stubb shrank back in his chair and grumbled. "Only speakin' my mind an' if ye don't expect that from me after all these years, then ye don't be knowin' *me* a'tall."

Rose sighed. "I expect you to be honest with me, which you are, most of the time."

"Bein' honest now," he muttered under his breath, undaunted. "You an' Billy: both addled as newts."

Billy was in the middle of peeling a mango and stabbed the tip of the dagger into the top of the table. "One more word and I vow it will be your last."

So it went on the fourth day. And the fifth. Most of that time the sky was thick with clouds and frequent squalls passed over the islands. The humid air did nothing to ease the heat or banish the swarms of vicious mosquitoes.

ARCHIE PENMAN SPENT those same long days exploring the island. He discovered the island's name, isle of bones, was exactly that. He trekked out daily with his sketch pad and found vast pits filled with human skeletons that had once been buried but were now exposed and bleached white by the tropical sun.

Thankfully, he did not find any graves that were relatively fresh.

He also carried with him his little string of baskets to search for leaves, herbs, and bugs to add to his apothecary supplies on board. It was during one of his treks he found a small freshwater pond that was cool and deep and seemed the ideal place to strip naked and enjoy a private swim away from prying eyes.

He was floating on his back, his arms stretched up behind

his head, eyes closed and a few contented sighs away from drifting off to sleep when he heard a splash nearby.

Jerking himself upright, he saw Billy by the water's edge a few feet away.

"Forgive me, I did not mean to startle you. I thought sure you must have heard me."

"No, I ... my head was half under the water. All I could hear was my own breathing."

"Would you rather I leave you on your own? I know how difficult it is to find some privacy on board a ship."

"Please, no. Don't leave. We haven't had the chance to spend much time together lately."

Billy offered up a knowing smile. "Our captains are each as stubborn as the other."

"Indeed. It is like standing between two panes of glass and wondering which one will shatter first."

She hesitated and looked like she might turn away.

"Please don't go," he said again. "The water is cool and lovely."

Billy noted where his clothing was laid out on a nearby rock.

"I promise to be a complete gentleman and keep my hands entirely to myself."

Billy debated the watery blur of naked flesh, then unfastened the thong at her waist. She slipped out of her short canvas trousers and dropped them in a crumple on the mossy bank.

Archie's tongue became stuck to the roof of his mouth as he watched her lift her shirt up over her head. Her body was lean and taut, tanned brown as a berry from the knees down and the arms up but with a sailor's snow-white skin in between. Her body was scarred in a dozen places, not the least of which was the continuation of the puckered burn on the side of her face and neck that stretched down almost to her breast.

"Why do you do what you do?" he asked, the question

blurted before he had a chance to think about it. "Why the guns? Why something so dangerous?"

She dunked her head under the water and scrubbed at her face and hair for a moment to remove the day's sweat before answering.

"My father was a gunsmith. He worked in a cannon foundry that also made various types of weapons. I knew how to load and fire a blunderbuss before my arms were strong enough to carry one. When I was six, he caught me trying to load one of the cannons. I was doing it all wrong and likely would have blown both my hands off, so he taught me the right way.

"Spain was very territorial and someone was always at war with a rival kingdom or principality. He was always being sent to teach the soldiers how to work the guns and I learned by his side until I was twelve or thirteen. Then one day he was accused of being a spy and shot. I would have been shot as well but I fled to Marselles and stowed away on board a ship disguised as a boy. The rest is a long and tangled story that brought me over to this side of the Ocean-Sea, and when I heard that a female captain was taking on a crew, I had to check it out. Rose was there, looking every bit a sea captain. She was overseeing the signing of the articles and when it came to my turn, somehow she saw beneath the disguise ... a disguise I had lived in for almost ten years. She told me to discard it, she had no use for pretense on board her ship. For that, I thank her every day for letting me just be me."

"I would add my thanks as well," Penman said, drifting closer to her. "Such loveliness should not be bound up to look like a scruffian."

She turned the ruined side of her face away. "I am hardly lovely."

"You are to me, and I've been told I have a very acute eye and extremely good judgement when it comes to the opposite sex."

"You are also a doctor."

"Yes. And I wish I had been on board your ship when this happened to you." He reached out and gently grasped her chin, forcing her to turn her face toward him again. "Whoever treated your burns ... well ... he wasn't very good. And that falls on him, not you."

He moved again, bringing his body close enough they shared the aura of warmer water between them.

Penman traced a fingertip from her chin down to her breast, holding his breath when he felt the tiny shivers beneath her skin. "Does it trouble you for your crew to know that we ... have become closer?"

"No. It does not trouble me one whit."

He leaned forward and kissed the tip of her nose. "I'm glad to hear it, because I would be quite happy to stand naked at the top of a mast and shout it to the world."

Now she was the one short on breath. "I've never ... I mean, I haven't ..."

He smiled gently and took her face between his hands, kissing her so tenderly and so deeply, she sighed into his mouth and wrapped her arms, her legs instinctively around him.

With their mouths still molded together, Penman lifted her and carried her out of the water. There, slick and sluicing water, with Billy's legs still wrapped tightly around his waist, he was beginning to press into her warmth when they heard a familiar voice through the surrounding fringe of vegetation.

"By Neptune's holy turds! I vow I be the last sane body on this island. All this frolickin' an' fornicatin.' 'Tis nay wonder aught gets done around here. There be a ship out in the Straits, ye lummocks. Did ye not hear the alarm?"

"I vow I will, one day, pin Stubb's nose to the mast," Billy said, breathless. "He pokes it in so many places where it is not wanted, I'm surprised he has kept it this long."

Archie started to pull away but her legs tightened and her hands grasped at his buttocks. "Don't you dare. Or I vow something of yours will be pinned on the mast along side his nose."

Archie grinned and much to Stubb's chagrin, did not respond to the first, second, or third conch-horn alarm that echoed across the island.

BY THE TIME they were dressed and had gathered up the baskets Penman had collected, the single ship had become a line of white dots neatly spaced apart, riding low on the horizon.

"Too many to be merchants," Billy said. "It has to be the English fleet."

They started quickly back to the bay. Both were grinning, too satiated and flushed with renewed energy to notice or care that the buttons on Penman's waistcoat were matched to the wrong holes or that Billy Burr had moss in her hair.

26

————

A jolly boat had been rowed to the hull of the *Black Wind*. Rose recognized the figure climbing down to board it and smiled smugly to herself. Six days she had resisted the urge to make that crossing. Six days she had resisted the temptation to join him on his ship or on the beach, fearing exactly where that temptation would lead.

Stubb was right. He was like a big sleek cat waiting to pounce and she had to be on her guard every minute.

Rose ordered the gangway to be opened. On further thought, she added, "When Captain Fonteyne comes on board, tell him I am in my cabin and will receive him there."

Digby Fitch was standing nearby and nodded. "Will do, Captain."

Rose returned, unhurriedly, to her cabin, where she drew the cork out of a fresh bottle of rum and set it on the dining table with two thick-bottomed glasses. She donned her vest and fastened all the buttons, then sat at the head of the table and propped her feet up on the corner.

Having another thought, she moved around behind her desk and sat down there, seemingly absorbed in studying a chart of

Florida and the Gulf coast. When she heard boots in the corridor outside her door, she picked up a thin graphite stick and started scratching notations on a piece of paper.

"Come," she said, responding to a knock.

She looked up as the door opened and Fonteyne's big body filled the entryway. He was dressed all in black, as usual, his hat on his head, his hair loose and wavy to his shoulders. At first glance, she noticed nothing out of the ordinary, but when she could calm her breathing and think past the heartbeats thudding in her ears, she noticed a fresh pink cut tracking across his forehead in almost the same location as the wound he had earned when the ships rammed together.

"Captain," she said by way of greeting.

"Captain," he acknowledged.

"There is rum on the table if like. Or wine. Or I could send for some lemon water if you prefer." She scratched a few more words on the paper. "If you'll just allow me to finish this calculation."

"By all means, don't let me interrupt."

She smiled and, after a moment set the graphite stick aside and wiped the smudges off her fingers. "Shall I assume you've come to discuss how to proceed now that we've found the British fleet?"

"I would agree some discussion is required," he said, taking off his hat. "We've already wasted six days sitting here doing nothing and I have a bad feeling that time is not in our favor. I also know from past experience that Nicholls does not sail through the night. He prefers to anchor his ships in a tight formation and wait for daylight. I, on the other hand, have had excellent results raiding at night, especially when there is no moon." He poured a glass of rum for himself, then filled another and set it beside the open chart. "There will be no moon tonight."

"Tonight?"

"The longer we delay, the greater the risk of being seen, and not just by the fleet. Never a humble man, Nicholls will cut northeast once through the Straits and keep within sight of land as he follows the coastline. He will want his presence to be known and celebrations prepared long before he makes landfall, regardless of where that might be. The same natives and spies who carry word of his impending arrival in Pensacola will also note a lone ship following in their shadow."

He moved behind the desk and leaned over her shoulder, placing a finger on the X that was marking Cayo Hueso and dragging it along the curve of islands toward the mainland of Florida.

"Most of these chain islands are barely inhabited, and then only by local native tribes. As you say, they send out small fishing flotillas, hardly a threat worth having revenuers regularly patrol the area. Higher up, however," he moved his finger to the mainland "you can almost guarantee there will be ships on patrol, and if the fleet is expected, those patrols will be thicker and more frequent than usual. We might only have this one chance to strike and get cleanly away."

"You have given this a lot of thought."

"I haven't had much else to do over the past few days."

She turned her head and looked up at him, realizing at once his face was too close, his scent was too heady, his eyes too direct. To distract herself, she focussed on the fresh line of scabbing on his brow. "Forget to duck beneath another beam?"

He touched it self-consciously. "Ah, this. Yes, well, I was drilling with the men, and I was momentarily distracted. It was the first time Archie's blade made it past my guard so he was quite thrilled and has been retelling the tale ever since."

He straightened, walking around to the front of the desk

again. "If we do this thing, I would suggest, in order to minimize the risk of being seen, that we only take one ship."

"The *Black Wind*, of course."

He shook his head and took a seat. "I leave that entirely up to you."

"Why?"

"Why what?"

"Why so obliging as to leave it up to me?"

He smiled and looked down into his glass as he slowly swirled the rum around. "Because it was your crack-brained idea. And whichever ship we choose to take, I have a complete set of black sails to refit the yards and render us nearly invisible. Conversely, every deck of every ship in Nicholls fleet will be ablaze with lamps; good for us, not so good for his sentries who will be at a disadvantage staring out into the darkness. The closer we can sail, the less distance the longboats will have to travel and the shorter the swim back to safety."

Rose took a sip of rum and studied Fonteyne's easy slouch, the long legs stretched out before him, black leather boots crossed at the ankles. He seemed altogether too agreeable today and that only made her all the more wary.

"I saw Billy on deck," he said, intruding on her thoughts. "She said you intend to be in one of the fireships we send against the fleet."

Rose gave a little shrug. "I never ask my men to do something I would not do myself. More to the point, I am an excellent swimmer, whereas, despite my best efforts to encourage all of my crew to learn how to swim, most flail about like beached whales if the water is deeper than their waists. Duardo will be with me. He swims like a shark."

"Once the fuses are lit, everyone will need to swim like sharks to get a safe distance away when the powder blows. A goodly number of redcoats will bail over the sides as well, choosing to drown rather than burn to death. Fireships are not called terror ships without good reason."

"I am well aware of the risks."

"As am I, which is why I'll be in one of the other longboats. Archie volunteered to come along as well, but he's too valuable to lose to mischance."

"And you're not?"

"I could ask you the same."

She tapped her fingers lightly on the desk. "I have been working for and with the Americans for the past few years. Whatever I need to do now, I will do it."

"Loyalty is an admirable quality."

She glanced up, fingers continuing to *tap tap tap*. "Stubb still doesn't trust you. He says his ballocks itch every time you are in the same room."

Sebastien pursed his lips. "What about you? Do you still have doubts?"

"Only about my judgement at times," she said quietly. In a louder, more firm voice she added, "Very well, Captain, we shall take your advice and set out tonight under the dark of the moon. We will take one ship ... the *Black Wind* ... saving the need to transfer sails. But so there are no misunderstandings, Billy will have absolute command of the fireships."

"I'll have the sails refit with the black sheets. If we leave at dusk, we should be able to catch them up by midnight."

Rose nodded and stood. "I will let Duardo know the plans."

Fonteyne set his glass aside. "Before you do, we have one other item of unfinished business to tend to."

She looked into his eyes—eyes that kept too many secrets and always had a curious effect on her breathing. For a man who kept his thoughts and emotions guarded against all intrusions, there was nothing hidden in the amber depths now and it was as if he had already reached out and run his hands down her body, stripping her clothes away as he went

"This is hardly the time," she managed to whisper.

"It is exactly the time," he said. He stood and moved toward her. "You never asked me what could have caused such a distraction as to have me let down my guard against Archie's blade. Shall I tell you? It was the sight of you climbing up the shrouds in a snow-white shirt and tight knee britches, your hair loose and streaming out in the breeze. You were laughing, racing one of your crewmen to the top of the mast."

When he came close enough, he touched her chin with his forefinger, his eyes clear and quietly searching hers. "It was the sound of that laugh. A laugh filled with the pure joy of knowing you were living exactly the kind life you wanted to live. I've not heard one in a hundred people laugh like that."

The words wrapped like a gentle fist around her heart and she felt something stirring within her. She'd spent half her adult life striving to prove she belonged in a man's world. It took her a moment to realize that over the past few weeks it had become more than just a longing to belong ... it was a longing to belong to *this* man's world.

MINUTES LATER, out in the corridor, Stubb raised his fist and was about to strike it on the door. He stopped mid-swing when he heard telltale cries and whispers followed by thuds as the berth moved in a lusty rhythm against the wall.

He clutched at both sides of his cap and pulled it down until it covered his ears and left only his nose and the scowl visible beneath. "Neptune spare me," he muttered as he walked away. "I vow I be the only sane one on board."

27

The night sky was thick with clouds and as black as the sails that now festooned all three masts. At first glance, it seemed as though there might be a moon up there somewhere. But as the *Black Wind* moved stealthily and invisibly closer, they could see it was the reflection of the lights blazing from the decks of the British fleet that caused the underbellies of the clouds to glow.

Fonteyne brought his ship to a gliding stop, cautiously well out of range of any possible glint or spark that might betray their presence. There were no lights on board, no cooking fire, not even a pipe. Cloths covered the huge brass deck lanterns at bow and stern, as well as anything else that might reflect a wink of light. Two longboats with their deadly cargo of black powder were being towed a safe distance behind. The casks were covered under a sheet of canvas on top of which were heaped dozens of pineapples and coconuts. Billy had set the fuses herself on each boat, winding them around the casks like long black snakes. Stern warnings were given to leave the boats the instant they were lit.

Four other longboats were lowered, these filled with baskets of fresh fruit and fish. They would approach the ships first to test their welcome and if all went well, the two fire ships would sail in after them.

Each boat had a fishing lamp on the bow, hung in such a way as to cast light over the produce. Earlier in the day, Digby Fitch had come to Rose and said he had been a fisherman long before he had signed on her father's ship as crew, and he would be proud enough to burst all his buttons if he could represent Alexander St. Clare in the daring raid. He was put in charge of the first four "fishing" boats while Rose and Duardo helmed the first fireship. Fonteyne and Jose Mercado worked the oars in the second fireship. They had darkened their faces and hands to look like local natives. All of them were dressed alike in loose trousers and striped shirts, with round woolen caps pulled low over their brows. Rose had a spot of trouble confining the full mass of her hair under the cap but that was remedied by tying the sides down with lengths of twine.

The water was smooth with shallow ripples on the surface, and the rowing was easy. Within a half mile of the fleet, Fonteyne stopped his boat and waited for Rose to come alongside. They watched as the 'fishing boats' went on ahead and approached the first brightly lit frigate, the *HMS Romulus*. They were hailed by several score of crew and soldiers standing at the rail. After some discussion took place between Digby Fitch and the quartermaster, nets were lowered and baskets were loaded and winched on board.

Rose wiped the palms of her hands on her trouser knees and tried not to think of the amount of black powder they were sitting on.

Fonteyne had raised his long glass and was studying the ships. "Bloody shame," he murmured.

"What is a bloody shame?" Rose asked quietly.

He smirked and reached across the gap to hand Rose his

spyglass. "Nothing except wishing I could make one raking pass with full broadsides. Look at how they are sitting ... like a row of skittles."

Rose raised her long glass and saw that the fleet was not grouped together in a lazy cluster as they had appeared to be from a distance. They were anchored a cable's length apart in a staggered, shallow crescent, nearly a mile long with their bows facing away from the distant shoreline.

Fonteyne shook his head. "Old naval tactics dictated that ships should meet their enemies head on and battle it out until the other was destroyed or fell away. Nicholls has apparently decided that any enemy ships they might encounter would abide by the same gentlemanly rules. Nelson blew those tactics out of the water at Trafalgar, which Nicholls might have known if he'd ever left port. The admiral cut through the line between enemy ships, which permitted one of his ships to fire broadsides from the starboard and port at the same time, causing twice as much damage in one pass."

Rose glanced across. Sebastien looked as calm as a choir boy.

"Aye," he said. "I'd give my weight in gold to have the *Black Wind* under my feet at the moment."

"Thankfully you do not," Rose murmured. She passed the spyglass back and felt the usual knot of tightness in her chest that was there before every battle.

"The last net is going up," she said. "I will aim for the bow, you for the stern." She turned to Duardo. "When the others are clear we row like the devil is in our wake and when we have enough speed for the boat to reach the hull, we light the fuses, tie off the rudder, and jump."

Duardo grinned and took up the oars.

The two longboats were heavy, and it took extra effort to get them moving toward the *Romulus*, but when they were within a hundred yards of the hull, Duardo discreetly shipped his oars and wrapped a length of cable around the rudder. Rose lit the ends of the fuses in the wick of the lantern and side by side, the two rolled silently over the sides of the longboats, arms and legs pumping furiously to swim clear.

Rose and Duardo were first to reach the escaping longboats and were thrown cables to catch. The men rowing did not stop to take them on board but dragged them behind for another hundred yards or so. At one point the rope twisted around her ankle and pulled her under, but she was able to cut herself free. She rose to the surface again, the knife clenched between her teeth, and felt Duardo catch her up around the waist and keep her head above the water.

When they were finally hauled on board, Rose knuckled the salt water out of her eyes and tried to see if Fonteyne and Mercado had made it away safely. At first she saw nothing, but then a series of tremendous booms thundered across the water as one of the fireships exploded in a massive, white-hot fireball of sparks and flame. It was short of the *Romulus'* hull, but a thick cloud of glowing hot sparks descended on the upper deck like a fiery hailstorm.

As more of the casks exploded, more sparks and flaming debris was thrown on board the *Romulus* accompanied by shouts and screams as the men scrambled to avoid the raining streaks of fire. Red-hot cinders landed in the bundles of sails furled in the yards, and stuck to the tar-soaked cables and lines tethering them. More explosions followed as casks were blasted apart and sent splatters of flaming pitch onto the hull.

The second longboat, however, was nowhere in sight.

"'He took it 'round the stern," Stubb informed her.

"Around the stern? That wasn't the plan."

"Mayhap he were thinkin' of a different plan."

Rose was about to unleash a volley of curses when there was

a second round of monstrous explosions. They came from the far side of the *Romulus*, where a sister ship was riding at anchor a hundred yards off her larboard beam.

"He went for a second ship," she muttered in disbelief. "The bloody fool will have twice as far to swim now!"

"There!" Stubb stabbed a finger in the air.

The glow from the erupting fireballs lit the surface of the sea like molten lava and Rose could see two bobbing heads as Fonteyne and Reed swam hard to circle around the hull of the *Romulus* and catch up to the longboats.

"Stubb, stop rowing!" Rose shouted. "Turn the boat around, we have to pick them up."

Explosions cracked the night air as the casks blew up in a furious display of hellfire. The crews on board the other longboats had stopped rowing to cheer the success and might have continued doing so if not for the sight of a dozen gunports opening on the *Romulus* and the black snouts of cannon being run out.

Even as Rose's boat completed the turn and started back toward the conflagration, she waved the other boats off and shouted, "Row, dammit, they're preparing to fire."

No sooner did the warning leave her lips when the upper bank of guns on the *Romulus* roared to life, spitting clouds of smoke and iron shot out of the muzzles. Most whistled by harmlessly overhead but one ball was lucky and smashed into the mast of one of the longboats causing it to capsize.

There were other popping sounds coming from the deck of the British ship and Rose could see soldiers leaning over the rails and firing muskets down into the water.

"The bastards be shootin' at 'em!" Stubb shouted. "They'll be shootin' at us soon if we don't turn around."

"Keep rowing!" Rose ordered.

The cannon on board the *Romulus* were pulled in and

reloaded. The second broadside whistled past so close overhead that Rose could smell the sulphur from the rush of hot air. It met with the same lack of success, and although the guns were hauled in again, the third round was delayed as all on board struggled to put out the dozens of fires on the deck and in the yards. All three masts were blazing like a Christmas tree. Men were jumping overboard to escape the heat and flames.

Rose kept her gaze locked on the churning surface of the water. Sebastien and Mercado had ducked under when the muskets had spat lead into the waves around them, and for longer than Rose thought they could hold their breath, they remained swimming under the water. Eventually, the two heads broke to the surface again, arms straining to widen the distance from the frigates.

AN HOUR LATER, when the longboats and crews were back on board the *Black Wind*, Fonteyne wasted no time in ordering the ship to get under way. While the great black beast shook out her dark sails, Sebastien and Rose stood on the quarterdeck, glasses pressed to their eyes, focussed on the distant glare of fires.

"What were you thinking going after the second ship?" Rose asked, her anger still high, having had little opportunity to confront him until now.

"I wasn't thinking, I was just doing. And it seemed a good idea at the time."

"There were soldiers shooting at you! You could have been killed."

He lowered the glass and looked at her. "A famous Roman general said: Death smiles at us all; all a man can do is smile back."

"I don't feel much like smiling. I feel like scratching your eyes out."

"Whereas I feel like taking you below and celebrating our little triumph properly."

"You barely had enough energy to climb on board the long-boat when we collected you."

He bent his head, lowering his mouth to within a breath of hers. "I assure you, Captain, I am so far from being exhausted at the moment that I may not be able to wait until we reach my cabin."

"Ah, Jaysus," Stubb said, coming up behind them. "Do the pair o' ye think about aught else?"

Rose sighed and glared at her navigator. "Indeed, I still think about tossing you overboard. A lot."

"Mout be a blessin'," he muttered as he kept walking past. "Wouldn't 'ave to listen to the pair o' ye actin' like cats in heat."

28

"**S**hip off the larboard beam!"

The day was eye-piercingly bright. The sun had washed the sky to a pale blue and the sea to a gleaming mass of silvery waves.

The *Black Wind* was a long pistol shot ahead of the *Cygnet*, too far for a hail to carry back across the open water but Fonteyne ran a warning flag up the mast. Rose, who had spent the last three days on board the *Wind*, joined him on deck. They had been enjoying their last few hours together before the ships parted company and Rose set a course for New Orleans.

Within the hour, they easily identified the silhouette of the *Pride*. But she was coming toward them, not sailing away in the direction of Barataria Bay.

"What on earth do you suppose that means?" Rose asked.

Sebastien shook his head. "I don't know. Either way, I expect I will be having my cabin to myself again."

Rose arched an eyebrow and smiled. "You could have had it back any time you wanted."

"Which should tell you something," he murmured, lowering the spyglass to look at her.

Rose felt her belly shiver and do a little flip as it did every damned time he looked at her that way. They had spent most of the last three days in his cabin and her belly had been doing a great deal of shivering and flipping.

One of the lookouts came swinging down from the shrouds and reported to Sebastien. "It's Reed, Captain. He's signalling to come aboard."

"Has he run up the proper flags?" Fonteyne asked.

"Aye, Captain. He's showed the right response to the code."

"Very well. Slow us down and hail the *Cygnet* to come alongside."

TWO HOURS LATER, Billy Burr, Stubb, and Duardo had joined them on the deck of the *Black Wind* and waited at the open gangway as Reed came on board.

"We've been tacking back and forth for the past few hours hoping to cross your path."

"We thought you would have been in Barataria Bay by now," Fonteyne said. "Was your arrival not a welcomed one?"

"We never made it that far. We were stopped by another ship before we came close."

"You were attacked?"

"No, Captain. We were stopped by Captain Sheridan on board the Kingfisher."

"Why the devil did he stop you?"

Reed blew out a breath. "He stopped us from going forward to Barataria Bay, because Barataria Bay is not there anymore. It was attacked and destroyed. Many ships were lost and many were captured. The *Kingfisher* was damaged in the fighting, but she managed to get away. Captain Sheridan also said that many ships had already left the Bay on Lafitte's orders, as though he was expecting troubles."

"Where is he now? Where is Lafitte?"

Reed shook his head. "Sheridan said he fled into the swamp."

"But the British fleet is days behind us," Rose said, frowning. "And they were headed for Pensacola."

Reed snatched the cap off his head and twisted the wool in his hands. "It wasn't the British who attacked Barataria. It was the Americans."

LONG BEFORE GRANDE Isle came into view, they could see the smudge of gray smoke hanging over the island like a low-lying cloud. There was wreckage floating in the water as far as a mile out and, when they entered the channel leading into the bay, the water was full of sharks circling, searching for their next feast.

The *Black Wind* led the way through the channel, followed by the *Pride*, the *Cygnet*, and the *Kingfisher*. The crews of all four ships were so horrified at the sight of all the sharks that they sought and won permission to fire down at them. With fresh blood in the water, the feeding frenzy remained outside the bay, although there was a greater horror waiting for them when the former thriving stronghold came into view.

Chimneys of black smoke rose from the charred ruins of the scores of buildings and warehouses Lafitte had painstaking built over the past two decades. The skeletal remains of wooden structures had collapsed into smoldering heaps. The wharfs were destroyed. The enormous tent city was gone. Wreckage from several ships had washed ashore and a pair of burned-out hulls lay beached, canted onto their sides. A dozen other sets of masts and yards jutted above the surface of the inky water, the sails hanging in scorched shreds above the sunken hulls.

At first, there had been no sign of life amongst the ruins.

But slowly, as the *Black Wind* was recognized and identified, figures began to emerge from the treeline. A half hearted cheer even echoed across the bay when all four ships had sailed into view. Men ran down to the edge of the water, waving their hats in greeting. Many of them wore filthy, blood-stained bandages.

"Good God," Penman said.

Fonteyne shook his head with quiet anger. "I suspect God was not good on this occasion."

"I will gather up what medicaments and supplies I have on hand."

"Whatever you need. What we don't have, we'll find." He turned to Reed, who had reclaimed his post at the helm of the *Black Wind*. "Drop the anchor, lower away the longboats. Ferry over what food and supplies we have."

"Aye Captain!"

Sebastien's steely blue gaze settled on yet another horror. What had looked like a heap of logs stacked on shore was, in fact, bodies. The crew had seen them too and the silence that had fallen over the ship was so complete they could hear the rustle of the flags and pennons overhead.

WHILE THE CREWS were loading supplies into the longboats, Fonteyne rowed himself and Rose ashore in a jolly boat. He did not wait for the bow to push up onto the sand, he jumped out in knee deep water and splashed onto the shale. A small grouping of men had gathered to meet him; most of the faces were familiar, all wore grim expressions.

"Not a very fine welcome back for you, Captain," one of them said. "But for our part, we're glad to see you, sir. Ye're a bloody welcome sight."

"My men are bringing over fresh food and the doctor should be on board the first longboat."

Hungry eyes looked out into the bay where the ships were lowering nets and baskets of food into the boats. "Don't suppose ye have a barrel o' rum to spare? Bloody bastards carried off every cask they could find."

"Pretty damned certain that would be one of the first things the men loaded." Sebastien looked around. "How long ago was the attack?"

"Six days, mebbe seven, hard to tell. Didn't get no warning. Ships opened fire before they was even through the channel. Come at us from both sides to cut off escape like they know'd how best to trap us. Blasted an' just kept blastin'. Ten or more gunboats. Dunno. Didn't wait around to count proper."

As they crunched their way across the shale, Rose was thankful for the gloom, for she could feel the blood drain from her face. In her mind's eye she could see the note she had shared with her father. The note Ramsey had penned detailing exactly how to make a two-pronged attack on Barataria Bay to catch them unawares. But that note had been found in a courier pouch intended for the British, not the Americans.

It was a piece that did not fit the puzzle.

Behind them came the *shoosh* and bump as several more longboats reached the shore and bit into the sand.

"Lafitte?" Fonteyne asked the sailor, drawing his startled gaze back. "Where is Lafitte? Is he alive?"

"Lafitte is here!" a voice boomed out from behind the ruins of a shed.

Jean Lafitte, as covered in filth as the rest of the men on the beach, limped forward, his right ankle heavily bandaged, a forked stick making do as a crutch.

"I am alive, my fine friend, and confess to having sprung a tear in my eye when I saw your ship."

"What the devil happened here?"

"What happened here was treachery! Pure treachery!"

Fonteyne's jaw hardened into a ridge. "Your men said they were American gunboats. Why the devil would the Americans attack Barataria?"

"The same question I asked myself, and the reason, when we saw the ships approaching, we let them into the bay unchallenged. Once inside—" he threw a hand up in frustration and anger— "there was little we could do. It was Claiborne, of course.

The arrogant fat bastard sent them in the hope, I'm sure, of destroying our base before Jackson arrived to take all the glory. I suspect his spies told him the British had approached me with an offer to join them and the swine convinced the council that I would accept it." Lafitte took the weight off his ankle and lowered himself gingerly onto an outcrop of rock. His dark eyes flicked to Rose. "What is she doing here? And why is she not in irons!"

"Captain St. Clare is here under my bond. Well-earned, I might add. And hardly what should be concerning you right now."

"This," Lafitte scowled, waving an arm wide. "This all concerns me, 'Bastien. Perhaps if you had been here instead of chasing this little thief around the Gulf—"

"My ship might well have ended up at the bottom of the bay along with the others," Fonteyne cut him off sharply. "You said Claiborne wanted to attack *before* General Jackson arrived in New Orleans. Does that mean he is here? Has he brought an army?"

Lafitte leaned over and spat into the sand. "Aye, the great general is here. Though I would not call a thousand Kentucky woodsmen and squirrel-hunters an army. He has put out a call for farmers and townspeople to join his militia. Faugh! Most of the bankers and shopkeepers have never even held a musket, let alone shot one." He paused and squinted up at Fonteyne. "We hear rumours of an English fleet arriving any day. If they were here now, they could sail straight up the Mississippi and capture New Orleans without firing a shot!

"It is not a rumor," Sebastien said. "We have seen it. Ten ships ... nine now, hopefully ... filled with seasoned troops from the Continent."

"*Merde!* Well, my friend, it appears we will have to find a new home." Lafitte scanned the smoking ruins. "Look at what they have done to us."

"You just said this was Claiborne's doing?" Rose said. "Perhaps he did it without General Jackson's knowledge to make himself seem loyal to the American cause."

The black eyes drilled into her. "And if the British capture New Orleans, he will speak out the other side of his mouth and flavor this attack in such a way as to say he did it to support the Crown. In either case, what would you have me do now?"

"I would expect you to fight to keep your home," Rose said.

"My home? I have appealed to Madison, to Jackson, to anyone who would listen because I would like to make it my home!" Lafitte was practically shouting and the veins in his neck were bulging. "To do so, I was willing to give my support to the defense of New Orleans!"

"Are you still willing?" She asked calmly.

"Willing? *Willing*? Willing to do what?"

"If I can arrange a face to face parlay between you and General Jackson, would you still be willing to support him?"

Lafitte scoffed and looked to Fonteyne. "Is she mad? Have you brought a madwoman back with you? Is this *puta* seriously suggesting she can arrange a meeting with General Andrew Jackson?"

Fonteyne cast a curious glance at Rose. "I have come to

believe she is quite serious when she says she can do something."

Lafitte looked from one to the other and threw his hands up in a gesture of disdain. "*Sacre bleu!* You are both mad."

Rose ignored him and turned to the men on the beach. Duardo was among them and when he saw her raised her hand, he came forward.

"I need you to take a message to Uncle Andrew. I don't want to risk exposing the *Cygnet* to any patrolling gunboats, so you'll have to find your way through the bayou to New Orleans. Tell him I am here with Lafitte and he is willing to meet. If my uncle agrees, we can arrange the meeting somewhere on neutral ground between here and the city." She turned and arched an eyebrow in Lafitte's direction. "Would you be agreeable to that?"

Lafitte was too stunned to do more than stare.

"I will take that as a yes," she said, then turned back to Duardo. "Have one of Lafitte's men guide you through the bayou."

Duardo nodded. "What if the general will not come?"

"You have your darts, do you not?"

He grinned, touched his brow and hastened away. When Rose looked back, Lafitte and Fonteyne were both staring at her now.

"*Uncle* Andrew?" Fonteyne asked after a full minute.

"Long story," she said with a dismissive sigh. "But I have known him most of my life. He and my father are close friends as well as allies in this war. Had the king of pirates given me the opportunity to mention this when I came to him a month ago, we could have avoided a good many misunderstandings and saved a good deal of time."

Lafitte waved a hand furiously to encompass his destroyed stronghold. "How can you expect me to lend support to the

Americans when they have done this to me? How do I know it wasn't Jackson who ordered the attack?"

"You said the attack was on Claiborne's orders. Then it happened before Jackson even arrived in New Orleans."

"They fly the same flag! How can I be certain Jackson will even want my help?"

"Because he is not a fool and only a fool would refuse it," Rose said calmly. "Most of the Continental Army is in the north fighting to reclaim Washington. And while the men who follow Jackson are loyal to a fault, neither he nor they know the swamps and bayous that surround New Orleans. They would not know *how* to defend it if the British send their fleet of warships straight up the Mississippi, whereas I'm guessing you would."

Lafitte snorted. "A fleet of warships would not make it over the shallow waters of the delta. Any vessel with a draught of more than eight feet would become bogged in the mud."

"There, you see? I doubt the general would know that."

Lafitte scowled. He pushed himself to his feet and limped a distance away then limped back, leaning heavily on the forked stick. He was muttering under his breath in Cajun, clearly not convinced or comfortable with the direction the conversation had taken.

Fonteyne patted a pocket for his tobacco pouch. "The British could ferry their soldiers through the bayou and land them on the Menteur Road. It leads straight up into the city."

"A dolt with a hundred men could block that road," Lafitte tossed over his shoulder as he paced. "The British would be forced into the swamps where the fevers and flux would get them if the snakes and alligators did not."

Rose frowned. "General Jackson was not well when I saw him on my last blockade run through to Charleston. He suffers from dysentery and has aged a decade in the past few months.

Yet Madison sends him from one end of the country to the other without rest, knowing he is the only truly capable general he has. And Jackson goes because that is who he is and because he loves this country and will give it his last breath if it is asked of him. Which I fear might happen if he fails to defend the city and the British break through."

Lafitte stopped to look her straight in the eye. "You are very good at wheedling and cajoling, little Rosie of the red hair. Are these the same guiles you used to convince my best and most cynical captain you were honest and trustworthy? Surely the simple act of opening your thighs to him was not the only trick you used?"

Fonteyne tossed his tobacco pouch aside and in two long strides had Lafitte's shirt collar bunched into a fist and had lifted the shorter man onto his tiptoes. Lafitte gasped as the air was cut off. His eyes bulged and his hands flailed against the iron-hard tension in Sebastien's arm. Two of his men stepped forward to come to his aid, but Rose brushed the edges of her coat aside and drew her pistols, quickly discouraging the pair from interfering.

Fonteyne brought his face close enough to Lafitte's that his spittle landed on the crimson cheeks. "She convinced me she was honest and trustworthy by *being* honest and trustworthy. Which is more than I can say for most of the bastards you rely on to speak the truth."

He released Lafitte with a jerk of his hand, nearly sending the coughing, choking pirate king onto his ass in the sand.

"We brought your damned ship back to you," Fonteyne added through a scowl. "If you decide to tuck tail and run for Galveston, you'll have to rename her *Poltroon*." He turned to Rose. "Come along, we're obviously wasting our time and breath here."

His footsteps crunched angrily over the sand but before he could disappear into the gloom, Lafitte shouted after him.

"Wait! *Wait*, you insufferable *bâtard!*"

Fonteyne paused, turned, and put his hands on his hips.

Lafitte straightened his collar and coat front. He muttered a few more oaths then nodded his head curtly in Rose's direction. "You must surely understand that all of this ..." he waved a hand again to encompass the smoldering ruins, "has been almost too much to bear. And so far I have heard nothing from General Jackson that would persuade me he would even be of a mind to seek my help *despite* my infinite knowledge of the city and surrounding terrain. Having said that, I cannot speak for the willingness of my men to fight for the Americans. But—" he paused and frowned, then scowled and moved his tongue from one side of his cheek to the other. "*But*, if you can arrange this meeting, I will listen to what he has to say."

Fonteyne looked at Rose. "Fair enough?"

Rose uncocked her pistols and slid them back into her belt. "I suppose it will have to be."

"YOUR RELATIONSHIP to General Jackson was a rather crucial piece of information you neglected to share," Fonteyne said as they walked back along the shoreline.

There were fires lit around the bay, the orange pyres surrounded by shadowy figures cooking, eating, drinking. Longboats continued to travel to and from the ships and Rose's gaze tracked them as they cut through the silvery streaks on the surface of the water.

"I didn't mention it sooner because I wasn't entirely certain I could trust you," she said honestly. "Not completely."

"I see." Then, after a pause, "Dare I ask what moment turned the tide in my favour?"

She smiled slightly. "The moment you told me you liked the way I laughed."

"Ah. Perhaps I should have told you that sooner."

She sighed and stopped to warm her hands before one of the bonfires. "I doubt it would have made a difference. I have never given my trust easily. A flaw in my otherwise predictable and completely guileless character, I suppose. Though I should think you, of all people, would know how difficult it is for a woman to gain the trust and respect of a ship full of men whose first thoughts are usually 'aye, she'd be a fine cunny to take to bed'? And how much trust and respect she loses when she does take a man into her bed? I could not afford to look soft or vulnerable or, God forbid, weak. I could not afford to give the smallest appearance of letting a man take control of my ship … or of me. I have fought too hard and long to be where I am right here, right now."

"I have seen the scars on your body and I know exactly how hard you have fought. But sometimes that fight can be shared. On equal terms. The devil knows I've never said that to a woman before, nor have I ever met a woman —" he hesitated as if tasting the words on his tongue before saying them— "that I would feel proud to say it to."

Rose felt something hot and stinging welling in her eyes but refused to believe it was tears. She hadn't shed a tear since that morning five years ago when she woke up alone in her bed and assumed Fonteyne had taken what he wanted and left without a word.

"Look at me," he commanded quietly.

She blinked away the threat of wetness, then slowly turned.

His eyes were waiting, staring into hers with a gentle fierceness that took her breath away.

"I'm not sure what else I can say or do to make you believe that I don't want to control you. I don't want you to feel obliged or obligated to accept without argument a word I say or an order I give. And I absolutely do not want to change single thing about you. I want you just the way you are: obstinate, prickly-tempered, and stubborn enough to drive a sane man quite mad. All I ask is that you share whatever small part of yourself you are willing to give me."

Rose stared up at him for another long moment. His jaw was as rigid as granite, his gaze burning with intensity that suggested a wrong word or a refusal would crush him.

"I am neither obstinate or stubborn," she whispered. "I merely make a decision and stand by it."

Some of the tension in his jaw eased. "I left out argumentative and annoying as hell at times."

She slid her hands slowly up his chest to his shoulders. "Said the pan to the kettle."

"Suggesting the perfect match," he said, lowering his mouth to within a breath of hers. "As Dulcinea was to Quixote."

"Good Lord, please don't tell me you've read Cervantes."

His arms went around her waist and he drew her close against his body. "Do I not espouse the errant knight?"

"The errant pirate, perhaps."

A heartbeat before his mouth covered hers, he murmured, "I'll settle for that. For now."

29

———

It took two days for Duardo and Stubb to locate General Jackson, another full day to gain an audience. During that same time word was carried on the wind that the British fleet had arrived in Pensacola where Major General Sir Edward Pakenham had assumed command of the infantry. Part of the fleet was promptly sent to Lake Borgne, one of three potential points to launch the invasion of Louisiana. They found access to the lake was blocked by the same gunboats that had so recently and successfully destroyed Barataria Bay. This time, however, the Americans were soundly defeated by the superior firepower of the British frigates.

Hearing of the loss of ships along with their captured crews —manpower he could scarcely afford to lose— Jackson grudgingly agreed to the proposed parlay with Jean Lafitte.

THE CLAMMY AIR was thick with fog. The crescent moon was somewhere above the canopy of cypress trees, all but invisible, and below it, the swamp was alive with the sound of frogs, the hissing of insects, the occasional splash of unseen creatures.

Perpetually damp earth was covered in a tangle of waterlogged roots and rotted vegetation that tainted the air with a pungent, sour smell.

A clearing in the bayou midway between New Orleans and Barataria had been chosen as the meeting place. Lafitte's men arrived first and set up a broad semi-circle of muted lanterns. The fog reduced the light to a brownish-yellow glow that barely served to break the menacing darkness that surrounded the small clearing. It was as eerie as a nightmare and, having lost all sense of direction in the bayou, Rose imagined Lafitte and his men could douse the lanterns and disappear into the fog, leaving her to wander forever in the swamps. To that end, she was thankful for Fonteyne's presence, hoping he, at least, might know the way back to the beach.

Jean Lafitte stood at the edge of a murky bank, his breath forming clouds in the chilly air. After straightening his waistcoat and adjusting the collar of his coat for the tenth time, he shook his head and scowled. "He is not coming. I knew this was a mistake. He is not coming."

"We only just arrived ourselves," Fonteyne said. "Give the man a chance. He's probably never ventured into the bayou before."

"I know how he feels," Rose muttered, slapping at a mosquito. "Each one of my boots has an extra ten pounds of mud and slime clinging to them."

"Someone is coming," Billy whispered. She melted back into the gloom, a pistol in each hand. At a nod from Lafitte, three of his men went with her, leaving four of Fonteyne's men standing in the ring of lanterns.

In a moment, Stubb's distinguishable voice could be heard through the mist cursing at the incessant clouds of insects. Moments later he appeared wearing enough wrappings of rags and clothing it would have acted as a barricade to bullets, let alone insects. Striding out behind him was Duardo, bare-chested but for his leather cross-belts, and two of Lafitte's guides.

"Ee's not human," Stubb protested, tossing a thumb over his shoulder at his nemesis. "Nary a single bite, nary a single sting, whereas I be itchin' worse than if'n a thousand fleas were nestin' in my crotch hairs!"

Any answer that might have been forthcoming was belayed as General Andrew Jackson emerged from the darkness behind them. He was a tall man, rake-thin, with a bush of graying hair over a face that was hard and uncompromising.

As he stepped into the circle of light, he gave his boots a final stamp to dislodge the mud. He wore a long black cloak with caped shoulders and a plain peaked bicorn hat. Other than a single row of brass buttons glinting from beneath the cloak, there was no gold braid or identifying insignia showing.

Piercing blue eyes scanned the small gathering of men to touch briefly on Rose before returning to the figure on the embankment and settling there.

"Jean Lafitte, the pirate king of Barataria, I presume?"

"I have been called worse."

Jackson nodded and scanned the foggy clearing again. "Quite the meeting place, you chose. I haven't been this cold or wet since Valley Forge."

"Unfortunately, I am not welcome in New Orleans, thanks to your ally, Governor Claiborne."

Jackson snorted a puff of mist into the air. "Claiborne has tucked tail and run north. As have most of his brave town council."

"My spies tell me you have already suffered your first defeat at Lake Borgne," Lafitte said.

"We could compare defeats, if you like," Jackson countered.

"But I have not come out here to exchange pleasantries with a pirate."

Lafitte stiffened when he saw the fog swirl aside to allow half a dozen armed militiamen to enter the ring of light and form up behind Jackson.

Rose quickly crossed in front of him and approached Jackson with her hands held out in greeting. Smiling, he grasped them and raised one to press against his lips. "Little Rosamund. I suppose it should not surprise me that you manage to find yourself in the thick of things. I could scarcely believe my eyes when I saw Duardo and the dwarf."

Stubb made an unintelligible squawking sound through the layers of a scarf covering his mouth, but he was ignored.

"They tell me you were the one who arranged this somewhat unorthodox meeting."

She shook her head. "I merely offered whatever small influence I might have to bring two stubborn heads together in order that they might help each other."

"What makes you think I need the help of a smuggler and his band of cutthroat pirates?"

"Because there are fifteen thousand soldiers fresh off the battlefields of France planning how to attack and capture New Orleans. And because Lafitte and his smugglers know the swamps and back channels in and out of the city better than anyone."

Jackson kept hold of Rose's hands as he looked past her shoulder at Lafitte. "I understand the British made you a handsome offer in gold. How do I know you will not sell us out or, like Claiborne, run if the tide looks to turn against us?"

Lafitte's mouth twitched. "I have enough gold, General. What I do not have, and what my men do not have is a country that does not threatens us with a hangman's noose at every turn. As it happens, the British offered me a pardon as well, an offer I trusted as long as it would take a flame to burn the paper it was written on." He took a step forward, his breath supplementing the fog that swirled between the two men. "I make no claim to be a patriot, General. Nor do my men. They will not fight for flags or politics, but they will fight for what is theirs and New Orleans belongs to them as much as it belongs to you. We do indeed know these swamps and bayous. We know the strengths and we know the weaknesses. The British will march right through your lines unless you know how and where to stop them."

"And you do?"

"Smuggling has its merits, General, but it is only part of the game. Ambush, misdirection ... that is how you win when you are badly outnumbered. That and not doing the enemy any favors by wearing bright red tunics and marching in straight lines across an open field with drums and bagpipes screeching your intentions."

"My Kentucky woodsmen are quite adept at ambushes, Lafitte."

"Look around you, General. Do you see thick, dry forests of oaks and evergreens? Here you must know how to take advantage of the swamps and inhospitable approaches to the city. For instance, I'm sure you are aware that mouth of the Mississippi cannot take ships with more than an eight-foot draught, and the narrow switchbacks and rapids in the river rule out most vessels apart from flat bottomed barques. The British have perhaps five or six of these, hardly enough to pose a threat that a hundred men placed along the riverbank could not destroy. Another possible avenue of attack is a direct march up the canal road, but there too, they would encounter resistance at Fort St. Philip. The only other option is to approach New Orleans overland from the south. The problem there lies in the fact they have to cross a lake that is thirty miles wide, then traverse two large bayous before they find enough solid ground to support their cannon ... assuming they can ferry cannon across the lake and push them through knee-deep mud.

"Further to this third option, my spies tell me the British general has already begun commandeering longboats and flat-bottomed barges."

Jackson's face was as unreadable as stone while he listened to Lafitte. After a full minute of not moving so much as a muscle, his gaze shifted to Rose, and then to Fonteyne, where it remained as if he was seeing the tall, black-clad privateer for the first time. "You concur with this remarkable assessment?"

"I do," said Fonteyne. "Moreover, his spies could probably tell you exactly how many men you have in your camp, the extent of your armory, and what you ate for dinner tonight."

Jackson absorbed this, then drew a slow deep breath before looking at Lafitte again. "You say you do not want gold, but in return for joining forces with us, what do you want?"

Lafitte, despite being a head shorter than the general, imagined himself an equal at that moment and drew himself up to his full height. "Full pardons for myself and my men. After it is done and we have won, we walk away free men, free to live where we choose without threat of persecution or arrest."

The two men stared at one another in silence, each gauging the other as to whether that rarest of all commodities ... trust ... was present.

Jackson put voice to his main concern. "Surely you must harbor some resentment after what the American gunboats did to your encampment?"

"I harbour a great deal of resentment," Lafitte agreed through the grate of his teeth. "And to that end I will settle accounts with Claiborne at some point. But for now, I am more concerned with keeping the British off my land and out of my country."

Jackson studied the shorter man in silence. Lafitte had made good points; the men in his militia were brave and would make a good accounting of themselves, but they were woefully outnumbered and no match for disciplined, battle-tested soldiers in open combat in territory as foreign to them as to the British. They were woodsmen and hunters, not swamp-dwellers.

As much as it galled him to do so, Jackson was the first to move. He took one measured step forward and held out his hand. "We have a deal, sir."

Lafitte accepted the gesture, matching the general's firm, solid grip with his own.

Before releasing him, Jackson leaned in and murmured, "But if you betray us, I will put the rope around your neck myself and hang you."

Lafitte grinned. "You would have to catch me first, General."

THE TREK back to Barataria Bay was decidedly more energized than the slow slog into the bayou. Lafitte was pleased with himself. Fonteyne was cautiously optimistic—they still had to convince Lafitte's captains and their men to aid the Americans. Rose was relieved the meeting had gone well, but wary. She knew Jackson's handshake was his bond, ironclad and unbreakable. But Lafitte?

The two had agreed to meet again in a week's time. By then, Lafitte would know how many men he could raise. There were some who would fight for the sake of defending the city against the British. Others would do so for the promise of full pardons. None, however, would consider joining the Americans if they were just there to bulk up Jackson's army without being recognized as a formidable fighting force in their own right, something Lafitte himself would not allow.

Upon arrival back at the Bay, Lafitte immediately pulled out maps of the city and the surrounding swamps, waterways, and farmland.

"New Orleans has very few defenses against an army of fifteen thousand infantry," he said, brushing a hand across one of his maps. "You may be certain the British will have the same maps and be aware of the same obvious obstacles to an attack. Since the building of Fort St. Philip, the city relies on its ability to control access to the river. In addition to the fort, here are stone emplacements constructed down each of the riverbanks where the bend is narrow and sharp. A hundred good men, with one or two heavy guns could, indeed, stop any attempt to get around that turn in the river.

"Over here—" his finger slid across the map— "to the north there are cypress swamps that only a madman would dare plan to march through. Impossible and impassable, not to mention the thousands of alligators who would chew those redcoats up like sweet treats. But here—" his finger slid down and circled a wide expanse of farmland— "there are two plantations, Lacoste and Villere, both left flat and dry since their crops were harvested. The British will always prefer dry land so they can march forward in their pretty red lines ... regardless if the swamps give them more protection and a more direct route to the city. A betting man, therefore, would place his gold piece here." He took a coin out of his pocket and placed it on the Villere plot of farmland. "It will support their artillery and allow the soldiers to march without having their boots sucked off in the mud."

"There is the small matter of the lake standing in the way," Fonteyne said. "As you said, that's a fairly huge undertaking to move an army across."

"Think like an English peacock. They have moved armies and dragged artillery across half the Continent of Europe. A lake would be a minor obstacle. And look here ... once across, they will see, and their spies will tell them, that there is only open field and beyond that, nothing but a puny fieldstone wall extending from the levy barely a quarter mile long. The owner of the plantation had his slaves build it a decade ago to keep his cows from wandering into the city, but he hasn't had cows for several years, so the earthworks are eroded and missing altogether in places.

"My men use those gaps to smuggle goods into the city while the excise men are busy watching the river. Those gaps will need to be filled and the rampart raised and, more importantly, extended a good mile or more to cover the full breadth of the field to where it ends in the swamp. Once fortified, we can put enough men up top to give the British a warm welcome ... if they make it that far."

Fonteyne arched an eyebrow. "If they make it that far?"

Lafitte offered up a crooked grin and pointed to another location on the map. "The levy runs parallel to the Chef Menteur Road and holds the river back to prevent flooding. Blowing a hole in the levy here," he tapped the map, "will bring the river rushing onto the lowland and turn half the farmer's field into a bog that will suck the boots right off their feet. I believe the phrase, 'Bastien, is ducks in a pond?"

Rose had been standing by, quietly observing, but she stepped forward now and looked down at the map. Lafitte and his men had been operating their smuggling enterprise for well over a decade, so it was no surprise that he should know where the city's weakest points lay. No surprise they could move like shadows in the darkness.

"Uncle ... er, General Jackson was sent here with barely a thousand men under his command. Even if you can bring a thousand more, the odds are still overwhelming. How did the

President think so few could hold a city against five times as many British soldiers?"

Lafitte's lip curled in disdain. "I expect Madison thought the general would put up a good fight and stall the bastards long enough to fortify a defense higher up the Mississippi. It is December. The north will be frozen and the British will wait for spring to mount another offensive. By then, Madison might stir his arse enough to send more men south. Until then, Jackson is on his own with only swamps and alligators as a deterrent."

Fonteyne tapped a finger on the map. "Supposing we are able to build up and reinforce these ramparts and supposing we are able to put two thousand men on top, the British will have artillery."

"Jackson dragged exactly five field pieces with him," Lafitte said. "About as useful as spitting in a bucket. We can take heavy guns from the ships and place them every ten feet or so on the ramparts as soon as they are fortified. We have enough powder and shot to give the redcoats a greeting they will not soon forget. We can also place one of our ships here—" he took another coin out of his pocket and placed it at the eastern edge of the farmer's field then looked at Rose. "Preferably a sleek little vessel with a low draught. We can use her cannon to blow the levy as well as bombard the field and cut them off from any attempt to reach the road."

Rose nodded. "If you think the *Cygnet* can make it up the river."

"Now hold on a minute," Fonteyne started, but Lafitte cut him off.

"Your ship has a hundred tons on the little swan, 'Bastien, most of it due to your flamboyant excess of guns; it would never make it past the delta. I happen to know you have tried and become miserably stuck in the sandbars."

"I can remove some of the guns for the ramparts."

"Indeed. And can you shave ten feet off the keel? You have twice as much ship below the waterline as you have above."

Rose almost smiled at the look of consternation on Sebastien's face. Not for the first time she gave thanks for the designers and shipbuilders in her father's company. Their ingenuity and skills dated back more than a century to the original fleet built by the Pirate Wolf himself.

"Without a formidable deterrent on the river," Lafitte was saying, "the British could easily veer off the fields and make for the road, and from there have a clear path into the city while we stick our hands down our trousers and wait for nothing to happen. It will be crucial to have accurate and fearsome firepower on our right flank."

"I agree," Rose said, cutting off another protest from Fonteyne. "However, I do not agree that you should be deciding all of this without General Jackson's input or approval."

Lafitte's frown crushed his eyebrows together in a straight line. "You saw what I saw tonight. A man whose strength is all but drained. His skin is gray, his hands shake, and he stinks of fever and squirting bowels. He needs rest, he needs food, and he needs to accept help where it is offered. While he recovers, *if* he recovers, we must gather every able-bodied man willing to start building and reinforcing that barrier, sooner rather than later. I will speak to our men at first light, but now, I need sleep. I've not closed my eyes for so long I feel like an owl."

Fonteyne saw the look on Rose's face and took a firm hold on her elbow, leading her away before the vein in her neck exploded.

"Did you hear that puffed up little snake?" she hissed. "*If* the general recovers?"

"Come away, come away. We are all of us tired and on edge. And he wasn't entirely wrong. You said yourself Jackson has been suffering from dysentery for several weeks now."

"Suffering, yes, on his deathbed, no. I know my uncle. He'll not take kindly to sharing authority when it comes to preparing for battle, and while he is canny enough to see the benefit of having Lafitte's help, he's not about to entrust the fate of his army to a thieving little blacksmith."

Fonteyne tightened his grip on her arm. "That thieving little blacksmith, my dear, might be the only thing standing between having the Stars and Stripes flying over Washington or the Union Jack."

30

"**I** don't like it."

Rose tipped her head from one side to the other in an attempt to stretch the kinks out of her neck. "What, exactly, don't you like?"

She felt his fingertips dragging lightly across the nape of her neck, moving her hair out of the way so his hands could gently massage the tension in her shoulders.

"You volunteering your ship and crew to blockade the river. I was hoping, now that Jackson had recovered enough to assume command, that he might counter some of Lafitte's wilder suggestions."

"You doubt the ability of my crew to hold the river? Must I remind you—?"

His fingers dug into her shoulder, pinching a nerve to cut off her words. "No, you don't need to remind me how clever you are creeping up on someone in a heavy fog. Or your vaunted skills running the British blockade twice."

"Three times," she muttered.

"This is war and the odds are stacked heavily against us."

"Women are always at war one way or another, and the odds

are always against us succeeding." She pulled away and turned around to face him. "I would, however, dare you to look Billy Burr in the eye and tell her she is not up to the task of blasting a few redcoats to kingdom come."

"I would not presume to tell her that upon risk of finding myself gelded."

"Then why presume it with me? Because we have just spent the night in bed? Because you think that gives you some misguided sense of control over me?"

He spread his hands wide and stepped back. "Fine. Forget I said anything."

"I already have."

They were in the great cabin of the *Cygnet*, having spent the first night in six days together. Fonteyne had been kept busy winching cannon off ships and transporting them through the bayou to the city defenses. Rose had used the *Cygnet* to ferry some of those heavy guns along with casks of powder and scores of muskets and ammunition up the river to New Orleans, and Sebastien had taken advantage of the opportunity to thoroughly and energetically make up for their time apart.

"These constant battles of wit do begin to test a man's sensibilities, however."

"Would you prefer it if I were docile and obedient?"

"It might be a pleasant change."

"You would hate it."

He held her gaze a moment longer then shook his head and turned away.

"I should go. Lafitte's men will be waiting on the wharf."

She bit down gently on the edge of her lip. "Do you know, yet, where the Baratarians will be positioned?"

"Wherever Jackson decides to put them. I doubt one man in twenty from his militia knows how to aim or fire a thirty-two pounder, so I expect we will have our own battalions along the line."

She watched as he took up his guns and sword belt, then snatched his hat off the peg by the door.

"I'll see you at the meeting tonight?"

He shrugged his answer and was gone.

Rose lingered a few more minutes by the gallery windows then took out her frustration in long brush strokes as she tamed and braided her hair. She donned her striped corset vest and laced the front tightly, then pushed her arms into her emerald green frockcoat.

"What did he want me to do?" she muttered. "Sail back to Barataria and darn socks while I wait to hear the outcome? Ships were not built to hide away in port, my dearest Captain Fonteyne. You, of all surly bastards, should know that."

Her hope was that General Jackson would not feel the same way, that he would have the good sense to put her and her ship to good use in whatever strategies they were planning. He had never treated her like a delicate rose and was well aware of her skill at the helm, her victories at sea. The fact her father supported her efforts should be enough to convince the general her guns were primed and ready to fire. Weakness was not an option and she had never flinched from the prospect of going into battle before.

Moreover, he had met Billy Burr and Rose suspected he was more than just a little terrified by her.

Smiling, she strapped her sword belt around her waist and snugged a brace of pistols into a second belt. A final glance at the pitted surface of the mirror assured her that she looked less like a woman whose lover had just left her bed, and more like Rosamund St. Clare, descendant of a long line of Pirate Wolves.

Back up on deck, she stood at the rail with Billy Burr and watched the men swarming around on shore. Fonteyne was in the thick of it, shouting orders, giving directions as the last of the wagons began to roll off the wharf. With clouds of dust boiling in their wake, he mounted a huge black horse and followed the wagons without a backward glance.

Archie Penman was a few cantered steps behind him and when he looked up at the quarterdeck, he gave Billy a little wave.

Instead of waving back, she glanced sidelong at Rose and asked, "Can I take my new toy out now?"

Rose returned the sly smile and nodded.

Together they walked toward the bow where the 'gift' her father had given her at the Nobbins was secreted beneath a thick canvas tarpaulin. Billy called two of the crew over to help unwind the criss-cross of cables. Men close by stopped what they were doing to watch as the canvas was peeled back, and as one, they gave off an enormous gasp.

Crouching beneath the tarp was a cast iron carronade with a two-foot-bore diameter. The walls of the monster gun were twelve inches thick and barrel-shaped; the base was seated in a sturdy wooden cradle. According to her father, it was capable of firing a sixty-pound hollow ball filled with gunpowder and shrapnel a distance of six hundred yards. The accuracy was questionable, since it sat in a fixed position, but the explosive force easily made up for any lack of mobility. Sixty pounds of metal scraps discharged on a battlefield would create terrifying chaos.

"They don't call it a hell cannon for no reason," Billy murmured, almost glassy-eyed with delight. "I pity anyone who marches into her path. They will pay one hell of a butcher's bill."

Staring at the enormous gun, Rose was twelve years old again, watching the men carry her brother ashore, his leg blown off by cannon fire, his body wracked with fever. Word had arrived before the ship that he had been sorely wounded, so mother, father, and daughter had stood side by side on the dock, hands clutched together, hearts beating like wild things. When he was carried ashore on a canvas stretcher, he had caught sight of Rose first and had held out a shaking hand. She had broken free of her parents' grip and run to his side, wetting his fevered face with her tears, sobbing with relief that he was alive. She had relived that moment so many times she could still see it clearly in her mind ... but suddenly, with the next stilted breath, it was not Ramsey's body missing a limb and wrapped in bloody bandages. Not Ramsey's face she saw twisted with pain.

It was Fonteyne's.

31

After studying the maps and riding around the farms, swamps, and bayous surrounding the city of New Orleans, the strategist in Andrew Jackson had reached the same conclusion as Lafitte. There were three possible ways the British could take to mount an attack, and all three were vulnerable, the current defenses woefully inadequate.

"Three routes," Jackson said, studying the map before him. He had set up a temporary headquarters in the city, in offices previously occupied by the absent Governor Claiborne. He had called a meeting with Lafitte and the leader of the militia, Rodney Lamb, who fought with the Kentuckians but had been born and raised in New Orleans. Also present were the captains of the two gunboats currently patrolling the Mississippi, the *Louisiana* and the *Carolina*.

Fonteyne and Rose, along with their second in commands stood quietly around the large table, their faces lit by the twin lanterns that hung over half a dozen maps and charts.

"The first point of attack, and the most obvious, would be for the British to attempt a direct approach up the Mississippi."

"Bloody well impossible for any heavy frigates to make it through the delta," Lamb reiterated. He was an older man with a face like a barnacle, who, like Jackson, had fought in the war for independence. "Won't stop the bastards sending lighter schooners or gunboats as a diversion, to take men away from the main assault. But that's all they'd be. A bloody diversion, mark my words. An' they'd have to get past Fort St. Philip to make any headway up the river."

"Armaments?"

"Twenty-nine long guns, two six pounders and a small mortar, thirteen-inch calibre. Also, a couple of thirty-twos mounted on shore, fairly well concealed behind a stone wall. The fort won't be easy to get past."

He marked the location of the shore guns by leaning over and putting an X on the chart with a stick of charcoal.

"The second point of possible attack," Jackson said as he dragged his finger across the map, "is by way of the Chef Menteur Road. That route would enable them to bring some of their lighter ships through the Rigolets passage into Lake Pontchartrain. Once there, they would be able to land their army a scant two miles from the city, but in order to get through the Rigolets, they would have to pass the fort at Petit Coquilles. I'm told it is neither a large nor imposing fort."

"Not worth the bricks it were built with as I recollect," Lamb declared, "but it stands where the river takes a sharp bend and I reckon some men with a few cannons might bottle them up for a goodly time. But it won't hold 'em, which is why, if I were the one making the decisions, that's where I would t'row all my forces."

Jackson frowned, not liking the pessimism, but inwardly agreeing with Lamb's assessment.

He turned his attention to the plantations south of the city. "Am I reading these distances and routes correctly?"

Jean Lafitte answered before Lamb could gather enough spittle. "The maps you have are as accurate as we could make them. However, the British have been given ... somewhat altered maps, obtained when they captured one of my men who was foolishly caught too close to the British encampment."

"How altered?" Fonteyne asked.

Lafitte waved his hand. "A few extra bends in the river, the bayou sketched little larger, roads removed or leading in the wrong direction. Without such discrepancies, the Rigolets canal might well be the clear choice."

General Jackson stared at the pirate for a moment before looking down at the map again. "That leaves the third option, which would involve crossing a lake and cutting through two bayous to the Villere Canal and would bring them to a point several miles south of the city."

"Seven miles to be precise," Lafitte said. "On the map they now have in their possession, however, the distance is marked as four. Moreover, the two largest farms in the area, Villere and Lacosta, would be tempting to an army more comfortable fighting on land than on canals or rivers. It offers flat, open fields to march across, especially since I expect they will be bringing artillery, yes?"

"Field pieces, I should think."

"Heavy and cumbersome." Lafitte smiled and touched a forefinger to the map where the Mississippi curved to follow the canal road, and beside it, the western boundary of the Villere farm. "Here, opposite the Chalmette Plantation, the levee is built closest to the road to prevent the river from overflowing the embankment. As I mentioned before, should it be blown open at an opportune moment, the force of the water as it comes around this bend will burst through the opening and flood the land as far as the cypress swamps a mile to the east. The British would find their temptingly flat fields turned to mud and their artillery pieces mired to the wheel axels. Should that become the apparent choice to mount an assault, I would suggest you place one of our ships on the river at that precise bend. After they blow the levee, they could remain in place to discourage the British from slogging out of the swamp and attempting to come up the canal road to attack your flank."

Jackson nodded, agreeing with everything Lafitte was saying. He looked around the circle of faces until he found the three he sought and waved them forward into the brighter light. The first belonged to Bryant Kelly, the captain of the war sloop, *Carolina*. He was short and stout with sparse bits of hair sprouting over his ears in a fuzzy circle that left the dome bald. Beside him was the captain of the schooner *Louisiana*, William Dollor, who was tall and skeletally thin, with an elongated face like a horse's snout.

The third face Jackson touched on belonged to Rose St. Clare.

"The three of you have met?"

Kelly har-rumphed and scratched his head. "Aye, that we have. Moored side by each in the river as we speak. The *Carolina* will go wherever she is needed."

"Aye," Dollar agreed. "As will the *Louisiana*."

"When the time comes, it will be up to the pair of you to ensure the British do not get past Fort St. Philip."

The two captains looked at each other, nodded, and puffed up their chests a little fuller.

"Rose? I'm going to post you upriver to blow the levee when and if the time comes it needs to be done. From there, you will be able to go downriver, should the *Louisiana* and the *Carolina* need assistance, or, indeed, stay put and defend the road should the English find the field approach too tempting to resist."

"It will be imperative that all three of you hold the river,"

Jackson continued. "If just one British gunboat breaks through, and gets behind us, we could find ourselves caught in an enfilade."

Kelly snorted and gave Rose's arm a little backhanded smack. "I've heard you have experience with blockade lines, lass. You can break through 'em, but can you hold 'em?"

He was at least a head shorter than Rose so she had to tip her head down to look at him. "I can hold them," she said with a smile. "As long as I don't have to ram anyone who gets in my way."

Kelly's eyebrows shot up. He was not entirely convinced that a woman could or should be included in any military actions. Despite having heard the astounding rumours concerning her capture of Sebastien Fonteyne's ship, he still was not completely convinced, although he had no solid grounds to argue.

He was, however, fairly certain the giant, Duardo, whose eyes were glowering at him from the shadows, would crush him like a bug if he voiced any of those doubts.

"Aye, we'll hold the river, General," he muttered. "To the last shot and cask of powder, we'll hold it."

Jackson nodded, gave Rose half a wink to acknowledge her restraint at not boxing Kelly's ears, then looked at Lafitte. "Everything you've said makes sense so far, apart from the fact that in order to reach these fields you've made look so appealing, Generals Keane and Packenham will have to row their entire army, including any artillery, across a lake 30 miles wide, in boats that hold perhaps twenty men each trip. That will take days, weeks!"

"Time we will need," Fonteyne said, "to reinforce the defenses around the city which, at the moment, are non-existent. We can bring cannon ashore from our ships, but we need somewhere to put them."

"Once again, if I may?" Lafitte moved the map a quarter turn and ran his finger along a line marked in broken dashes of ink. "You see this line? It is known to the locals as the Rodriguez Canal, though it is not much more than a dry, shallow ditch and no one remembers who Rodriguez was. There are partial earthworks that run along the northern edge. They rise about four feet and were kept mainly as a property demarcation line for the Chalmette Plantation, which is now adjoined to the Villere land. If the British take the bait and choose to come across those fields, the best ... and possibly only defensive position to take would be along the Rodriguez Canal. Much work would have to be done, of course, to build the wall to a secure height, but as you pointed out, we would have time while the English ferry their men across the lake."

"*If* they decide to come that way." Jackson's craggy face looked even more sunken as he sucked in his cheeks and studied the map to ponder his options. "Today is December sixteen. The British generals will undoubtedly be flush with their victory at Lake Borgne and will want to press their advantage. I am acquainted with the reputations of both men and surmise that Keane will urge haste, whereas Packenham is more experienced and, like me, not one to rush into a situation he does not control and has not thoroughly examined.

"I dislike guesswork, gentlemen. Before I am prepared to commit every resource we have to building up those earthworks, we need to know for a certainty which of the three alternatives they have decided on to launch their main assault. We could build ramparts twenty feet high, but they would be useless if the British attack from the north and our guns were facing south."

"My best scouts are Choctaw Indians," Lafitte said. "They move like wraiths in the darkness and can smell Englishmen ... and Americans ...a hundred paces away. I will send them out tonight to glean what information they can. But as a betting man, General, I would put my coin here." He stabbed the long straight double line of the Rodriguez Canal. "Along with my heaviest guns. When they cross that open field with no cover, nowhere to run? The earth will be red with their blood."

32

The next day, map in hand, Fonteyne walked the length of the Rodriquez Canal with a small group of Lafitte's men and local townspeople. Jean's description of it being not much more than a dry ditch was generous. The shallow basin, once used as an irrigation ditch, was clotted with weeds and brush. The ground was uneven, the banks crumbled. It was little more than a boundary line that marked the northern edge of the Chalmette-Villere Plantation. It was as high as four feet in places, and as low as scattered clods of dirt where it ended a half mile short of the huge cypress swamps to the east. The many vulnerabilities were obvious. With the lack of height, a strong leap could put a man on top of the earthworks. British scouts would undoubtedly pinpoint the weakness where the wall dwindled to flat ground and the army could simply circle around and outflank Jackson's defenses. From there, they would have a clear path into New Orleans.

"We need to build this up," he said to Rodney Lamb. "We need a stout barrier all the way from the canal road to the swamp."

Lamb's mouth gaped. "You're talking near two bloody miles."

"If not more. Which is why we will need a work force of men, women, children ... Lafitte's men, your men, Free Blacks, Indians ... anyone who can hold a shovel because it is going to be a damned huge job. This—" he bent over and picked up a handful of dry dirt, "would never support our guns. We need proper breastworks reinforced with timber and clay, built high enough that when we dig out this ditch they will need fascines and ladders to get to the top of the ramparts."

Beside him, Arthur Penman whistled softly under his breath. "You've discussed this with Jackson?"

"It doesn't take a general to know we need to be above the enemy shooting down and the enemy unable to climb up to us."

"Not quite the same as firing a broadside from a ship."

"Yet not entirely different. We put gun emplacements every ten feet, fix the elevation to cover the open field, then unleash hell to discourage the pretty rows of redcoats when they march forward in their precise formations."

"You sound as though you're looking forward to it."

"In truth, I never look forward to causing bloodshed. But I have no qualms against creating bloody havoc when I have to do so."

He stood and glared at the ditch, the field, the enormity of work that lay ahead, then at the smattering of lights that were twinkling to life along the distant banks of the Mississippi.

Archie followed his gaze and smiled a little. "I thought I detected a bit of a chill in the air earlier today. Are you two quarrelling again?"

"The woman doesn't quarrel. She hisses and spits and scratches."

"She sounds like the perfect match for you."

Fonteyne muttered and started retracing their path along the dry ditch. Aloud, he said, "She's too damned eager to prove to

Jackson she's as good as any man in this fight. And Jackson is too ill and desperate to deny her."

"She did manage to outfox you, which is a daring achievement in itself." Penman reminded him gently. "And she does seem to have won over the little pirate king. At least he hasn't threatened to skin her alive for oh, six hours or so. As for Jackson, he has the constitution of a horse despite the streaks he leaves in his britches. I can get his dysentery under control once he starts eating proper meals again."

Fonteyne walked a few more paces in silence. "I suppose you are pleased and overjoyed that Billy Burr will be in the front line of gunners defending the river access?"

Penman's smile faded. "Not at all. But there is very little I can or, indeed, would do about it. That entire crew has been a fierce fighting team since long before we came along. My suggesting that Billy step back, sit down, and let someone else command her guns would be met with such a depth of disdain I fear I would end up crushed like a roach under her boot. I warrant the same would happen to you if you told Rose she should find a cozy chair and pick up her embroidery needles."

"I reckon he'd get that needle in the eye," Lamb declared with a chuckle.

"Both eyes," Penman said. "So he could be 'sewn' the error of his ways."

Fonteyne turned and glared for a moment as the pair shared a snort of laughter, then shook his head and carried on walking, his stride long enough to eat up the distance and leave the other two fools far behind.

By the time Sebastien returned to the river, having spent an hour with Jackson recounting his findings along the Rodriguez

Canal, it was near midnight. The *Cygnet* was still at anchor, but she was well lit from stem to stern and there was plenty of activity on board.

The *Carolina* had already departed to take up a position downriver with her sister ship, the *Louisiana*.

Billy nodded to Sebastien as he came through the gangway. She was supervising the placement of the largest carronade he had ever seen on land or at sea. It was a monster gun wrapped in a webbing of cables necessary to winch it across the deck, yet Billy was treating it like piece of delicate porcelain directing and maneuvering it into place. Working alongside her, Duardo was stripped to a loincloth, his tattooed muscles gleaming in the lanternlight.

Rose was observing from the quarterdeck. Her shirt was a splash of white against the darkness beyond the rail, and when Fonteyne was finally able to catch her eye, she tipped her head in what he assumed was an invitation to join her.

"I'm almost afraid to ask where you came by that beast," he said when he joined her.

"My father acquired it, goodness only knows where. Billy can hardly wait to test it, whereas I'm hoping the recoil doesn't blow a hole through the deck. That hammering you hear is from the carpenters reinforcing the deck beneath with timber."

"I didn't come to disturb your preparations. I came to ask if you have any men you might be able to spare for a few days; we need them to work on the canal. Most of my crew will be there along with around eight hundred of Lafitte's 'volunteers'."

"I heard the earthworks need a lot of work to rebuild. Billy would skin me if I sent any of her gun crews, but I can spare a score or two from the rest of the crew, so long as I get them back without too many blisters."

He nodded. "Good. Thank you."

She smiled. "Here I thought you were coming to wish me luck."

He looked down at his hands, which had reflexively tightened on the top of the rail. "No. No, I don't expect you rely too heavily on luck."

He felt her eyes boring into him.

"That was almost a compliment, I think," she murmured.

He resisted turning to look at her for ten or so heartbeats. "No need to think too long or too hard on it."

"I fear I must, since it doesn't happen too often."

"My dear Captain St. Clare, I compliment you more than I have ever complimented another human being, man or woman."

Her pale eyes twinkled seeing how uncomfortable such an admission was for him to make.

A moment later, he shook his head and laughed.

"By Christ, you are, by far, the most aggravating, irritating ..." he stopped, took off his hat and threw it on the binnacle then grabbed hold of her wrist and dragged her into the deeper shadows behind the bulkhead. He pressed her up against the boards and pinned her there, kissing her so thoroughly she had to gasp to catch a breath between each fiercely possessive thrust of his tongue. Any resistance she might have tried to feign melted away as she flung her arms up and around his shoulders, holding on for dear life as her knees buckled and her belly slid in shimmering ribbons down to her toes.

When he finally broke the kiss, he kept his mouth a scant hair's breadth from hers. "For what it's worth, I don't like you sitting here so exposed on the river but not because I doubt your ability to hold off the entire British navy if you encountered them. I just don't like you being out of my sight for any length of time."

Her eyes caught little pinpoints of light and sparkled up at him.

"Have you always been so protective of your other women?"

Standing in the shadows, he looked as ominous as the devil himself, but his hands, when they cradled her face between them, were so gentle she could almost swear she felt the slightest of tremors in his grip.

"There hasn't been any other woman who has managed to wheedle her way under my skin and into my blood like a damned fever."

He looked like he wanted to kiss her again, but a familiar squawk drew his hands away as Stubb came up onto the deck.

"Captain? Belly-gun's in place, solid as my arse, an' Billy says we be ready ... whup, ho!" He stopped short as Fonteyne and Rose stepped back into the light. "So that's why ye're not where ye were a blink ago."

"Stubb—"

"Nay, nay," he waved his hands dismissively. "I was sent to tell ye an' I've told ye, so now ye've been told. Not my never mind ye'd rather grope 'n fondle in the shadows like country bumpkins."

Fonteyne looked like he might draw his sword, but in the end, he plucked his hat off the binnacle and snugged it on his head. "I guess I should go. If you can spare me those men?"

Rose nodded. "I will even send Stubb along, if you like. I'm sure he would be more than willing to share his vast expertise on the proper way to dig a ditch and build a wall."

He noted the laughter in her eyes and the smile on the reddened lips he had so recently kissed.

"I would rather eat a bucket of nails."

Rose followed behind as he walked to the ladderway, but did not descend with him to the main deck. She stood at the rail and watched him stride across the deck to the gangway.

There, he paused to exchange a few words with Billy and to take a closer look at the carronade, but then he was gone. Hearing Stubb shout, her attention was drawn back to the men laying the rails that would support the Beast and allow for the firing position to be adjusted without the need for wooden wheels or bracing bars. When she looked ashore again, there was no sign of the tall, devilish figure in black striding into the darkness of the night.

33

I took six days and nights for the British to ferry eighteen hundred soldiers from one side of the lake to the other. The crossings requiring ten hours of rowing each way. The men who landed in the first flight included General Keane, who had been given command until the rest of the army joined them. A detachment of his men established a small camp at the edge of the lake, but the main complement of soldiers marched north to the plantation owned by Gabriel Villere. They quickly commandeered the house and erected neat rows of canvas tents on the land surrounding it. Villere himself was placed under house arrest but managed to squeeze his bulk through an upper storey window and made good his escape. He went immediately to Jackson's headquarters, which had been moved to the McCardy House a stone's throw from the Rodriquez Canal.

~

"ALMOST TWO THOUSAND SOLDIERS ALREADY ASHORE," Jackson said. "With more being ferried across the lake every damned hour. You were right," he said to Lafitte. "They have chosen to fight on dry land. And if their scouts were worth their shillings' pay they will know how ill-prepared we are and will push forward without delay."

Rodney Lamb scratched the top of his head. "Lafitte's Choctaws tell me they have only what weaponry they could carry on the boats. Very little artillery has been ferried across as of yet but more will surely come soon, so mayhap they'll be waitin' on that."

"Waiting for them to increase the number of artillery pieces is not in our best interests," Jackson said. He paused and looked at the three men gathered to hear Villere's report and his hawk-like gaze settled on Fonteyne. "How is the work coming at the Canal?"

"We have every able-bodied soul working on the ramparts day and night, building them up, reinforcing them with bales of cotton, timber, logs, barrels of packed earth, anything solid they can use to add height and strength. It is up to ten feet high and eight feet wide in places, well able to absorb cannon fire and provide cover for our men. But we could certainly use more time."

"Time we may not have," Jackson muttered.

Lafitte shrugged. "Unless we consider—"

"Attacking first," Jackson said, his voice sharp and clear.

Lafitte blinked. He exchanged a hasty glance with Fonteyne. "That was not what I was about to say, General, but—"

"If we attack first, we will have surprise on our side. The English would not expect it, especially not if we mount an assault under cover of darkness. Not very gentlemanly of us, according to the British idea of warfare, but if we delay, we give them time to land more men, more artillery, and our odds of success go incrementally downward. In my experience, however, surprising them, overwhelming them with the first assault, their confidence can be shaken if not shattered completely."

"We also know the lie of the land," he continued, looking at each solemn face as if challenging them to argue. "We know the gulleys, the swamps, and patches of trees that offer cover. If we attack tonight, when they least expect such a bold move, we can cause enough confusion to set them back on their heels."

"Tonight?" Rodney Lamb's bushy gray eyebrows folded in a frown. "We've not even had our bloody noon meal yet."

"Tonight," Jackson said firmly. "Before common sense gets the better of me. When I was a lad of six, barely able to carry a drum, let alone beat out a signal, a wise man told me I should always go with my first instinct, for it is usually the right one. And so far, General Washington's advice has served me well."

"We have your Kentucky frontiersman and we have Lamb's militia, which amounts to about eight hundred," Fonteyne said, not exactly arguing, but wanting to point out possible drawbacks. "We can pull another hundred or so local townsfolk and shopkeepers off the ramparts, a few dozen New Orleans businessmen in frockcoats and beaver hats, as well as a handful of free coloreds, some Indians, and a few hundred Baratarians more comfortable fighting at sea than on land. Hardly what one might call an overwhelming attack force."

"Boldness is in our character, gentlemen," Jackson insisted. "It is how we rebelled and won against the tyranny forty years ago, and by Christ, it is how we will drive it off our shores once and for all." He pointed a long finger at Lafitte, who had remained uncharacteristically quiet through most of the discussion. "Send your Choctaw spies out again. We need to know exactly where they have picket lines, how many sentries they have guarding the camp, and where they have those artillery guns. If we can capture the guns and bring them away with us, all the better."

He leaned over to study the map again, his large hands splayed flat. His focus was on the location of the Villere manor house and surrounding fields in relation to the river. "It would help to have a little chaos to blast open the night. I heard a rumor that my niece had a beast of a gun on board the *Cygnet* capable of firing a sixty-pound ball full of explosives and shrapnel. How far would such a shot carry?"

Fonteyne glanced over and hesitated long enough for Lafitte to offer his estimate. "I only just heard of this weapon myself and have not seen it, thus I can only make a fair guess at its capabilities. But with the proper elevation I expect such a missile might travel between five and six hundred yards."

"Fonteyne?"

Sebastien's expression darkened. "Aye. That sounds reasonable."

Jackson nodded and consulted the map again. "We have currently placed the *Carolina* and the *Louisiana* on this bend in the river." He slid a small pot of black ink onto the map to mark the location. "If we bring one of them, the *Carolina*, north to join the *Cygnet*—" he slid the pot up the river until it was parallel to the British encampment— "their guns would certainly cause some confusion and chaos, giving us cover for a three-pronged attack. One third of our force from the river, one third striking on their right flank, and one third charging in a direct assault to center.

Fonteyne stared at the map and for the first time in the many years he had spent roaring his victories at the helm of the *Black Wind*, he cursed his ship's size and weight, cursed the fact it sat at anchor in Barataria Bay unable to sail up the Mississippi.

But there, in the thick of it again, was the red-haired wildcat.

He laughed out loud, startling the other three men in the room. None of them cracked a smile. Indeed, they stared, wondering if he had lost his mind.

At length, Fonteyne gave a final chuckle and shook his head.

"It is a good plan, General, and if anyone can cause confusion and chaos, it is certainly Rose St. Clare."

Jackson nodded and blew out a breath. "Very well, gentlemen. If there are any doubts, any questions, put voice to them now."

The enormity of Jackson's presence, his reputation, his confidence allowed for not one single word of dissent.

"Good. Good! Then we shall settle the details and meet along the canal at dusk," Jackson said. "With as many men as we can muster."

FONTEYNE LEFT the meeting torn as to whether it was a good plan or a foolhardy one. It was not that he was against a nighttime ambush. Hell, his ship carried a set of black sails for exactly that purpose. To that, Jackson was right: surprise was a coveted advantage.

Lafitte was a few hasty steps behind him, the haste required to keep apace with the strides from Sebastien's long legs.

"So the minx has ingratiated herself with Jackson as well. Hearing of this great iron beast of hers, I was tempted to laugh with you. A gun that size is meant to be fired on land. It will blow her ship to splinters."

Fonteyne kept his voice even. "She has had the decking reinforced."

"She can reinforce it as far down as the bilges, it will make no difference. How does she expect to load a sixty-pound ball down its throat, never mind put a big enough charge to it to fire. Six hundred yards? I will eat the shirt on my back if it even gets out of the barrel."

Fonteyne smiled crookedly. "A fair wager, Jean. I'll supply the wine to wash all that fine linen down."

ROSE RECEIVED the dispatch from General Jackson mid-afternoon. A few hours later, Captain Kelly had moved the *Carolina* upriver and was anchored alongside, settled in to wait until the stroke of midnight.

It was a warm, still night, the air along the riverbanks thick with a hovering fog. Frogs croaked and cicadas chirped. The long dragon-like creatures who favored the swamps splashed into the river and slid across the surface searching for food, their eyes catching the faintest hint of light and glowing a luminous green.

Rose had ordered absolute silence on board. No lights, no cooking fires, no pipes. The larboard battery of thirty-two-pounder guns were loaded with ball shot and incendiary congreve rockets. With her stern to Rose's bow, the *Carolina* was similarly dark and quiet, her guns loaded, her crew waiting with nervous anticipation.

As the minutes ticked past, the tension grew. The men sweated into the fog and swatted at the incessant clouds of insects. There was no relief below decks from the bugs or humid air, so they sat and waited; some managed to sleep propped against the bulkheads, others checked and rechecked the guns and powder charges, ensuring the latter stayed dry.

The iron Beast crouched ominously by the rail. Along with the gun, Rose's father had provided six hollow iron shots filled with scrap metal and explosives but since there were no other guns of its size or purpose to be found this side of the ocean, Billy knew that when the six shots were gone, that would be the end of it until she could locate a foundry capable of making more. She wanted desperately to fire the gun, to see what it could do, but she was also reluctant to do so because of the size, the unknown recoil, and the uncertainty of any damage the blast might cause the *Cygnet*.

"A shame to have it just sitting here," she said to Rose, her voice barely above a whisper. "If ships were meant to sail, guns were made to be fired."

"Aye, an' women were made to bake bread an' hatch babies."

Both women looked down at Stubb, who raised his pudgy hands in self defense. "N'owt my sentiments, o' course. But mark my words, that be where the pair o' ye will end up if ye keep moonin' over them two piraticals."

"No one here is mooning over anyone," Billy said.

Stubb raised his voice to a falsetto. "Oh, doctor, doctor, can I come catch bugs wi' ye? Can I play wi' that big snake in yer trousers?"

Stubb laughed and was quick to duck away, but Billy was quicker as she reached out and grabbed a fistful of his leather vest. She hauled him back and raised him into the air, then watched him flail his arms and legs for a moment before swinging him around until he was directly above the gaping maw of the Beast. From there, it was a simple matter to drop him into the wide mouth of the barrel, cover it with the wooden lid, then hop up and sit on top of it.

"If I can't fire it," she said, "at least I can put it to good use."

Rose tried not to laugh when the muffled protests began. But a glance over Billy's shoulder quickly stifled the urge. A light appeared on shore, a single lantern light swinging back and forth. Billy followed her gaze and grinned.

"Blow up your fuses, boys, we're about to have some fun."

The whispered order was passed along the line and at every gun placement, the crews jumped up to take their positions. Gun ports were opened and the cannon were hauled forward by thick cables until the black snouts protruded from the ports. Men with wooden mallets knocked chocks out from behind the wheels and to a man, each member of each crew touched a hand to a cold iron barrel and murmured the motto of the Dante family, the same motto that had been whispered, cried, shouted, and cheered in victory for over two hundred years.

"De sanguine, ferro et honore!" With blood, steel, and honor!

A lad with a shielded lantern went down the line so the gun captains could light the wicks in their linstocks. Wads of cotton were twisted and stuffed into ears, shirts were stripped off and bandanas tied around the foreheads to soak up the sweat.

In a final act, Rose ordered the Dutch flag hauled in and the stars and stripes raised up the main mast.

DESPITE HIS SIZE AND BULK, Fonteyne moved with the grace of a big cat. He led his contingent of Baratarians through the woods, using hand signals to spread them out like a carpet of black beetles. They came close enough to the edge of the British camp to taste the bite of smoke from their fires and count the neat rows of tents pitched across the green. Jackson and his frontiersmen had claimed the center; Rodney Lamb's militia was on the right flank.

Somewhere in the rear, one of the Choctaw Indians lit the tip of an arrow dipped in oil and shot the flaming missile in a bright arc overhead. Rose and Kelly saw the signal and commenced firing. Almost instantly the fields on the right erupted with explosions of earth, followed a heartbeat later by the thunderous booms rolling over the plantation grounds and vibrating through the tents. Soldiers, half dressed, stumbled out into the night, confused and disorientated, scrambling for the neat pyramids of rifles that were stacked outside the tents. Once armed, they ran in circles diving behind wood piles and wagons, anything that might offer protection as all three prongs of Jackson's army started firing out of the darkness.

Continuous volleys of shot came from the two ships on the river, tearing up the ground, deliberately creating chaos and panic. Jackson's men charged forward across the field and out from behind the verge of trees, the three-pronged attack catching the British in a brutal crossfire.

Taken completely by surprise, the British retreated behind the manor house and outbuildings. There, discipline and experience overcame confusion and the soldiers regrouped to begin battling back.

From his position on the left flank, Fonteyne spied the small clearing where four big artillery guns had been brought across the lake and left there.

"Sheridan!" He called out to his fellow privateer captain and pointed. "We need to get to those guns."

"Aye, I'm right with you."

They culled half a dozen men from their company and, keeping low to avoid the zinging shots that were flying overhead, crab-walked through the fringe of long grasses at the edge of the trees, then ran across the open space two by two until they reached the clearing.

If there had been a guard placed with the guns, he was gone now to fight alongside his comrades. With fires burning behind them, the two captains were exposed, but they ran up close to the guns, keeping their pistols in hand.

Fonteyne realized the problem the same time as Sheridan.

"Temporary caissons. They've taken the guns off their carriages for easier transport."

"Not even bolted down," Sheridan said with disdain, checking the barrels. "We can't move them."

Fonteyne reached into his belt and drew a knife. "I was

hoping not to have to do this, but it would appear we have no choice."

He went to the gun closest to him and pushed the blade of the knife into the priming hole, jamming it in as far as it would go. He then picked up a rock and smashed the handle of the blade hard enough to snap it off, leaving the length of broken steel wedged tightly into the gun.

Sheridan nodded and ran for the two guns on their left. While Sebastien stood watch, Sheridan spiked them both using the blades off two bayonets. He picked up a third discarded musket, but Sebastien took it from him and waved him back toward the cover of the trees.

Fonteyne drove the bayonet blade into the touchhole and snapped it in half, but as he was about to turn and follow Sheridan to the safety of the woods, he saw something else in the shadows behind the artillery pieces. Something no sailor would ever want to see.

He started to walk toward it when he felt a tug on his coat sleeve and a burning slash across his upper arm. A soldier had been crouched behind the caisson, and as Fonteyne turned to see where the shot had come from, the shooter stepped out from cover and took a hobbled step back. He was young, not yet twenty, fresh-faced and owl-eyed as Fonteyne's arm came up, strong and steady, his thumb poised on the hammer of his pistol.

The lad licked his lips and started trembling as he stared into the black hole of the barrel.

"What is your regiment, boy?"

"T-Twenty-first Foot, Sir."

After a long, tense silence, Sebastien waved the nose of the gun. "Get the hell out of here and at least find some boots to put on."

The soldier looked down at his bare feet, turned and stumbled away. Too late, Fonteyne heard running steps from another direction and a few seconds later, a hail of bullets struck the side of the caisson, sending splinters of wood flying into the air. There were four soldiers coming toward him, all of whom had fired at the same time. Fonteyne ducked down and estimated the time it would take them to reload, then ran back into the trees and caught up to Sheridan. The two joined the rest of the Baratarians and spearheaded another attack on the British camp.

34

———

I t wasn't the lack of fighting spirit that forced Jackson to signal a retreat. After three hours of skirmishing, burning tents, destroying supplies, his army was running low on ammunition.

Another flaming arrow arcing through the air marked the end of the assault and left the British dazed, counting the hundreds of dead and wounded laying on the field.

Five miles away, Jackson marched back to his headquarters at McCarty House at the head of a robustly confident contingent of two thousand men comprised of militia, Indians, pirates, and townspeople, having lost only twenty-four souls. He was cautiously delighted but not bursting with confidence, for he knew it was not an absolute victory. The British had managed to regroup enough to defend and hold their position. Moreover, there was another eight to ten thousand men on their way to reinforce General Keane, and those eight thousand would be under the command of General Edward Packenham, brother-in-law to the Duke of Wellington, and a fearless veteran of the Continental War.

But a victory was a victory and one that his troops needed to see them through the next days and weeks.

They had returned with a score of British prisoners, most of whom sat stoically silent when questioned. Lafitte offered to introduce them to shipboard persuasion by swinging the cat-o-nines a few times, but Jackson declined and simply locked them in jail.

The general removed a glove and inspected a deep cut on his hand. Archie Penman started toward him with his medical box, but he waved the doctor away. "See to your captain first, he has leaked far more blood than this paltry scrape."

Penman changed direction mid-stride and carried his box to where Fonteyne sat. Sebastien had tied a kerchief around his arm, but the sleeve of his white shirt was soaked red. He said nothing as Penman cut away the sleeve and inspected the furrow the bullet had made in his skin.

"In my humble medical opinion, I believe you will live," Archie said, smiling. When neither the smile nor the quip was acknowledged, he pursed his lips and set about cleaning and stitching the wound then dressing it with a roll of bandaging.

"I suppose we must assume there will be no white flag of surrender coming forth from the enemy camp," Jackson said. "But by God we did show them our colors. Hopefully that will disabuse them of the notion we are ill-prepared and unwilling to fight."

"Not to mention buying ourselves a wee bit more time to reinforce our defenses," said Rodney Lamb.

"The Rodriquez Canal," Jackson said. "How is the work progressing?"

Fonteyne seemed to snap out of his thoughts and nodded. "I'm amazed how much we have accomplished in such a relatively short time. The rampart is ten feet high where the canal has been dug four, five feet down. Anyone attempting to breech will need ladders. The wall itself is roughly eight feet thick and strongly reinforced with earthworks. We've mounted and tested half a dozen guns and the base has held. We've extended it almost half a mile to the edge of the cypress swamp, where we've moved most of the workers now; it is still the weakest part of the line. And speaking of which, it might interest you to know the men are calling it the Jackson Line now, casting aside the unknown Senor Rodriguez."

"The Jackson Line," the general repeated. "There have been more than a few in the past. Let us hope this one holds as well as the others. I fully expect Keane will regroup and come at us again. We must be ready."

"We've moved some heavier guns to the fort at the Rigolets," Lamb said. "An' we've built a temporary redoubt on the main canal road, the Chef Menteur Pass, but if it's attacked with any great force, it won't hold fer long."

"With each boatload he ferries across the lake, Packenham is formulating his plan of attack. Tonight will be a setback, but a temporary one. He will choose his time and throw everything he has at us."

"At the first sign of movement, we should blow the levee. The longer the water soaks into the ground, the deeper the mud."

Jackson nodded at Lamb. "I have men up on the roof with long-glasses keeping a close eye for any activity across the fields."

From the far side of the room, Jean Lafitte lit a thin cigar and blew smoke into the air. "I'm told the Captain's lady did a fine job on the river tonight. And you as well, of course."

"Captain's lady?" Lamb looked puzzled for a moment then glanced at Fonteyne. "Oh. Aye. Aye, she did that. The thunder of them bloody thirty-fours scared the shite out of me, an' I were on her side!"

Fonteyne was watching Lafitte, not convinced in the least by the smile or flattery. He suspected that behind both was still a bristling urge to punish the woman who had humiliated him by stealing his ship out of Barataria Bay. Lafitte was not one to forgive or forget easily.

"Had you been there," he said, "you would have seen for yourself how the bombardment went and not relied on *being told*."

Lafitte shrugged. "It was necessary to fetch more supplies and casks of powder from the bayou."

"At any rate," Jackson said, "Captains de Clare and Kelly did an excellent job creating confusion in the Villere encampment. My niece does love to blow things up."

"So do the British. When I was spiking the guns, I saw a hot-shot furnace in their arsenal."

Lamb and Lafitte both sat a little straighter in their chairs. Jackson looked from one to the other, then to Fonteyne. "I see. That could pose an unpleasant threat."

"Heatin' a twenty-pound ball of iron red hot then firin' it at a wooden ship, aye," Lamb agreed. "It would be mighty unpleasant."

Fonteyne flexed his arm when Penman finished bandaging it then pushed out of his chair. His whole body ached and his eyes felt full of sand. It was tempting to grab an hour's sleep and a hot meal. "If there is nothing else ...?"

Jackson waved a hand in dismissal while his other hand came under threat with needle and thread by Penman.

"I'll walk out with you," Lafitte said, rising from the chair.

When he stepped outside, Fonteyne turned to look up at the faint blue smear of dawn beginning to spread across the western sky. He drew in a deep breath of the chilled morning air and started walking toward the stables.

"I hope my slip of the tongue did not embarrass you in

there," Lafitte said, taking two steps to every one of Fonteyne's long strides.

"By calling Rose St. Clare my lady? You would have to do a great deal better than that, my friend. And the only time your tongue ever slips is when you're licking a gold bar."

Lafitte laughed. "Touche. I see she has improved your sense of humor even as she tames you into becoming one of her lapdogs."

Fonteyne stopped and turned so abruptly the shorter man nearly walked up his shins. "What did you say?"

"Only that she is changing you, my friend. There was a time you and I would have sailed away and left the British and Americans to fight it out between themselves and come back when it was all over to share the spoils. Yet look at where we are now?"

Fonteyne took hold of Lafitte's coat lapels and pushed him so hard against the wall, the cigar flipped out of the Cajun's mouth and his hat flew off his head. "Where we are now is on the land you claimed to want to make your home. Where you have tried to bribe your way into being accepted as one of *them*."

"*Mon ami, mon ami*, there is no need to threaten violence." Lafitte raised his hands in submission. "You must know, as my friend and ally, that I only wish to look out for your wellbeing. I wish only to be useful."

"Useful? If you truly want to be useful you will stop skulking away into the bayou whenever you think your fine clothes might get smudged with dirt."

Lafitte gasped again. "Skulk away? I did no such thing! I was fetching—"

"Yes, yes, you were fetching more supplies. As it happens, I know where all your hidden caches are and first thing in the morning, *mon ami*, you and I will make certain every last barrel and crate is brought to the city so there will be no further need for you to fetch *anything*."

Fonteyne released his lapels with a small shove and turned away but stopped again and glanced back over his shoulder. "By the way, I also know *exactly* what you have squirreled away in those caches, and I don't just mean weapons and powder. After the *Pride* was returned and you went on board, did you happen to notice anything missing from your cabin?"

Lafitte's expression darkened, and he said quietly, "You have my ledgers?"

Fonteyne smiled crookedly. "Rose has them, but I've read what's in them and I'm sure the other captains would be just as interested as I was to learn exactly how much profit you make off every one of our shipments."

"You would not do this," Lafitte said on an expunged breath.

"Oh, I absolutely would do it. Then stand back and watch them tear you to pieces."

Lafitte suffered Fonteyne's hard stare for a moment longer, then squared his shoulders as some of the knuckles along his spine stiffened again. "She means this much to you? Enough to throw away ten years of friendship?"

Fonteyne's mouth curved slightly. "We were never *friends*, Lafitte. Our association was mutually convenient and I used you as much as you used me."

"I see. Will that ...association ... be at an end now?"

Fonteyne laughed. "If we both live through the next few weeks, you can ask me again."

ROSE WAS NURSING a row of blisters on the palm of her hand. She had been working with one of the gun crews to vent some of her pent-up tension. Touching the hot barrel of a cannon was never a wise idea, but difficult to avoid when she stumbled slightly and needed to brace against it to keep from having her face burned instead of her hand. Billy had supplied some of her special salve, which smelled like monkey dung but instantly cooled the raging heat of her skin.

A few rounds of linen bandaging and she was fine and fit. Along with one of the men who had dropped a ten-pound shot on his foot and broken a toe, theirs were the only two injuries on board. Since they had not been under direct attack, and speed was not a critical factor, Billy had unleashed thirty full broadsides over the span of three hours, allowing time for the guns to cool between every five volleys. Each round tore up broad swaths of land and sent debris flying in all directions. If a redcoat was spotted trying to sneak onto the canal road, the guns were loaded with chain shot, which cut through trees, shrubs, bodies like the devil's own scythe.

Not many redcoats had attempted to breach the road.

When the flaming arrow signaled the end of the skirmish, the guns were thoroughly swabbed but not hauled in. Nor were the gun crews told to stand down. Instead, they sat in tired huddles around the wooden carriages and caught what rest they could. Being so far from the main battleground, the silence that followed was only broken sporadically by the occasional distant cry. Those on board the *Cygnet* and the *Carolina* had no idea how the attack had gone on land and were unsure as to whether the arrow had signalled a victorious end or a staggering retreat.

As the silence stretched to thirty minutes, Captain Kelly had his gig lowered and was rowed over to the *Cygnet*. The first sound he made when he came through the gangway and saw Rose waiting to greet him was a loud *har-rump!*

"I am not one to give idle praise, but by God our crews worked well together, lass. Well indeed! I vow there isn't a tree or twig standing between here and Lake Borgne! Pity old Villeres, I do. He had some fine fields of tobacco before all this."

"On the bright side, he won't have to till the soil as deep come spring."

Kelly barked out a laugh and accepted a cup of grog from the crewman passing out drams to the men. He touched his cup to Rose's and together they looked out at the distant ribbon of glowing red that indicated the broad swath of fires that were still burning in the British camp.

"I confess I had my doubts," he said.

"Doubts?"

"Aye. A woman at the helm? A woman in charge of a crew of piratical scallywags? Aye, I had my doubts."

"Well, if it helps, we are not actually pirates. We do sail under legitimate letters of marque." She paused and glanced up at the flag of fifteen stars and stripes that now flew from the masthead. "At least, we did."

"Riders coming," Duardo called down from the bow. "Four. On the canal road."

Rose quietly ordered six of her best marksmen up into the yards with their muskets. Kelly gulped down the last of his grog and bustled back to the gangway to return to his gig.

Duardo came down onto the main deck and took Kelly's place at Rose's side. "I think it is the captain of the *Black Wind*. He rides a horse like a string-puppet bouncing on his balls."

Rose tried not to laugh. "I shall be sure to pass your observation along."

The big man shrugged. "I only say this to warn you in case he cannot perform well later."

Her grin faded under a flush of heat and she muttered, "Is there anyone on this ship who doesn't gossip like a fishmonger's wife?"

Duardo looked down at her, his expression as blank as always. "No. It is how we know to protect you."

Uncertain how to respond to that, Rose ran to the gangway

and caught Kelly before he could row back to his ship. She lowered herself over the side and joined him and together they were rowed across to the riverbank.

Fonteyne met them on shore. Archie Penman was with him, having left the wounded in the capable hands of the three town doctors.

"We would have come across to you."

"It was quicker this way," she said. "We've had no news."

"Jackson sends his thanks and his praise to both of you for a job well done. We didn't exactly scare them back across the ocean, but we gave them a fair thrashing to think about."

"Casualties?" Kelly asked.

"We lost far fewer than they did," Penman said. "About two dozen, and twice that many wounded. The men fought hard and proved we would not easily be pushed aside."

"There is still the line that must be held in order to keep the British out of New Orleans," Fonteyne said, "and we are none of us foolish enough to believe one skirmish will dissuade them from throwing everything they have at us the next time."

"Aye, aye," Kelly nodded in agreement, but he could not keep the grin off his face. "For now, our lads will be wanting to know what happened out there on the field tonight."

Rose agreed. "I'm going to return to New Orleans with Captain Fonteyne. You can carry the news back to the men and will you also tell Duardo he has command of the *Cygnet* until I return."

Fonteyne turned to Penman. "Any objection to staying here with the *Cygnet* so Rose can have use of your horse?"

Penman brightened, for his eyes had not strayed from the dark silhouette of the ship. "No! No objection at all."

Kelly *har-rumped* one last time before the two of them headed back to the jolly boat.

Fonteyne and Rose walked over to where the other two

riders were waiting, both men she recognized from the crew of the *Black Wind*. Sebastien gave her a leg up into the saddle, which brought forth an involuntary grunt as a sharp stab of pain reminded him of the wound in his arm.

"Are you hurt?"

"A graze, nothing to worry about," Fonteyne said, then looked at the linen wrappings on her hand. "Are you?"

"A few blisters. Nothing to worry about."

He touched the brim of his hat and swung up onto his own saddle. Rose nudged her horse into step behind him and couldn't help but agree with Duardo's description of his riding skills.

WHEN THEY ARRIVED BACK at McCarty House, they were told, in no uncertain terms by General Jackson's valet that he was asleep and not to be disturbed by anything short of a cannonball crashing through the roof.

After a very long, exhausting day and an equally debilitating night, Rose and Fonteyne were too tired to try to argue or bribe the valet. Fonteyne had a room above a nearby tavern, where they ordered large tankards of ale. But that wasn't what they wanted either. Having not said a single word since leaving Jackson's headquarters, Fonteyne took her by the hand and led her up the stairs to his room. Although they were soon twined together in his bed and fast asleep within minutes.

35

When Rose woke up, she was alone. She lifted her head to look around, needing a moment to remember where she was. The mattress was thick and soft and smelled faintly of chicken feathers, but she snuggled back down, too damned comfortable to complain or move. The room itself was tiny, with half the space taken up by the bed. There was a washstand in the corner, a rail-back chair, and small writing table beneath a single window with shutters and no glass.

It was obviously late afternoon, to judge by the thick beam of sunlight streaming through the window. A million floating dust motes swam up and down the length, moving with the drafts.

She rose up onto her elbows and pushed the tangle of hair off her face. Her clothes were folded neatly on the chair, her hat, sword, and gun belts hung on pegs by the door.

When she lifted her head higher, she could see a rolled chart and some papers scattered across the tabletop and beside that, two tankards half-filled with unfinished ale.

Grumbling with reluctance to leave the cozy warm bed, Rose threw off the blanket and swung her legs over the side. It was always an odd sensation waking up in a room that was stationary and did not roll with the waves. It generally took four or five halting steps to adjust as she made her way across the room to the chair and slowly started dressing. A quick glance told her there was no thunderpot under the bed, but an urgent need sent her to the door to peek out. In boots, breeches, and shirt she went down the stairs, gave a look of askance to the servant in the tavern and was directed to the door that led out back.

Returning in far more comfort, she ran back up to the room and finished dressing. She had no idea where Fonteyne had gone but another brusque encounter with the general's valet had her hitching a ride on a wagon that was being driven out to the newly christened Jackson's Line.

She could hear the sounds of hammering, sawing, and shouting before the wagon came around the last bend in the road. Her eyes popped wide at the sight of all the activity: men with shovels filling flour bags with dirt they were digging out of the canal, men working with saws and awls trimming stakes and sharpening the ends into lethal points.

She thanked the wagoneer and started walking along the earthworks that had, barely ten days ago, been a crumbling fieldstone wall running alongside a dry dirt ditch. Now she had to walk up an incline to get to the top of the rampart, which was fully wide enough to walk six men abreast. More than that, she saw cannon that had been moved from the ships placed along the top of the fortification every twelve paces with bales of hay and bags of sand beside the barrels to give the gunners protection.

Walking closer to the first gun, she peered over the edge and saw a steep drop into the newly excavated ditch below ... a ditch that was now ten feet wide and laced with crossed, sharpened stakes. The field beyond the ditch had been cleared of any vegetation higher than a man's ankles, giving the gunners alarmingly clear, broad sight lines. The field itself stretched out a thousand yards or more; flat, open, barren.

Andrew Jackson's deep baritone came over her shoulder. "Impressive, isn't it?"

"Bloody astonishing," she agreed. "And frankly, I wouldn't want to be the ones coming across that field trying to attack this wall."

"Come. Walk with me."

Rose fell into step beside him. As they walked, he paused to point out some of the stronger and weaker points in the fortifications. He stopped to consult with parties of men with shovels and picks and gave words of thanks and encouragement to women carrying buckets of water and trays of fish pies. The faces they passed were sweaty and dirty, but each one smiled in response to his frequent words of encouragements. There were even children running up and down the line carrying shot and lengths of cable, fuses, pails of nails.

"Captain Fonteyne is working at the far end of the line," Jackson said, stopping. "He is not happy with the slow progress so he has an extra fifty men there to help with the digging. If you are going that way, will you let him know I will send more as we can spare them? And you might mention that Lafitte has gone into the bayou again, for what reason I know not. Quite the annoying creature. I almost hope he intends to stay there."

Rose sighed; her similar dislike of the pirate king obvious. "I will tell him."

"On the point of being annoying," Jackson said, "I have discussed it with Captain Lamb, whose militia will be in one of the more vulnerable positions on the right. We have spies keeping watch every which way, but not everyone can see everything under cover of darkness, and should the British attempt to move up the Menteur Road and establish a redoubt, Lamb's battalions of militia would be in grave danger."

He stopped and faced her. "Captain Fonteyne suggested you and Captain Kelly move your ships back down the river, a half mile, no more, and harass the British by keeping up a steady bombardment of the road and adjoining field. He assures me that Lafitte has more than enough powder and shot to keep both ships well supplied. He also assures me that you and your crew are more than able to annoy the hell out of the British."

Rose smiled. "Billy Burr and her guns will be delighted to oblige, General."

A small group of men had been following them as they walked, most wanting Jackson's attention to some detail. He gave Rose a gentle peck on the cheek and tucked a finger under her chin. "You are your father's daughter, and for that we are all very grateful." He started to walk away but stopped again. "I like this fellow, Fonteyne. I grant you, I've only known him a short time, and he has a reputation that makes grown men quake, but his first thought, after coming off the battlefield, was to go and see you to make sure you were alright. He seems to be quite taken with you, my dear, and unless my eyes deceive me, the feeling is mutual?"

Rose felt her cheeks warming and, noting it, Jackson smiled. "I only hope you won't make the same mistake Alexander made."

"Mistake?"

"The next time you see your father, ask him how long it took him to gather enough courage to tell your mother he loved her."

Rose's blush darkened, but he had already walked away to respond to a persistent harangue from one of the carpenters.

⁓

ROSE FOLLOWED the stream of men going in the direction of the distant fringe of the cypress swamp. She found Fonteyne at the far end of the canal, where furious efforts were being made to extend and heighten the wall. He was stripped to the waist and covered in dirt head to foot. He was one of several dozen men working with picks and shovels, first to loosen the hard-packed earth at the bottom of the ditch, then to fill the buckets and barrows that would then be used to build up the ramparts above them. They had already lowered the ditch by five feet and added nearly half a mile to the wall, but there was still a gap between the wall and the swamp that could present a vulnerability.

Woodcutters and carpenters had constructed stout timber foundations eight feet apart and another beehive of activity was working to fill the empty space with rocks, dirt, bales of hay, anything that would form a solid base for mounting the men and cannon.

Rose was accidentally bumped by a woman carrying two heavy buckets of dirt hanging from a wooden yolk across her shoulders. They each apologized to one another before Rose moved hurriedly out of the way. Behind her, there were more buckets being unloaded from carts and wagons, and without giving it much thought, she stripped off her jacket, her sword and guns, and set them aside, then dug in to help.

She was thankful, after the first three trips ferrying buckets to the wall, that her hand was wrapped in bandaging. Even so, after two hours, the linen was stained red, her shirt and breeches were sweat-soaked and smudged brown, her boots were filthy, and she seriously thought of taking a knife to the braid hanging down her back that kept swinging forward to smack her in the face. She also had cause to be thankful for Billy Burr's insistence that everyone on board the *Cygnet*, captain included, was required to participate in arduous daily training.

Her muscles ached, but apart from short breaks to drink a ladle of water, she kept going.

Several of the women working alongside Rose carrying the buckets and dumping them into the foundation, wondered that she could work so steadily and make so many trips back and forth without gasping for breath on every turn or stopping to rest. Rose, on the other hand, wondered how so many men, women, and children could carry and dump so many buckets of dirt and rubble yet the filling in of the earthworks seemed to progress by mere inches.

When an enormous basket piled high with bread and pasties came by, Rose did finally stop. She sat on a crate with a cup of water and a pie and was inspecting the tattered condition of her bandaged hand when Fonteyne saw her and strode over. He crouched down in front of her and took her hand in his.

"Let me have a look at that."

"It's fine, really."

"I can see that." He gently unwound the strip of linen and frowned at the raw, bloodied condition of her palm.

As soon as the air hit the ravaged blisters her hand began to shake. Pain returned with a vengeance and she merely shrugged at the accusing glare in Sebastien's eyes. "I wanted to help."

He muttered a few curses under his breath and waved down one of the lads they used as runners. "See if you can find some bandages and a pail of clean water. Clean, mind you. Not out of a field barrel."

The boy, no more than five years old, filthy as an urchin, saluted and ran off.

"It is okay for him to work the rampart but not me?"

"I doubt his hand will have to be cut off from putrefaction."

She frowned and tried to pull her hand out of his, but he held fast. "I've had worse injuries."

"I'm sure you have and I'm not faulting you for wanting to

help. But your skills are more valuable and of more use elsewhere and if you fall sick with a fever or require Stubb to fashion a hook in place of your hand, you won't be of much use to anyone on or off your ship in the coming fray."

When she said nothing, he glanced up and caught the smile.

"I wasn't aware I said anything amusing."

"You didn't. But as you once told me, your bedside manner is sorely lacking, Captain Fonteyne."

His eyes narrowed but there was humor lurking behind them. "Have I also told you how much I dislike having my own words thrown back at me?"

"Have I told you how much I dislike waking up naked and alone in a man's bed?"

He contemplated the sparkle in her eyes. "Believe me, I did ponder the moment. But you looked so warm and cozy, all curled up and snoring contentedly."

She drew back and scowled. "I do not snore, sir."

His grin widened. "Indeed, no. My mistake. You purr like a kitten with a ball of fur caught in its throat."

Luckily for him, the boy returned at that moment with a small pail of water and a roll of clean linen strips. He also brought a spike of cactus that had healing properties. "Mam says to squeeze the cactus and spread the jelly on the wound then wrap it real good."

Fonteyne pressed a silver coin into his hand before he scampered away.

He bathed the wound thoroughly first then did as instructed, spreading clear jelly over her palm before wrapping the bandaging twice as thick as before. Thick enough, she could not move her fingers or make a fist.

As she watched him tending her hand, Andrew Jackson's words came back to her.

Ask your father how long it took for him to tell your mother he loved her.

She felt the peculiar tightness constricting her chest again, not unlike the one she felt before an impending battle when every nerve ending in her body prickled and her belly took slow rolls around and around. This time the battle was inside her own head and she didn't know how to fight it, or if she even wanted to fight it.

"Did Jackson tell you about the plan to move the ships downriver?"

"Yes. Yes, he did. He also wanted me to tell you he would send more men as soon as he could spare some, and to let you know that Lafitte has scurried away into the bayou again."

"He hasn't scurried. This time. I sent him. We need at least a dozen more cannon and he has actually agreed to cannibalize the long guns on the *Pride.*"

"Billy will be pleased all of her hard work at cleaning them will not go wasted."

"He has enough powder and shot squirrelled away to keep you and Captain Kelly well supplied." He glanced up as he tied off the knot on the bandage. "It is crucial to keep the British confined to the fields. More of the bastards are disembarking every day and we will be hard-pressed to fight them on too many fronts. Jackson gives a good impression of a confident man, but he knows the odds are stacked immeasurably high against us. If one section fails, we all fail. We have to hold the river, and we have to hold the wall. If there was any way I could be in both places at once—"

She held up her good hand and pressed two fingers against his lips. "You have the wall, Captain Fonteyne; I have the river. Neither one of us will fail."

He smiled at her bravado but the same assurance did not quite touch his eyes. Those amber eyes that had not given her one moment's peace over the past weeks now seemed to be searching, questioning, wondering ...

He drew a breath and, ignoring the dozens of eyes watching, gathered Rose close for a kiss that was long and deep, one that left her lips throbbing and her body drowning in heat.

"Yesterday," he murmured, his lips not quite relinquishing hers, "Lafitte called you my woman. I have decided I rather like the sound of that."

Rose suffered the tightness in her chest a moment longer before she felt it ease. The giant hand that had been squeezing it full of doubt and hesitation suddenly let go and flooded her body with certainty.

"I like the sound of it too," she whispered.

He grinned and pulled her close again, and this time, when the kiss ended, there was laughter and cheering from the onlookers.

"I ... I should get back to my ship," she said through half a breath.

Fonteyne helped her to her feet and watched as she fetched her coat, guns, and hat from the crate where she had left them.

"I have no way of knowing when I'll have the chance to get downriver again," he said.

"You have more than enough here to keep you busy."

"Rose—"

She reached up on tiptoes and kissed him. "I will wait for you, Captain Fonteyne, no matter how long it takes. For now, however, it will be dark before I get back to the ship and God only knows if Billy has hung Stubb up by his ears yet."

He laughed and sent her off with playful slap on the rump. She took a few steps, slowed, then stopped and looked back, "Just don't make me wait another five years, Sir."

But Sebastien had already vanished into the crowd of workers.

36

Rose did not catch so much as a distant glimpse of Fonteyne during the following two weeks. The *Cygnet* and the *Carolina* moved downriver and took up positions opposite Fort St. Philip. There, they were joined by the schooner *Louisiana* and the three ships kept up a steady barrage of shots day and night to discourage the British who attempted several times to creep up the canal road under cover of darkness. Rose had men hidden in the trees on shore to send warnings to the vessels, at which time, full broadsides would be unleashed and maintained until the threat passed and the British retreated.

On Christmas Day, General Edward Packenham finally landed with another four thousand soldiers and took charge of the army. Angered by the cat and mouse games Keane was playing with the Americans, he had the hot-shot furnace moved closer to the Mississippi riverbank along with nine large artillery guns. Two days later, under cover of darkness, the guns were placed behind a temporary fieldstone redoubt where they could see the river and the three anchored American ships through the trees, but their location would not be so easily visible from the other side of the canal.

That same night he sent a trio of British gunboats up the river with express orders to turn Fort St. Philip into a pile of rubble.

"Captain, we've got company."

The gray mist was drifting slowly across the river like shreds of a torn bridal veil, sometimes thin enough to reveal shapes and shadows, other times as dense as clouds. The air was heavy with moisture, barely starting to lighten with the approach of dawn. Rose had placed lookouts at the top of all three masts in the hope of seeing above the wafting layers of fog, for they had been hearing sounds throughout the night that suggested the British were getting bolder in their effort to claim the canal road.

The crews on board the *Louisiana* and the *Carolina* were on full alert. Similarly, on board the *Cygnet*, there was absolute silence broken only by the creaking of the cables and the slap of wavelets on the ships hull. They were positioned slightly behind the two American ships, only lightly moored so they could move at a moment's notice. The guns were loaded, brass monkey racks were filled with shot. Barrels held felt charges full of black powder while smaller casks were filled with Billy's pre-filled quills. She prowled up and down the line of guns, checking and rechecking, but she knew her crews were the absolute best.

Stubb stalked up and down the deck as well, hopping up onto every cask or coil of rope as if willing the fog to speed on its way.

Captain Bryant Kelly had claimed the forward position on the *Carolina*; thus he was two hundred yards in front of the *Louisiana* and four hundred yards in front of the *Cygnet*. It was the muffled sound of one of his lookouts that broke the oppressive silence.

What the lookout saw was three British gunboats advancing through the purplish haze of dawn. When they caught sight of the *Carolina*, they made no attempt to hail. Two of the gunboats split from the other and maneuvered into position. Their forward guns were run out and fired, leaving no doubt as to their intentions. The first few shots fell harmlessly into the dark water, but with the second volley the guns were adjusted, the range was found. Shots found their marks and punched into the *Carolina*, tearing through sails, cracking yards and rails, lifting guns off their carriages.

The third gunboat began firing at the walls of the fort, their shots exploding in sprays of stone and mortar.

The big guns mounted on the fort boomed out their answer. Jackson had increased their number from six to fourteen and placed Baratarian gunners on each cannon with the result that few of the shots fired from the fort missed their mark and the gunboat was quickly rocked back with repeated strikes.

Before the Americans had a chance to cheer, the crews of the *Louisiana* and the *Carolina* came under heavy fire from the second threat on shore. The twenty-four-pounder naval guns were close enough to inflict serious damage, but what raised the hairs on the back of every sailor's neck was the sight of red hot cannon balls screaming through the air and exploding in a fountain of fiery sparks on deck.

"Bastards are using the hot-shot furnace," Billy said.

"Can you see where it's coming from?" Rose asked.

They heard another screaming shriek and caught the direction of the arc as it came over the trees. This one landed squarely on the main deck of the *Carolina*, blowing a hole through the boards and lifting the ship with a tremendous series of explosions. At the same time, the naval guns concentrated on her masts and rigging, tearing both to shreds. In under two minutes, her masts were gone and fires were raging from bow to stern.

While the war sloop burned, the British guns took aim on the *Louisiana*. Her captain was firing broadsides as quickly as his crews could reload but from his angle on the river he had trouble pinpointing the location of the guns firing the hot shots. Chain shot cracked the top of his main mast and slashed through the sails. Shot smashed into the rails and sprayed her crews with dagger-like shards of wood. But they kept firing and the mist was soon thick with clouds of acrid white sulphur smoke.

Rose had agreed to hang back until and unless Kelly and Dollor needed help, but seeing they were under heavy fire, she was not about to wait for any signal to bring the *Cygnet* forward.

"Away aloft," she shouted. "Cut the anchor and reset the top gallants to give me steerage!"

Duardo took an axe to the anchor cable, splitting it in one strike. The helmsman, Mercado, cursing a steady stream of Spanish epithets, spun the huge, spoked wheel to bring the *Cygnet* downriver to join the fray where the two British were concentrating their fire on the *Carolina* and the *Louisiana*, sensing easy kills.

The gunners seemed not to be aware of the *Cygnet* until she broke through the clouds of drifting smoke. With a shout and the drop of her arm, Rose's crew unleashed a tremendous broadside firing from both decks at once, exploding along the riverbank where red-coated soldiers had crept out of the shadows. A second thunderous broadside loaded with chain and bar shot scythed through a stand of trees that had concealed the position of the naval artillery.

"Billy!"

"Aye, I see it!"

Rose heard the crunch of the *Cygnet's* foremast taking a hit as the gunners on shore found their new target. One of the heated, red hot balls came screaming toward the ship and landed in a spout of hissing steam a mere arm's width from the hull.

Billy cursed at the insult and ran over to where the Beast was crouched by the rail. She had ordered the big carronade loaded earlier with no real thought of having to fire it, but now she knew it was the only gun with a high enough arc to clear the trees and smash down behind the British position.

She snatched up a burning linstock and held it close to the priming hole. For the smallest moment of hesitation, she held her breath, hoping she'd put enough reinforcement under the deck boards so she didn't blow her own ship to smithereens. Using the rule of three, she had estimated a charge of twenty pounds of powder wase needed to fire a sixty-pound shot, but she had no real way of knowing if the force of the recoil would propel the gun up or down...

"Fuck it," she said, and lowered the linstock.

The powder caught with a spark and puff of acrid smoke followed by a loud hiss and fizzle as it scorched its way to the barrel where the charge of powder ignited.

The *BOOM* was like ten cracks of thunder exploding simultaneously. Billy was thrown back on a surge of hot air as the heavy gun reared back on its haunches. The shot—loaded with iron cuttings, nails, bolts, spikes, and incendiaries that would combust on impact—erupted from the muzzle in a blaze of shooting flames. It flew on an angle that sent it four hundred yards up and over the trees, landing almost on top of the artillery position. The enormous explosion that followed sent a towering orange fireball into the sky, accompanied seconds later by two, three more explosions as casks of powder and shot were struck and ignited. The hot shot furnace was lifted into the air by the impact, crashing down and scattering its red-hot contents in a deadly spray. The stone barrier was ruptured, exposing the gun emplacement. Men screamed as sprays of shrapnel spread out in a circle dozens of feet wide. Most staggered away with hideous wounds, their clothing on fire, their bodies scorched from the heat and flames.

Back on the river, Rose maneuvered the *Cygnet* past the burning hulk of the *Carolina*. Taking full advantage of the current to build up her speed, Rose aimed her bow at the gap between the two gunboats. Instead of backing her sails and slowing to present her broadside, as the British gunners expected, Rose kept her ship moving forward.

The gunboats started firing at the *Cygnet,* but she was moving too fast and presented too narrow of a target to inflict much damage. When she had closed the gap and was about to cut through the two ships, Rose passed a signal to Billy, who ordered both the starboard and larboard batteries on both decks to open fire, blasting full broadsides at the two British ships at the same time.

On board both gunboats, masts were blown apart and came crashing down, sections of rail were torn away and decks erupted in splinters and shattered boards. Guns were blown off their carriages, crushing men beneath them. Some of the shots hit stores of powder and exploded in flames, while other volleys of chain shot spun across the deck like scything dervishes. The damage from such point-blank barrages was deadly and horrifying and at least one of the gunboats started to fall away, shattered and broken, letting the current carry them back around the safety of the river bend.

Mercado worked the helm like a madman, forcing the *Cygnet* into a tight, sweeping turn, hoping to carry her momentum through to a second pass between the gunboats. If the crews needed incentive, they had only to look further up the river, where the *Carolina* was battered and on fire. Her masts were gone, her yards and rigging chopped and dragging in the water. Her guns were silenced under boiling clouds of black smoke and scorching flames.

Billy's guns took lethal revenge. By the time the *Cygnet* made her second pass, one of the gunboats had taken a direct hit on the armory and erupted in a two-hundred-foot pillar of flame. Their forward progress slowed now by the river current, the crew of the *Cygnet* managed three more full broadsides off both beams, leaving the second gunboat in shambles. Most of the crew either jumped overboard or ran below to escape the carnage.

Billy's crews reloaded, eager to carry on the fight, but what little remained of the British attacking mettle was already staggering away back down the river.

On board the burning hulk of the *Carolina*, the body of Captain Kelly and most of his officers lay crushed under the trunk of the broken main mast where it had smashed through the foredeck.

Rose ordered her crew to lower away the longboats to pick up survivors, then, seeing *Louisiana* drifting rudderless downriver, sent more boats with heavy cables to tow her to safety on the opposite shore.

By then, having heard the gun battle on the river, a regiment of Jackson's militia had come pouring down the canal road. They swarmed onto the field and through the charred remains of the trees to overrun the British artillery position and scatter what was left of the British offense.

ROSE TIPPED her head from one side to the other, hearing the crackle of tiny bones grating in her neck. Billy, Duardo,

Mercado, and Stubb were in her cabin and they all seemed to be talking, but their voices sounded like they came through a tunnel of water. Judging by the hand gestures that accompanied the conversations, they were as deafened as Rose but still determined to discuss the day's events. The normal twists of linen stuck in their ears had been scant protection against the incredible concussive boom of the Beast and because the five of them had been standing closest, it would likely be several hours, even days before they could hear clearly again. Billy's arse was bruised purple and yellow from when she was thrown back onto the deck. Stubb's eyes could not seem to hold their focus, they kept rolling up and down, side to side. Mercado looked like he was reciting the whole of Dante's Inferno—in Spanish—with flying hands and broad gestures.

Only the stoic Duardo seemed unaffected, but then he was not one for lengthy conversations at the best of times. Rose did notice a small trickle of blood that leaked from one of his ears, but that was not uncommon after a pitched battle.

Looking around, her cabin had not escaped unscathed. Most of the glass panes in the gallery windows had been shattered, the broken bits scattered like diamonds across the floor. During battle, her berth had been raised and hooked on chains to the wall to give access to the cannon beneath, but it had taken a hit and the gun port had been blasted off, leaving a gaping hole. Damage to the rest of the *Cygnet* was remarkably minimal. Eighteen of the crew were wounded, three dead, a few dozen more with minor scratches and scrapes. Two of the heavy twenty-four-pounders had been blown apart but Billy assured her by hand gestures that they could be repaired.

The *Louisiana* was beached on the west bank of the river. She'd suffered a good deal of damage, but her guns would still be a threat to anyone attempting to breach the canal road. Fort St. Philip had stood strong against the British assault, proving the Americans could maintain control over the river as well as the west bank.

Rose sighed …she could hear that rush inside her head well enough … and refilled her cup to the brim with rum, then pushed the bottle down the table for the others to help themselves. She'd already had two refills, but it didn't appear to be having an effect.

There had been intense fighting on shore between Lamb's militia and the British soldiers. Neither the *Louisiana* nor the *Cygnet* could fire in support for fear of hitting the American forces. At one point, it looked as though the British might have been able to push on up the road to breach Lamb's defenses, but the effort failed and the drummers had to beat a retreat.

She felt someone tag her arm and looked up at Billy. She was gesturing that she needed to go and check on her crews and Rose nodded. Stubb and Mercado scraped to their feet as well and followed her out the door, leaving just Rose and Duardo sitting at the table. The liquid brown eyes were intent on her face and she attempted a small smile.

"I'm fine, really. Apart from this—" her hand made a whirly motion around her ear—"I'm fine."

He grunted and pushed to his feet. There were cuts and bruises on his bare torso and arms, and a gash on his thigh that had bled through his breeches. Rose knew better than to ask or express concern. Warriors of his tribe, he had told her once, consider all wounds won in battle well earned and should never be boasted or complained about.

She suspected he would tell her the same thing if his leg was hanging off by a few bloody veins.

Having seen Fonteyne brush away any questions about the myriad scars on his body, she was fairly certain he shared Duardo's disdain for showing any weakness and, if not for Archie Penman, he likely would have bled to death long ago.

Rose had not seen Fonteyne since the afternoon on the rampart. She received reports almost daily on how the fortifications were progressing, but they always came from General Jackson. Having all but confessed her feelings for the bastard, he might have at least had the grace to send her a personal note. Or a cherry pie on Christmas Day.

"Lucky for him, I hate cherries," she muttered.

Duardo looked over but she waved her hand. He apparently heard a knocking on the cabin door and when he opened it, a boy was standing there balancing a large tin platter in his hands. On it were thick slices of mutton, a round of bread, cheese, and some sugared figs.

Rose lost interest right away and turned to stare out the broken gallery windows again, so she did not see the shadowed figure standing in the corridor behind the boy. He ducked through the doorway and removed his battered leather hat, then stood with his arms crossed over his chest, content to simply watch her for the longest thirty seconds of his life.

Fonteyne had heard and read the reports of the battle on the river. He knew the part the *Cygnet* had played in helping to win the day both on the river and on shore. If the artillery guns had not been silenced and the British had not fled the canal road in a panic, Lamb's militia might well have been driven back to Line Jackson. As it was, Packenham had attempted a frontal attack on the earthworks, probing for a weakness in their defenses, but the Line had held ... barely ... and the English had withdrawn.

No one doubted they would be back and in greater force than before as more and more troops were ferried across the lake every day.

Rose felt a tingle across the back of her neck and glanced over her shoulder. When she saw Fonteyne standing there, her breath escaped her lips in a rush and she was on her feet in a heartbeat.

"You're alive!"

He glanced down the length of his body. "I believe so, yes. As are you, I see."

"I sent messages."

"I did receive them."

"Then why did you not answer?"

His mouth stretched to a crooked smile. "Why, Captain St. Clare, you were not worried, were you?"

She glared. "No, of course not. But it would have been the polite thing to do."

"Polite?" His amber eyes narrowed. "Of the many things I have been called, polite has never been one of them."

"Informative, then. I believe I asked several times how the work on the Line was progressing."

He seemed to remember he was holding his hat and tossed it aside. He glanced at the berth, chained up against the wall, then at the desk.

"And I will tell you, in the most polite, informative terms I know. But first ..." in a soft, husky, meaningful voice he advised, "you might want to move the inkwell."

Duardo, standing by the open door, looked from one to the other then quickly walked out of the cabin and pulled the door closed behind him. Standing out in the corridor were Billy, Stubb, and Archie Penman, all with questioning expressions on their faces.

"Well?" Stubb asked. "Did she rip him top to tail?"

"They are ...discussing manners," Duardo said.

"Manners! What d'ye mean manners?"

"Since you have none, and are likely not to acquire any, you would not know." Duardo snatched the little man up by the scruff of the neck and carried him back down the corridor. "Come. All of you. Leave them. They have much to discuss."

TWO HOURS LATER, utterly exhausted, laying on the floor in a crumple of tossed bedding and discarded clothing, Rose struggled to open her eyes. Sebastien was sprawled out beside her, arms and legs spread wide, his body covered in a sheen of sweat. A breeze was coming through the broken gallery windows, but it was laden with too much Louisiana humidity to be refreshing. The sound of the river lapping against the hull was too tempting to resist and she rolled up onto her feet and walked barefoot to the narrow door. The sun was already well below the treeline on the west bank and the water was black with shadows. She scowled, seeing the gap in the balcony rail, and, careful not to step on any splinters of wood or shards of glass, stepped to the broken edge of the narrow gallery and dove cleanly into the river.

The water was cool and silky against her bare skin. She rose to the surface then ducked under again, wishing she'd thought to bring a pot of soap with her. Even without it she combed her fingers through her hair and scrubbed away some of the dirt and ash that had formed a dull film on the strands. She rubbed her face and her arms then swam a dozen yards toward the middle of the river, where she paused and tread water so she could look back at her ship.

The carpenters had already replaced any broken yards; sailmakers had taken down the torn canvas and fixed new rolled bundles in place. Men were busy on deck in the waning daylight to mend cables, clear the last of the debris, and check each gun for any signs of damage, for there would be no lights on board tonight. Farther down the river, the hulk of the *Carolina* had sunk, leaving only the top of one charred mast poking up above the surface. Jackson had sent two smaller support ships down the river from New Orleans, the steamboat *Enterprise* and the schooner *Eagle* both of which had taken the rescued crew from the *Carolina* on board. Neither was heavily armed, the schooner carrying ten guns, the steamboat with six. But the mere presence of them on the river might discourage any further attempts by the British to mount a river assault.

Rose heard a splash and saw Fonteyne's head bob above the water a few long arm strokes away. She swam back to meet him halfway, happy to let him wrap his big arms around her.

"I have to get back to camp soon," he said. "I've already been gone longer than I should have been."

Rose twined her legs around his waist, pressing herself against him. "I'm glad you came. I wasn't exactly worried, when I didn't hear anything from you, but ... well ... I was worried. And I am still not entirely convinced I should forgive you."

He grinned. "I don't believe I've had a more energetic reprimand."

She felt his flesh stir and harden against her. "Apparently not energetic enough."

He made a growly sound in his throat and slid his hands down to her hips, guiding her, lifting her up then settling her down over his flesh.

She glanced over at the ship, wary of any eyes that might be watching, but they had drifted a ways in the current and were shielded by the overhanging branches of a willow tree.

She angled her hips to bring him more firmly inside her then touched her brow to his and closed her eyes, savoring the cool sliding of the water and the pulsing heat of their joined bodies. She started rolling her hips, feeling him grow bigger, harder, more determined to keep them both floating above the water. They were caught briefly in a swirl of current that spun them around and he had to let go long enough to use his arms to keep them from sinking.

"I don't think this is going to work very well," he said through a rueful laugh.

"I don't need it to work," she whispered. "I just need to feel you there, inside me."

He threaded his fingers into her wet hair and held her through a deeply possessive kiss. But once again the river sabotaged their efforts and, after half laughing, half sputtering through nosefuls of water, they broke apart and swam back to the ship.

BACK IN THE CABIN, they gathered up their scattered clothes. When they went up on deck it was almost fully dark and lights were twinkling into view from high up on the walls of Fort St. Philip and from the small camp on shore behind the grounded *Louisiana*.

Billy and Archie Penman were standing by the Beast, conversing in intimately low voices. They both looked quite normal apart from the usually fastidious doctor having his cravat askew and not all of the buttons on his waistcoat aligned.

In the distance, they could hear the rumble of guns as the nightly exchange of fire began between the Americans and the British, neither side wanting to give the other another chance to make a surprise attack.

Wary of the crew's eyes on them, Sebastian touched Rose's shoulder then skimmed his hand down her arm until he was able to grasp her hand briefly in his. He gave it a little squeeze, before reluctantly letting go, then crammed his hat on his head.

"I don't know when ... or if ... I'll be able to get away again any time soon," he said, then added in a louder voice for the benefit of the crew. "We're mounting another dozen guns on the earthworks tomorrow, which should pretty much bolster the defenses for the entire length of the Jackson Line. Also, as soon as General Jackson sends word, your captain will be blowing a hole in the levee to send the river onto the plantation fields to flood them."

The information was met with a rumbling of approval interspersed with a few *huzzahs!*

"We don't expect the British to sit on their haunches much longer, so be ready, my hearties, to fight the good fight!"

A second round of cheers rolled like a wave through the crew, and, after a last lingering glance in Rose's direction, Fonteyne strode to the gangway and climbed down to the waiting longboat. Penman followed, but not before he startled the entire crew by snatching Billy Burr into a tight embrace and kissing her long enough and passionately enough to earn hoots and whistles and a score of caps thrown up into the air.

Stubb, watching, grabbed his cap with both hands and pulled it down over his ears.

37

New Years Day began with the British moving their guns forward to the edge of the plantation and firing in earnest on the Jackson Line, hoping to soften the defenses or open a gap for the army to breech in force. Jackson's headquarters at McCarty House was leveled and if not for watching the birth of a new foal in the stables, the general and his officers might well have been blown away with the building.

Redcoats lined the distant edge of the field like a bright red ribbon, cheering each time an explosion sent up founts of earth and rubble.

With Fonteyne in charge of the Baratarians, he ordered the twenty-four-pounders to fire high, at an elevation that would cause the shots to fall well short of the British line. Noting the harmless spouts of earth damaging little more than the American's pride, the British cheered even louder and hurled insults across the field. The officers in charge of the artillery gleefully ordered their guns to be moved a hundred yards closer, at which time, Fonteyne not only corrected the elevation on the lighter long guns but ordered the heavy thirty-fours into action.

Lured into the ideal target zone, the British lost thirteen

guns and four wagon loads of powder casks and shot. The exploding wagons caused confusion and panic, resulting in scores of wounded men and fifty dead.

While the Line suffered some minor damage from the English bombardment, it was not the victory Packenham likely hoped to achieve. After three hours of fighting and having done little more than disturb clods of dirt from the earthworks, he ordered the army to withdraw back to the Villere encampment. There, he vowed in terms that sent his officers cringing under the tirade, that the next time they crossed that field the city would run red with American blood.

EIGHT DAYS later in pre-dawn darkness and heavy fog, three Choctaw scouts came running into Jackson's headquarters from three different directions, bringing word that the British army was in motion. Two battalions had crossed the Mississippi during the night, marching upriver on the west bank, and it was not difficult to anticipate their goal. Jackson had worried, because they had concentrated their heaviest defenses on the Rodriguez Line and if the British attacked in force and captured the guns protecting Jackson's right flank, they could then use those same guns to attack the main American force from behind.

With scant warning, Jackson moved five hundred militia from the central lines to reinforce the right bank. He also sent the order to the *Cygnet* to blow the levee and flood the canal road as well as the plantation field. Billy Burr unleashed a concentrated barrage of ten guns at the wall, opening a gap wide enough for the river to burst through like a tidal wave. Within minutes the water was a foot deep and the fields had become a four-hundred-yard-wide stretch of ankle-twisting mud.

. . .

As dawn approached, a signal rocket was launched from the British line lighting a red arc through the fog. Moments later, their artillery opened up on two fronts. The battalions that had succeeded in moving upriver during the night began firing on the American defenses across the river. As luck would have it, when they launched their boats to make the crossing, they sorely underestimated the strength of the current. While their field guns kept up a steady bombardment, many of the boats they had laboriously transported through the night were carried a thousand yards further downriver than their intended landing. At the same time, a second force of light infantry was marching up the east bank of the river on the canal road.

The gun crews on board the *Cygnet* as well as the *Louisiana* began bombarding the riverbank, the canal, as well as the plantation field.

A larger artillery attack was centred on the earthworks of the Jackson Line, where the British hoped to soften the defenses in advance of the main infantry assault. From the top of the ramparts, Jackson, Fonteyne, and Lamb had a clear view of the undulating lines of red uniforms amassing on the far side of the field. All three knew the sheer number of soldiers advancing on them was staggering. Jackson had slightly over two thousand men facing off against eight thousand seasoned British troops.

The British artillery, while fierce and thunderous, did almost as much damage to the now flooded fields as to the earthworks. After an hour of pummelling the American line, the sodden earth was churned up which made it difficult, once the order was given for the Foot regiments to advance, to slog through ankle deep, uneven ground. Adding to the confusion, the company that was supposed to carry the ladders and fascines needed to scale the ramparts, had advanced empty handed, having been told the wrong location to find the ladders. When they ran back to fetch the equipment, the soldiers advancing behind them thought the army was in retreat and stopped where they were, less than six hundred yards from the American guns in the prime killing zone.

Fonteyne and Jackson observed this through long-glasses, and had the Baratarians load the cannon with chain shot and ball shot which raked through the red lines with merciless effect. The British soldiers, mired in the mud, still attempted to march forward in straight, disciplined lines, but they soon became fodder for the privateer's guns ... guns that made no distinction between soldier and officer.

ON BOARD THE *CYGNET*, the air screamed with the volleys of shots exchanged between ship and shore. Rose stalked up and down the length of the main deck, ignoring the exploding rails and cracking yards overhead. Her path crossed with Billy's and together they encouraged the crews to shoot at will. The best marksmen were sent up into the tops to fend off the boats full of soldiers that had been carried downriver by the current. Rose could hear the cannon booming from the grounded *Louisiana* and she could hear the distant, rolling waves of thunder from the guns pounding at both sides on the main battlefield.

One hour ...two ... three ... and she was soaked head to foot in sweat. The air was thick and hot with smoke, burning eyes and lungs. Great white clouds of it hung over the river, hung over the land reducing visibility. Billy began to worry they would run short of ammunition. Two of the long guns had cracked under the pressure of repeated firing and they had expended all but one of the sixty-pound shots blasted out of the belly of the Beast. The canal road was torn to shreds. The river continued to rush through the gap in the levee making it difficult for the British to pass, and soon it became obvious they were no longer trying to do so.

In fact, what troops they could see through the haze on either bank of the river appeared to be moving south.

"Retreating ... or regrouping?" Billy asked, her voice hoarse from shouting.

Rose shook her head. "I don't know. Is it possible? Could they possibly be pulling back? And if so ...does that mean ...?"

The question was cut short as a scream from an incoming shot smashed through the rail behind them, blowing both Rose and Billy off their feet.

SEBASTIEN FONTEYNE PROWLED the top of the ramparts like a big black cat. His gunners were working furiously to answer the heavy British guns, but the rifle brigades had not yet been given the order to open fire. Jackson had commanded them to wait, to hold off expending ammunition needlessly until the advancing infantry was within range. The men on the line sweated profusely intimidated by the thick wall of redcoats coming closer and closer. They crouched behind bales of hay and timber planks, looking to Fonteyne, looking to Jackson, waiting, waiting for the order ...

"I know you're impatient, boys," Jackson shouted as he paced back and forth. "But wait ... wait until you see the whites of their eyes and make every shot count!"

Jean Lafitte, in command of a battalion of guns next to Fonteyne, cursed in every language he knew and some that were made up upon the moment. He had long since taken his hat off his head and stomped it into the ground, and the cigar he clenched between his teeth was chewed to shreds.

Rodney Lamb wiped sweaty palms on his trousers and kept glancing at Jackson, but he had fought under the general before and trusted his instincts. Mostly. But the sea of red kept coming despite the carnage created by the cannon, despite the fact that even if the soldiers reached the ramparts, they would have no means of clearing the ditch and climbing the ten-foot high redoubt.

When the front line of infantry was ordered to break rank and charge, Jackson waited until they had almost reached the ditch at the base of the rampart before he nodded and calmly said, "*Now! Now*, boys, give them hell!"

The order rippled down both sides of the Line and the men with muskets rose over the barricade to start firing ruinous volleys down at the advancing infantry. Women crouched beside the men, loading and firing alongside, barely having to aim with the soldiers so close. Those shot down in the front ranks created obstacles for the redcoats behind with the result that many stumbled and fell, some choosing to hide behind the bodies of their fallen comrades. The few who made it as far as the wall were easily picked off by the Americans firing from the top of the ramparts. Without ladders, the soldiers tried carving steps into the earthworks with their bayonets, but when that failed, when men were screaming and dying all around them, the soldiers turned and started running back across the field, shouting a warning to others that it was hopeless, to save themselves and retreat.

Adding to the confusion, most the officers had been cut down alongside their men. Packenham was shot dead out of his saddle, as was Keane. A troop of Highlanders, mired in the mud, had been decimated by half before a junior officer screamed a command for the drummers to beat out the retreat. Like a wave pulling back from shore, the soldiers peeled away and staggered back across the field. Wounded were helped to their feet and dragged or carried back. Men wept and reloaded as they ran, pausing to turn and fire in an effort to defend the retreating army.

One of the badly wounded soldiers, propped on a knee in the muck, managed to raise his musket to his shoulder. He desperately searched for a target and found one in the tall, black-clad devil who leaped on top of a bale of hay to encourage his gunners to keep firing through the chaos. Seconds before the soldier died, he saw his shot strike the bastard high on his chest, sending him cartwheeling back off the bale of hay to fall out of sight.

38

With an enormous effort, Rose managed to roll onto her side. She was confused, disoriented. At first, she thought she was blind, for she could see nothing but blank white space. She squeezed her eyes shut and opened them again, but it still took a few moments to realize she was lying beneath a sheet of canvas, pinned down under a sail that had been torn from an overhead yard. Her head was aching, and when she raised her hand, she saw that her arm was soaked red with blood. The front of her shirt was also crimson and she was able to trace the source of the blood to a deep gash above her left ear.

She could feel the juddering of timbers beneath her and knew there were still some guns firing, though not in full broadsides. Taking a breath drew more smoke and dust than air into her lungs, and she coughed to try to ease the thickness in her throat.

She made a quick assessment of her arms and legs, moving them enough to know there were no broken bones. But she could feel cuts where slivers of wood had sliced into her legs and thighs. When she tried to push herself upright, the tightness of the canvas prevented her from gaining more than an inch or two of space and the effort sent a searing pain lancing through her mid section.

There was another body sprawled beside her, pinned under the cocoon of canvas and it took Rose a full minute to recognize the slender shape.

"Billy!" She reached over but her hand fell inches short. Gritting her teeth to fight against a wave of nausea, she pushed and dragged herself close enough to grasp a fistful of Billy's shirt. "*Billy!*"

There was no answer, no movement, and when she pressed her hand over Billy's chest, she could not feel her heart beating or her lungs breathing.

"Dammit, Billy don't you dare die on me! Don't you dare!"

She heard a groan and saw Billy's arm twitch. "I thought I was already. I can't see anything."

Rose expelled a huge sigh of relief and rested her brow briefly on Billy's shoulder. A quick check along her gun captain's body and she felt a clutch as she saw one of Billy's legs bent at an unnatural angle.

"We're stuck under a bloody sail."

"Aye, well, I didn't think we'd be bound for the white clouds of heaven."

"I... I think your leg is broken."

Billy's voice started to fade out. "As long as it's still there."

Rose kept her hand flat on Billy's shoulder as she tried drawing the canvas back but something was weighing the heavy sheet down. Sounds were muffled but she thought she heard shouting nearby, voices searching through the wreckage as it was lifted and shoved aside.

"Here!" she croaked. "We are here! And we need help!"

A frantic shuffling soon lifted away the broken spar that was holding the sail down and Duardo was there to help her up onto her feet. Stubb, his cheeks wet with tears, was bending over Billy, but when he saw she was alive, he dashed the wetness off his face and plumped his hands on his hips. "No surprise the pair of ye decide to take a rest while we finish the fight."

Then he saw the twisted leg. "Oh, my Christ. Aye. Aye, careful now. Lift her careful lads an' take her straight the way down to the surgery."

Rose watched as Billy was gently lifted onto a canvas stretcher.

"What the hell happened?"

"What happened," Stubb said, "was the pair o' ye were standin' in the path of a ten pounder. Lucky fer both, the rail took most o' the damage; even luckier ye were flat on yer faces when a brace o' spars came down on top."

"The ship?" Rose asked, leaning heavily on Duardo.

"She's fine. Crew is hale n' hearty. Four wounded, aside yersel's, there be only two dead."

"Has there been any word from ... from shore?"

"N'owt a sign ner signal," Stubb said, "But if I were a bettin' man, which I be not, I'd say by my eyes, the redcoats appear to be runnin' back down the road as quick as their bony arses can take 'em."

"*Back* down the road?" Rose was not certain she heard him correctly through her half-deafened ears.

"Retreating," Duardo said. "With all haste."

Rose nodded and the strength drained out of her legs. Duardo scooped her up into his arms and shouted for the crew to clear a space as he carried her across the deck behind the stretcher bearing Billy.

Stubb followed, chiding the sailors carrying the stretcher

each time it dipped or bumped into something. He stayed with Billy as she was taken down into the lower deck while Duardo took Rose to her cabin.

There, her patience lasted barely long enough for Duardo to wrap a wad of linen around the gash in her head to staunch the bleeding. Ignoring her protests, he inspected the multitude of cuts on the rest of her body and decided at least one of her ribs was badly bruised, if not broken. After brushing away his suggestion to wrap her midsection up like a mummy, she stripped off her bloody clothes, washed as best she could, then donned a clean shirt and trousers.

"I need to check on Billy."

"You need stitches," Duardo said.

"I need to see Billy, then I need to go up on deck and see to my ship and crew. My head is fine, it's barely a scratch."

Considering the fighting had been long and vigorous, there were only half a dozen wounded men waiting in the corridor outside the surgery. Rose passed through the door in time to see Billy pushing aside a vial of laudanum in favor of a large cup of rum. The ship's doctor was leaning over the table inspecting the break in her leg.

"Seems clean enough. A good snap halfway twixt the ankle and knee. Don't think we need the bone saw."

"Ye cut off her leg, old man," Stubb warned, 'an' I'll chew both o' yorn off at the knees."

The doctor's bushy eyebrows twitched but he mumbled something to his helper, who produced four straight lengths of wood. "I need to fit the bones back together in a straight line then wrap these sticks around the calf to hold it firm. Might need to hold her down."

"I don't need anyone holding me down. Just give me a minute." Billy finished off the cup of rum in several deep swallows then nodded to Stubb to fill it again. He did so, but when she wasn't looking, added a healthy dollop of the brownish laudanum elixir.

Digby Fitch, appeared in the doorway and snatched his cap off his head. "I heard Billy was dead."

"Not quite yet," Billy said, her words starting to slur a little. She gave Fitch a crooked little smile. "When we were leaving the Nobbins, you said you wanted more adventure. I hope we managed to give you some."

He chuckled. "Aye, I thank you for that. Intending no offense, but I'll be perfectly happy to take my place back on the *Nighthawk*." He turned to Rose. "Captain, there's summ'it up on deck ye might want to see."

Rose looked at Billy, who was starting to hum a little ditty, then to the doc, who tipped his head toward the door. "Go where you're needed. She'll be fine."

Rose nodded and followed Fitch back up onto the main deck. There they, along with every other member of the crew looked at the riverbank where a troop of soldiers was marching south along the road behind their leader, who had skewered a large white handkerchief on his bayonet.

Rose held her breath for a moment. "Do you suppose that means …it's over?"

"Aye, for them, I warrant," Digby said.

As if to reinforce that pronouncement, Rose was called to the port side of the ship, where a dozen small boats were passing downriver, each carrying wounded men, each floating past showing a white flag.

They could still hear the sound of cannon from the main battlefield, nothing had slowed or stopped to suggest the fighting had ceased.

"I need to go ashore," Rose said.

Duardo curled a lip to express his disapproval. "It is not safe yet. An army in retreat will have moods like stuck pigs and shoot everything that moves."

He was right. Of course he was right, and Rose knew it. But every nerve and muscle in her body was so tight with anxiety, she felt like a pane of glass about to shatter.

"I need to go now. Lower a boat and find me six stout volunteers to row me upriver. Arm them with muskets and pistols as well."

Despite growling another protest, Duardo ordered the men to lower a boat over the side. He called for four volunteers but twenty stepped forward to join him and Digby Fitch. Fitch also ordered one of the small calibre chasers to be mounted in the bow of the boat along with a sack full of fist-sized shot filled with nails and metal scraps.

Bowing to at least one of Duardo's stipulations, she went below again and dressed in the plain garb of a sailor. She wound her hair in a tight spool and tucked it up beneath a woollen cap. Before she left the ship, she stopped in at the surgery again, where the doctor had finished setting and binding Billy's leg. She thought Billy was out cold, but when she told Stubb where she was going, the jade green eyes popped open again.

"Have you heard ... anything?"

"No," Rose said. "Nothing yet."

Billy's hand swam outward to clutch at Rose's sleeve and Rose nodded. "I will find them. I promise. I will find them."

She looked at Stubb. "You have command of the ship. Fire at anyone or anything that looks like a threat from the river or the shore." She paused and glanced at Billy. "If anything changes ..."

Stubb puffed up his chest and laid a hand gently on Billy's shoulder. "You go about yer business, lass. Ye can count on me to take care o' the ship an' everyone on board."

THE MEN LABOURED hard to row up the river against the current and it took nearly two hours to reach the first intact jetty north of the Chalmette plantation. They had met with no trouble on the way, but even from well out in the middle of the river they could see the extent of the damage along the shore. The two British battalions that had made it this far had all but destroyed the battery of American guns defending Jackson's right flank. There were bodies from both armies littering the shore, some frozen together in hand to hand combat for all eternity.

After being hailed and identifying themselves, some of Jackson's Kentuckians rose from places of concealment behind bushes and damaged sheds to greet them as the boat pulled in to shore. They were not inclined to let her crewmen keep their weapons but they agreed to escort Rose, Duardo, and Digby Fitch to Jackson's Line.

Most of the cannon that comprised the American battery had been overrun and, after realizing they could not hold the line, had been spiked by their own men before withdrawing. Why the British had not pressed on was a mystery, as it was clear they had taken command of the east bank of the river. A further push of half a mile would have seen them in a position to attack Jackson's main army from behind the defensive ramparts the rebel forces had labored so long to build and reinforce.

McCardy House, which had been nearly leveled the week before, was now smashed and roofless. There were fires burning in the surrounding trees and outlying sheds, great gouges in the earth where British artillery had exploded behind the Line. The rampart itself appeared to be holding, and though the cloth was shredded, the American flag still flew strong and proud.

Rose was led past the first two battalions of cannon that were now only firing sporadically. Most of the gunfire was coming from the rows of militia and musketmen who kept up a steady barrage against the British assault. The air was thick with smoke, the top of the earthworks were crowded with men firing, moving back to reload, replaced by men stepping into the gap to fire.

Rose crept to the wall of hay bales to look out at the field, but all she could see was hundreds of red-coated soldiers firing up at the rampart, dropping to reload their muskets, then charging forward to fire again. Some never managed to rise but fell and joined the other dead and wounded lying as far as the eye could see.

"General Jackson?"

The Kentuckian who had escorted them from the river, pointed east. "Getting hit the hardest, but holding the center. *Watch out!*"

He pushed Rose unceremoniously out of the way as the stovepipe cap of a British soldier appeared above the bales of hay. He brought his rifle up and fired, at the same time as Duardo raised his pistol, both shots hitting the soldier squarely in the forehead.

Spurred into action again, Rose kept low as she ran along the top of the rampart. She weaved her way through the chaos of fighting men until she spied a familiar figure in the distance. Andrew Jackson was unmistakeable in his caped greatcoat and shock of thick gray hair that seemed to have gone snow white in the past few weeks. He was pacing back and forth, followed closely by a small wolfpack of officers who took his orders and passed them to runners, young lads who ran off in full flight to carry those orders down the line.

He looked like a young man and an old man inhabiting the same body. He was in his element, a general in charge of an army defending his country and while he hated the death and devastation happening out on the battlefield, he was thriving on the danger and excitement as well.

Rose was all too familiar with those two conflicting emotions. She felt them every time the guns on board the *Cygnet* blasted to life.

She dared not approach the general while he was strategizing and organizing, but she saw another face she recognized further along the rampart.

Jean Lafitte was striding back and forth between two gun emplacements, shouting words of encouragement to his Baratarian gunners and marksmen alike. He wore a white open-throated shirt and white breeches with a yellow striped waistcoat, all of which were remarkably clean despite the raining ash and dirt and smoke.

He saw Rose and raised a hand that was wrapped in bandages. Up close, she could see a bloody tear in his breeches and a scorched line of soot on his sleeve. He was shouting something to her, but the guns chose that moment to fire in unison, drowning out his voice, leaving only the gestures he made pointing further down along the rampart for her to interpret.

She ran past, her bruised rib stabbing her with shafts of pain at every step. Her heart was pounding, her blood was drumming through her ears, and twice she stumbled over craters in the earth. Somewhere along the line she had become separated from Duardo, but she kept running forward, kept searching the faces of the men, some she recognized but most were too grimy and sweaty, blackened by the smoke.

She passed close to a gun that had been shot off its carriage and stopped for a moment to try to catch a breath. She ripped the stupid cap off her head and shook out her hair, a tumble of red curls in an otherwise brown and gray world.

Then she saw him. He was still a few hundred yards away, but the shock of blond hair drew her eye like a magnet.

Archie Penman!

He was well behind the line tending the wounded men, and as she gathered the last of her energy to run closer, she could see the man he was crouched over was dressed all in black, his long black hair streaked in red, scattered over the edge of the makeshift canvas cot, his chest a bloodied mess from shoulder to waist.

39

———

The Line had held.

Despite being far outnumbered, the Americans had won the day.

On the far side of the battlefield, the bulk of the British army was in full retreat. There was still sporadic gunfire on both sides, but the fighting was over.

Now there was laughter and back-slapping all along the top of the earthworks. Casks of ale were being rolled out and the weary fighters sat with their backs propped against bales of hay, bleeding and dirty, but toasting one another and savouring their victory.

General Andrew Jackson rode the length of the Line on a great black stallion. He waved and paused every few feet to acknowledge and respond to the cheers as he passed. His wolf-pack of officers followed close behind, Rodney Lamb amongst them, his craggy face split in a wide grin as he too shared the astounding victory with his militiamen.

Duardo had found Rose again and stood close by, keeping the area clear, growling ominously if anyone came too close to where she was crouched by Fonteyne's side.

Rose neither cheered nor celebrated as she dipped a cloth in a basin of cool water and blotted Sebastien's forehead. He was unconscious and, according to Archie Penman, likely to remain that way for some time. The bullet that had caught him in the shoulder had also sent him tumbling off the wall, where he struck the side of his head on the wheel of a gun carriage. It was impossible to know how much damage the blow had caused, and while Penman had cauterized the wound on his shoulder and stitched the gash that nearly took off Fonteyne's ear, there was no recourse but to wait and see when ... or if ... he regained his senses.

"He has a hard head, Rose," Archie said after insisting on putting a few stitches in the cut on Rose's temple. "It's been bashed one or two times when I've thought ... well, I didn't make any wagers that he would come out of it, but he did. As soon as things calm down here we can move him somewhere quiet. Back to your ship, perhaps." He hesitated a moment then asked for the fourth time, "You're certain Billy is okay?"

"It was a clean break," she assured him, also for the fourth time. "When I came away from the ship she was sleeping easily, probably easier than I've seen her sleep ever before."

He nodded and left her sitting by Sebastien's side, tasked to watch for any sign of shaking or fits. She had bathed the blood off his chest and arms, had dabbed a wet cloth over his lips and watched the dark lashes flicker and shiver but not open.

"Captain."

Rose looked up at Duardo, who touched a finger to his ear. She was still somewhat deafened from all the gunfire and it took a moment for her to understand his gesture.

Rose stood and looked around. The frantic activity of only moments ago had gone completely still. Men and women stood like statues on top of the rampart, barely breathing, almost afraid to shatter the moment by moving.

Curious, Rose followed Duardo cautiously to the top of the earthworks. What she saw would be relived in nightmares, for the battlefield was covered in red, littered with the bodies of the dead and wounded soldiers. Jackson had ridden down onto the field and some of those red bodies had began to rise up, their weapons abandoned, their arms raised high in surrender. One badly-wounded officer was helped to his feet and steadied himself long enough to withdraw his sword and offer it to Jackson.

The general dismounted, his face reflecting the horror around him, and with tears streaming down his cheeks, accepted the officer's sword but returned it almost immediately, sliding it back into the young man's scabbard.

"I will not take the sword from a man who fought so bravely. Nor will any of my officers or men do so."

As if on cue, some of the American fighters jumped down off the wall and began helping the wounded to their feet and supporting them if they could walk, or lifting them onto canvas stretchers if they could not.

Andrew Jackson nodded at their compassion in victory, then he too walked into the muddy field to help with the wounded.

EPILOGUE

For four days Fonteyne drifted in and out of consciousness fending off a fever that had burned scalding hot. Apart from short breaks to check on her ship and crew, Rose stayed by his side, and, not knowing what else to do, talked to him constantly, keeping him abreast of the events that had followed the battle. She told him of the victory on the river, the victory on the field, the care and generosity Jackson had shown to the wounded prisoners, of which there were many.

The British had lost whatever ambitions they had brought ashore from their warships. Most of their experienced officers had died on the field and those who were left showed no signs of wanting to attempt another attack. Every scout in camp confirmed their withdrawal and Jackson was confident there would be no more attempts to storm the ramparts. True to his word, he had personally written letters of pardon for Lafitte and all of the Baratarians, with a promise to have official grants of amnesty drawn up in Washington. He then enlisted their help in shoring up the broken levee to stop the river from continuing to flood the muddy field, which was making it difficult for the British to recover their almost two thousand dead.

By comparison, the Americans had lost less than a hundred.

Rose didn't know if Sebastien could hear any of her ramblings. Despite Penman's optimism, it had been four days and nights without more than the shallow, albeit steady rise and fall of his chest to offer hope that he would recover. Archie had plied him daily with his potions and tinctures, but there was always the danger of a piece of cloth having been driven into his wound by the musket ball. Archie had cleaned it well at the time and was reluctant to reopen it and search around the torn flesh unless it became absolutely necessary. To that end, each time he changed the poultices, he sniffed them like a bloodhound for any signs of putrefaction seeping from the wound.

They had moved to a quiet house in New Orleans, not far from Lafitte's original blacksmiths shop. Rose would have liked to take him to the *Cygnet*, but there was too much hammering and banging while repairs were being made. The Beast, as it turned out, did make a great hole in the deck after being fired six times and it had taken a full day just to winch it out of the wreckage and set it on shore.

Rose slept in snatches with her head resting on the side of the bed and her hand on his chest to assure herself his heart was still beating beneath. Sometimes the tips of her fingers would trace absently through the soft mat of dark hairs and she would smile, remembering how such a slight touch could rouse him from a deep sleep. Within moments he would be inside her ...

"Come back to me," she whispered, turning her face into the blankets. "I still haven't said the words. I haven't told you that I love you. And I do. I have been afraid to say it out loud but I'm not afraid anymore. I'm not afraid because you told me once that all you would ever ask from me was that I share whatever part of me I was willing to give. Well ... if you ask me now, I would tell you that I would gladly give you everything I have, everything I am. I would even try not to argue so much, though I must admit I have enjoyed some of our more heated discussions. And the way we make up afterward."

Even though she wasn't expecting a response to her heartfelt admissions, she gave a tuft of his black chest hair a vicious little twist.

"Damn you, Fonteyne," she whispered. "Don't do this to me. Not now. I'm sure it has already occurred to you that we are very much alike, both stubborn, both pig-headed, both living lives we built for ourselves rather than accepting what others expected of us. You walked away from a captaincy in the Royal Navy; I turned my back on the genteel life of a plantation wife. And it was your fault, you know. When I first saw you at that bloody ball, I thought: that's who I want to be and that's what I want to be doing. I think I've been trying to live up to that vision ever since. I've blocked out all the softness in my life. I haven't allowed myself to weep in ... God knows how long. I just pushed all that womanish stuff aside, as if it was a weakness.

"But it isn't. It isn't a weakness to ask for help when you need it, or to shed a tear when your heart feels like breaking. Or ... or to worry about someone you love when ... when you just get used to having them around and they decide to play hero and get themselves shot."

"It wasn't my choice, believe me."

Her head jerked up and she was shocked to see a pair of clear amber eyes looking at her.

"You're awake!"

He smiled weakly, "Difficult to sleep when someone is pulling out the hairs on your chest."

She withdrew her hand, then pressed it over his forehead, then his cheek. Both were cool to the touch. His fever had broken.

"Welcome back," she said softly. Then to ward off the threat of tears she added in a sterner voice, "It's about bloody time too."

"How long—?"

"Four days."

"Four? Damn. I vaguely remember you saying we won the day, but—?"

"It's all over. The British have abandoned their camp. They are loading their longboats and rowing back to their ships as fast as they can work the oars."

"Jackson?"

"He is basking in his well-deserved accolades. He has stopped by a few times to check on you. As has Lafitte, when he was sober, who seemed almost annoyed that you hadn't died."

"I shall offer my apologies for disappointing him. What of the others? Archie and Billy?"

"Doctor Penman has been much in demand. Billy has a broken leg and refuses to stay in bed. Stubb lost three toes when he dropped an axe on his foot. Duardo is ... well, Duardo. As for the others, Fitch and Reed have a few cuts and scrapes. Oh, and for a bit of a mystery, Mercado has miraculously started speaking English without a trace of a Spanish accent."

He noticed the bruising under her eye and lifted a hand with a wincing effort to brush aside some strands of hair that were hiding an even darker bruise around the row of stitches on her brow. "What happened here?"

"Hardly worth the thread to stitch it," she said. "Unlike the entire spool it took to sew your ear back onto your head. Between that and the hole in your shoulder, I was ... we were worried your pirate's luck may have run out."

He smiled weakly. "I'm sorry I worried you."

She shrugged. "I wasn't really. Archie kept insisting you were much too obstinate to die."

"Me obstinate? You have a firm grip on that attribute, my love."

"I absolutely do not! You are without doubt, the most stubborn, the most overbearing, the most bull-headed—" She paused to search for more words and his eyes narrowed.

"So much for promising to mend your ways and not argue so much. Though I must agree that making up afterward can be exhilarating."

She blinked. "You heard all of that? Exactly how long have you been awake?"

He reached for her hand and laced his fingers with hers. "Long enough to know what I want. And what I want is you. This. You and me. Everything we are, everything we will be. I want you to know and *believe* that while I have breath in my body, my everything belongs to you. My life, my heart, my love. For as long as you'll have me."

Rose felt the hot shimmer of tears that had gathered in her eyes start to spill over. "That could be a very long time, Captain Fonteyne."

"In that case, Captain St. Clare, I would very much like to kiss you right now ... and I would if I could lift my head without a thousand banshees lighting rockets behind my eyes."

"I believe I can help with that." Rose said, leaning forward. The flood of tears bathed her lips as she pressed them against his and whispered the words she was free to say now. Over and over and over ...

THE END ... or ... Just the beginning.

ALSO BY MARSHA CANHAM

China Rose

Bound by the Heart

The Wind and the Sea

Swept Away

Under The Desert Moon

Pale Moon Rider

Straight for the Heart

The Dragon Tree

The Black Wolf Series

Through A Dark Mist

In the Shadow of Midnight

The Last Arrow

The Mark of the Rose

Highland Wolves Series

The Pride of Lions

The Blood of Roses

Midnight Honor

The Pirate Wolves Series

Across A Moonlit Sea

The Iron Rose

The Following Sea

The Far Horizon

The Black Wind

ABOUT THE AUTHOR

MARSHA CANHAM currently resides in Toronto, Canada. Her sweeping, swashbuckling, awardwinning romances reflect her love of many periods in history, from Medieval England to the pirate-filled waters of the Caribbean.

She is the USA Today Bestselling writer of nineteen books and has won multiple awards, including a starred review from Publishers Weekly touting the sizzling pirate adventure *The Iron Rose* as one of the six best mass market books for the year.